The Impostor
(Book Two in the Liar's Club)

Celeste Bradley

St. Martin's Paperbacks

THE IMPOSTOR

Copyright © 2003 by Celeste Bradley.
Excerpt from *The Spy* copyright © 2003 by Celeste Bradley.

ISBN: 0-312-98486-3

Printed in the United States of America

St. Martin's Paperbacks edition / October 2003

St. Martin's Paperbacks are published by St. Martin's Press, 175 Fifth Avenue, New York, NY 10010.

10 9 8 7 6 5 4 3 2

Dalton had a problem. And it was growing larger by the moment . . .

Her warm firm little body was driving him mad. He'd bent his head slightly to whisper to her, and he hadn't been able to make himself move away afterward. She smelled like warm heaven, like woman and rose petals and, rather suddenly, like passion.

The skin of her neck was so close that he could feel the heat on his lips. A fraction of an inch more and he would be able to taste her. And dear God, how he wanted to taste her.

He succumbed. Just a brief stolen taste. Just a whisper of his tongue on her fragrant skin.

She jerked slightly and he pressed her still with his palm on her firm rounded hip. Held her still with strength and the fear of discovery for this tiny ravagement. God help him, if she had objected further, he was not sure he would have listened.

Instead, she let her head fall back on his shoulder, exposing more soft neck to his exploring mouth.

A near silent sigh escaped her, a sigh of submission and longing, or so he chose to hear it.

Clara had no sense available to her but touch and scent. The darkness was comforting in its anonymity. If even they couldn't see what they were doing, then perhaps on some level, it wasn't truly done.

Yet the heat of his mouth on her flesh was very real . . .

St. Martin's Paperbacks Titles
by Celeste Bradley

The Pretender

The Impostor

Dedication

This book is for Monique Patterson,
because she loves Dalton even more than I do.

Acknowledgments

As always, I must thank my husband and children for their patience and their gullibility in ever believing that "I'm almost done with the book." I love you, B, H & G!

And my wonderful friends and family who never seem to tire of supporting me and telling me where the book has gone wrong: Darbi Gill, Robyn Holiday, Cheryl Lewallen, Joanne Markis, Michelle Place, Alexis Tharp, Cindy Tharp, and Cheryl Zach.

The Liar's Creed

In the guise of knaves we operate on the fringes of the night, forsaking home, hearth, and love for the protection of all.

We are the invisible ones.

Prologue

England 1813

She stood upon a pedestal, a Hellenic goddess gone grievously bad. Her pouting lips and exaggerated pose were far too carnal for classical statuary. And although a gossamer drape properly covered her curves, the very way her rounded limbs narrowed to her tiny hands and feet only led one's mind to imagine the voluptuous swells hidden beneath the fabric.

At her feet knelt three worshipful men, two easily identifiable as pillars of London Society, one partially hidden behind the luscious figure. All three men were captured in the act of showering the idol with gold and jewels, their hands attempting to grasp her even in the act of giving.

Below, drawn in tiny scale compared to the goddess and her admirers, crawled the plainly recognizable wives and children of the two foremost gentlemen. Their wretched, ragged state was in startling contrast to the wealth piled at the feet of the temptress above.

"Fleur and Her Followers" read the caption beneath the drawing.

Gerald Braithwaite shoved away the pile of paper and string that had come wrapped around the stack of political cartoons, in his enthusiasm knocking the engraved sign that read "Editor" to the floor. The simply clad servant girl who had delivered the package knelt quickly to return the plaque to its proper place, but Braithwaite ignored her as well.

With loving care he picked up the topmost drawing with one hand while he rubbed the other across his mouth as if to repress his response. A gleeful chuckle escaped anyway as he gazed down at the drawing that was going to sell more newspapers in one day than the *London Sun* had ever seen.

"Sir Thorogood, you do me proud, you do," muttered the editor. What a drawing! It had lust, sin, and pathos. Three wealthy men squandering their wealth on a woman—likely some current favorite opera dancer—while they beggared their families in the process. It was superb mockery, razor-edged in its detail, all rendered in skillful lines that might more likely be found in the sketchbooks of the masters.

"The devil take them all, those pompous toffs. In fact, they'll wish he had when this one hits the streets." Braithwaite gave a happy sigh and tossed a thickly stuffed envelope to the servant without so much as a glance.

The editor smiled, then chuckled once more. Finally, his laughter echoed through the halls of the building that housed the press of what was fast becoming the most widely read news-sheet in all of London.

As the mousy young delivery woman passed through

the door onto the street, only the smallest twitch of her lips betrayed her satisfaction at the editor's merriment.

The next afternoon, a certain gentleman opened the *London Sun* to peruse over his breakfast. He'd slept quite late in the day, but he'd managed to find time to grope one shivering chambermaid, batter one footman, and profoundly insult his butler. All in all, he'd worked up quite an appetite.

Perhaps that was why he nearly choked on the giant mouthful of ham he was chewing. Or perhaps it was the lethal quill of Sir Thorogood.

Reddened with rage, the gentleman summoned his butler with a howl. "Bring the carriage round! I'm going out."

The butler nodded obediently, but as he turned to go his gaze fell upon the paper clenched in his master's hand. Even the very real possibility of reprisal could not stop the grin that grew upon the butler's face as he left the room.

Slap! The paper landed on one very consequential lord's supper plate.

"Here, now! I was eating that!" The fair-haired lord glared up at the two men who had disturbed his evening.

"I daresay your appetite will be gone in a moment. Look at this!" The taller of his visitors unfolded the news-sheet to reveal the latest cartoon by Sir Thorogood.

The lord was halted in the act of wiping his mouth as he realized what was exposed in the sweeping lines of the caricature.

"Bloody hell," he whispered.

"Precisely," said his visitor.

"What are we going to do?" whined the second man, who up until now had hung in the background, wringing his hands.

The lord grunted. "What else? Find this Thorogood and discredit him. He must have some dry bones rattling in his closet. A family scandal, a gambling problem."

The first man seemed doubtful. "Will that be enough, do you think? I move for a more permanent solution."

"It's a beginning," the lord said grimly, tossing his napkin down over the cartoon. "But you may rest assured, gentlemen, that there will be an end."

Chapter One

Dalton Montmorency, Lord Etheridge and Crown spy, strode into the ballroom in his first appearance as the reclusive cartoonist Sir Thorogood and became instantly aware that he had somehow seriously angered his valet.

As he passed through the large arching doors of the Rochesters' ballroom and down the elegant spiraling stairs, the clamor of voices halted and a sea of faces turned upward toward him like flowers turning into the sun.

Perhaps it was due to the brilliance of his evening wear. Compared to the somber black worn by the other men in the room, Dalton was dressed with theatrical excess as a fop.

A dandy.

A flaming tea leaf with delusions of manhood.

"Dress me as a flamboyant artist," he'd told Button, the valet and onetime theatre costumer he'd borrowed from his good friend and ex-spymaster Simon Raines. "Make me look like one of those idiots who cares for nothing in the world but clothes."

Upon reflection, Dalton realized that those were perhaps not the wisest words to use to a valet.

Button was a costuming genius and was fast becoming the outfitter of choice of the members of the Liar's Club operating covertly. He was also a bit on the sensitive side, to understate the matter. Quite frankly, Dalton wished Button had gone for a simpler revenge.

Poison, perhaps. Hired killers, even. Dalton would much rather be facing armed thugs in an alleyway than be standing in front of this crowd, clad in all his "artistic" glory. In the abruptly silent ballroom, close to one hundred people stood with their eyes fixed on him as he paused at the top of the spiraling entry staircase.

His coat alone should have blinded them. It hadn't seemed so garish in the dimness of his rooms, or the darkness of his carriage. However, in the blazing glow of the fully lighted chandeliers that hung above the crowd, there was no denying that Dalton was wearing a particularly malevolent shade of chartreuse.

That coat, combined with his shimmering violet silk waistcoat and his peacock-blue pegged breeches, convinced Dalton that he resembled nothing so much as a nightmarishly enormous tropical parrot.

Button was a dead man.

For now that "Sir Thorogood" had made his long-awaited public appearance in this guise, there would be no choice but to continue the entire charade costumed like a pirate's pet bird.

To make matters worse, he had serious doubts about the necessity of his mission. True, for nearly a year those reformist cartoons had incited much ridicule of certain powerful men. And true, the British government did not need such a drain on its credibility during wartime. Not to mention the secrecy shrouding the man, which gave Dalton's instincts a decided twinge.

But restraining a fey artist with a penchant for exposing the underbelly of the aristocracy was not on Dalton's list of priority objectives. He felt very much as if he was being used as a villain to keep some lord's personal agenda.

But the Liars were on shaky ground these days, and the eclectic band of spies dared not upset the hierarchy if they wished to remain banded. Dalton was still new as the head of operations, and the Royal Four who ruled above him were not at all sure about his innovations.

Nor were his own men entirely sure about him.

Dalton had taken on this mission for a reason beyond the usual obedience to orders.

The spymaster of the Liar's Club normally worked his way up through the ranks, earning the admiration and loyalty of his fellow intelligencers by years of work and camaraderie.

He, on the other hand, had taken over upon the retirement of Simon Raines. Although Dalton had been a member of the Royal Four for over a year, none of the Liars were aware that he had been the Cobra—one fourth of a powerful coalition of lords that decided in what direction to aim the weapon that was the band of thieves and assassins called the Liar's Club.

When he'd stepped down from the Cobra's seat a few weeks ago, eager to get back into the game of intrigue, the men he now commanded had looked upon him with rank suspicion.

In the past weeks he'd managed to win some degree of compliance from them, but not yet the respect that would turn one commander and fifteen men into a close-knit crew.

So he'd vowed to take on the very next mission himself, to prove to his men that he not only was one of them, but that he was damn good at it.

Of course, when he'd made that vow, he'd had no idea how excruciating a mission it would be.

I am the weapon of the Crown, he told himself as he stood dreading the next few hours. *A terribly colorful weapon wearing high heels.*

Everyone was waiting, staring at him in anticipation. He could almost hear their thoughts: What would someone so outrageous do first? Would they all decide to slavishly adore him, or just as capriciously declare him an undiluted fool and cut him dead?

Since the success of Dalton's mission depended on the first option, he knew he'd better make an impression. Well, in for a penny, in for a pound.

Pasting a superior leer onto his face, he flipped back the lace cuffs cascading from his sleeves, and made a theatrical bow to his hostess, managing not to totter in his high-heeled shoes. Then he stood and flung his arms wide to the crowd on the floor below.

"I . . . have *arrived*," he intoned haughtily.

The men present merely raised brows and cast one another amused glances, but the ladies sighed in unison and immediately began to pester their escorts for an introduction. Excellent.

Let the game begin.

Clara Simpson sat between two rather overblown ladies and practiced her invisibility. It certainly seemed to be working on her seatmates, who talked over her head with enthusiasm.

Pity the skill no longer worked on Beatrice, her sister-in-law, or she might not have been subjected to this evening's entertainment at all. To think she could have been free for hours on end this evening, secure in the knowledge that there would be no interruptions while the family attended the ball.

Bea had burst into her room this afternoon, bent on prying Clara away from her pen and paper. Her sister-in-law's broad face had already been arranged in an implacable expression and Clara had known there would be no getting out of whatever Beatrice had in mind for her.

"Bitty and Kitty will be accompanying me to the Rochesters' ball tonight, Clara. I'll need you to come along as chaperone."

Clara had given refusal a try, even knowing it would do little good. "I don't wish to go to the Rochesters' ball. I'm still in mourning."

"Must you continue this, Clara? My brother has been gone for well over a year. One would think you were still pining for my poor Bentley."

"Perhaps I am." Or perhaps she had no desire to purchase a new wardrobe, as she was hoarding every penny for the day she moved out of this house.

Beatrice had sniffed. "Well, it doesn't show much consideration for my sensibilities, now does it? Reminding me of his loss every day? And what do you think people say when they see that I'm already out of mourning?"

Ah, therein lay the truth. "Perhaps if you wore—"

"Oh, pish. I look horrid in anything near black and you know it. Bentley would never have expected me to wear something so unbecoming for long."

"I'll consider it, Beatrice," Clara had said, as she always did when this topic came up.

Personally, she didn't much care what she wore. It

wasn't as though she was interested in attracting a *man*. Clara barely repressed a shudder at the thought.

No, all she wanted was the freedom of being self-supporting and perhaps, just perhaps, to make some small bit of difference.

But Beatrice was a force to be reckoned with, rather like a hurricane wind. Clara simply wearied of resisting sometimes. Furthermore, tonight was an opportunity to observe and that was not to be wasted.

So here she sat with the spinster aunties, keeping her eye on two girls who were hardly going to drive young men to take liberties, despite their sweet, uncomplicated natures.

She was quite accustomed to the wall, in fact she preferred it. There was always something interesting to see from here.

All around the room there was a flow of people, moving in clumps for a time, only to break apart and join other groups. Clara watched the dance of pretty gowns and dashing frock coats, secure in the complete lack of anyone's attention. As she'd planned, her own rather dull half-mourning gown blended nicely with the upholstery, her hair was tucked neatly away beneath her cap, and her face was as bare as a chambermaid's.

There was no telling what interesting bit of information might be dropped in her presence. *Now you see me—now you don't.*

When an odd hush becalmed one portion of the room, she noticed long before her companions. Yet even they broke off their chatter when the wave of silence swamped the room and made their own voices suddenly loud.

On the heels of the silence, the whispers began. Like the child's game of Tattle, where what is told in the beginning means something entirely other by the end. Clara smiled at the irreverent thought, but to be truthful she was as curious about the cause of the disturbance as the others.

Then the wave of whispered information reached the rear of the room. Ladies bent heads and tittered appreciatively all around her, while gentlemen huffed and pretended not to be craning their necks at the newest arrival.

"Who is it? Who has come in?" bellowed the lady on Clara's left. Clara winced, but listened for an answer as intently as did her seatmate.

"It's him!" gushed a woman from the edge of the crowd. "He's actually here! Sir Thorogood!"

It can't be.

Outrage swept Clara in a heated rush. Her invisibility evaporated. When several of those nearby turned questioning gazes to her, she realized that she was standing and that the protest had come aloud from her lips.

Flustered, she stammered something to remove the gaze of all those curious eyes. "I mean to say, how— how unusual! I've never heard of . . . Sir Thorogood attending social events before."

"Well, I think it's marvelous," prattled one of Clara's seatmates. "We haven't had a new face around here for simply ages! And with so clever a man as he, I daresay we'll be mightily entertained now. Why, I have collected *all* of his cartoons! Original clippings, mind you, with not a tracing among them."

Clara wasn't listening. She was already deep into the crowd, slipping in and around until she stood on the foremost fringe, not ten feet from "Sir Thorogood" himself.

He was very tall. How loathsome. Clara despised men

who loomed over her and treated her as though she were both twelve years old and not very bright.

Not to mention the fact that he was very handsome, in an overdone, foppish way. Despicable. Thick dark hair—it was much too long. And those eyes—unnatural, to have eyes so silvery. Eyes like that would go a long way toward convincing others of his depth and sincerity.

What a peacock! The fact that he didn't look nearly as ridiculous as he should have only frustrated her more. There was no hiding those shoulders, or that flat stomach, or the intriguing cut of his silly pantaloons. . . .

But of course, he was a scoundrel. The only thing worse than a tall, handsome man was a tall, handsome man who was not telling the truth. And he was most certainly not.

Liar, thought Clara wildly, though she was careful to keep her face expressionless.

Liar and *thief* and—

She caught herself just before striding forward to denounce the rogue. Why was he here, using that name? What could possibly be his purpose?

He must have desired to bask in the attention of novelty-starved society—to manipulate the mystery that had long shrouded Sir Thorogood, the source of the scathing cartoons that society loved so well.

She must think. She could not publicly denounce him or she would lose her own anonymity. She would lose the work that had come to mean so much to her. She must expose him in another way. She needed to get closer to this stranger, close enough to trick him into revealing his lies.

She edged up to the fringe of the crowd of women now surrounding him like pigeons to a handful of seed.

A few escorts were being pressed into service to make any number of introductions.

In a moment Clara was lost in the rustle of fabrics and the miasma of mingled perfumes. To either side of her, ladies pressed ardently forward, dying to get the attention of the tall stranger. When one of the ladies looked Clara's way, there was a moment of surprise, followed by a feline assessment and subsequent dismissal of her charms.

A silken elbow caught Clara in the ribs. She edged away, only to have her toe stomped by a high-heeled shoe. She could get no farther in the swarm of women. Her practiced unobtrusiveness worked against her now.

She went unnoticed among ladies in costly gowns and elaborate hairstyles, all calculated to minimize brains and maximize bosoms. Clara stepped back, and the space she left was immediately filled by another spectacular lady. Over the plumed heads that surrounded the stranger, Clara could see the cunning knave smile winningly at the brightest plumage and the finest bosoms, while the rest hung desperately on the outer fringe.

How could she get closer? She had reason enough to seek some answers, for this man could ruin everything she had accomplished so far. How could she wrest his attention from the cream of London's beauties?

How, unless she was one of them—

Well, if that was what caught his eye, then that's precisely what she would use. She had a bosom and a pair of lashes after all. What she needed was some help in using them well.

Abruptly, Clara felt better. It was truly quite ingenious of her. If they were dazzling, she would be more so. If they were silly, she would be the silliest of them all.

After all, who could possibly suspect a dazzling, silly woman of being anything but useless and ornamental? Truly, it was a much superior disguise than that of invisible bluestocking. Why had she never thought of this before? She mustn't let the world think her at all serious-minded. Indeed, she must seem the very opposite.

With determined strides, Clara set off to find Beatrice. She had an impostor to unveil.

Dalton moved through the sea of ladies who crowded about him, his eyes on the gentlemen. Somewhere, in some drawing room or ballroom this night, there stood the man who was Sir Thorogood. Dalton was determined to rub his own obnoxious presence into the faces of every man in Society until he found the fellow.

He approached a knot of gentlemen who parted for him with curiosity. Well, most of them anyway. One of them sent him a venomous look and stormed away without a word.

"I say, I hope that fellow isn't ill," Dalton said smoothly in Thorogood's fruity tones. "One does so dislike catching something from attending a simple ball."

The men looked at each other. The youngest, a tall bloke barely out of school, cleared his throat. "I should think you would recognize Lord Mosely, Sir Thorogood. It was your drawing that cost him his position on the board of the orphanage."

Bloody hell. Dalton had looked over the drawings but not well enough, apparently. He covered his slip with a lofty wave of his hand. "I portray my cartoons as the muse directs me. I can scarcely remember every blackguard my art uncovers."

One of the others nodded. "You've done the lot, that's

true. From Mosely to Wadsworth, and everyone in between."

The youngest man was obviously burning with curiosity. "Wadsworth?"

The others looked at him. "Wife left him over the cartoon," one of them explained.

The young man only seemed more interested. He looked at his companions, who were decidedly more restrained, then back to Dalton. "Can you tell me how ... I mean to say, where ... where do you get your information? It must be rather difficult to learn everyone's secrets. After all, they *are* secrets."

Dalton allowed a slow, slightly evil smile to cross his face. He leaned forward, and despite their aloofness, the others leaned toward him. "Nothing," he said with dark intention. "*Nothing* is secret from Sir Thorogood."

A number of the group swallowed in unison. Dalton only smiled and took note of their faces in order to check them out at his leisure. He had no interest in their whoring and gaming, but one never knew where one would uncover treason.

Then the ladies descended once more. "Oh, Sir Thorogood!" they caroled and fluttered about him like butterflies without the sense to get out of the rain. The gentlemen scattered under such a feminine barrage and Dalton cursed to himself. He'd not accounted for Sir Thorogood's magnetism with the ladies.

How could he have, when women had treated him like a rather frightening menagerie lion for most of his life? He'd sometimes wondered how to bridge that distance, but now he was beginning to miss that intimidated awe with all his heart.

Put a pair of high heels on a fellow and just look what he was reduced to.

• • •

With one hand, Clara dragged Beatrice into the ladies' retiring room. The rose-and-cream-furnished room was supplied with several wall mirrors that only served to multiply the many ladies within to dizzying numbers.

Bea put a hand to her hair to protect her array of ostrich plumes as she ducked through the doorway. "What are you on about, Clara?"

Clara didn't bother to answer. Instead she towed Bea through the crowded room to a free corner.

"I need to look different," she whispered urgently to Bea. "I need to look like them." She gestured toward the other ladies. "Only better."

A smug gleam lit Beatrice's eyes. "I knew it. I knew you'd regret not coming out of mourning sooner. It's that Thorogood fellow, isn't it? He's a handsome one, I'll grant you that."

Clara waved off the question. "Help me, Bea."

Bea looked her up and down. "Well, we can visit Madame Hortensia tomorrow morning and order some things, though I'm sure it will take weeks at this time of year—"

"No, Bea. *Now.*"

Beatrice blinked. "Now? You want to impress a man in that dress, with that hair, and your face unpowdered—"

It was time to bring out the big cannon. Clara half turned away, letting her shoulders sag. "If you don't think you can, I suppose I could ask Cora Teagarden—"

"That goose? Are you mad? She doesn't have the fashion sense of a flea! You'd look a sight worse—" Sputtering in indignation, Beatrice grabbed Clara's arm and dragged her to a mirror.

Standing behind her, Bea examined Clara in the glass with alarming intensity. "The gown's well enough, if we lose the lace. Heavens, girl, why bother with a corset at all if you're not going to lace it nice and tight? Pull the shoulders down—no, lower . . . hmm . . ."

She turned to gesture at a waiting chambermaid, assigned to help ladies who wished to unlace and freshen up a bit. "You there! Fetch some rice powder and kohl. And some pins!" she called after the retreating maid.

Turning back to Clara, Beatrice smiled with fierce glee. "I've been dying to get my hands on you for years."

Clara swallowed. Oh, dear holy *drat*. What had she gotten herself into now?

Chapter Two

Dalton's feet hurt and his jaw ached from smiling, and he wanted nothing more than to burn his shoes and relax with a snifter of brandy and a fire, yet he forced himself to smile insincerely at yet another fawning female. "I'm entirely shocked, my lady. How could one so lovely as yourself ever doubt . . ." Blah, blah, blah. He could hardly keep track of all the moronic things he'd said this evening.

He felt an abrupt desire to go shooting. Or perhaps go a round in the boxing ring—*anything* reassuringly masculine. Preferably something exhausting and dirty that involved not an inch of lace.

Time to leave this conversation and move on to another, anyway. Preferably in a card room or smoking room. Sir Thorogood must be somewhere among the elite, for no one on the outside could ever know so much about the scandals and goings-on among the members of the *ton.*

Enough. He made a pretty excuse to the lady currently monopolizing his attention and moved away before she could capture it once again.

He turned, only to nearly trip on another. Catching himself quickly from trodding upon the gown of yet one more overdressed female, he quickly reached for a gloved elbow to support her.

The faint scent of flowers came to him, reminding him more of soap than of perfume and sending tiny jolts of alertness to his male instincts. Startled, he removed his supporting hand and stepped back, making an apologetic bow as he did so. "Please pardon my clumsiness, dear creature. Might I beg an introduction?"

"On your knees would be perfectly acceptable."

Dalton looked up quickly. He couldn't have heard those crisp acid words in truth, could he?

But the lady before him was as overdone and silly as any in the room. Sillier, in fact, for her hair was piled high upon her head in a tumbled style and sported three ostrich plumes that topped even his own height.

She was probably attractive enough, if one could see past the heavily applied powder and rouge. At least there didn't seem to be any obvious deformities. But her gown, dear God, the silly things ladies got up to!

She'd pulled the small cap sleeves down to her elbows, trapping her own arms to her sides, and her breasts were thrust up nearly beneath her chin by a corset surely too tight to allow natural breathing. Since he was obviously meant to notice those breasts, he took a moment from his busy evening to appreciate them.

After all, he was only working. He was not dead.

Very pretty, considering the rest of her. Smooth and creamy, with just the right amount of plumpness. Not so much as to ruin the cut of an elegant gown, not so little as to disappoint a fellow. Dalton suppressed another round of glimpses. He was only looking, not buying.

Finished with his appraisal, he looked up into the

woman's eyes. She stood with her head tilted, batting her overly kohled eyes at him slowly. No, not a sharp tack, this one. More like a dull pin.

"I am Mrs. Bentley Simpson, sir. I don't think we really need an introduction now, do you? After all, you're the famous Sir Thorogood, so there, you see?"

He didn't see at all, but rallying to his cause, he bent deeply over the silly twit's hand. "It is my pleasure, Mrs. Simpson. Might I add that Mr. Simpson is undoubtedly the luckiest man in this room tonight?"

He was answered by a decidedly unladylike snort. Was that sarcasm? Still bent, he looked up in doubt, only to see the brainless creature tilting her head so far to the right to meet his eyes that she appeared about to fall right over.

Dalton straightened quickly, and Mrs. Simpson bobbed right up with him. One of her plumes had come unfixed, and now bent gracefully forward to dangle before his nose.

Backing away while retaining his smile, Dalton gave the thing a surreptitious bat. The lady only smiled and stepped closer, bringing the damned feather to tickle his cheek and ear.

"I know how you can make it up to me," Mrs. Simpson said with a gleeful clapping of hands. "You can draw me a picture!"

Good lord, was she twelve? Glancing down at those admittedly mature breasts again, Dalton had to say no to that. But her girlish squeal had brought the attention of several other ladies nearby, and soon he was once again surrounded by trilling ninnies galore.

All clamoring for him to demonstrate a talent which he did not possess.

And at the center of it all, eyes alight, stood the silliest female of them all, Mrs. Bentley Simpson.

Oh, he was a smooth one. Even as Clara urged the other ladies to plead for drawings, she had to admit that the impostor was a very good liar.

With charming smiles and pretty words, he begged off from displaying his talents here at the ball, when they had all come to hear the music and dance with fine young men. Not for him was it to steal their attention, he said.

That was rich. Clara almost kicked him in the shin on the spot. Stealing attention was precisely what he was up to.

For the first time, she was forced to admit to herself that she had enjoyed the public's response to her work. Although her original purpose had truly been to stop injustice, over the last months she had begun to cherish Sir Thorogood's popularity like a secret jewel.

She didn't like knowing that she was less than entirely altruistic in her purpose. She didn't like it one little bit. One more reason to hate the outrageous poseur for pointing it out. Scarcely able to hide her sneer, Clara stood among the teeming ladies and added her pleas to the clamor.

One drawing was all it would take to expose him. Her talent might not be much more than a parlor trick, but it was a parlor trick that she was very good at.

And it was something that not everyone could do. Caricature was not a straightforward representation of a person. It was an exaggeration of a few key features, and a minimization of all others. To know *what* to draw was the difficult skill.

The press of ladies behind her thrust Clara even closer to the fiend in question, and a whiff of his scent came to her. She wanted to hate it, to claim to herself that he smelled of pungent cologne and lies, but he smelled rather nicely of sandalwood soap and clean, healthy male. She liked it very much. Very annoying.

Was there no end to his perfidy? Even his scent was a lie!

Her anger seemed to be choking her. Clara tried to shake off a sudden spell of dizziness, but it only worsened. Perhaps it was her corset that wasn't allowing her to breathe. Bea had pulled the dratted laces much too tight.

Clara tried to take deep even breaths to stem the dizziness and it seemed to help for a moment. She turned her attention back to the crowd around the impostor but found that something else had captured the man's attention.

Over the shoulders of the ladies, Dalton saw a man enter the ballroom. He was a lean older fellow, not very tall, but the guests seem to part before him like a well-trained sea.

The Prime Minister of England.

Dalton knew his godfather rarely made appearances at anything but royal events. Apparently, he was about to find himself in some trouble.

After greeting a few of the more important men in the room, Lord Liverpool raised his gaze directly to Dalton's. Liverpool seemed anything but surprised to see him there.

Oh, yes, trouble indeed. When Liverpool's gaze flicked to a nearby set of terrace doors and back, Dalton gave a tiny nod.

With sugary platitudes he excused himself from the

company of his fawning admirers. He'd thought the clinging Mrs. Simpson would put up more of a struggle, but she seemed a bit distracted and pale. Dalton made his escape and strolled leisurely to the terrace doors.

As this was a town house, the scale of the terraces was small. Each had its own entry into the ballroom, and a set of stone stairs leading to the gardens below.

Dalton found Lord Liverpool leaning against the balustrade, gazing down to where a box-hedge maze cleverly gave the small area of gardens more scale for the wandering admirer.

Although Dalton hadn't made a sound, Liverpool began speaking immediately, though he remained turned away.

"What in the seven reaches of hell do you think you're doing?"

If Liverpool was resorting to bad language, Dalton was in for even more trouble than he'd thought. "I'm investigating the latest case given to the Liar's Club," he replied stiffly.

Liverpool snorted. "*Personally*. You left out *personally*. Which you are not supposed to be doing. Have you given any thought to the repercussions if your true identity is revealed? You've lived quietly these last few years, but not that quietly!"

Despite the fact that he'd worried over that very point, Dalton felt obligated to defend his decision. It wouldn't do for Liverpool to know precisely how tenuous his hold over the Liars truly was. "It isn't likely that anyone will associate the somber, reclusive Lord Etheridge with the flamboyant Sir Thorogood. In the event that they do, I shall admit my identity and claim Thorogood was merely my nom de plume."

"And how do you intend to explain away the humiliation and degradation of several dozen peers of the realm at the hands of that reformist agitator? What about the connection that will inevitably be made to *me*?" Liverpool turned swiftly, his black eyes glittering in the half-light. "It is no secret among those who matter that I raised you when your father died!"

Dalton looked down at his godfather. *Raised* was perhaps too strong a word for the man's participation in Dalton's childhood. *Supervised,* perhaps. *Arranged,* even.

Liverpool had personally selected a highly distinguished school, where he ordered that his charge remain through every lonely holiday while the other boys had joyfully returned to their homes. Every six months Lord Liverpool had made an appearance there to check on the young Lord Etheridge's progress. Dalton knew this because the faculty had never failed to inform him of his esteemed guardian's visits.

He himself had never had much conversation with the man until he'd finally left Oxford to take his place in the House of Lords.

Once there, he'd been expected to back Liverpool at every turn, to vote with the man's vote, and generally add to the power and influence that Liverpool had already accumulated.

Liverpool would have had his support anyway. The man was the glue holding the government together, what with a mad king and a profligate prince who was more interested in art and women than in government.

In the past several years, Dalton had run many a mission under Liverpool's direction. His esteem for Liverpool's political acuity had only grown.

But England's most powerful man was not Dalton's

intimidating guardian anymore. Nor was Dalton a lonely boy, desperate to please.

"I fail to see how any of this could come to reflect on you, my lord. My identity will not be revealed. I had the best of costumers, and honestly, would anyone dream that the sober Lord Etheridge would use a quizzing glass?"

The attempt at levity fell flat in the silence. Though the gathering was plainly audible in the background, the high terrace seemed very much like a chill mountaintop at that moment.

"However you and that ragtag lot care to go about it, I want Thorogood run to ground. Do you hear me, lad?"

Before Dalton could protest that he was no longer a lad and had not been for fifteen years, Liverpool had slipped back through the doors, leaving him in the darkness.

Dalton pulled a cheroot from his pocket and leaned back into the shadow of the house. "Poor Thorogood. You don't stand a chance, old man," he murmured to the night.

Drat Beatrice! Clara's lack of oxygen had distracted her long enough for the impostor to get away. There was no way to know when she would gain another chance to corner him.

"Are you quite well, madam?"

Clara glanced up to see a man gazing at her with a concerned look upon his face. Thankfully, it wasn't the impostor, though this man was handsome as well. Goodness, attractive men were just climbing from the woodwork this evening, weren't they?

She blinked at the fellow, her dizziness making her

feel rather disconnected. The man was fair, as Bentley had been, but much better looking. Bentley had been boyishly appealing. This fellow was verging on beautiful. Only the masculine contour of his classic features kept her from resenting that such beauty had been wasted on a man.

If she'd had breath enough to feel anything but a mounting panic.

"We haven't been introduced—"

"No, we most certainly have not." She wanted him to go away so she could find Beatrice and have her ease the dratted corset strings. She tried to step to one side to see around the fellow, but he only moved before her again, his brow etched with concern.

"Where is your maid? May I help you to a retiring room?"

She must look a sight to have a stranger so worried. Clara fought down her panic and tried to regain some measure of poise. "I apologize, sir. Perhaps if you could seek out my sister-in-law, Mrs. Trapp?" she gasped out. Her breath was shallow, too shallow to feed her brain.

"Of course. Then, perhaps, later I might pursue a more usual introduction?"

"But . . . of course. I could never . . . deny so persistent a knight errant." Oh, dear. That hadn't come out right. Her brain was fogging over. She glanced at the man worriedly. He maintained his air of concern, yet for a brief instant she imagined she saw a flash of a somewhat different emotion. Scorn, or perhaps simply recognition of her irony.

Then he was gone, and Clara was finding it more and more difficult to take a breath. The ballroom seemed to waver about her, and the once oppressive air now seemed to have been entirely used up by the people swirling about her. It gave her lungs no nourishment.

And she'd lost the dratted impostor to boot.

She would find him later. Now she needed her sister-in-law. As she cast her gaze desperately around for Beatrice, she saw a wiry older gentleman entering the ballroom through a set of doors. He seemed so familiar . . . the Prime Minister? But what could he be—

The cool night visible through the doors distracted her for a moment before he closed them behind him.

Clear night air.

Air.

Clara stumbled the short distance to the terrace exit. Leaning against the gilded doors, she dimly tried to manage the latch. After fumbling for a moment, the door fell open before her. She staggered through to the terrace, trying to drag breath into her lungs.

It wasn't working. The corset was too tight. Tiny particles of gray began to come between her and her view of the evening gardens. Blindly, she reached for the stone balustrade, only dimly aware that she was in danger of falling to the ground far below.

Dalton couldn't believe it. This was no dainty feminine show. The silly twit was *fainting* her way off the terrace! Tossing his cheroot to one side, he made a grab for her.

His right hand caught only a wisp of silk, but his left managed to wrap itself around one pale arm. With a yank, he pulled her away from danger, back against his own body. She sagged, forcing him to shift his grip hurriedly.

Unfortunately, that left him with one arm wrapped around her ribs and a handful of soft breast.

"Damn." All he could think of was facing her likely

equally brainless—though undoubtedly well-armed—husband at dawn. Quickly, he spun her and tossed her over one shoulder..

Back into the house? The draped doorway led directly to the ballroom, her husband . . . and Liverpool. Not an excellent option.

Instead, Dalton headed for the stone stairs at the end of the terrace that led to the gardens below.

Bloody ladies and their bloody fashion. Whatever possessed them to sacrifice sensible comfort for some illogical physical ideal? Then he winced as he nearly turned his ankle when his high-heeled shoes failed to take purchase on the graveled pathway.

Of course, *he'd* never be dressed so by choice.

The white gravel path shone in the lamplight coming from the windows of the house, making it fairly easy to see. The brightness also made it easy to be seen.

Damn. What the hell was he to do with the woman?

She stirred on his shoulder. Having her head down was apparently bringing her back to life. With a muttered curse Dalton ducked down a darkened path, hauling his irritating burden away from the betraying light.

The maze of hedges led him to a turn, then opened to display a gazebo of some sort ahead, barely outlined in the dimness.

Perfect. He'd dump the woman, fix her blasted corset prison for her, then slip away before she came to. She hadn't seen him, so she'd likely think she'd wandered off in her daze. If she bothered to think at all, which he doubted.

Stepping up onto the marble floor of the garden structure, Dalton heaved Mrs. Simpson off his shoulder to half-sit her on a crescent-shaped bench.

He supported her upper body with one arm wrapped

beneath her breasts, this time avoiding taking a handful of soft flesh into his hands. She lay limp against him, her breath shallow on his neck.

She smelled good. Stupid she may be, slovenly she was not. Dalton had never understood the habit of some people layering costly clothing over unwashed bodies. Mrs. Simpson smelled sweetly clean. Even her hair smelled pleasant as it tickled his ear.

Oh, that was those damn plumes. Restraining a growl, Dalton plucked them from her hair and tossed them to the ground. Then he turned his free hand to unfastening the tiny buttons that ran the length of her back.

With skillful fingers he soon had them free, even in the dark. Then he tugged at the knot in her corset strings to no avail. Some idiot maid had tied them into a great snarl that he had no hope of undoing without plenty of light and time.

He could leave her here and let someone know . . .

With the shrug of one shoulder, he flipped her head from its roost and changed the angle of her body to look into her face. It was too dark to see well, but he was very much afraid that she was paler than ever, right down to the color of her lips. There was no time.

There seemed no end to the stupidity of slaves to fashion. Dalton held her tightly with one arm while he tore the corset strings with one mighty yank. With a series of pops, the garment gave way.

Even though she was unconscious, her body sensed its freedom and drew in a deep breath. When he was sure she was breathing normally, Dalton eased her flat on the bench.

Standing, he arranged her as comfortably as possible, aware that she was likely to awaken at any moment and take umbrage at his liberties.

She was somewhat pretty in the faint starlight, he had to admit. Without the overuse of cosmetics—not to mention the fervent glint in her eye and that annoying titter—she might even be attractive.

Then again, almost any woman would look good lying sprawled wantonly on a bench with her bodice gaping, revealing that pair of perfectly intriguing—

Her head rolled to one side, then back, and her eyelids quivered.

Time to go. Dalton stepped back into the shadow of the hedge, then quickly made his way back around the turn, walking close to the maze wall to avoid the crunch of gravel under his feet. Then he paused in the darkness, unwilling to leave her untended until she was fully conscious.

Clara drew one breath after another of cool blessed air deeply into her lungs. At first she was content simply to breathe with ease, so it was a moment before she realized that the only sound she heard was her own breathing against a backdrop of rustling greenery and the chirping of crickets.

She was outside? She opened her eyes, looking about her in bewilderment. The gardens? She'd come so far in her search for air?

Sitting up swiftly, she felt the bodice of her gown slide away and the cool air of night caress her breasts. Swiftly, she grabbed it back and covered herself. Her face was hot against the cool breeze as she realized that she must not have come to the gardens on her own.

Fumbling behind her with one hand, she discovered the snarl of corset strings and the torn lacing holes. Had she been attacked? Deep inside her, something cried out with age-old feminine fear.

Yet she was unhurt, and her gown had been carefully unbuttoned, not a single tiny pearl gone astray.

The back of her neck tingled. She looked about frantically, but there was no sign of anyone. Only her crumpled plumes, trod negligently onto the inlaid marble floor of the gazebo. The sight almost reminded her of something, or someone . . .

Well, whoever had brought her here had disappeared for the moment. She'd best do likewise in case they decided to come back. With quick movements she retied the corset loosely halfway down, then did up her buttons as well as she could.

She looked a scandal, she was sure. She'd go round the house and wait in the carriage, she decided, unwilling to search for Beatrice in the crowd. Picking up her skirts, she ran from the gazebo, back down the path toward the noise and light of the assembly, that same prickle down her neck speeding her on her way.

Chapter Three

Dawn was attempting to break through the sooty skies of London when Dalton Montmorency let himself into Etheridge House after his painful night of posturing. Although no one met him at the door, he could tell by the smells of cooking and the faint noises from belowstairs that his household was up and about.

He could have called for his majordomo to take his hat and light cloak—his own somber black ones, thank goodness, for he'd changed back into himself at the Liar's Club—but Dalton didn't bother. The Sergeant would only castigate himself for allowing "his lordship" to sully his own hand with a lowly door latch.

He'd not been allowed to open many of his own doors in his lifetime, for Dalton had been a lord since the tender age of twelve, an unusual state of affairs within the aristocracy. Apparently the Montmorencys had a tendency to run through their male heirs rather quickly.

He himself had only one possible heir, so he hoped that his nephew Collis Tremayne intended to take good care of himself. Dalton didn't relish the idea of bringing

the chaos of a wife and children into his carefully ordered world.

And it was so very ordered. He looked about him with
satisfaction. Etheridge House was very fine and filled
with items of beauty and value, just as it should be.
Dalton could see living out his years in this house, a
peaceful haven from the unpredictable element of the
Liar's Club.

Yes, his life was in perfect balance. At least now that
he was out of those intolerable high heels.

The Sergeant came bustling into the hall, his face pen-
itent at missing his master's arrival. "Oh, milord! I
thought you'd be staying at your club tonight or I'd have
been watching for your carriage."

Dalton handed the man his hat and cloak. "Sergeant,
I know how to open a door."

A clatter on the stairs drew the attention of both men.
Collis Tremayne trotted down the wide curved stairway
in a manner guaranteed to create maximum noise. Dalton's head throbbed in response and he flinched.

"Honestly, Col, one would think you were nearly thirteen, not nearly thirty."

Collis grinned and finished up his descent with a one-
armed flourish onto the marble entry hall. "You're a sour
sod this morning. Is it because you are coming in so late
or going out so early?"

"Collis, you live here on my generous forbearance. I
suggest you refrain from inquiring what is not your business to know." Dalton caught himself in a yawn.

"Well, let's see . . . if you're yawning, then my wager
is on coming in late." Collis threw his good arm over
the militarily rigid shoulders of the Sergeant. "What's
the hob, Sergeant? Am I right?"

The Sergeant rolled a pained glance toward Dalton but apparently couldn't bring himself to shrug off the Heir Apparent, despite the crimp in his own dignity.

Dalton wanted his bed with sudden ferocity. Collis's insouciant energy was more than he could stand at this hour. "Stand down, Collis," he snapped. "The Sergeant has work to do and so do you."

Collis blinked and his grin faded. He slid his arm from around the Sergeant. "*I* have work to do? How so?" His expression suddenly bitter, he rubbed his other, deadened, near useless arm with his good hand. "Unless you've a job for a crippled man?"

At his nephew's change of manner, Dalton damned himself for being so curt. Collis covered his anguish so well that even Dalton sometimes forgot what the younger man had lost to Napoleon. Dalton hadn't been close to Collis's mother, for his sister had been years older than himself and long married when he'd still been in school. He and Collis were actually closer in age, close enough to be like brothers . . . had Liverpool allowed it.

Stiffly, Dalton nodded to acknowledge his gaffe. "I only meant that you should pay a call on James Cunnington today. He's working on a most interesting puzzle for me."

Collis was never able to stay somber for long. The customary glint reappeared in his eye immediately. "I'd be happy to. James isn't nearly as much of a stiff rod as you, O Mighty One."

With a mock salute and bow, Collis was off. Dalton watched him go with a weary scowl and the feeling that he ought to be doing more for his nephew. If Collis didn't find useful occupation to take his thoughts from his infirmity, his light-minded ways bid fair to making him one very idle and useless Lord Etheridge someday.

Dalton noticed the Sergeant still waiting for instruction. "I'm going to bed," he stated with finality. "If anyone wakes me in the next four hours, behead them."

The Sergeant nodded. "It'll be my pleasure, milord."

Clara had greeted the dawn with a yawn and a quick cup of tea before spreading her drawing supplies out across her desk and setting to work. She'd been awake long into the night plotting wild acts of revenge against the impostor. Her favorite was still one involving replacing all the seams of his ridiculous clothing with cheap thread. The next time he performed one of those flourishing bows, he would split his breeches and reveal his true nature to the world and whatever highly shockable ladies of influence might be standing behind him.

It was a lovely image. Positively joyous.

Her lips twitching still, Clara bent to her final, more realistic plan. Surprisingly, it had taken her several hours to come up with the single most obvious way to expose the man.

Sir Thorogood would do it.

Clara chewed her pencil end in thought. She could show a stalwart, dignified Sir Thorogood tossing the poseur into a rubbish bin. She stroked a few lines onto the page and studied them.

She wasn't terribly comfortable with the idea of actually portraying herself as a man. That smacked too much of outright lies. Best to leave the details of her alias as vague as possible.

What about a hand, drawing the ridiculous fake with a quill . . . well, the fellow was absolutely crying out for caricature with his outrageous costume and his flamboyant ways. He'd been wearing more cosmetics than she had, for pity's sake! And if she were not mistaken, he'd drawn in a mole upon his cheek, like a beauty mark.

The drawing began to take shape. First the hand, neither masculine nor feminine—and if the public chose to take the cuff of the sleeve as a shirt rather than a gown, well that was their option, of course.

Yes, that was just the thing. . . .

Only the impostor didn't turn out quite as ridiculous as she would have liked. In fact, he looked almost handsome with those long legs and those shoulders—

Clara tossed her pencil aside in a burst of frustration and crumpled the drawing in her hands. Once more, this time concentrating on the powdered hair and the man's fluid catlike grace and his silvery eyes—

The drawing met the same fate as the first, as did the next, and the next. She wasn't concentrating! Just when she thought she'd pinned down the very features to exaggerate, she would start to think on the breadth of his frame, or his eyes, or something else entirely useless to her plan.

Perhaps she was still distracted by the other episode last night. Yes, of course. How could she possibly concentrate for wondering who had loosened her corset and left her half-naked in the garden? Honestly, anyone would be diverted by such a question.

Clara pushed aside her sketching materials and leaned back in her chair. Well, who could it have been? She didn't remember anything beyond being unable to breathe and making for the air outside. She had obviously made it to the garden, and someone had come upon her there.

Not another woman, for it would take a man's

strength to tear the strings from their holes.

Though it gave her a shiver, she forced herself to consider that a strange man had touched her and half-undressed her. But only to help her, surely? Once she had been safely freed, hadn't he discreetly left so as not to cause her further embarrassment?

But who?

She knew the names of most of the men in the ball-room last night, though she had been introduced to very few. After all, she could hardly do her work without a thorough knowledge of her subjects. She even vaguely recalled seeing the Prime Minister himself there.

But he had come inside before she had gone out. Sir Impostor had been about somewhere, but she didn't see him as the rescuing sort. And there was that fair-haired man who had been so concerned—

Oh, dear.

Clara bit her lip. Perhaps she didn't want to know what had happened. After all, she was fine now. Nary a bruise to show rough handling, and she was no child. She knew what handling felt like and she was quite prepared to vow there had been none of it.

So some mysterious gentleman had come to her aid and left her once she'd been aided. There was nothing more to it than that.

She shook off the thought and bent to her task once more. Perhaps if she concentrated more on the dandified clothing and not so much on the man within it . . .

Dalton Montmorency tried not to wince as James Cunnington took another brutal fall to the mat. The Liar's Club fight instructor was not one to spare James just because he was second in command. If anything, Kurt would be all the harder on him.

James lay panting on the mat that stretched the entire length and width of the room that had once been the cellar. The house that now held the spy school had been gutted and refitted with classrooms and bedchambers abovestairs, all very ordinary to the outside world once the highly irregular books and maps were stored away.

However, the belowstairs had been converted to a very strange sort of gymnasium, apart from the kitchens. This area was covered by the mats that Kurt had made from sailcloth and straw, and the walls were lined with racks that held every weapon known to civilization and a few that were not. Straw-stuffed mannequins stood at attention beside the racks, ready to do battle with un-suspecting students. Someone had painted curling mus-taches on the canvas faces and a few even wore scraps of tattered French uniforms.

James groaned. Dalton left his position holding up the wall to step carefully onto the mat and bend over his second. "Are you still with us, then?"

"No. Sorry. Quite dead, I'm afraid."

Kurt planted broad hands on broader hips and grunted. "Still got a mouth on 'im. He'll do for another round."

James shuddered. "Dalton," he gasped. "Have mercy. Kill me now."

Dalton shrugged. "Can't be done. If you don't work that shoulder, you'll never be ready to return to work." Then he looked up at Kurt. "What do you think? Is he ready?"

Kurt would have looked almost sad—if mountains could show emotion. "Not a bit of it, milord. A kitten'd take him out now."

"Damn." Dalton looked down at James. He'd been a good operative before he had taken a bullet in the shoulder for the Prime Minister. Dalton had hopes of getting him back in the field soon.

Crestfallen, James gazed back up at him from the mat. "My apologies, Dalton. I know you wanted me for the Thorogood mission."

"That I did. It had to be someone who could pass in Society. With you still recovering and Ren Porter out, possibly forever, there wasn't a Liar available who could do the job."

James managed a grin. "But you did look fine as the fop last night. And I must give Button my compliments. Today's costume bids fair to being yet more eye-popping."

Tugging at the wine-red frock coat that he wore over tangerine breeches, Dalton gave James his best "watch yourself" squint. James only grinned unrepentantly back. Dalton's lips twitched reluctantly. "Humph. If you don't discuss my costume, I won't discuss the amount of time you've spent on the floor today."

"Agreed." James rolled his head to turn a roguish gaze on Kurt. "I've decided I should change my Liar nickname, Kurt. Instead of 'the Griffin,' what do you think of 'the Wolf,' since I'm so lean and fast now?"

Kurt gazed down at James impassively. "More like the Scarecrow, you bein' more skinny than lean. Methinks a man gets named when he's earned it, and he takes the name he's given." He sent an impenetrable glance to Dalton. "Just ask the gentleman if that ain't the way of it."

Dalton held the big man's gaze with composure but inwardly he wondered what the big assassin truly thought of the new spymaster.

Kurt had seen a few spymasters come and go, for he'd been here since before Dalton's own predecessor, Simon Raines, had joined as a boy.

Had Kurt tested Simon so relentlessly when he'd taken over for the Old Man? Possibly, although Simon had been groomed by the Old Man himself, taken from the streets and trained alongside the men at every turn. Like a son taking over a business from his father, since the story held that the Old Man's own son had wanted none of it.

Dalton had no such advantage of familiarity with the Liars. Even James was less friend than comrade, for the bond they had was one forged during their accidental adventure a few weeks past when James's sister Agatha had so desperately needed Dalton's help.

With one hand Dalton pulled James to his feet. The younger man still weighed too little. His health was slowly returning, but his wound and previous imprisonment had drawn him to his finest line. He wasn't half up to fighting weight yet.

Another life shattered by the war against Napoleon. Would that madman never stop costing England her sons?

James had caught back some of his breath and was dusting himself off, although the half-furnished gymnasium was spotless. Tactfully, he changed the subject. "I still don't see why I couldn't have done it. If I were playing an artist type, I wouldn't need to be very athletic."

Kurt grunted as he gathered up the last of the equipment they had used. "Weak as a girl. Even Button'd make pudding of ye, like as not."

Dalton gazed evenly at Kurt. "Will you be joining us across the way, Kurt?"

Kurt cast a glance over his shoulder and snorted as he lifted the heavy gear with one hand and toted it toward the weapons storage room. One could possibly construe that as agreement, if one were a bloody optimist.

Dalton watched Kurt leave the ring, then turned back to James. "There were two more reasons you weren't chosen. First, you were made overly visible recently when you took that bullet for Lord Liverpool. Second, it's common knowledge that you've been out of the country much of the past year. Sir Thorogood has been in operation for at least that long." Dalton shook his head. "Sorry, James. I know you think you're ready for the field, but there is too much at stake with this case."

"I thought you called it a make-work errand for some overstuffed pompous idiot?" James toweled off and pulled a shirt from his stack of clothing.

Dalton handed James his waistcoat and cravat. There was a meeting of the Liars in a few minutes, but Kurt had insisted that James not miss a day of training. "It is. But dissenters come in many sizes. Even a small character like Thorogood could have surprising power to drum up sympathy for a cause. The popularity of those cartoons is growing by the day."

James grinned as he created a cursory knot in his cravat. "I think they're rather good, myself. Remember the one that skewered Sir Mosely for taking the orphanage funds for himself? How he was portrayed as a reverse St. Nicholas, stealing the stockings? I pinned that up at home."

"Don't forget the furor which ensued from that, costing Mosely his position on the board and embarrassing several other lords."

James was affronted. "As it should have!"

"Precisely." Dalton nodded. "As I said. Power."

"So far, Sir Thorogood's cause has been to aim the public eye at the unfair differences between the classes," James protested. "You yourself are something of a reformist, remember?"

Dalton raised a brow. "That I am. Still, there exists the possibility that the reformist platform is being used now to gather popularity, and that something other is motivating Sir Thorogood. Else why the secrecy? Why can't we discover who he is?"

"That editor Braithwaite still won't talk?"

Dalton shook his head and held James's coat for him. "There's nothing for him to tell. The caricatures are delivered by a servant roughly every two weeks at no specified time. He pays cash at delivery, and no addresses or accounts are used at all."

James shrugged into his coat. "So follow the servant."

They climbed the stairs from the lower training level to the main floor. Dalton wanted to collect one other Liar for the meeting.

"I've put Feebles onto that already. He'll be watching the *Sun,* and Braithwaite has agreed to give him a sign if the servant shows up. It may take a while, for the last delivery contained enough drawings for several issues. In the meantime, we've moved on to the secondary plan."

When they entered the outer rooms of the "school," they spotted the founders of the Lillian Raines School for the Less Fortunate in the front study. A lean dark man stood with a curvaceous woman turned out in the latest fashion. James stepped past Dalton to sweep the lady into a most improper hug, considering that her husband stood not two feet away.

"Aggie!"

"Jamie, put me down! You know Simon hates it when you do that."

"You never should have married the old codger, Aggie. He's made you boring." James bussed his sister's cheek.

Agatha laughed and cast a plea to her husband. "Simon, do I bore you?"

Dalton watched as Simon turned his head to give his wife a profoundly smoldering glance. Agatha blushed in response, her jest with James forgotten, her eyes only for her husband. The two were the very picture of a newly wed couple in love.

Dalton smiled tightly. It hadn't been all that long ago that he himself had imagined a very different outcome with Agatha Cunnington for one impulsive moment. He'd done his best in the end to keep Simon and Agatha together and a good thing, too. Agatha had proven to be far too unpredictable to make a proper Lady Etheridge.

Then again, women like Agatha seemed to be something of a rarity. Oh, there were plenty with generous figures and pretty faces, and perhaps even a few with brains—but he couldn't seem to find one with heart.

Real heart, an understanding of true loyalty and allegiance—at least to something other than fashion and gossip.

"I don't suppose there are any more like her around, are there?" Dalton raised a brow. "All I seem to be able to meet are silly creatures like Mrs. Simpson."

Agatha, who had come close enough to reach her fingertips to Simon's sleeve in a tiny unconscious gesture, tilted her head and frowned. "Mrs. Simpson? Clara Simpson, the widow?"

"Widow?" Dalton considered that. "I suppose that makes sense. Why do you ask?"

Almost absently, Agatha tucked her arm into her husband's and moved as close to him as was proper. Then she moved a little closer. "I don't know her well, but I always thought her a sensible woman. Kind, as well."

Dalton doubted any such thing, but he only smiled at Agatha's radiant happiness. "You think well of everyone right now, I daresay."

Simon chuckled. "He's right, damsel. I even heard you say a kind word about Lord Liverpool yesterday."

Agatha looked shocked. "I did not!"

Dalton shook his head. "I don't want to hear this. You know I don't agree with the opinion you two hold of Liverpool."

"But only a few weeks ago, he was going to blackmail Simon into a lifetime of service!" Agatha declared hotly.

"Not to mention ruining Agatha's reputation in public," Simon added.

Dalton snorted. "And you had nothing to do with that, I suppose?"

Simon said nothing, but Dalton could have sworn his friend's eyes took on a faraway look of remembered delight. Damn, but the man was in love. "Never mind. No matter how you two feel about Liverpool, you can't deny that he is the strongest Prime Minister that England has seen in a century. We need him right now, warts and all."

Agatha grumbled, "Well, if you want to reduce *ruthless* and *manipulative* to mere warts—"

"Damsel," Simon said softly.

Agatha rolled her eyes. "Oh, very well. I concede that Liverpool is both strong and effective as Prime Minister, but—"

"Let's just leave it at that, shall we?" Dalton nodded

brusquely. "I'd rather discuss Sir Thorogood before the meeting."

Simon grinned. "Yes, let's talk about Sir Thorogood, shall we?" He eyed Dalton's costume. "What did you do to earn Button's vengeance?"

Dalton closed his eyes and shook his head. "Don't ask."

James cleared his throat. "Actually, I have something for you there, Dalton."

He moved to a cabinet on the far wall of the "classroom" and pulled out a sheaf of political cartoons. "I've noticed that a good third of the caricatures feature Mr. Edward Wadsworth. Once I noticed that, I realized that many of the others depict those known to associate closely with Wadsworth."

Dalton nodded. "Excellent." He studied the file for a moment. "James, I would very much like to know who wanted us sent on this fool's mission. Do me a favor and check out all the subjects, will you? One of them is our offended party. I think it might be useful to know who."

James wilted just a bit. "*All* the subjects?"

Dalton looked down at the stack. "I think we can limit our search to cartoons that appeared during the last month, don't you? This seems like a counteraction at best. I think it must have been something quite recent."

Simon frowned. "Edward Wadsworth . . . do you know him, Dalton?"

Dalton shook his head. "Not personally. I know of him. He's an arms manufacturer for the military. Supposedly he has the Midas touch with his affairs, if he is as wealthy as is believed."

"A merchant, then."

"Yes, but not a middle-class one. Wadsworth keeps

company with the elite, I've heard." Dalton considered the options for a moment. "I can hardly get close to him socially, now that I've taken on Thorogood's identity."

James snorted. "Not now that Wadsworth's been lampooned any number of times. He likely wouldn't let Thorogood past his threshold."

"No, he wouldn't." Dalton narrowed his eyes. "But there is more than one way to get into a house."

Chapter Four

"Aunt Clara, please may I have a piece of that very thin paper you use for tracing?"

Pulled from the depths of concentration, Clara looked up from her drawing to see Kitty eyeing her hopefully from the doorway. "I'm sorry, dear. Did you knock? I didn't hear."

"Yes, Auntie. May I have a sheet of trace paper, please?"

Clara slid the blotting sheet over her latest Sir Thorogood drawing as Kitty approached. Hope sparked within her. Could Kitty be showing artistic tendencies? "If you want to draw, I have some very nice paper—"

"La, you know I hate to draw. But Bitty claimed the Sir Thorogood cartoon today, and I wanted to make a copy for myself."

Clara abandoned disappointment for artistic pleasure. "You liked it very much, then. What is it of?"

"Oh, it's most amusing, Aunt Clara. It's a Society mama and she's putting her daughters on the marriage mart, only it's really an auction block, and the daughters are really—"

Cows. Oh, drat. Guilt beat artistic pleasure on the head and threw it out of the door. That drawing had been the result of a particularly grueling chaperoning session that Beatrice had forced her into. She'd forgotten to take it out of the last packet she'd given to Gerald Braithwaite.

Well, if she had ever considered sharing her secret life with her in-laws, she could forget it now.

Kitty left with her trace paper and Clara returned to work, but the interruption had ruined her concentration. As fond as she was of Kitty, and even Beatrice, at times there was nothing she longed for more than a place of solitude and silence. It need not even be a real artist's studio, though that was her ideal. Merely a place that she could truly call her own, from which she could rule her own destiny.

That was what she had thought to achieve by marrying Bentley in the first place. A home of her own, a future, a family.

As the indignant shrieks of a sisterly argument penetrated the walls, Clara snorted and began to pack up her drawing supplies in defeat.

She'd certainly acquired the family portion of her dreams.

A reminder to oneself—be careful what you wish for.

James found himself wishing he'd waited until after the meeting to allow Kurt to pound him into the floor. Sitting in the chair was allowing his muscles to stiffen abominably and he was aware that his aroma was none too fresh.

James forced himself to look away from the empty chairs that would be filled if not for him. *My life for yours.* The promise wasn't worth much, but it was all the amends he could make. His life for the Liar's Club.

If that club lasted the year.

The ragtag bunch that half-filled the meeting room was of the old club, the men hand-picked by Simon Raines and some even by the spymaster before him.

Men who had yet to truly give the new spymaster their support.

James watched as Dalton led the meeting—saw how the refined Lord Etheridge had to draw grudging answers and suggestions from the men as if with hooks and line.

"There has been an increase in French recruitment efforts among the merchants and manufacturers, according to our informants. Some are suborned with financial promises, some with French imperialist propaganda."

"What—some poor draper sellin' out his country 'cause he wants to be as good as the toffs? Can't imagine it." The dry comment came from behind James, its originator probably not intending it to reach Dalton's ears. James hoped it hadn't.

Dalton's gaze flicked to the heckler without hesitation. "Dissatisfaction with one's station should not excuse treason, justified though it might be. Don't you agree, Mr. Rigg?" His voice was cool, not rising in the slightest, but James felt the ridiculous urge to duck out of the line of fire.

Rigg blustered his way through a sort of agreement and James relaxed slightly. Open defiance and insubordination did not seem to be on the menu today, thankfully. Still, there was no comparing this stiff, uncooperative gathering with the camaraderie and teamwork of old.

He wanted to jump up and shout at them all, these men who had seen him through years of working together, who had searched for him when he'd been imprisoned, who had taken him back without a word even after his revelations under capture had cost several their lives . . .

He didn't say a word. Not for him to order them to listen. Not for him to force their loyalty when his own hung by a damaged thread.

Dalton must forge his own chains of loyalty to the hearts of these men. James looked around the room, gazing at each recalcitrant face in turn.

God help him.

That meeting had been an improvement, Dalton told himself as the men moved from the room. This time there had been no bloodshed between arguing factions. In addition, not a single stick of furniture had been broken. Nothing that a bit of glue wouldn't fix, at any rate.

All in all—another worthless attempt to bring the Liars together. *Patience.*

Unfortunately, Napoleon wasn't going to wait while Dalton ironed out insubordination and inter-faction rivalry.

Dalton straightened his peacock finery and donned his plumed hat. Time to leave the club for the outside world and the smarmy existence of Sir Thorogood.

Dalton walked from the club with a tip of his hat to Stubbs, who was minding the door while he anxiously waited to begin saboteur training with James Cunnington. Unfortunately, until the Griffin recovered, the Liars were still drastically undermanned.

Once Dalton had settled the ambiguity of his place with his men, he was going to have to look into serious recruitment. Agatha was pushing to recruit some women.

While Dalton wasn't averse to the idea, he had no idea where to even begin. If he couldn't seem to find a suitable woman for himself, he didn't see how he was supposed to locate them for intelligence training.

Simon had found Agatha while searching for her brother.

Then again, Simon had given up everything for Agatha. Dalton couldn't picture himself throwing away the Liar's Club for anyone. The club was his now, if he could hold it.

From where Dalton stood across the street, he could see the two of them leaving the school. He watched as Simon handed Agatha into their carriage with such tender solicitousness that Dalton's throat tightened.

Then Simon looked up to see him loitering outside the club. Dalton nodded to him, and Simon nodded carefully back, as if he were greeting a slight acquaintance, although there was an admonishing cast to Simon's brow. Dalton could almost feel Simon's thoughts, that Dalton was not careful enough in hiding his trail to and from the club.

Dalton shook his head at the notion as he turned to be on his way. As if anyone would suspect anything from Sir Thorogood's presence at a extravagant gentlemen's retreat like the Liar's Club! In truth, it fit this persona perfectly.

As he walked down the crowded street, Dalton struggled with the unfamiliarity of his new identity. Not for Sir Thorogood the subtle passage of an anonymous gentleman. No, thanks to Button, Dalton found himself in full rainbow grandeur, complete with shoot-me-now pantaloons and a monocle. Every eye was upon him.

Then a prickle up the back of his neck gave him pause. Instinct cut in, making him slow his pace and extend his senses. That feeling meant only one thing. *Trouble.*

Dalton paused to let pass a boy with a barrow full of coal. Then he turned into a tobacconist's shop as if it had been his destination all along.

He spoke to the proprietor for a moment about his latest shipment from the West Indies, and about the woeful loss of American trade lately. All the while, he kept one eye on the front window. The street was full at this late morning hour. Servants and gentry, merchants and vagrants, all passed before the large shop window in the subsequent minutes.

Yet only one person glanced at the interior of the shop as he passed. A tall man, fair-haired, of perhaps thirty years of age. A gentleman by his fine boots, although by the workingman's cap pulled low and the casual knotted neckcloth, there had been an obvious attempt at a more disorderly ensemble. Still, there was a certain something in his carriage . . . was it military training?

No. Dalton smiled slightly. The fellow's walk reminded him of the sort of posture and carriage drilled into the students at some of the finer schools. A gentleman, indeed.

The fellow passed on by, but Dalton remained within for a moment more. The shopkeeper had a truly fine array of cigars. Soon Dalton was strolling from the establishment with a box of excellent smokes under his arm.

Instead of hailing a hack he decided to walk a bit more, purely to see if his shadow returned to task. As he left the mercantile district to head back to Mayfair, he turned down a less crowded side street. Perhaps he could isolate the fellow from the crowd again.

The cobbled way was more of an alley, he realized as the high buildings on both sides cut off the daylight. Suddenly the city sounds seemed far away and his own boot heels rang loudly in the near silence.

Until he heard the slight grate of a shoe on the stones just behind him. Swiftly he turned, flinging the wooden cigar box up before him like a shield.

The point of a blade splintered through the printed lid of the box to gleam just before his eyes. The impact caught him in mid-turn and cost him his balance. Leaving the impaled box behind, he fell with a roll and was back on his feet in an instant.

There was no one there, only a dark shape at the far end of the alley rounding the corner and the fading sound of running footsteps on the cobbles.

A box of very fine cigars lay forlorn on the ground before him, stabbed through the heart.

Dalton rubbed his own chest in sympathy. That had been entirely too close. He stooped to recover the knife from the box without much hope of using it to identify his attacker. After all, the fellow would hardly have left it behind had it been engraved with his name.

He was quite correct. It was an ordinary knife with a Sheffield stamp, the sort that was available from any number of shops in and out of London.

The assailant could simply have been an ordinary footpad as well, simply seizing a likely moment.

Or perhaps Simon had a point about concealing one's trail.

"Clara! Claaa-*ra*!"

Clara cringed at the yodeling up-note in her sister-in-law's call. She didn't waste time answering, since Beatrice knew precisely where she was. Instead, she used the few seconds of warning to blow softly over the still-wet ink lines of her latest drawing.

As the door to her room opened Clara casually laid a blotting sheet over it, then turned to face Beatrice.

"Good morning, sister."

Beatrice stood puffing loudly and fanning her face. Clara remained unmoved by the guilt that she was supposed to feel about putting her sister-in-law to the trouble of climbing the stairs.

In her own mind, she considered Bea's daily climb something of a constitutional. Such exertion could only benefit someone so sedentary of habit.

When she saw no reaction, Bea snapped her handkerchief down and dispensed with the dramatics. "Well, I see you're up and about already."

"Indeed. I've already been for a walk. How are you this fine morning?"

It wasn't morning any longer, for the clock had since struck two, but Clara saw no sense in encouraging Bea to rise any earlier than absolutely necessary. The morning hours when she had the house to herself were far too precious.

"Humph. I suppose you went shopping while you were out? Wasting more money on ink and such for your silly scribbles?"

" 'Tis my money to spend as I please, Bea. I had another . . . investment pay off recently."

"Well, if you've money to throw away, you might consider helping with the household expenses. I vow I don't know how Mr. Trapp bears the burden of all these women to support. The cost of launching twin daughters into Society—mercy!"

Clara glanced over Beatrice's fine silk morning gown and the flashing rings that were never removed but for bathing, but said nothing. Oswald Trapp couldn't spend his wealth in this lifetime if he tried. Still, the Trapps had not had to take her in when Bentley had died.

She truly must keep that in mind. Clara tuned out the rest of her sister-in-law's complaints as she gathered up her drawing supplies and tied shut her portfolio. There'd be no more time to work until the next morning came blissfully, quietly round again.

". . . Sir Thorogood himself will be here!" Beatrice's triumphant crow shattered Clara's calm like a hammer on glass.

The ink bottle slipped from her suddenly numb fingers to bounce harmlessly on the carpet.

"Oh, my! You've ruined the rug, you careless thing!"

Clara knelt to pick up the well-corked bottle with shaking hands. "No, Bea. See? Not a drop spilled."

"Well, you'd best be glad of that, Clara Rose Tremont Simpson! That carpet is very valuable!"

It wasn't, but Clara had no interest in arguing the point. The carpets were a sensitive subject. After the last stray cat that Clara had rescued, the house had become infested with fleas. It had taken soaking every carpet with benzene to rid them of the pests. After that, Beatrice had put her foot firmly down and Clara had brought home no more strays.

"What did you say about Sir Thorogood?"

"I declare I don't know what you think you're about, tossing ink around my home this way. You'd think this was your house—"

Clara sighed. "Sir Thorogood. What were you saying about Sir Thorogood?"

"What? Oh . . . oh, yes. When I met him at the ball last night I invited him to dine with us tomorrow. I just received his acceptance! We shall finally have an individual of wit at our table," she caroled.

"At last," Clara seconded weakly. She was fairly sure Beatrice didn't spot the irony of her own statement.

"I thought you were partial to him. What's wrong? You've gone pale of a sudden. Are you ill?"

Beatrice blinked at her in real concern. Clara took her sister-in-law's hand, grateful for the reminder that Beatrice was not bad, simply more concerned with a part of life that meant nothing to Clara.

If she didn't wish to be judged, she ought not to judge. "Dear Bea. You are so kind to me and I am so indebted."

Beatrice actually blushed. "Well, of course you are. But I wouldn't have it any other way. Bentley was very fond of you, and it's only right that I should look out for you."

Clara gripped her hand and smiled. "Well, then, you must take me shopping for a new gown. I rather think I'll need something much prettier for our esteemed guest."

Beatrice clapped her hands together. "We should go now so they will have time to fit you properly."

"No, tomorrow," Clara said absently. She had much work to do today and then there was tonight's venture. She would shop tomorrow, she decided, then draw until the time came for dinner with the impostor.

Then Clara saw the disappointment in Beatrice's face.

"But you must help me choose just the right gown. Perhaps something . . ." Clara concealed a shudder. "Pink?"

The cloudy night was perfect for a thief. Dalton leaned back onto the warm chimney at his back and watched the dusk overtake the square below him.

Wadsworth's residence was one of a row of brick houses, all connected by their side walls. The fronts faced across the cobbles to the square with its manicured lawn and white graveled paths winding through graceful trees.

Wadsworth's house was fine, if a bit ostentatious. It stood at a respectable address, in a part of Mayfair largely occupied by what Stubbs would call "the Quality." Wadsworth was in manufacturing. Not all the money in the world would buy him into the *ton,* although presumably nothing could prevent him from living next door.

The back gardens ranged from the floral explosion of the house at his back to the grim formality of Wadsworth's perfect lawn and flawless walk. Apparently not a blade dared grow out of place. Even the slates on Wadsworth's roof were fitted with military precision.

The lamplighter came into the square below, trundling his oil cask and his apprentice, whom he sent shinnying up the posts like a monkey. All around the square the two figures went as the twilight deepened, until the center of the square glowed golden in the bluing night.

The light was enough for those at street level to see their way, but Dalton knew it didn't reach as high as the rooftops. In his dark seaman's wool and black silk mask, he was merely another shadow among many. On a cloudy night like tonight, not even the waxing moon would betray him.

Still, there was no point in making his entry too early. Londoners kept late hours, and Wadsworth was no exception, according to the servants. Dalton had approached an elderly footman earlier in the day and struck up an idle conversation.

"Sorry, me lad, but 'is lordship don't 'ire outside 'elp."

"That's too bad. I been lookin' for anythin' to keep the little ones fed. I'll shovel coal, sand, or horse apples, I ain't choosy. Me wife's right pretty and well spoke. She could serve sometime when 'is lordship's 'avin' a do."

"Nay, son, you don't want to put a pretty girl in this 'ouse, not by far! Late hours and little to show for it, and not every guest behaves as he should."

Dalton had pressed for details but the old fellow had only warned him off again and shuffled back indoors. That alone had been something odd, for even the most base servants tended to boast about their employers to others in service, if only to make themselves more important.

So he prepared himself for a long wait and slouched comfortably against the toasty bricks behind him. At least this resident kept his house warm. He pondered the pretty grounds behind "his" house in the very last of the dusk. A woman lived here, likely more than one.

A warm house. A pretty house. You needed a woman for that. His own rather austere mansion was very fine, the best. Built by his grandfather for his grandmother upon their wedding, it was still new enough to be sturdy, but old enough to have become a fixture in its own elegant square.

But it was neither pretty nor warm. Nor would it be soon, for Dalton had no intention of marrying for many years, if at all. He simply couldn't imagine his life with a wife and child in it. There would be too much distraction, too much disorder.

Besides, he had a nephew to inherit someday. Collis Tremayne would make a fine Lord Etheridge in his turn, or father one of his own. Families were for another sort of man altogether, not for him.

Still, the garden below was very nice, indeed.

Chapter Five

Clara trod as softly as she could along the carpeted hallway passing before the family bedrooms. Although it was past midnight, there was no guarantee that everyone was soundly asleep. Beatrice liked to think that they kept "town hours," though their social calendar wasn't quite *that* full. Privately Clara believed that if one slept until past noon, one didn't have much choice about staying wakeful into the night.

Once she passed the tricky section of hall, she breathed much easier. The few servants that the Trapps employed were long in their beds on the third floor. As long as she was careful, they were not likely to wake for anything but a furious ringing of the call bell or their mistress's demanding bellow.

Still, they were paid well and seemed happy enough with their service, unlike poor little Rose.

Clara checked under the cloth in the basket she carried over one arm. The beef rolls were no longer warm, unfortunately, but the crockery flask full of chocolate was still hot. And she'd managed to save a few teacakes back from the twins.

Anticipating Rose's delight with a great deal of pleasure, Clara made her way up the final narrow set of stairs
to the attic. She fished the key from her pocket and un-
locked the door. As far as she knew, no one had missed
this key in the year and a half that she had been making
this trip, likely because no one in the sedentary Trapp
household wanted to climb one more stair than was necessary.

The attic was even darker than the hall, but Clara
didn't light her candle. By now, she knew every trunk
and box by heart, and could whisk her way through the
long narrow attic without a single stumble.

At the far end, she stopped before a bare plank wall—
all that separated her attic from that of the adjoining
house. She tapped her knuckles softly on it three times,
then stepped back.

Before her, one of the widest planks shifted to the
side, swinging on its last remaining nail. A small hand
holding the stub of a candle came through, and Clara
blinked at the sudden radiance as she took the holder
and set it on a nearby trunk. Rose wasn't nearly as comfortable in the dark as she was.

Then a small head covered in a large cap emerged,
and the rest of a slender young chambermaid slipped
sideways through the narrow hole.

"Hello, Miss Clara!"

"Hello, Rose," Clara replied warmly. "I've brought
your payment. And this time, there's lemon seed cake."

The girl's thin face lighted at the mention of the
sweets, but she politely waited for Clara to sit down and
begin spreading the contents of the basket before she sat
herself.

When Clara had first met the next-door housemaid,
she had been putting the last of Bentley's things away

in the attic after his death. The sound of muffled crying had been very startling, especially as she had been shedding a tear or two of her own at the time.

At first, she thought Beatrice had come upstairs to help her after all. Then she'd realized that the quiet, secretive sobs were coming from the wrong direction, not to mention they in no way resembled Bea's theatrical wails.

She had followed the sound to the far wall of the attic, where she had remembered that the Trapps' house was one in a terrace of connecting houses around the rather exclusive Smythe Square.

She'd never heard a sound from the houses on either side before, but the walls between were thick stone and quite impenetrable. For some reason, this wall had been left unfinished and planked over instead.

The sound of weeping was growing more desperate, but eerily no louder. Her heart moved by the sad sound, Clara knelt beside the wall and knocked softly.

"Hello? Are you ill? Is there anything I can do for you?"

The sobs cut off immediately, and there was only silence from the other side of the wall, but somehow Clara knew that the weeper was listening. She sat down on the floor with her back to the wall, unwilling to leave someone alone in such pain.

"I've been crying myself," she said to the wall, leaning her cheek against the rough wood. "I know being sad is harder when you're by yourself."

She heard nothing for a long moment, then came a mighty sniffle. Encouraged, Clara continued. "I'm sad because someone has passed away."

There came another sniffle, then a small voice. "Who?"

"My husband. He is—was a soldier, fighting on the Peninsula."

"Napoleon got 'im?"

Clara shook her head ruefully. "No. No heroic finish for Bentley. He slipped in the mud and broke his neck on the way to the latrine."

There was a long moment of silence. Then Clara heard a muffled snicker. It was a terrible moment to laugh, Clara knew that, but she couldn't help a giggle of her own. Then her pent-up sense of the ridiculous took over and she laughed with the stranger on the other side of the wall until more tears tracked her cheeks.

When her helpless half-tearful giggles finally died down, Clara wiped her eyes, trying to feel bad but truthfully feeling a good bit better.

"Did you love him?"

Clara didn't reply right away, because she truly didn't know. "I liked him. He was a bit light-minded, and not terribly responsible, but he was kind. Perhaps if we'd had more than a few months together I would have come to love him. But he was called up soon after the wedding."

Before, actually, which was why she'd married him in an uncharacteristic bout of romantic and patriotic fervor. *Your typical wartime marriage*, she thought. The stuff of jest and ridicule. Poor Bentley. All the most important moments of his life had been a series of hackneyed japes.

She wiped her eyes again, then turned back to the wall. "Why were you crying?"

"Me back. It hurts."

"Your back? Did you injure yourself?"

"No, miss. 'Twas the whipping."

Clara was horrified. "You were *whipped*?"

"Oh, it ain't so bad," the little voice quavered. "Not like the time I spilt tea on the master's guest."

"You were whipped for spilling *tea*?"

"Well, it were *real* hot, miss. And I'm terrible clumsy. But I never spilt tea again," the voice went on to assure her. "This time it were for leavin' dust on the newel post."

Clara couldn't bear it. Here she'd been pitying herself, thinking her life so terrible now that she was dependent on Bentley's sister and brother-in-law. She was ashamed as she recalled her spacious new room in Beatrice Trapp's comfortable home, where she had no duties more onerous than helping Bea watch over two quiet girls.

She shifted uncomfortably at the thought, and felt the plank behind her wobble loosely. That gave her an idea. "Listen—what is your name?"

"Me name's Rose, miss."

Clara was startled. "Why, so is mine! Clara Rose." Then she bent to the wall once more, tapping softly. "Rose, I want you to push on this plank." She tried to edge her fingers around it, but could get no purchase. Then a shove from the other side moved the plank out enough for her to gain a grip on the sides. Disregarding the splinters that sank into her fingertips, Clara gave a mighty yank. With a screech of dry wood giving up its long relationship with old nails, the plank swung inward and sideways.

The wavering light of a tallow candle shone through the gap, then was blocked by a floppy white mobcap and a starveling little face.

"Hullo, miss."

Seeing the tear-streaked visage and thin cheeks, Clara

could only hold out one hand. The girl took it gingerly and let Clara pull her through the gap.

When the maid stood upright, Clara was a bit surprised to see that she was much the same height. In fact, they were much the same in many ways. The girl was of a similar age, and had nearly identical coloring to herself. And there was the matter of her name.

Struck by these odd similarities, Clara had a moment of odd displacement, as if she were looking at another self, a girl she might have been had she not had the few advantages she'd been born with.

" 'There, but for the grace of God, go I,' " she whispered.

Rose blinked at her, rubbing one wrist beneath her nose and giving a great sniff. "What's that, miss?"

Clara shook her head and smiled. "It doesn't matter." She tugged on Rose's hand. "Come down to the kitchen. We'll have a nice cup of tea, and Cook will tend your back."

Rose pulled back. "Oh, no, I dasn't! 'Tis a kind offer, and I thanks ye, miss, but if I don't get back to me duties, I'll be whipped again, or sacked!"

"Well, let—" Clara almost said, *Let them sack you,* then realized how unthinking that was. If the girl had other options of employment, she'd hardly stay in such an untenable situation in the first place.

The poor creature *must* go back to work, even in pain as she was, or be mistreated further. Clara couldn't bear the thought.

"Let me take your place," she had blurted.

And that had been the beginning of it all. She persuaded Rose to allow her to don her uniform and cap, and had seen for herself the awful conditions in which the girl existed.

Her room was a bare pallet in a corner of the attic, one much colder than the Trapp attic. The master of the house, Mr. Wadsworth, was a skinflint of the highest order and only allowed a single fire at a time—in whichever room of the house was occupied by him, naturally.

Rose's dinner was often nothing but a crust, and she was worked from before dawn to long after the sun set.

Clara didn't learn all that in one night, of course. That first encounter was merely the inspiration for a permanent bargain with the willing Rose. Clara "paid" Rose to let her take her place once a week or so, thus overcoming the girl's unwillingness to take charity, and in return Clara had the priceless opportunity to view the underbelly of "good" Society.

She'd tried to draw her brother-in-law's attention to the problems that Rose faced, hoping to get her hired away from Mr. Wadsworth, but Oswald Trapp had only patted her head and chuckled that she ought not to think about such unfortunate things, for he surely never allowed himself to.

So Clara had taken her cause to the *London Sun,* submitting her first scathing drawing of Mr. Wadsworth under the facetious nom de plume Sir Thorogood.

The cartoon had been printed immediately, as had every one succeeding it. Eventually it had occurred to Clara to ask for payment.

She'd donned a servant's simple dress and had hand-carried the next packet of drawings to the news-sheet herself, along with a note from Sir Thorogood naming his fee. She'd thought perhaps there would then be a process of bargaining down, since she doubted that the drawings were terribly valuable.

Instead, Gerald Braithwaite had paid without protest and had sent a note back stating that if Sir Thorogood was of a mind to do so, the paper would be happy to buy the drawings in greater quantity, enough to print one every other day.

Now, as she watched a much-improved Rose enjoying her chocolate and cakes, it occurred to Clara that she had almost realized her dream. Under her bed there was a box brimming with banknotes, someday to be enough to live on comfortably, if not luxuriously, for the rest of her life.

It was an intimidating goal, one that she often despaired of reaching. Then she would remember the people that she had helped with her investigations, such as the children in the orphanage that Lord Mosely had been systematically cheating. And dear Rose, who would be the first person she would hire should she ever reach her goal.

"Well, I must be getting to work," she said cheerily. "I'll be late, so do sleep here where it's warm. I'll wake you when I come back."

Rose nodded. "Yes, miss. I thanks you for the seed cakes."

"Nonsense, you've earned them. I could never do my job without your help." Clara rose and squeezed her way through the gap. "Keep the candle, I do fine in the dark," she called through the hole, then fitted the plank back into place.

At the far end of Wadsworth's attic was the trunk where Clara hid her costume. She dressed by the faint gleam of light that came from the street lamps of the square through the large window in the eaves.

Thankfully, the window was far too grimy to see through, she thought. Then she laughed at herself.

The attic was four floors up. There would scarcely be anyone out there to see!

• • •

Dalton found himself clinging to the highest ledge of Wadsworth's house, grinning fiercely at the night and thinking that this was much more the thing. This was what he had wanted when he'd stepped down from the Royal Four—this feeling of being completely alive.

Around him, the quiet square slumbered but for a few lighted windows, and the incoming fog turned those into blurred rectangles of gold. He could likely dance a reel on the rooftops and no one would ever spot him.

Swiftly he crept along the ledge. There was a large square of glass panels set into the first slant of roof. The center panel would open, he'd noted from the street this afternoon as he'd leisurely strolled the square.

The panel did have hinges and a latch, but it was fixed from the inside with a simple drop hook. Reaching into his jacket pocket while clinging to the fog-dampened ledge one-handed sent his heart racing and made his grin stretch wider.

The rush that danger sent through his blood made him long for more of this sort of adventure in his life. At that moment, he wished that he might never be forced to total a ledger book or examine a law proposal again.

He closed his eyes and slid the flattened blade of the tool through the invisible gap between window and frame by feel. The blade slid freely upward for a moment, then caught in the drop latch.

If he was lucky, the latch would simply flip up and unlock the window. If it was even slightly stuck, he would be looking at a very dangerous climb down the slippery stones of the building.

The blade would not go further. Patiently, Dalton jiggled it, first slanting it this way, then that. The latch gave suddenly, and the window released toward him with a slight creak.

Chapter Six

Clara shed herself as she shed her own gown, and settled into the persona of Clara Rose.

Clara Rose was not the real Rose, of course, for Mr. Wadsworth's battered chambermaid was entirely too mild and fearful to suit Clara's mission.

Her Rose was a bit on the saucy side, at least in her own mind. She worked hard, but owed no loyalty past that of paid servant. She was brisk and opinionated in the way that Clara had never dared be. Rose would laugh in the face of Beatrice's demands, and make faces behind Oswald's back when he waxed overpompous.

Clara felt the irreverent confidence of Rose seep into her bones. She needed to affect the scuffling fearfulness of the real Rose when others were around, of course. But that Rose would never dare to climb into a cupboard to overhear the master's private conversations, nor would she make free with the drawers of his lordship's desk.

Only Clara Rose had the confidence to sneak a stub of pencil and a scrap of paper into her pocket to make a quick sketch of a visitor, or the crest on a carriage—

though most of Mr. Wadsworth's familiars came in anonymous hackney coaches in the dark of night.

With quick motions, she tied her apron round her back and turned to dig in the trunk for her cap, searching by feel in the darkness. With her head deep in the trunk, she could hear nothing but her own scuffling movements.

But the tingle of cool night air across her neck—when had she felt that exact sensation before?—caused her to jerk upright from her search.

A man stood there, silhouetted against the dim light filtering through the grimy attic window.

For a moment, she couldn't grasp the image. It was a trick of the night, a shadow. Just another dark flicker in the corner of her vision, as had happened so often in her attic hiding place.

But the shadow didn't fade, didn't transmute into an old hat-rack, or her own figure in a wavy looking-glass. It was a man, a very large man.

Clara's pulse froze still, then raced. She was alone. No one knew she was here. And no one would hear if she screamed.

The man's profile turned this way and that. He was listening for her, she realized. She made no sound, not even allowing her breath to rasp the way it most certainly wished to.

She almost stepped backward and rang her heel into the trunk, but stopped herself just in time. The empty trunk would have boomed like a cannon in the silence.

The empty trunk.

Before she even truly completed the thought, she'd hiked her skirts and lifted one foot over the side. If he didn't know she was there, if she could hide quickly enough—

She carefully lifted her other foot over the high side of the trunk and lowered herself inside, never taking her eyes off the silhouette that stood mere yards before her. The bottom of the trunk was lined with an old bit of wool and she made no sound as she settled herself within.

She'd oiled the hinges herself long ago, for she'd never wanted to alert any wandering servants to her presence in the attic when no one was supposed to be up there. When she slowly lowered the lid, not a squeak came from the old forged iron, not even when the lid settled home.

Clara curled up on the old blanket, which was clean if a bit mousy smelling. She was rather small and the trunk was rather large. All in all, she was quite comfortable. She'd no fear of small places. On the contrary, she rather liked them. Heights now, that was another matter.

She cocked her ears to the outside world, but not a sound made it through the thick wood. Had the man left—passed through the attic on the way into the house? Had he gone back through the window?

Then the lid creaked just above her ear and she started violently. He was opening the trunk!

Instinctively, she shut her eyes and shrank down, waiting to be dragged from her hiding place by hard hands. Nothing happened. The trunk remained closed. She heard a faint grating sound as if someone was idly shuffling their feet on the dusty floor of the attic. The lid creaked again above her head.

Was he *sitting* on her? Hysteria began to bubble up within her. Did he require a rest after his strenuous evening of breaking and entering? Even mad intruders needed to relax, apparently!

There came a very polite knock on the lid of the trunk. "Oy, there! Anybody 'ome?" The voice was deep and not terribly loud, for all that it vibrated right through the heavy wood.

Did he truly expect her to answer? *Oh, yes, kind sir, do come in.* She held her breath for fear of him hearing her, then realized how absurd she was being. He obviously knew she was inside and was simply toying with her.

Even as these thoughts were skittering through her mind, another part of her was becoming very aware of the closeness of the air. Every breath she took was becoming more labored. She'd not thought the trunk might be airtight!

She must get out. Listening carefully, she heard nothing from above her. Perhaps he was already gone. Then a sound reached her. A tuneless humming, an idle sort of sound.

Drat. He was most definitely still there and he wasn't leaving anytime soon. Time ticked slowly on and the air in the trunk became heavier and less satisfying. She tried her mightiest to wait the invader out, but finally she could not deny that shortly she would be in certain danger of suffocation. Could the alternative be any worse?

In a resentful panic, she rapped sharply on the lid.

"Yes?" came that deep voice.

Her lungs were beginning to burn and her head was swimming. In panicked anger, she slammed the side of her fist against the lid. "Oh, just get off, you great bugger!"

The deep chuckle barely reached her consciousness as her mind began to buzz unpleasantly. Then the lid no longer resisted her efforts and the air became blessedly clear.

Breathing deeply, she blinked, her eyes straining in

the darkness. Where was he? Fighting the last of her dizziness, she rose to a crouch and looked about her. Where had he gone?

Then she saw motion in front of the window again and realized he'd retreated to his former position. Still, she had the feeling that he could see her every bit as well as she could see him.

Giving up entirely on stealth, she clambered noisily from the trunk. After all, if he'd wanted her dead, he'd only have needed to leave her in the dangerous position in which she'd put herself.

She stood and straightened her skirts with a swish, in no mood to be toyed with further. " 'Twas a dirty trick," she hissed at the shadow. "You nearly done me in!"

The man didn't move. "I'll not harm you, girl."

She flinched at his voice, though it was warm and even, and he made no move toward her. Clara realized that she had never heard a masculine voice in this attic, never known the way it could rebound from the slanting walls and low ceiling until he sounded as though he were standing right beside her, murmuring into her ear.

Then she took in his meaning. He could not truly see her, she was sure of it. How then had he known that she was female?

"I can smell your scent, my flower," he said with a chuckle, though she had not spoken the thought. "And I can just see your pale bit of a face."

The fellow shifted his stance, slowly moving his hands up and settling them into his pockets. With his form clearly in profile now, Clara could see that he was a fit fellow, tall and powerful.

Oddly, that didn't add to her unease. If he'd wanted to attack, surely he could have done so by now. As it was, he reminded her of a man trying to ease his way into acquaintance with a gentle wild thing.

"Will you not come forward then, little one?" the fellow said softly after a moment. "I'd not meant to frighten anyone."

His deep voice eased her fear with his soothing tone. The knot of fear in her belly untied itself, but the strings still thrummed with tension. She felt dizzy, unsettled by him, although that could be the result of scarcely breathing for so long.

"Why are you here?" she whispered.

"Not to do you harm, I swear to ye."

"Well, you're not here to clean the windows," she retorted.

He laughed softly, still maintaining his position. "True enough, my rose."

Rose? "Why—why do you call me that?"

"I smell roses on you."

The soap she'd used for her bath this eve. A tiny joke with herself, using rose soap when she would be playing Rose.

The nightmare feeling was becoming more dreamlike by the moment. Here she stood, conversing with an undoubtedly dangerous stranger in a dark attic in the middle of the night.

Hardly the place for a proper lady to be.

She was not afraid of him, she realized, but was not startled by that, still caught up in the unreality of it all. She felt pulled to him, drawn by his attempts to reassure her. She wished the moon would come out from behind the clouds the better to see him, but the sky was impenetrable and the lamplight from the square was entirely inadequate. There was only the dimness and the man.

As if he had her insides on a string, he pulled her

with his voice. "Will you not come closer, pretty rose? There's no need to hide in the shadows."

She took one step, then another. He turned his head as if to listen to the gentle grating of her shoes upon the floor and she saw the dark mask wrapped round the top of his face.

"A thief." She froze once more. "You're naught but a thief."

He said nothing for a moment, then nodded. "You could say that, but I've not come to steal from you."

"Not from me? How do you know I'm not the lady of the house, and will call down the law upon your head?"

"You may be a princess in your own right, my rose, but you're no fine lady, by your voice."

Clara realized that she'd kept Rose's uncultured accents throughout the exchange, and blessed herself for unwitting cleverness. He thought her a simple chambermaid, and therefore of little consequence, as long as he could persuade her not to give alarm to the household.

And truly, a thief in Wadsworth's home was hardly a bad thing, was it? If anyone deserved a stiff robbing, it was the master.

"No, I'm no princess, nor a lady fine." She stepped closer once more, her curiosity overcoming the last of her fear. "And you're no gentleman, but a common parlor thief."

"Nay, not common at all." He chuckled. "Are you not afraid, then?"

"No." She truly wasn't, though she was foolish to be so trusting. Still, aside from his teasing with the trunk he'd been nothing but respectful so far, though he had her quite alone. Which was more than she could say of the majority of Wadsworth's guests. Many was the evening she took home a few bruises from fingers pinching in unmentionable places.

"I ought to call out," she mused aloud. "I ought to run for the stairs and scream down the house."

"But you won't." He seemed very sure.

She smiled at him. "No, I won't."

Dalton was having difficulty grasping the situation. No one should be in the attic at this time of night. Especially not a female person in an apron and cap, standing saucily before him with a smile.

He was surprised by the white gleam of her teeth in the dimness. He'd thought himself coaxing a shivering maid from calling an alarm, but now found himself the recipient of a conspiratorial grin.

This one was not in the manual.

"Are you sure you're not afraid?" he asked again, trying to catch up.

She laughed out loud. "If you was to throw me over your shoulder and carry me away from here, I'd likely shout me thanks to the top of Westminster."

Dalton relaxed. A disgruntled servant he could believe, knowing what he did of Edward Wadsworth. Heaven knew what this girl was forced to put up with in this household, although it apparently hadn't broken her spirit.

She plunked something on top of her head, a cap of some kind, then held out her hand.

"Best we get on, then."

He hesitated. "Get on where?"

"The master's safe box in his study, o' course. Or is it jewels you're after? They're in the master's chamber."

"N–no, the safe box'll do." He took her outstretched hand in his own and allowed her to lead him on a winding path through the crowded attic. How . . . unexpected.

"Good. The master don't hold with jewels much, anyway. But I think there might be something in the safe box."

"Does he use the safe often?"

"Every Thursday night, and the first Sunday of the month, as well."

"Why Thursday?"

"It's when he's after having his meeting."

"His meeting . . . every Thursday eve?"

"Aye. So he's just had it last night."

How perfect. If the girl was correct, Wadsworth wouldn't even be checking his safe for days. If Dalton was able to get the contents away undetected, he could examine them at his leisure before he had to put them back.

"You never told me your name," he said.

"Nor have you."

Dalton smiled, charmed by her pertness. "Monty," he said, his nickname from school long ago.

"It's a nice name," she said softly, "for a thief."

"Only in good cause, my rose."

She tilted her head and looked back at him soberly. "You know, I believe you mean that."

They came to a narrow door that opened onto a set of even narrower stairs that wound down into complete darkness. Dalton spared a fleeting moment of pity for the poor souls who had to carry all the flotsam of the household up those tight turns. Were the stairs in his own house so inaccessible?

They traveled down, taking turn after turn. Dalton realized that she was leading him straight to the ground floor.

With one hand held by the girl and one hand trailing along the wall to keep his bearings in the darkness, Dalton had no way to tell that she had stopped short before him until he ran into her.

His arm swung to catch himself, and wrapped right about her waist. She inhaled sharply in response, which only served to tighten his grasp.

She was taller than he'd thought, for her head fit just under his chin. If he bent down, he could kiss the top of her silly mobcap. Not that he wanted to, of course, though she smelled of flowers and warm woman, and fit so nicely against him.

The thought scampered across his mind that this was the second time in two days that he had been in this position with a woman.

He felt her let her breath free in a slow, controlled exhalation, then she calmly peeled his arm away and moved on, never losing her grip on his other hand.

"I'll thank you not to be thievin' from me, masked man. *My* safe box is not for your pilferin' hands."

Dalton grinned in the dark. She was a bold thing, this attic rose—dainty and poised, but saucy. He decided that he liked saucy.

He heard a click, and a rectangle of pale light appeared before them. He'd made it into the house.

For a brief moment, he felt regret at leaving the scented intimacy of the dark stairwell. This fearless maid had him somewhat enchanted, and he was frankly a bit afraid to see her clearly.

Her face could never live up to her clear lilting voice and her lithe graceful form. She'd have a large nose, or bulging eyes, and his enjoyable moment of fancy would be quite spoiled.

She turned briefly, lit from beyond by the few sconces still burning in the hallway. Her cap was pulled low and she ducked her head but Dalton saw enough to reassure him. There was no bulbous nose in view. Only a delicate profile, one with a decidedly firm little chin.

She was no beauty, perhaps, but apparently fine featured and clear skinned. Pretty, he decided, in an understated way. Hiding it like that likely did her good in this house of men.

He was glad that she was pretty, even as he laughed at himself. What a fairy-tale fool he was, to fancy her a dream girl, a secret beauty formed just for him from midnight magic.

She was only a maid, and he was only an idiot who'd gone too long without the caress of a woman's hands.

Still, he was enjoying this adventure. He was Monty, sneak thief and charmer of pretty chambermaids. His life was chancy but free, and he made the most of it.

No responsibilities, no seat in Parliament, no national security needs laid at his doorstep. Lord Etheridge would return to his life in a few hours, but for now Monty would relish his freedom and flirt with a pretty girl.

She led him down the hall, moving too quietly for words. Was she required to be so silent in her duties? Dalton realized that he had little idea what a chambermaid's life was like.

The girl stopped before a set of double doors that looked very much like the ones that led to Dalton's own study. Pushing him back and motioning him to stay, she pushed one open and entered, ducking her head and shuffling as she did so.

She popped back out immediately, flashing him that same gamine grin in the dimness. "His lordship's gone to bed hours ago," she said. Then she took his hand and towed him into the study.

"How can you tell?"

"The fire. 'Tis cold as ice. He don't allow a fire to

burn unless he's in the room. Wasteful, he says."

"Chilling," muttered Dalton. In more ways than one. Now that he thought about it, the attic had been uncommonly cold, as was the rest of the house. And this poor girl had to work in this unheated place?

Wadsworth was even more close-fisted than Dalton had realized. Not to mention uncaring to the point of cruelty. Dalton decided that he would enjoy pilfering Wadsworth's safe box.

Without being asked, the girl moved to open the draperies of the street-facing window. The glow from the lamps on the square provided enough light for Dalton to examine the safe box.

It wasn't a very complicated one, he soon learned. Apparently Wadsworth couldn't bear to part with his brass, not even for good security. Dalton removed two picks from his pocket and slipped them into the keyhole of the lock.

He smelled roses, and looked down to see that the girl was standing almost in his armpit, gazing raptly at what he was doing.

"Thinkin' of takin' up a new career?" he teased.

She flashed him that pirate smile again. "None o' your cheekiness, Mr. Monty Thief-in-the-night! I've always wondered, is all."

Dalton wasn't sure what possessed him, but he pulled the picks from the lock and reached for her hands. "I'll show you."

Willingly she moved in front of him and allowed him to manipulate her hands while she held the picks. "Y'see," he said softly into her ear. "You hold this one still whilst you find the tumbler with this one. Then you turn it till it gives in to you."

It wasn't very gentlemanly of him to move still closer,

pressing himself to her back. But then again, Monty was no gentleman, was he? The maid's hands went motionless beneath his, then she shifted slightly against him and bent to her task once again.

The lock clicked and sprang open, but Dalton's senses didn't absorb it for a moment. He was still somewhat dazed by the unexpected rush of desire that had swept over him at the light brush of her bottom against his groin. Startling and . . . somewhat confusing.

Triumphant, she turned in his arms, holding the picks aloft. "I did it!" Then she froze when she saw his face.

Her own face was a pale oval in the dimness, only her brow, cheekbone, and chin catching the glimmer from the street. The shadows added mystery, so that all he could see of her eyes was fathomless darkness.

As if on its own, his hand lifted to her face. She didn't move, still gazing into his eyes. He let his knuckles skim along her soft cheek and she started slightly. Did she feel it, too?

The silence pulsed around them and he could hear her breathe. He let one finger drag along her bottom lip, just to see if it was as soft as her skin. Her lips parted and a small breath escaped her. Dalton liked the way her lips felt. He especially liked the lower one, which was just a shade too plump for refinement, but which suited him very well.

She made a tiny sound at the contact, a small catch of her breath.

It was enough to wake him from his daze of lust. Dalton became aware of two things simultaneously. She smelled better than any woman he had ever known, and she had suddenly begun to shake against him.

She was alone with him, and he wanted her. She had good reason to be afraid, were he anyone else. It sick-ened him to know he'd caused fear in her. He'd never taken advantage of a woman in his life, not even a chambermaid, and in his position of wealth and power he easily could have.

With a physical wrench, he stepped back and dropped his arms, forcing a weak laugh. "Well, you can't blame a bloke for dreamin', now can ye?"

She only looked at him, her eyes dark and wide in the dimness. "Best you don't dream of me, Monty Thief-in-the-night. For you'll dream in vain."

Then she moved neatly away from him, stopping only when she had placed a large chair between them. "Go on with your job. 'Tis gettin' late."

Dalton stared at the open safe for a moment, feeling foolish. He was on a mission. He was not here to cuddle chambermaids. Angry at himself and at her for being more focused than he was, he began rifling through the contents of Wadsworth's safe, sorting by feel.

Keeping his back to her, he left the lovingly wrapped banknotes alone, taking only the tightly bound portfolios. Wadsworth's files would be worth more to this mission than all his wealth.

Swiftly he stuffed them into the small bag that was strapped over his shoulder, keeping them in the precise order in which they had lain in the safe, and closed the clasp. He shut the safe and held out his hand.

"My picks."

Clara looked down at her hands, surprised to see her fingers still tightly wrapped around the long metal picks. The metal had bitten into her skin and her fingers opened stiffly after clenching for many minutes. She likely had red marks driven deeply into her palms.

He'd frightened her worse than she'd thought.

Frightened, were you? Is that why your knees are weak and you can't catch your breath?

Of course it was. What else could it be but fear?

Fear and a tall, broad-shouldered, slim-hipped male body that was made all the more tempting by the black mask above . . .

Clara shook her head before that sharp little voice could answer. There was something quite seriously wrong with her. Watching Monty warily, she stepped forward to drop the picks into the dim blur of his waiting hand, then retreated behind the chair once more.

He'd touched her so . . . longingly? No, it hadn't been mere longing. There had been something darker and more intense in the delicate sensuous strokes of his fingers.

Bentley had desired her physically and she'd been willing enough, if never terribly enthusiastic. But he'd never *ached* for her, the way that Monty's silent touch had revealed that he did.

And she had certainly never responded so to a simple touch. For a moment, she allowed herself to wonder what it would be like if she really were Rose.

Rose could carry on with a thief, if she were careful. And if she were caught, she'd shame no one but herself. Of course, poor little Rose would never dream of doing such a thing. Almost the only thing the girl had in the world was her virtue.

Monty finished locking the safe box and turned to her. "I know the way out. You don't have to show me the door," he said softly. His voice was gentle, almost apologetic.

Suddenly Clara felt silly for fearing him, if that was indeed the emotion she'd felt. What had he done but touch her? He'd not harmed her at all, despite every opportunity.

"No, I'll take you back." She smiled and reached for his hand once more.

This time, however, she was profoundly aware of how large his hand was, and of how warm. There was something new in his grasp. Awareness and . . . caution? He held her fingers carefully, as if to let her know that she could pull free at any time if she wanted.

He was kind, she decided. Kind and daring and very, very . . . interesting.

Chapter Seven

The girl said not a word as she led Dalton back up the black stairwell to the attic. They stopped before the window where he had entered.

"My master will be opening his safe in a few days' time." She cocked her head and smiled slightly in the faint glow through the sooty window.

Dalton found that he missed that wild-child grin.

"You'd best get all them papers back in there by then," she added. Then the wicked smile flashed all too briefly in the dimness.

Startled, Dalton realized that she hadn't been fooled at all. Had she seen him take only the files, or had she guessed?

She stepped back, almost disappearing in the attic shadows. "Fare thee well, Monty." The soft scuff of her shoes moved away, and she was gone from his sight.

"Wait. You didn't tell me your name."

Her soft laughter came dancing back to him through the darkness.

"Why, 'tis Rose, of course."

The stews of London smelled nothing like food. This portion of the city reminded James Cunnington more of decay than cooking. The loose community that had built up over the years around the estuaries of the Thames—long since shortened to *stews*—attracted the lowest rung of civilization. Excrement, both animal and human, could be found in the gutters. Everywhere was the pervasive stench of urine, both new and old. Coal smoke mixed with the miasma to cause a choking brew that nearly blocked the sun, even at the hour of noon.

There was no sun now, for the hour neared midnight. Torches lit the entrances of those establishments that could not afford lanterns or perhaps did not want to risk almost constant theft and breakage.

He and Collis were here to investigate the subjects of yet another Sir Thorogood cartoon. They'd identified more than two dozen such subjects today and they were bloody tired of it. Now they were on the hunt for a whore who went by the name of Fleur.

The public houses lined the street and whores lined the alleys. For a penny, one could even lie down with one of them on a straw pallet in a tiny wretched crib. If a bloke only wanted to spare a ha'penny, or perhaps just a swallow or two from his flask, he could take a whore up against the alley wall and never so much as wrinkle his trousers.

James had tried it once in his younger and more drunken days, but the odor from the woman's rotting teeth had doused his lust like a candle. He'd paid her anyway and ducked off into the night, half-shamed but mostly relieved that he hadn't followed through.

Still, he could read the thoughts in Collis's mind as if they were his own, not so long ago. It was not easy for a gentleman to take care of his satisfaction. Young ladies were off limits, as they should be. Mistresses were expensive and James had spent too much time with Simon—son of a Covent Market whore—to ever wish that life on a woman. Widows were a possibility, but they often expected marriage. Wives were the most convenient but the trickiest, having husbands who tended toward jealousy.

Lavinia had been a wife. Of course, Lavinia had also been a vicious, kidnapping, murdering French spy who had brought about the deaths of several of the Liars before she was stopped, but when James had met her he hadn't known that. All he'd known was that she knew how to do things he'd only heard about and that seemed character reference enough for him.

He would never be that stupid again. And neither would Collis if James had anything to do with it.

"Put your eyes back in your head, Col. Those bosoms are constructed from whalebone and that laughter comes from opium."

Collis pulled his head back into the unmarked carriage, grinning and unrepentant. "Don't worry, James. I'm only looking. I won't go blind from looking."

James snorted. "No, not from *looking*."

They spared a moment for boyish snickers, then returned to the discussion of their plan, which had been interrupted by Collis's distraction. James wasn't sure how much Dalton had revealed to his heir about the Liar's Club, so he'd kept the origin of his quest secret, only telling Collis that he needed to track down Sir Thorogood's most recent subjects. Collis had agreed so willingly and unquestioningly that James suspected his friend would have come along on any excuse in order to occupy his mind.

"We're two young louts with more money than brains, and we've a wager at White's that we'll be the first to find the mysterious Fleur."

Collis raised a brow. "I like it. Original."

It wasn't original at all, they soon learned. The first publican they hailed answered almost before they got the question out.

"Don't know any Fleur, she ain't here," he recited as if by rote. "But there's a girl in the corner over there that'll let you call her anything you want."

James and Collis peered through the smoky pub to spy a young girl sitting on the corner bench. She was pretty and fairly clean, but her eyes held a level of emptiness that bordered on idiocy. Collis whistled low. "I don't think she's a French spy, do you?"

James flinched. His affair with Lady Winchell and her subsequent treasonous acts had been made all too public by Lavinia herself. Her defense had been that she had never meant to shoot the Prime Minister, but had truly been aiming at her former lover, James. The gossip sheets had outdone themselves for days, although the furor had subsided when the Prince had decorated James at the same time he had knighted Simon Raines.

Collis sent him an apologetic glance. "Oh . . . sorry, old man."

James forced a careless smile and shrugged off the familiar burn of humiliation and regret. He was simply going to have to get used to this sort of thing.

Collis turned back to the publican, adopting a slur and waved the wrinkled bit of newsprint with the cartoon on it. "Want the real Fleur. Want her! Got the brass to pay her well, and you, too."

The man shrugged as if he'd heard it all too many times to care. "No Fleur. Nobody knows her. Damned paper sending you sods all over the city, lookin' for some whore what don't exist." He turned his back, muttering about wasted time and sorry sods.

That was the story all over the stews, and finally James and Collis called it an evening. Or rather, a morning.

"These girls change their names more often than they change their drawers," James complained when they were back inside the carriage. "She's long gone, if she ever existed. Who's next on the list?"

Collis pulled out the file and flipped through the cartoons within. "We've identified everyone in this lot except for two of the four people in the Fleur cartoon. I'll wager anything that Fleur is a figment of Sir Thorogood's imagination."

James nodded. "Sounds good to me. I doubt we'll ever identify the third man, with only half his face to go on. We've two hours until dawn. Let's get some sleep now. I've much to do tomorrow."

"You mean today." Collis yawned. "Well, if you wanted to cure me of ever visiting a whore, you just did." Shuddering, he glanced out the carriage window at the women still wandering the streets. "What a life."

"I wouldn't call it that." James shook his head. "That's no life at all."

There was no reason for Dalton to be looking behind him every step of the walk to the club the next morning, yet he was. He felt compelled to check under every cap, every tall hat, that filled the streets around him.

A great many people were about today, both walking

and driving. Carriages and carts on the cobbles, people of all sorts on the walks. Dalton had his own money tucked deep inside his waistcoat, but he knew that many of those around him would lose their purses today.

A glint of light hair caught his eye as a gentleman doffed his hat to some ladies and Dalton squinted to see through the crowd. No, the bloke was too old . . .

Dalton was beginning to wonder if he was losing his mind. He had seen the fair-haired man twice more since the attack in the alley yesterday, or at least he thought he had. Both times had been a mere flicker of an image at the corner of his vision, yet when he'd tried to get a better look, the stranger was not there.

He'd described the fellow to the Liars in detail, but none of them had any help to offer, nor had they seemed terribly impressed by his urgency. After the first time he hadn't mentioned it to them again.

He would deal with this one on his own, as he was dealing with the Sir Thorogood case.

Which was going nowhere fast. He'd spent two evenings attending every ridiculous ball and excruciating musicale that he could bear, and still he had not flushed out anyone who made protest of his posturing.

Except perhaps the blond man. He could very well be associated with the fellow, or even be the artist himself, though he looked more like a cricket master than a flamboyant artist.

Still, unless the fellow left a drawing of himself behind, Dalton didn't stand much chance of identifying him by description alone. It was too bad that the Liars didn't have an artist of their own . . .

He stopped in his tracks. What a brilliant idea. An artist could supply every Liar with a sketch of suspicious characters. The identification rate would soar. No enemy operative would be safe within the boundaries of London or Westminster!

Dalton realized that he was standing stock-still in the center of the walk with a stupid grin on his face, like a child who had spotted the confectioner's shop. Two ladies stepped around him with a whisper and a twitter, followed by two footmen laden with shopping. Dalton removed his hat and bowed deeply in his best Sir Thorogood manner.

"My apologies, dear ladies. I was only struck still by your brilliance. Do forgive me."

The twittering increased, but their gazes turned from judging to flirtatious as they walked on. Dalton returned his hat to his head and turned to cross the busy thoroughfare.

He'd been traversing the dangerous streets of London for many years, and the way of it was second nature. Keep one's attention focused on both lanes of heavy mid-morning traffic, watch for oncoming carriages, carts, and riders, and run for one's life.

He'd almost made it across when a man on horseback veered suddenly to cut him off. Backpedaling, Dalton cursed under his breath and made to dodge around the horse's rear.

The heavy rattle of wheels sounded far too close and Dalton jerked his head to the left to see an ale wagon bearing directly on him at high speed. He leaped forward out of the way, his coattails clearing the rushing vehicle by mere inches.

Only to find himself in the path of a coal cart coming fast from his right. The lead horse threw up his head in alarm. There was nothing that Dalton could do but to reach for the harness and pray.

His hand closed around the leather strap at the horse's

jaw and he was jerked from his feet. With all his might, he pulled down on the strap, using the leverage to swing one leg up on the cart horse's back. There he hung sideways on the wild-eyed animal feeling like a circus fool, but at least he was not lying chopped beneath sixteen iron-shod hooves.

The carter called halt and Dalton felt the horse come to a shuddering stop. Gratefully, he slipped off to land on his feet and released his death grip on the chin strap.

"Oy, there, guv'nor! You all right, sir?" The drover stumped forward to hold the horse, his sweating face horrified and fearful. "I din't see you 'tall! The coal's that heavy, it don't stop easy. Tell me you're all right, sir."

Dalton dusted himself off. "I'm very well, my good man. That was fine driving. Couldn't have done better myself."

Profound relief crossed the stout man's face. No doubt the fellow had dealt with "the Quality" before. Many a gentleman of the *ton* would have had the fellow up on charges, even for something so unavoidable.

Yet had it been an accident, or something more sinister? Pedestrians were struck so often in the London streets that under any other circumstances, Dalton would have thought it was just bad timing on his part. After all, if it hadn't been for the man on horseback—

A fair-haired man, well dressed, with his hat pulled low. Dalton had only had the merest glimpse as he'd dodged behind the horse. He hadn't seen the fellow's face at all. He honestly couldn't be sure. And yet, the ale wagon hadn't so much as slowed its pace.

Had the mystery man purposely herded Dalton into danger? If so, it was the perfect crime. Murder by ale cart would never be investigated. He would have simply been another unfortunate story for nannies to tell their charges, a cautionary tale about looking both ways before crossing the street.

After reassuring the carter once more, Dalton headed onward down the street to a hack stand. From now on, he'd be taking a carriage to work. His daily constitutionals were becoming deadly.

Morning sunlight streamed into Oswald Trapp's study, illuminating dust motes into flakes of gold and making Clara's eyes water as she glared at Oswald's stubborn safe box.

She blew her straggling hair from before her eyes and bent to the lock to try again. Had Monty told her to hold the top pick still and move the bottom one, or was it the other way around?

Perhaps Wadsworth's safe box worked differently from the Trapps'. Or perhaps she was simply no use at all at this sort of thing. Fortunately, she had decided to practice on Oswald's safe first.

She wiggled her new homemade lock picks in the keyhole once more, but nothing happened. She sighed. What she needed was a set of real picks. A hatpin and a dismantled scissor blade were never meant to be put to such purpose.

She changed her approach and began again, even as she berated herself for her stubbornness. This was a terrible idea. She was losing her mind. There was nothing interesting left in Wadsworth's safe.

Except that Monty would be returning the papers soon, she was sure of it. And somewhere in that stack of documents might just be the ticket to striking a real blow for her objective. She'd been combing Wadsworth's desk for months, hoping the man would accidentally leave something useful for her, but she'd never dreamed she'd be able to get inside his safe.

Not to mention that it would be a lovely excuse to see Monty again.

"Oh, shut it," she muttered to the little voice. "You've no idea what you're talking about."

Monty. You recall, with the mysterious mask and the roguish grin and the way he has of making your toes curl when he stands close to you in the dark?

Clara sighed. "Oh. That Monty." She was becoming as silly as Beatrice, drat it. All atwitter over a man.

Worse. All atwitter over a thief.

Clara bit her lip and forced herself to concentrate on her task. Now was no time to be thinking about the heat of his hands over hers, or the way she'd felt when his arms were around her as he had demonstrated the picks. Or the touch of his slightly rough fingertip on her mouth, and how her body had responded, warming and aching between her—

The lock tumbled, something clicked, and the door of the safe box opened into her hands. She'd done it!

Clara's fingers twitched with curiosity, but with ruthless self-control she quickly closed the door and worked the lock back into action with her makeshift picks. She wasn't here to snoop into the Trapps' business, but to practice what Monty had shown her last night.

Now, again.

But the picks felt like pikes in her clumsy fingers and no matter how she concentrated, nothing she did seemed to work. How had Monty held this pick, and how had he moved that one? She ought to have paid better attention, but he'd been scrambling her thoughts with his large hard body pressing to her back. She'd felt the heat coming from him through the fabric of her gown, felt it sink into her and warm her from a certain spot within. He was a big man, bigger than Bentley. She wondered if his size corresponded—

The lock went *snick*. Clara blinked as the door popped open. She'd done it again, but she'd been so busy thinking of a certain masked thief and his certain parts that she didn't even remember doing it. . . .

Aha! She grinned and shut the door, working the picks to lock it once more. Then she purposely concentrated on nothing but the dark need in Monty's touch when she'd turned in his arms to face him. With sudden intensity, she wished she'd kissed him. Kissed him and wrapped her arms around his neck and pressed her body close enough to feel his bulging—

Click. Clara pulled her thoughts from the fascinating contents of Monty's trousers with difficulty, then smiled as the door released once more. It seemed that all she needed to do was think terrible, scandalous thoughts about Monty and nothing would be safe from her picks.

She'd just jimmied the lock tight again when she heard the knob of the study door rattle. Quickly, she stood and straightened her skirts. By the time the door opened and Kitty entered, Clara was serenely examining a shelf of books, her head angled to read the titles.

"Oh, there you are, Auntie. Mama said she's ready to go shopping if you are."

"Oh . . . yes, shopping." Drat. It was her own fault. She'd committed to purchasing a new gown yesterday. And she did need something appropriately featherheaded to impress Sir Impostor with her inanity. She turned a smile on Kitty. "I shall be ready as soon as I've fetched my bonnet and spencer."

Kitty smiled back as if surprised that Clara was actually going through with the outing. "Wonderful! I shall fetch Mama and Bitty at once."

A quarter of an hour later, Clara stood outside the front door of the Trapp house tugging on her gloves. Inside, Beatrice was still haranguing the twins into preparing themselves for a day of shopping.

Clara had come outside to take a moment away from the hullabaloo and because she'd noticed that most of Wadsworth's servants were out front unloading a delivery cart.

It wasn't nosy to take a moment of air when one's neighbor happened to be receiving something, she told herself primly. Besides, she'd seen Rose out there with the others and wanted to give her the signal to trade places with her again tonight.

Mr. Wadsworth certainly ate well, she noticed, as yet another bushel basket of greens was unloaded. A string of plucked birds came next, then a large wooden trough of organs.

The scent of the tripe wafted to Clara and she wrinkled her nose. *Ick.* Perhaps she didn't want to sneak into Wadsworth's tonight to serve after all.

Rose took the trough from the servant before her and turned toward the narrow stairs that led down from the street to the kitchen entrance. The huge wooden platter was so large it dwarfed the little maid. She could scarcely see over it.

Clara almost held up a hand to protest the obvious danger of such a move, then remembered that she could hardly be expected to know that Rose had an unfortunate habit of—

Rose stubbed a toe on the cobbles and stumbled forward. The trough went spinning from her grip. Clara couldn't watch. She squinted her eyes shut, but that didn't do a thing to hide the squelching splat of the wet meats hitting Wadsworth's front steps.

"You useless wench!" Wadsworth's roar sounded over the street noise. Clara opened her eyes.

Oh, no. Mr. Wadsworth stood in a sea of quivering creature parts. They mounded over his shoes and clung to his jacket and waistcoat. Strands of something unbearable hung trembling from the man's hair and muttonchop whiskers.

Clara felt the snicker rising from somewhere reprehensible within her and firmly tried to suppress it. If she laughed and embarrassed Wadsworth yet more, things could only go worse for poor Rose.

Even now Rose fluttered about her master, attempting to clean him up with the corner of her apron. The man raised his fist.

"Get off, you stupid cow!" He swung a blow at Rose, who ducked with the ease of long practice, dispelling the worst of the impact. Wadsworth's swing took him off balance. His shoes slithered in the slime at his feet and he landed with his large bottom directly on the pile.

Clara pressed her gloved fist hard to her lips, but a strangled snort escaped her. Wadsworth lifted his head and glared about him to see who was laughing.

A bedraggled orange tabby cat, attracted by the free banquet spread upon the cobbles, ran out to steal a bite from the mess. Wadsworth roared and took his rage out on the innocent animal in one savage swipe of his foot that sent the cat twisting and yowling through the air into the center of the busy street.

"No!" Clara cried and started forward. It was too late.

The poor creature's cry was cut off abruptly as it landed hard on the cobbles.

Sick with pity, Clara dodged an oncoming cart and ran to the still form. Gently, she laid one hand on its thin side. There was a faint heartbeat, wasn't there? There had to be.

Carefully, she gathered the limp cat into her arms and carried it to safety. Beatrice stood on the steps with the twins, watching in horror.

"Oh, no! No more strays, not in my house. Clara Simpson, you drop that filthy creature right this minute! Goodness, what are you thinking, running into the street for such a thing?"

With dismay, Clara looked up at Bea standing above her on the steps. She'd thought to nurse the poor cat if she could, but she'd forgotten. This was not her house. If Bea wouldn't allow the cat inside—and she wouldn't—then Clara had no recourse.

If only she had her own home. . . .

Well, she didn't. She was dependent on Bea and Oswald, at least for now.

"Here, miss," came a soft voice at her elbow. "Let me take that dirty thing. I'll put it in the rubbish for you."

Rose stood beside her, a bruise already darkening her pale cheek. The maid held out her apron to catch the cat.

Bea stamped her foot. "Well, give it to her, Clara! And then go change your gloves. I hope you didn't get any vermin on that gown. New carpets don't grow on trees, I'll have you know!"

Clara eyed Rose, who gave her a small wink. "I'll put it far away, miss. No one will ever see it."

Clara hid a smile. Good old Rose. The cat would be

waiting in the attic tonight, she'd wager her stockpile on it.

"Thank you. I'll let you see to it, then." She placed the cat gently into Rose's apron and watched as the maid returned to the kitchen, her bulky apron convincingly wadded up to her bruised cheek as if to soothe it.

Bea's housemaid trotted forward to hand Clara a new pair of gloves. After donning them and giving the girl the bloodied pair to dispose of, Clara turned to Bea, who was now leaning from the carriage window. The look on her face did not bode well.

The footman opened the door and held out a hand. With yet another sigh, Clara stepped up into the vehicle, sure that her afternoon of fashion was going to be a tedious one.

Chapter Eight

"My God, Etheridge. Don't you look the first stare of fashion!"

Dalton forced a pleasant smile on his face while he bowed low to the Prince Regent. Being called unexpectedly before England's ruler was always a bit nerve-wracking. Being forced to show up in full Thorogood finery ranked somewhere just past nightmarish.

Especially since Prince George the IV *liked* this hideous costume. With every fiber of his being, Dalton prayed that the Prince would not decide to adopt such rainbow-hued regalia, thereby sending every gentleman in England to outdo each other in slavish imitation.

He straightened to find George regarding him with greedy eyes. Oh, hellfire. Male dignity was doomed. Then Dalton pictured Lord Liverpool dutifully rigged out in poisonous colors and high heels. Perhaps there was a bright side . . .

Feeling better, he was able to greet the Prince with a very sincere smile. "Good afternoon, Your Highness."

"I say, you do look fine, Etheridge." The Prince Regent walked once around Dalton, finger tapping his chin.

"Bother that Beau Brummell anyway, making us wear funeral dress all the time." George sniffed. "I used to wear a waistcoat like that, back when a man was allowed to show a little color. Who is your tailor, anyway?"

"Dead," stated Dalton flatly. "Fell over dead last week, just like that." He snapped his fingers.

George furrowed his brow. "Pity. I could have made him a very rich man." He sighed. "Ah, well, I suppose such ostentatious dressing would look bad in wartime, eh?"

"Very wise observation, Your Highness."

"Humph." George didn't look as though he appreciated such speedy agreement. "Still, your *shoes*! You must give me the name of your cobbler."

Dalton supposed that another sudden death for the cobbler might cause suspicion. He nodded. "I'll send his direction to your valet." Poor Button. Dalton didn't want to be nearby when the little valet learned that he'd missed a royal opportunity due to his own untimely death.

Casting a glance down at the results of Button's latest act of vengeance, Dalton wondered if perhaps he ought to leave town for a while.

"So, sit and share my tea," invited George, waving Dalton to a table absolutely groaning with food. Tea for the portly Prince Regent was apparently a week's feasting for anyone else. "Tell me about this Thorogood. Found him yet?"

It wasn't policy to give his report over Liverpool's head like this, but who was he to refuse a royal edict? So Dalton related the entire case history to George, aware that he had little to show for several days' work.

George nodded and grunted here and there while he polished off platter after platter. One would have thought he was scarcely listening had it not been for the occasional probing question and intelligent aside. Dalton never underestimated the Prince Regent. He was a brilliant man, swift and decisive when he wanted to be.

Pity for England that he so rarely wanted to be.

"I see," George said as he dabbed his mouth with a regally monogrammed napkin and tossed the priceless linen into a puddle of prune sauce. "A two-pronged investigation. I approve. Well, carry on then. I want to meet Thorogood when you find him, by the way. Preferably before Liverpool gets him. Our dear Prime Minister never wants anyone else to have a bit of fun."

The Prince shook his head. "I really don't know how you managed to survive being raised by the man. He *still* thinks he can scold me like a boy. Just this morning he was waxing livid over some boyish prank I committed when I was sixteen." George chuckled. "Perhaps I can convince Thorogood to do a cartoon about Liverpool. Damned funny fellow. Damned funny."

Which one? Liverpool or Thorogood? Dalton didn't ask, not sure he wanted to know.

The Prince Regent walked from the room laughing, leaving Dalton amid the wreckage of their "tea," feeling rather like he'd had another near miss with an ale wagon.

Anyone looking at the three men gathered next to the stall of a promising two-year-old gelding would have thought they were perhaps discussing the virtues of the horse.

Anyone would have been wrong.

"He was seen being admitted to the Prince, I tell you! For all we know, he could be spilling everything he knows this very moment!" The portly man was red of face and virulent of manner. "He must be removed from the field of play!"

"First of all, we don't know that he has anything to tell. The drawing was damaging, true, but it could have been worse." The tallest man, a fair-haired gentleman, leaned indolently on the post at the corner of the stall, never taking his eyes from the horse. "By the by, who is your informant in the palace?"

The third man, small and thin, looked from side to side fearfully. "Oh, who gives a damn? The point is, we should leave now! If the Prince gets wind of us, if he remembers *Fleur*—"

"He isn't likely to connect Fleur with anything," the fair-haired man said soothingly. "I still think our best course lies in discrediting Thorogood. That way, everything he says will be suspect."

The fat man growled. "Now that he's made himself a spectacle, all the more reason to remove him. With as many enemies as he's made, no one will be able to trace anything back to us."

The fair-haired man gazed worriedly at the gelding. "Don't do anything rash. This is not the time. Shall we meet tomorrow night to discuss it? The pieces are not yet in place, you said so yourself."

"The pieces are *my* players. Don't forget who invited you into this game."

The fair-haired man turned to look at his companions for the first time. His gaze was calm but direct. "I may be new to *this* game, my good man, but I have been playing since I was born."

He pushed himself from his slouch against the stall. "Now, if you'll kindly excuse me, I believe I shall go buy this horse."

The modiste's boutique was stuffy and overly warm. Clara found herself rather inclined to yawn. After she had chosen a half-dozen styles from Madame Hortensia's pattern book, she submitted to being measured. Of course, Beatrice insisted that it be done while Clara's corset was tightly laced, although not as tight as it had been the other night.

Madame, a severely stylish lady whose once heavy French accent had mellowed since war had been declared against Napoleon, nodded and clucked approvingly over the measuring process. However, she protested when Clara chose from the shop's slim supply of ready-made gowns.

The overly flounced dress was made in a girlish pink satin and vastly overdecorated. It had clearly been a custom order, for flounces had been out of fashion for years. Even Clara knew that much.

Madame Hortensia paled. "Th–this one? But madame, you will look like an overturned feather duster! The style this season is a narrow silhouette. One must drape, madame, not flounce!"

The woman was so distraught that Clara almost felt sorry for her. "I need a gown tonight, and this one fits." It also cost the moon, with all its bows and tiny pearls. It hurt her to spend so, after saving so carefully. But all her work would be for naught if she didn't maintain an adequate disguise. "This dress is perfect. I shall have it, or I shall go elsewhere."

Apparently taste was no equal to profit. Madame Hortensia nodded. "Very well. But if Madame will indulge me . . . perhaps if anyone asks where you obtained this gown . . ."

Clara smiled. "I shan't breathe a word."

"Thank you, madame." Looking dazed, the modiste wandered off to note the rest of Clara's order.

Through all of this, Beatrice had only nodded approvingly. "Silly fad, this Grecian style. I myself like a flounce or three." She looked thoughtful. "Perhaps I'll have Madame Hortensia make a few up for me, as well."

Outside the curtained fitting area, the silver bell that hung over the door rang. A familiar voice called out for Madame Hortensia. Beatrice flew to the slit in the curtain and peeked through.

"Oh, it's that horrid Cora Teagarden!" she hissed over her shoulder. "And she has a man with her. He's handsome and young, but not too young for you, Clara."

She straightened and tugged her neckline tidy. Then she swept through the curtain. "Cora, *darling*! How lovely to see you. And who is this handsome fellow?"

Clara rolled her eyes as she pulled her plain black gown back on. It was going to hang on her with the corset laced this tightly, but she simply didn't feel like waiting one more moment to leave this torture chamber.

She'd just about worked her head to the neck of the gown when it was snatched directly off her.

"You are *not* going out there in this rag," whispered Bea furiously. "That's Cora Teagarden's cousin's nephew out there, and he's a *lord*! With a house on Grosvenor Square!"

"Shall I greet him in my corset, then, Bea? Give me back my gown."

"No. I've sent for Madame. She'll help us."

Clara snatched for the gown, but Beatrice flung it to the floor and stood on it.

"Bea! You've ruined it with your shoes!"

"Good. It's naught but a rag anyway." She grabbed

Clara's arm. "Listen to me. Sir Thorogood is a fine target, but with your looks and figure you could do better. Out there is a perfectly gorgeous lord, who's likely bespoken to no one as he's been in Vienna until a few months ago." She leaned close. "If you land him, it will open doors for Kitty and Bitty."

"Then let Kitty and Bitty have at him."

Beatrice pursed her lips. "I love my girls, Clara, but we both know they aren't quite up to a lord. Perhaps if they had a brain between them—" She shook her head. "It doesn't signify. The important question at this moment is, *what are you going to wear out of this shop?*"

What she wore was a very elegant walking suit in green satin that made her eyes gleam like emeralds, despite their usual rather muddy color. Clara stared at herself in the mirror, turning this way and that. The gown even came with a hat, for the original buyer had asked for it to be trimmed in the same green satin.

"Oh, Auntie Clara," breathed Kitty. "You look like a duchess!"

"Indeed, madame. And not a flounce in sight!" Madame Hortensia was practically cooing with satisfaction, both from aesthetic joy and from the hefty bonus Beatrice had forked over for another customer's finished gown.

Clara turned to her sister-in-law. "Bea, I can't let you do this."

"Consider it an investment. When you've landed a rich husband, you may pay me back. With a tiny bit of interest, of course."

Vintage Beatrice. Clara hugged her impulsively. "Of course."

Then Bea swept back the curtain and greeted her life-long nemesis once more. "Cora, you remember Bentley's darling widow, Clara, don't you?"

Clara ducked to manage the bonnet through the curtain. Then she straightened to come face to face with the fair-haired gentleman from the Rochesters' ball.

He smiled. "Ah, I see I have managed my proper introduction after all!" He bowed deeply as introductions were made.

Clara froze. *Rochesters' ball—solicitous gentleman—unstrung corset—*

This had to be the single most humiliating moment of her life.

Nathaniel Stonewell, Lord Reardon—and persistent knight errant—rolled his eyes at his cousin's boasting and Beatrice's avid curiosity. "I feel rather like a prize pug," he murmured in an aside to Clara. "What do you suppose would happen if I bit you?"

There was nothing but playful interest in his eyes. Not a speck of prurient awareness, not a single knowing gleam. It could not have been him. Clara smiled in relief as much as at his mischief. "Beatrice would no doubt consider that tantamount to an engagement."

He grinned and offered her his arm as both parties concluded their business in the shop. "The day is fine. Would you care to take a turn in the park?"

Clara tucked her arm into his. Why not? He wasn't serious-minded and he was far too well-born for her, not to mention much too handsome. No danger of a true match at all. And it was surely an improvement over shopping.

Looking at his perfect profile from the corner of her eye, she decided that it was a vast improvement. Besides, she was tired of contemplating Sir Thoro-rat's ruination at dinner tonight.

Clara felt conspicuous in the elegant walking dress, although she suspected that she now fit in better than she ever had. She was dressed much the same as the other ladies walking down High Street with their escorts.

Perhaps it was the way the other gentlemen's eyes slid in her direction and stayed. Perhaps it was in Lord Reardon's solicitous attitude—the way he kept his fingers touching lightly to her elbow as they walked, as if she were so delicate she was scarcely able to walk on her own.

"Think you these are my first steps?"

The look he sent her was priceless, equal parts surprise and suspicion. She was laughing at him again and he knew it. "I beg your pardon?"

"My lord, I am quite able to walk on my own. I have been practicing for years, you know."

He snatched his hand away. "My profoundest apology, Mrs. Simpson. I did not mean to offend."

Clara sighed. "What a shame."

"What is?"

"That a man as well endowed as you should lack a sense of humor."

His jaw dropped. "Endowed?"

"But of course! You are a handsome, titled man of means and obvious education."

"Oh," he said faintly. "*That* endowment."

Clara's thoughts hadn't taken that particular path until that very moment. She shot him an embarrassed glance at the same moment he sent her a look of barely repressed hysteria.

Her lips twisted mightily but she could not hold back her snicker. That broke the dam for them both. Clara was forced to turn away with one gloved hand over her mouth, but Lord Reardon frankly leaned upon a lamppost and brayed.

Clara slapped him on the arm with her reticule. "Do stop," she choked out. "Or I shall . . . not be able to."

With a last weak chuckle, Lord Reardon handed her his handkerchief to wipe her streaming eyes. Clara handed over her own bit of lace in return. He took it into his large square hand and stared down at it, his jaw working.

"Is it not manly enough for your taste, my lord?" Clara smiled. "Do you not share Sir Thorogood's penchant for lace?"

"That is not the case at all, Mrs. Simpson," he replied, dabbing at his eyes, then tucking her hankie into his pocket. "I shall have it cleaned, and therefore I shall have an excuse to see you again."

Despite herself she was flattered. She shouldn't be so affected by pretty words, but after all, she'd never had a great deal of male attention in her life. Not many fellows spared interest for bookish girls with poor-quality clothing and a notorious father.

Could it simply be the dress? Had she indeed been wrong all this time about the unimportance of fashion?

Could Lord Reardon indeed be that shallow?

"My lord, perhaps you should understand that I do not normally look this way."

"No? How so?"

Toying with her parasol handle, Clara glanced away. "I mean to say that . . . this is not how I often appear. I tend to ignore fashion for function, and I seldom care for—for figure improvement."

He stopped walking and turned to her, smiling. She felt her jaw begin to drop and quickly picked it up again. He was simply too beautiful for words.

When she'd encountered him two nights past, her first thought had been that he ought to be required to share his beauty with some deserving woman. Now, she wondered if perhaps he'd been fashioned purely to ornament a woman's days. Lord knew she could happily stare at him for hours.

Her fingers twitched. Did she have a pencil in her reticule?

"What do you care for, may I ask?"

She held up one hand for silence. The way the sun struck his hair showed many golden glints among the light brown . . .

Oh, if only she were a painter! Unfortunately, she had never taken to oils well. But she could and would capture the magnificent line of his cheekbone and jaw.

"Don't. Move." She fumbled in her bag for the pencil and then stooped to unwrap the topmost layer of brown paper from one of her parcels.

Spreading the paper out over a bench seat took only a moment, then she was ready to begin. She looked up to see him staring at her oddly.

"Oh." She'd forgotten to ask his permission to draw him. So many times she'd stolen clandestine drawings, she'd forgotten that it was mannerly to ask first. "May I sketch you?"

His only reply was a tilt of his head. She jumped up and moved it back into the proper position by cupping his jaw in her bare hands. She'd removed her gloves to draw without even realizing it, but the heat of his skin on her palms shocked her back to her position.

She snatched her hands away, very much as he had earlier. He must have remembered, as well, for he grinned. "I am quite able to move my head by myself. I've been practicing for years."

Chagrined, she shook her head. "You've been practicing to be very patient, as well. I'm sorry. It is just that you are so nicely . . . formed. I only thought to capture the way you looked just now."

"By all means."

She smiled, then dove back to her paper. "You see, I find it interesting why some people are considered handsome and some are not. A slight difference in the nose, perhaps. Or too much chin or not enough—"

With quick sure strokes, she'd captured him on paper. As she quickly delineated that particularly Grecian angle of his jaw, the part of her mind not occupied with drawing wondered where she'd seen it before.

Well, he had spoken to her once before today, she mused as her fingers still moved swiftly over the paper. Likely she'd noticed it then.

Yet she felt as if she'd drawn it quite recently, though the only subject she'd sketched lately had been Sir Thorogood—if one didn't count her many idle sketches of Monty.

From her brief moments with him in the dimness, all that she'd really taken away was the memory of how Monty's jaw was more rugged, his chin more chiseled and square. And that particular dip to his bottom lip, which took his masculine mouth one step over the line into sensual. She wondered if the rest of his face was nearly so perfect. The silken mask covered everything above the tip of his nose, even his ears, which was unfortunate. She burned to see Monty's ears. If there was one flaw she was unforgiving about in a man's appearance, it was a pair of jug-handle ears.

It made her shallow, she knew, and it was a flaw that she someday fully intended to eradicate from herself, but for now, the artist in her hoped mightily that Monty's ears pinned down close to his skull—

"Have you done yet?"

Clara yanked herself back to the moment at hand. She looked up to see Lord Reardon, not Monty, before her. She looked down, however, to see variations of her masked thief covering the brown paper, overlapping her sketch of Lord Reardon, some with large ears, some not.

Quickly she rolled the paper and stuffed it under her parcels. "Not yet. I was simply doing a few—preliminary studies." Not quite a lie. She unwrapped another layer of the thankfully generous shop wrapping from her topmost parcel and began again.

This time she kept her mind firmly on her subject, and in a few moments she had a very acceptable drawing of Lord Reardon as he leaned one elbow upon an elm.

"There." She sat back and looked from the man to the sketch. When she took it home and used it to draw from, she would widen his shoulders a tad . . . and his boots hadn't come out precisely correct. He wore low heels, unlike so many of the dandies, which gave a square and manly quality to his stance. She quite preferred it to Sir Thorogood's mincing posture.

"What do you think, my lord?" Lord Reardon had come behind her to look over her shoulder. He didn't respond immediately. Worried that he was not pleased, she looked up into his face and froze.

There was something in the back of his eyes, something hot and black, like coal that was about to ignite. . . .

Then it was gone, and there was only a genially smiling fellow reaching over her to lift the drawing from the bench seat. "My word, you are a talented creature! It's the very image of me!"

Clara shook off the odd hunted tremor she'd felt. She

truly was not used to the presence of men, to be so threatened by what was probably a simple moment of attraction.

It was likely only the dress, anyway.

As Lord Reardon continued to exclaim over the drawing, Clara began to relax and even to enjoy his fulsome words. He was full of wind, of course, but for once it did feel nice to be on the receiving end of praise for her work.

"May I keep this?"

She nodded, although she'd thought to use it to draw from. Still, his attention was flattering and he'd been very patient. She rolled the drawing and handed it back to him.

He accepted with every evidence of delight. "You must show me more of your drawings, Mrs. Simpson. Do you have a large portfolio of work?"

Not at all, as she hadn't kept one for nearly a year. "I fear not, my lord. I don't often sketch my friends anymore." Entirely true, if a bit misleading.

"Well, you must draw someone else for me. A mutual acquaintance perhaps, so I'll not have a stranger looking at me from my study wall?"

He meant to hang something of hers in his home? A bolt of pure artistic joy shot through her, far exceeding the minor pleasure she'd felt in his flirtation. Eagerly she leaned forward.

"Whom do we both know, then? Shall I draw your cousin Cora?" Not the first subject she would choose, for Cora Teagarden was rather ordinary. Pleasant, but not much artistic scope there.

Apparently Lord Reardon felt the same. "Ah—I think not." He settled next to her on the bench.

Clara felt that nervous tremor move through her once

more. She was being a bit silly about this. After all, she was a widow, not a green girl. The proprieties were much relaxed for her now. She could certainly sit with a gentleman on a public park bench and feel not a moment of disquietude.

Of course, that depended on the gentleman, didn't it? Was it Lord Reardon's extreme good looks that had her so unsettled? And was this a good unsettled or a bad unsettled? Was she fearful or stirred by his nearness? She honestly did not know. He was terribly attractive—

"—Sir Thorogood?"

Clara's habit of keeping her thoughts to herself came in most handy at that moment. She was quite sure that the look she sent Lord Reardon was merely a blank look of misunderstanding, and not the panicked glazed stare of a captured rabbit.

She forced herself to inhale, then exhale, in a natural fashion. Next, a slow blink and an apologetic smile. "So sorry. I was woolgathering. Did you say that you would like me to draw Sir Thorogood for you?"

Lord Reardon had his gaze fixed on her face. Was he watching her closely, or simply pondering her lack of intelligence?

"Yes. I saw you speaking to him at length the other night, and thought perhaps you knew each other well, as you are both artists."

"Yes," she said, her voice faint. "Both."

"Have you known him long?" Lord Reardon's voice and manner took on a boyish eagerness. "I have been collecting him for some time. I should very much like to have him sign some of his work for me."

Goodness, Lord Reardon was a *devotee*? He was pursuing her to get closer to Thorogood?

Sickening relief swept through her, leaving helpless

hysteria behind. Well, wasn't this his lordship's lucky day! He was about as close as he was ever going to get to Sir Thorogood, at least without a bouquet of flowers and a wedding proposal!

"I . . . shall recommend you to him at dinner tonight, my lord. Although I do not know him well, he seems a friendly sort of person." More like a fame-grabbing monstrosity, but who was she to quibble?

Lord Reardon was most appreciative, and carried on some more about her talent, but for Clara the fun had gone out of the afternoon. All she could think of was tonight's encounter with Sir Thorogood, and her mission to expose him for what he was.

After one too many times of having to recall her attention, Lord Reardon gave up on conversation and walked her back to where Cora Teagarden waited with Beatrice and the twins. Clara managed to say goodbye in an unexceptional manner despite her occupied thoughts, but she scarcely remembered the ride home.

How in the world was she going to be able to expose the impostor tonight?

Chapter Nine

Dalton Montmorency, Lord Etheridge, flipped back Sir Thorogood's puce coattails and sat his blinding yellow satin rear on the seat of his plainest carriage, the one he used to blend into the crowded streets.

Even the horses were nondescript, right down to their middle-aged hooves. No livery, no crest, no way to distinguish his vehicle from hundreds currently on the streets of London.

Still, he pulled the shades tight, for his finery would certainly not blend in. Traveling from his own home in costume was a risk, but he couldn't spend every moment at the club, either. His own affairs required his attention, although harvests and granaries were duller than dull.

How he wished he were contemplating harvests and granaries at this moment.

Instead, he was looking forward to an evening at the Trapps'. How could he have known that the annoying Mrs. Simpson lived there, as well? He'd accepted the invitation after learning that Oswald Trapp lived in Smythe Square, thinking that questioning Wadsworth's neighbors might turn up something interesting.

If only he had known . . .

Dalton rubbed the back of his neck, feeling the tension grow between his shoulder blades at the mere recollection of Mrs. Simpson's shrill titter. Perhaps Trapp was a drinking man, he thought desperately. Perhaps he would be offered a whisky before dinner.

Perhaps he could turn around right now and send his regrets.

He actually twitched with eagerness at the thought, his fist rising to bang the roof for Hawkins's attention. Then long years of training took over.

One did not neglect an accepted invitation. One did not disappoint a hostess at the last moment.

One did not turn tail and run from the field of battle.

God, he hoped Trapp was a drinking man.

The dress was enough to drive any man to drink. Even Clara had the urge to toss back a sherry at the sight of herself in the looking-glass.

When she thought of how much she'd paid to look—how had Madame Hortensia put it? Ah, yes, like an overturned feather duster.

A giant pink feather duster. With feet.

Mercy, perhaps she'd have a whisky herself.

Or three.

She was nearly as wide as she was tall. Flounce upon flounce of tongue-pink organza rose to the high waist, just under her bosom, which was pleated pink satin encrusted with tiny silk bows and pearls.

"Oh . . . my." Bea's voice from the doorway was breathless.

Clara turned to see her sister-in-law standing wide-eyed, with one hand pressed to her throat. If even Beatrice was struck speechless, then Sir Thorogood was likely going to be turned to stone.

I am a pink organza Medusa. She chuckled. Then she did a quick spin so that Bea could get the full effect of the flounces. "Do you like it, Bea?"

"Ah . . . well . . . what a charming color on you!"

It was, actually. Clara examined herself in the glass. Pink made her look fresh and young and turned her hazel eyes to deep green.

Oh, *lovely,* she thought irritably. It wouldn't do to actually *win* Sir Thorogood, now would it? What she wanted was to get close enough to discover his motives and to expose him as false, if possible. Still, if he found her attractive in this monstrosity, then he was even sillier than Bea and therefore of no threat whatsoever.

Perhaps a silly hairstyle to go with the dress? She grinned at Bea in the mirror and piled her hair high upon her head. "Have you any more ostrich plumes, Bea? And may I borrow your face powder and kohl again?"

Dalton stopped counting the ticks of the clock perhaps an hour into dinner. He'd lost count between the soup and the roast. He then pondered formulating the mathematics behind the placement of the flowers on the dining room wallpaper, but then decided that even he was not that bored.

Mrs. Simpson seemed somewhat more composed this evening, though as silly as ever. Her gown was proof of that, for he had never seen a more overdecorated garment in his life. It was as if she could not decide between the pearls, ribbons, or flounces and had therefore chosen all three. The woman looked like a cake, for pity's sake!

A pink cake, topped by pale shimmering cleavage.

His memory veered back to when he had seen those same breasts bare and gleaming in the starlight. Saliva flooded his mouth and his throat tightened.

Perhaps it was time to take a lover. If he found himself tempted by a woman as empty-headed and annoying as Clara Simpson, then he was surely a man on the edge of celibacy-induced madness.

Even now her annoying titter scraped along his every nerve as she misinterpreted a perfectly serious statement made by Mrs. Trapp as a jest.

"So amusing, Beatrice! I'm sure Sir Thorogood doesn't think we volunteer at the hospital because we feel strongly about the war effort!"

She leaned close to Dalton as if to impart a secret. Dalton restrained himself from leaning away, although he did find his gaze dropping a bit lower than her face, just for an instant.

"The twins and I are looking for husbands!" she said in a whisper that could have been heard across the Covent Garden piazza on Market Day.

Mrs. Trapp stared open-mouthed at her sister-in-law for a moment before turning to Dalton and stammering a meaningless comment on the weather.

Gratefully, Dalton turned to support his hostess's change of subject. Though not the most intellectual of women, Mrs. Trapp seemed a sane and solid relief after the past hour of enduring the shallow twit who sat beside him.

When had he begun to yearn for a woman whom he could talk to?

A woman, not a wife. A lover would be pleasant but he was against the use of mistresses, nor did he want to dally with one of the wandering wives of the *ton*. He still believed in solemn vows, even if they didn't.

The alternative was to approach a widow of independent means, so he would not feel as though she were selling herself to him for security.

Wonderful. Now he had it all figured out. But where in the world was he going to find an attractive widow of means and a certain age, who possessed brains and heart and absorbing conversation?

Not to mention a few bedroom skills, reminded his baser nature. For a brief moment, Dalton tried to imagine sharing Mrs. Simpson's bed. Despite her obvious penchant for him, she was a respectable woman. A widow, but not poor by the look of her sickening gown. Of a certain age—well, Mrs. Simpson could be no more than in her late twenties.

He eyed her as she chattered and preened, hardly stopping to take a breath. She was healthy, of good figure, and interested. She was too vapid to be a danger to his clandestine work. And he had been without a woman for a very long time.

Perhaps—

Her spine-altering laughter shattered his contemplation like a hammer on glass, making his shoulders rise in an involuntary attempt to protect his hearing.

Perhaps not.

Clara refrained from rolling her eyes. What a buffoon. What a waste of a tall, good-looking man. It was simply too much to hope the fellow might have a brain to go with those muscles.

And those eyes. She'd had difficulty all evening keeping herself from being mesmerized by the matching silver glimmer of his eyes. He would turn away and she would recover herself, remind herself of his lies, convince herself that there was nothing unusual about a pair of light gray eyes.

Then his gaze would swing back to her and she would almost stop breathing at the beauty of his eyes. He was handsome enough without that hypnotic gaze. It was truly quite unnecessary. Wasn't that just like a man, to claim more than his due?

So she assured herself of time without his attention. All it took was a little boredom. Clara watched "Sir Thorogood" cringe as she tittered and prattled away. She wanted to laugh for real at the hunted expression on his face.

Beatrice's reaction to all this was priceless, as well. She was staring at Clara as if she were contemplating calling in religious assistance.

It was time to move in for the kill. With only the Trapps for witnesses, the timing was not as good as a more public event would have been, but Clara was tired of waiting. She wanted this liar unveiled.

She opened her mouth to pin him down and force him to draw for the company—but Kitty beat her to the punch.

"Did you know that Auntie Clara draws as well, Sir Thorogood? She's very good, almost like a real artist!"

Clara sent the girl a glare, and the poor thing retreated in confusion. Clara felt terrible, since Kitty was her favorite and was obviously trying to help Clara in her "pursuit" of Sir Thorogood. Yet her drawing ability was the last subject Clara wanted aired right now.

"Oh, *my* scribbles are nothing compared to Sir Thorogood!" Clara simpered. "Why, sir, *you* are a *genius*! A *master*! Those cartoons are so full of wit, as well as skill!" This was fun. "Why, I've heard that the Prince himself never misses one of m—*your* caricatures!"

She could see the dread growing on his face. *Yes, you had better be worried, you fake.* "We would simply love for you to draw something for us tonight, wouldn't we, Bea?"

Beatrice began to chime in, obviously seeing an opportunity to best her rival, Mrs. Teagarden. To have an original Sir Thorogood drawing on display would be quite the social coup. Of course, Bea already had a number of them stored rather disdainfully away, but Clara could hardly tell her that.

"I spent all morning tracing one of your drawings, Sir Thorogood, and my hand was utterly exhausted," Kitty said. "However do you manage to draw hundreds of each one for the newspaper?"

"They're not all hand-drawn, Kitty," explained Clara absently. "The original is taken to the engraver, who carves the lines into a metal sheet which is then inked and used to print—"

Halting with dismay, Clara looked up to see everyone at the table regarding her with surprise. Sir Thoro-fake had one eyebrow nearly to his hairline and Beatrice had stopped with a forkful of food halfway to her open mouth.

Even Kitty was astonished. "Why, Auntie Clara, how on earth did you know that?"

Eek. How could she make such an idiotic slip? "Ah— I—visited a newspaper once to—to place an advertisement. I learned about it there." Time to change the subject. "Sir, do tell us how you began your work. With whom did you study? Ackermann?"

"Oh, I never studied at all," Sir Thorogood said airily. "I always felt that formal tuition would only sully my style."

Sully his style? She, who had longed all her life for real instruction in art, wanted to sully more than his style, the blackguard!

Dalton was ready to leave now. These people knew little or nothing about Wadsworth. In the entire evening, he'd only managed to learn that the man was a faultless neighbor, if a less than friendly one.

Every time he'd brought the subject up, Mrs. Simpson had pointedly returned the topic of conversation to himself. The woman obviously thought that he would find such attention flattering.

She was almost frightening in her zeal. Dalton was quite sure he had never been pursued with such determination. The woman was like a terrier, never releasing her prey until it was dead. An admirable trait in a colleague. Not attractive at all in a paramour.

In fact, he was beginning to feel downright claustrophobic in this small overdecorated dining room, fixed in the hunter vision of a small, overdecorated predator.

He was forced to wait until the ladies rose from the table, but as soon as he was able, he bowed over their hands in turn. "I despise parting from your lovely society, Mrs. Trapp, Mrs. Simpson, but I must make my way home. There is such scope for inspiration in your exquisite company that I find myself quite overcome."

He thought he heard a tiny derisive snort greet his words. Dalton looked up, only to see Mrs. Simpson gazing at him with single-minded devotion.

"Oh, do come again soon, sir. We take such delight in learning about your art. Next time, you must draw for us. Promise you will, for me?" She batted her eyelashes at him until he would have sworn that she blinded herself.

"Ah—yes, of course. Next time." He turned to take his coat and hat from the butler. The door was mere steps away. He could make it—

"Oh, Sir Thorogood! Clara was just telling me how

very much she wished to take some air in Hyde Park tomorrow. Do you think you might be available to escort her?"

Dalton was so surprised by Mrs. Trapp's bad manners that he hesitated a fraction of a second too long. The woman clapped her hands together in delight.

"Oh, wonderful. The two of you will make such a dashing couple—as you drive, I mean to say."

Hellfire. Once more in the company of the huntress. He was going to feel like a fox before the hound all morning, just waiting for her to take a bite out of him. The only comfort was the expression on Mrs. Simpson's face. Apparently, Mrs. Trapp hadn't consulted her sister-in-law either, for Mrs. Simpson looked truly disconcerted.

He bowed to her. Anything to get out of this house. "Tomorrow then, my dear lady. Shall I call for you at noon? Good night, Mr. Trapp, ladies."

Then he was through the door and free. Until tomorrow morning, at any rate.

Still, his step lightened as he thought of his last task for the evening. He had a few things to return to Wadsworth. Things that, while they gave no hint as to Thorogood's identity, did prove that the man was one nasty player in a very vicious game.

Idly he wondered if Rose would be up and about tonight. But he never stopped to ponder the fact that the corners of his lips were lifted in a smile at the thought of her.

Clara rushed through her own attic and into Wadsworth's, only pausing a moment when her laden basket snagged in the narrow hole between the boards.

The light of a single tallow candle lit the shadowy space, and in its glow she could see Rose kneeling beside a small battered crate.

"How is it?" Breathless, Clara knelt next to Rose and peered down at the still form of the injured cat.

"It's still breathin', miss, but it ain't opened its eyes once since I been here."

Pity filled Clara. "I blame myself. If I hadn't laughed, Wadsworth might not have been angered into striking it."

Rose made a cynical sound. "The likes of him don't need an excuse to hurt things. He just fancies it, is all."

Clara thought about Rose's dismal life in this house. Wadsworth had struck more than the cat today. "You must think me silly, to care for a dumb animal when people are suffering around me."

Rose looked up quickly, her dark eyes somber. "Oh, no, miss, never you! And carin' for things, well, that's just who you are—a caring sort, the way the master is a hurtin' sort."

Clara was humbled by the uncomplicated admiration in Rose's eyes. "I thank you, dear one, but I cannot take so much credit." She turned back to the cat before Rose could make her feel worse.

"I've some broth for the cat," she said. She pawed through her basket and lifted out a small jar. She set it next to the crate and dug into her things again.

Then she snapped out a napkin and laid it over her arm like the master at a fine restaurant. "And for milady's feast, we have a lovely kidney pie, accompanied by your usual chocolate of course." She sucked in her cheeks and served Rose with snooty formality. The little maid giggled.

"Now when you're done, I want you to go into my

attic where it's nice and warm. You should rest until I come back." Rose looked so weary that Clara felt a bit guilty that her primary reason for the offer was that she was fairly sure Monty would be returning tonight and she wanted to see him alone. Then again, Rose would only be frightened by the presence of a masked thief in her attic.

"I thanks you, miss." Without another word, Rose dug into her meal. Clara changed into her maid costume, then turned her attention to the cat.

The poor slat-ribbed creature looked near death. Yes, it was breathing, but only just. Carefully, Clara lifted its head with its poor tattered ears and spooned a bit of broth between the slackened jaws. She waited, gently stroking the filthy neck with one thumb, until she felt a contraction that meant the cat had swallowed.

If it—Clara quickly checked—if *she* could eat, then she would live, Clara was sure of it. Patiently, she dribbled the broth into the cat, spoonful by spoonful. Rose finished her meal and bid Clara good eve. Clara answered absently, her entire attention focused on the slowly reviving animal.

Finally the broth was gone and the cat had even roused enough to lick her jaws and Clara's fingers with a rough tongue. Letting the creature's head relax to the blanket in a more natural sleep than before, Clara stood and stretched.

It must be later than she thought, for she'd gone quite chill as she'd sat there.

Perhaps Monty was not coming after all.

Thinking that she could hear the watchmen call the hour if she opened the window, she crossed the attic to the high mullioned glass and unlatched it.

Monty was waiting just outside when she swung open the glass panel.

She started, her heart leaping from more than simple surprise. "Goodness, Monty, you near scared me to death!"

He leaned one arm over the sill and hoisted himself up to sit on it with his long legs dangling outside, putting his eyes on a level with hers. The light of the candle in the far end of the attic only lit his face enough for her to see the gleam in his shadowed eyes.

"You're not surprised to see me, my flower."

"That I'm not. Seemed to me you might be wantin' to return what you took out of the master's safe." She grinned at him. "Get a good look at it, did you?"

He smiled back and leaned close to her ear, though there was no one to hear and they were nearly whispering already. "Maybe I came back to see your smilin' face."

His breath was warm on her neck and tingled within her ear. She licked her lips and swallowed. Without truly planning it, she tilted her head to reveal more of her neck to him. He obliged by leaning closer, hovering just a hairsbreadth over her skin. Time seemed to last, stretching on while they lingered in that almost-touch moment. Clara's eyes drifted closed the better to absorb the pleasant sensation of his breath on her skin.

Then they flew open again and she drew back to glare at him.

"None o' that, sir! I'm a good girl." *Oh, no I'm not!* "You'll not be talkin' me out of it." *Please talk me out of it!*

He drew back, his lips slightly parted, and for a moment she thought he would kiss her. Then he grinned and leaned closer, dangling comically by one hand grip-

ping the window frame until his face nearly nestled in
her bosom. "Just one kiss, my flower, and I'll die a
happy man."

"You'll die all right," she replied tartly. "With me fist
in your nose, you'll die."

He clapped a hand to his heart, and swayed on his
perch on the sill. "I'm done for, then. You've broken
me heart with your hard-hearted ways. Goodbye, cruel
maiden!"

He moved as if to throw himself from the window,
but Clara caught the lapel of his short wool coat and
dragged him back.

With a lithe twist, he was standing within the attic
and her tug had him pressed nearly to her front. His big
body blocked the dim light and she could no longer see
his eyes behind his mask, but she could feel his soft
chuckle as if it came from her own body.

"She says yes, she says no, she says yes again," he
murmured. "Reel me in, little fisherwoman. I'm well and
hooked."

His voice was low and intimate, and although he kept
his hands to his sides, she could feel him lean closer.
He tilted his head and she felt the brush of his lips warm
on her forehead.

She had only to tilt her own face up to invite the kiss
she wanted. The pull was strong, as strong as her grip
on his coat, and it would be so easy . . .

She stepped back once. Then again. The second one
was easier, but not much. She released her stranglehold
on his lapel. The third step was easier still. In a moment,
she would begin breathing again, surely.

Clara forced herself to fill her lungs. Why did he
make her so breathless? And why did she want him to?
This was not why she was here.

"Enough of your play, Monty. Do you have the master's papers or no?" She had every intention of using her new-found lock-picking skills to open the safe herself and read them after Monty had gone.

He slid his hand down to the deep pockets that all such rough coats had on each hip. "Here. I've 'em all here."

"Good, then. The house is well asleep. Let's put them back where they belong."

He caught her hand. "I know where to go. You'd best be out of this, for your own good."

"And if someone hears a noise, will it be you claimin' to be sneakin' to the kitchens for a bit of bread? That would be convincing, wouldn't it?" She cast her gaze up in impatience. "Would you get steppin', Monty? We've not got all night." She turned and left him there.

Chapter Ten

Dalton followed that determined little backside down to the door and into the dark stairwell. As the blackness closed around them, he was reminded of his wayward thoughts the last time they'd been here.

His bout of flirtation had been meant to distract her from her questions. Instead, he was fair to distracting himself from his mission. His arousal stirred at the soft scent of roses in the air. It was really past time to dally with some widow or another.

The image of Mrs. Simpson hovered in the blackness before him. She lay half-dressed upon a garden bench in the moonlight, only this time her eyes were open and so were her arms.

Forcefully, Dalton shunted that image aside and replaced it with one of the annoying widow braying loudly at the dinner table while her in-laws regarded her with dismay.

There. Lust all gone.

Until the woman before him turned abruptly and placed her palm on his chest to stop him as he followed her down the steps. His body continued two steps until it came into contact with hers and he was forced to wrap one arm around her for balance. Or something.

"Wh—"

The small hand fumbled quickly to his mouth and pressed gently to his lips. Then she wrapped her fingers around the back of his neck and pulled his head down to hers.

Oh, yes, the lust was back.

"—the hall," she whispered into his ear. Dalton realized he'd missed the first part of what she'd said in the roar of all his blood leaving his brain for other regions.

He shook his head quickly. She leaned closer until her small bosom contacted his chest and breathed softly into his ear. "I think I heard footsteps in the hall."

He heard her this time, although he still didn't give a damn what she said. All he wanted was to wrap his arms about her and pull her close for a deep breathless kiss.

Or a damp and breathless rogering would do.

She remained where she was, breast to chest with him. She was listening for danger, he managed to think. Good. She could listen.

He would lust.

Her hand still lay gently on the back of his neck. His head was still bent down to hers. One small tilt and he could capture her lips with his. . . .

She likely wouldn't protest too much, if at all. She might claim that she was a good girl, but she was daring enough to meet him in the attic past midnight and show him through the darkened house.

She was no lady, no protected debutante. With his wealth, he could more than compensate her for any distress. His lust struggled to convince him that she was fair game. A saucy servant girl, without a soul to protect her—

From him.

With deep gut-chilling shock, Dalton realized that he was actually contemplating seducing an innocent servant girl, of breaking down her protestations of virtue and taking her right here on this dusty attic stair.

He despised men who did such things. Reviled them for rutting selfish beasts who thought dependents were nothing but playthings.

How could he be so base? To even think such a thing about a bright brave young woman like Rose? Filled with self-loathing, he took a step back, shaking her lax hand from his shoulder as he did so.

He was a Montmorency. A peer and a gentleman. "Monty" was nothing but a fancy, and a dangerous one at that.

Her attention still on the hall, Clara reached for Monty's hand again. "Come. They're gone now."

As she carefully opened the door to step into the hall with him, Clara wouldn't allow herself to think about the chance they were taking. The cause of damaging the cruel Mr. Wadsworth was reason enough. If Monty wanted to clean the man out completely, all the better.

She wondered, however, why someone as honorable and kind as Monty would stoop to thievery. With his quaint gallantry and his mannerly behavior, he seemed rather more like some knight of old than a criminal.

They entered the study and Clara again opened the street-side draperies.

As she watched Monty swiftly return the contents of his pocket to the safe box, it occurred to her that an ordinary thief would no more take papers than he would firewood, for that was all the use the papers would be to an uneducated man.

"Who are you, truly?" She kept her voice low, but it seemed to startle him all the same. Or perhaps it was the question itself.

He hesitated for a moment, keeping his back to her as he finished returning the safe to rights. Then he turned, his smile rueful in the dim glow of the street lamps.

"You're thinkin' that a thief'd be more like to take banknotes than papers?"

She nodded, wishing she could see him—all the better for observing all the small signals of a lie in progress. Most people never noticed the little things that liars did, the flick of the gaze, the tiny frown that marked the forehead for the merest instant.

However, she was an expert on faces. Bentley had never been able to keep the truth from her and she had caught the twins many times in their girlish fibs.

Monty's voice was clear, his gaze unshakable. "I'm only doin' as I was told by the man what hired me," he assured her. "This fellow don't want alarm raised over somewhat missin' from the safe box. He wants to read them papers, is all."

Clara narrowed her eyes. Helping Monty relieve Mr. Wadsworth of his ill-used wealth was one thing, but she had no intention of assisting a stranger in what might be dastardly doings.

"This man, who is he?"

Monty shrugged. "Just a fellow what works for them that's suspicious of your master. You know, Bow Street sorts."

"You're working *for* the law?"

He seemed affronted. "O' course I am!"

Clara considered this. It fit well into her perception of Monty so far. Whoever had thought to assign him to this task was little short of brilliant, she had to admit. What could be better than to read Mr. Wadsworth's nefarious plans from his own files? After all, that was what she was interested in as well.

That and being alone with Monty.

Still holding Dalton's hand as they entered the attic a few moments later, Rose turned right instead of left to the window.

"I want to show you somethin'," she whispered. She released his hand. His fingers felt cold without her small warm ones within. In the dimness, he saw her kneel and remove something from behind a crate.

"Come to the light so you can see," she urged, as she carried her surprise to the open window. He followed, intrigued. What would Rose consider an important secret? Something she'd found in the house? He leaned closer to see, then drew back slightly in dismay.

What she'd found was a cat carcass. It didn't smell much yet but by the look of it, it wouldn't be long. She'd bedded the thing carefully in a basket, tenderly placed on soft rags. The entire matter was somewhat awful.

He didn't want to hurt Rose's feelings. "Was this your cat?"

She laughed softly and stroked the animal's side. He flinched. "*Bah!* Don't touch it. It'll still carry the sickness what killed it."

Turning her face up to him, she grinned. " 'Tisn't dead at all, squeamish Monty. And if it were, I don't think the master's kick is catching."

He didn't know how to break it to her. That was one singularly dead cat. "Wadsworth killed it?"

"Monty. It. Isn't. Dead." She placed the basket on the ledge and reached for his hand.

Dalton gritted his teeth and touched the cat. Its fur was matted and filthy, and he could see the creature's ribs even in the forgiving moonlight, but he was still quite certain he was fondling a feline of a deceased nature.

That is, until a low growl issued from beneath his hand and a lightning strike from a set of very lively claws drew blood. He snatched his hand away to bring the back of it to his lips. "Bloody rat-catching—"

"Monty!" Rose batted him away. "To say such a thing about my marmalade darling."

Dalton restrained a sigh. Rose was a cat lover. Bloody hell. "Yes, it's right lovely, rosebud. A fine animal."

She nodded, her attention still on the fur-covered hand assassin. "I know. She's wonderful, isn't she? But I can't keep her, for B—the master would never allow it." She turned a wistful gaze on him.

He should have seen it coming. He should have seen that look in her eye and run for it. Instead, he found himself caught by the heavily lashed darkness of her eyes. What color were they? He'd yet to see her in anything but dim light. Would he even recognize her if he saw her in the day—

"Would you take care of her for me? Just for a little bit?"

He found himself nodding before he'd even realized precisely what she'd said. Then it hit him.

Oh, hellfire. The Sergeant was going to kill him.

The next day dawned quite chill and foul. Dalton hoped that Mrs. Simpson would send a note begging off their drive. Unfortunately, she seemed all the more eager when he arrived promptly at noon to take her out. Her footman accompanied them, clinging to the back of the low, open carriage.

He'd chosen this carriage hoping that she would become uncomfortable enough to end their outing early. It went against his every inclination to purposely displease a lady, but the sooner he scraped off this particular clinging vine, the better.

So he limited his conversation to monosyllables and shrugs and kept his horses to a slogging plod. If the weather wouldn't discourage her, perhaps he could bore her to death.

If he didn't die from boredom himself first.

She prattled. She giggled. She tossed her plumes this way and that until he sneezed repeatedly. She pointed out people that she didn't know and begged him to introduce her. She waved vigorously to people she did know until even they looked askance at her behavior.

Finally, the horse stopped of his own accord, his nose dragging sleepily near the ground. Dalton couldn't blame him. If not for the Merry Widow's screeching giggle, he'd be near sleep himself. Every time he began to nod off, she would peel the paint from their surroundings with her shrill laughter.

The horse had stopped near the promenade that led through the trees and over the Serpentine. Perhaps a bit of exercise would enable him to keep his eyes open. "Shall we walk for a bit?"

Mrs. Simpson bounced down with alacrity, brimming with energy. Her eyes were bright with enjoyment as they walked and her step was light. Dalton examined her in the pearly daylight, realizing that he had never seen her in the sun.

Of course, with all those cosmetics, he wasn't truly seeing her still. She might even be an appealing female under all of that, but there was no way to know.

She was certainly being a good sport about his lack of attention. Feeling guilty for his behavior, Dalton made a sincere attempt to be entertaining, only to find that it made no difference to her whatsoever.

She was looking this way and that, at the sky and at the ground, making no pretense of listening to him at all. How discourteous. If he was forced by propriety to show false interest, then so should she be. "You seem distr—"

"Where are the birds?"

Damn, the silly twit was making him miss his noon meal for this nonsense? "I'm sure I don't know what you mean."

"They're gone." She finally met his gaze, her eyes wide. "The birds. Where did they go?"

Dalton looked about them. By God, she was correct. Where just moments ago had clustered flocks of sparrows and pigeons there was nothing but crumbs and droppings on the grass.

Oh, no. "Quickly, move off the path. There are too many carriages near." He took her arm. "We must get to the footbridge." He turned to call to her footman. "Get to the bridge, man! The fog is coming!"

Mrs. Simpson gasped, then grabbed up her skirts and broke into a run. Dalton had to grant that she knew how to move when it was required of her.

The air was thickening even as they drew near the gateposts of the small bridge that crossed over the Serpentine. A stench of coal smoke and sewage fell upon them along with the damp cloak of thick brownish fog. Within seconds, Dalton could see nothing but the bridge planks beneath his feet and the pale face of Mrs. Simpson.

"It's like twilight at noon," she marveled as she caught her breath. "I've never been outside in it before."

"Don't be frightened. It's only the 'London particular'," he explained. "That's what the locals call it. It may pass quite soon."

She turned to look at him. "I know what the 'London particular' is, sir. I have lived here all my life."

"My apologies. So many people leave the city during the cooler months and never see this phenomenon. It's unusual for it to strike at this time of year."

She put her hand on his arm. "Oh, do be quiet. I want to listen."

Surprised, Dalton eyed her through the growing murk. Gone was the fluttering admiration and the coy flirtation. Instead, she stood tall, clinging with one hand to the bridge railing with her eyes half-closed and a slight smile. A private smile of enjoyment—really only a tilt of the corners of her lips.

In truth, her lips were rather fine when she wasn't using them to speak nonsense. He wondered how they would look swollen and flushed after a long hard kiss . . .

It was definitely time to find himself a lover.

For Clara, the moment was rather thrilling. To be frozen in time in day-turned-to-night was very exciting. She only wished Sir Thoroughly Unbearable wasn't with her. If only—

If only Monty were here.

Monty would see the adventure in this moment. He would feel the magic in the sudden muffling of the city's frenzy, in the cloaking of the world—

"Madam? Madam, where are you?" John's cry came over the water from their right.

Clara opened her eyes to find the impostor gazing at her soberly. Struck by his expression, it was a moment before she could tear her gaze away to search the dimness by the bank. "John? John, come no closer. You'll fall into the water."

"Aye, madam. Are you well enough where you are?"

"Yes, John. We're fine."

"Get you to a tree, John," called the fake. "It will shield you from a trampling."

Indeed, Clara could hear the sounds of panicked horses coming from various directions. "That was quick thinking, to head for the footbridge," she admitted grudgingly.

"Thank you." His tone was dry. "You don't seem quite as easily impressed as before."

Oh, drat. She'd forgotten she was supposed to be fawning over him. The very notion of laying one more flattering remark upon his lying head made her weak with exhaustion.

"Don't let's speak just now," she pleaded. "Let us simply listen to the fog."

He nodded, still gazing at her oddly. She turned toward the lake once more, but her thrill in the moment was gone. The way he studied her was alarming.

Did he suspect? After all her work, had she ruined her pose of silly uselessness with one terse comment?

Well, more than one, to tell the truth. Where was her self-control these days? The old Clara would never speak with such asperity. She was becoming as outspoken as her Rose persona.

Abruptly, she wished she truly was Rose. Rose had the freedom to be a bit saucy. Rose had the nights in her attic. Rose had Monty.

Monty Thief-in-the-night. The man would be horrified if he knew who she truly was. He would avoid her, fear her even, for she was part of the world that disdained men such as him. He would never believe that she didn't give one whit about that world.

She was in great danger, she knew it. Not from Sir Thoro-knave. Not from discovery. From herself.

She wanted to take Monty as her lover. And why shouldn't she take a lover? She was no maiden that she must save herself for marriage. She'd likely never have an opportunity to wed again, nor did she want to.

Then again, if all she wanted was to take a lover, she could choose from any number of gentlemen. From what she could see, there was no shortage of men looking for bedmates.

For a moment the thought of Monty in her bed made her breathless. His mouth . . . on her. His hands . . . on her. His lean body, his wide shoulders, his hot skin beneath her fingertips. . . .

It was scandalous. It was shameful. It was, oh, so very tempting.

"What are you thinking?" Monty's voice was low and warm in her ear.

"Mmm, you'd be surprised—"

Monty? Clara's eyes flew open to meet the searching silver gaze of Sir Thoro-snake close to hers. How odd, that she could mistake that, even in such an . . . unusual moment. Two more different men had never been born.

She shook her head and took a step back, reducing him to a misty blur. "I'm s-sorry. What did you say?"

"Don't move away. The fog is growing thicker. I don't want to lose you in it."

I do.

He reached for her hand. Clara calmed herself firmly. She was being a goose. This was no time to be alone.

Reluctantly she placed her fingers in his, only to be surprised by the strength of his grip. Somehow, she'd imagined him to have limp-fish fingers.

He tugged slightly on her hand and she stepped closer. It truly was growing more difficult to see. For the first time she began to wonder how they were going to get home. "If the fog doesn't lift . . ."

"I should think as the afternoon warms it will pass. It is a cold-weather phenomenon. Today dawned colder than usual, that is all."

"Oh. You seem well informed on the subject."

"Yes, I can speak intelligently on many topics. Quite boggles the mind, does it not?"

Was he joking? How odd. She'd never witnessed the slightest sign of a sense of humor in the man before. Well, she certainly couldn't respond in kind. Henbrained Clara had no humor in her at all.

She decided to take him literally. "Oh, *yes*! I've never understood the weather, not one little bit. I mean to say, why does it rain? Wouldn't it be so much more pleasant if the sun shone all the time? Except when I'm out without a bonnet, of course. Then a cloudy day would be much more appropriate, don't you think?" There, that ought to dispel any suspicion of a brain in her possession.

Dalton sighed. The Widow Simpleton was off again, traipsing down paths of illogic that only she could follow. Every time he thought he just might be attracted to her, she lit off on some inane burst of silliness.

Well, at least she wasn't laughing. Then he might very well be driven to push her directly off the bridge.

The muffling effect of the fog had isolated them for many minutes now, masking the sounds of the city and the other park occupants until it seemed to Dalton that they stood alone in the world.

Therefore, when the thud of a footstep sounded on the planks of the bridge, it seemed to vibrate right through him. Another thud followed the first. Mrs. Simpson started, as well, her fingers tightening on his.

"J-John?" she called toward the sounds.

"Aye," came the grunted reply.

Dalton relaxed. But Mrs. Simpson released his hand to grab his arm. She leaned close.

"That is *not* John!" she whispered urgently.

Dalton didn't have time to do more than thrust her behind him before the men were upon them.

Chapter Eleven

"No!" Clara's protest came too late. The idiot had thrust her behind him with such force that he'd pushed her past the visibility point. Or had that been his intent? If she could not see him, then the strangers couldn't see her.

She heard the grunt and scuffle of a fight just beyond her vision. The bridge shook from an impact on the railing, then another. Curses and the thick sound of blows on flesh issued from the dimness, but she couldn't hear Sir Thorogood's voice among them at all.

Then came a great splash, followed by the sound of running footsteps on the bridge. Someone very large ran past Clara, brushing against her in the swirling mist and spinning her quite around with the impact. Then the figure was gone and only silence remained.

"Sir Thorogood?" Her voice sounded thin in the dimness, even to her. "Sir, please answer me." Was he all right? Had he sacrificed himself to protect her?

Well, wasn't that just perfect. If the dratted man turned honorable at this late date, she was throwing up her hands at the whole confusing mess.

She stood still for a moment, trying to get her bearings. Then she thought to kneel and feel at the planks beneath her feet. They ran perpendicular to the length of the footbridge. Therefore she should be able to follow them to—there!

The post of the railing appeared just inches before her eyes. But was it the right-hand railing or the left? She tried to feel the faint arch of the bridge beneath her feet, but she was simply too disoriented to tell.

Suddenly, a low groan came from behind her. She turned, then stopped. "Sir? Is that you?"

Following the railing with one hand, she kept the other out before her and moved closer. She kept onward, feeling nothing there at all. Had she imagined the sound? Was she now quite alone on the bridge?

"Mrs. Simpson, I'm sure those are very lovely shoes," came a voice from the vicinity of her feet. "But would you mind removing them from my hand?"

Clara stepped back quickly. "Oh, dear! Sorry!" She knelt where she had been standing and reached toward the voice. She found suit cloth beneath her hands and clutched it. The suit howled.

"Unhand me, you tw—dear lady!"

She jerked her hands back. "I'm sorry! Are you wounded there?"

"I wasn't," he gasped.

"Where did I . . ." She stopped. "Perhaps I don't want to know."

"No, you don't," he wheezed.

Free to clutch his bruised privates in the fog, Dalton suppressed a moan of pain. Bloody hell, the little idiot had nearly unmanned him! He was *definitely* not going to pursue an affair with the woman. She had a grip like a vise!

"Are you better now?" came a hopeful voice a few seconds later.

Only a woman would ask that at a time like this. Then Dalton forced down his irritation with a pang of guilt. It wasn't her fault they were in this position. He never should have agreed to this outing, knowing there was likely someone after him.

"I'm sorry I shouted at you. Yes, I'm much better now." He felt for the railing and pulled himself upright. Immediately his vision darkened and he swayed under the attack of a blinding headache. Taking stock, he realized that he wasn't all right.

He'd taken a bad knock to the head at some point. Now the pounding in his head combined with the swirling fog to completely disorient him. Dizzily he slid back to sprawl on the planks. Even with the solidity of the bridge beneath him, he couldn't seem to steady himself.

"I—my head—"

"Shh." Soothing cool hands came to cup his cheeks, then softly felt through his hair to find the tender spot. There must have been a lump indeed, for the fingers immediately moved away to gently and efficiently travel down his body searching for other injuries.

He didn't think there was anything seriously wrong elsewhere, but his voice didn't seem to be responding well enough to tell her so. And her touch did feel good.

His mind began to wander. He pulled himself back. Fog. They were in the fog, which may have been more aid than hindrance to him in the attack. Things had been so confusing that half the time he'd been convinced the two men were fighting each other. Then one had landed in the lake below and the other had run for his life. Dalton was sure he himself had suffered a slight concussion, nothing more.

Unless one counted the damaged family jewels.

Clara tried to keep her objectivity as she ran her hands over him to search out further damage. There was no denying the fellow was very nicely put together. Not a tailor's padding thickened his chest and shoulders, but hard muscle. Not whalebone and lacing made his waist fit and flat, but it was ridged and hard of its own merit.

There was no sign of a wound on him, not a tear in his clothing, not the sticky welling of blood. Still, she knew that a bad blow could injure without a sign. Worry began to spike through her, and she wondered how much longer the fog would last.

What if there was something seriously wrong with him? He might be a liar and a fake, but he had placed himself between her and the footpads without hesitation. She very likely owed him her life.

Drat it.

Finished with her examination, she felt her way back up to sit where he leaned his head upon the hard railing of the bridge.

"I think I can do better than that," she said. Gently she coaxed him to lay his head upon her lap. He came willingly enough and collapsed limply upon her. This worried her. She knew from volunteering at the hospital that those with head injuries should not be allowed to sleep until all danger of unconsciousness had passed.

"Sir?" He didn't respond. She patted his cheeks lightly. "Sir Thorogood? Sir, please answer me."

Real alarm was beginning to join with the dismay in her stomach. "Oh, do wake up. You mustn't sleep now." She patted him again, this time more firmly.

He stirred, rolling his head on her thigh to lean his cheek against her waist. "You smell good," he murmured.

Relief made her laugh. She was so happy that he wasn't unconscious that she only stroked his hair once more. "Stay awake, please. I should have a great deal of difficulty explaining how I came to be sprawled on this bridge with an unconscious man."

She could feel his chuckle against her torso. "Tell them that I expired . . . from an excess of devotion."

She snorted. "Romantic twaddle. I'll simply tell them that you tried to take advantage and I was forced to defend myself with my parasol."

He nestled closer, pressing his cheek intimately into her. "Ah, but where is this great weapon of yours? You brought no parasol with you."

"Hmm. True. I shall have to say that it fell into the river. Actually, I could solve the entire matter by pushing you in right now."

"A crime of passion. How . . . theatrical of you . . ."

His voice faded. Alarmed once more, Clara patted his cheek. "Do wake up, sir!"

He didn't respond. "Sir Thorogood!" She gave his cheek a right wallop in her fear.

"Ouch." His hand came up to cover hers on his face. "Careful . . . I'll start to think you like me again."

"Don't be silly. Of course I like you. I'm saving your life, aren't I?"

"Oh, is that what you're doing? I thought . . . I was going to end up in the river."

"I was simply teasing," she said softly. "You took this blow defending me. I should be an ungrateful wretch to let you go now."

"My head . . . is it bad?"

"There's a lump." She took his hand to cover the damage. "I should think you'll be right as rain tomorrow. In the meantime, it's important that you remain awake."

He shuddered. "God, yes. I must stay awake. Someone I know took a bad blow to the head a few months ago . . . he has yet to wake from it."

Compassion welled in her at the dread in his voice. His predicament would seem doubly grim then, with his friend's situation foremost in his mind.

It seemed as though she'd heard of such a case herself at the hospital not too long ago. A gentleman had arrived with a cartload of wounded soldiers, so badly beaten that they hadn't expected him to last the night.

The man had lived, but hadn't awakened in the remainder of his time there. Eventually someone had claimed him, she supposed.

Who would claim this man? If she were to take her impostor to a physician, she would not even be able to give his real name. She knew nothing about him at all.

She'd been going about this all wrong, she realized. She should have been gaining his confidence, charming him into sharing his purpose with her. She'd seen him admiring her figure on occasion. If she exercised her little-used feminine wiles, perhaps she could finally determine whether he was truly a threat or not.

His head lolled on her thighs and she realized that he was fading out again.

She rummaged in her reticule for the smelling salts that she had begun carrying after her unfortunate experience with the overly tightened corset. She found pencil stubs, scraps of foolscap, a ribbon from Kitty's bonnet that she'd promised to sew back on, and sundry other items, but no salts.

In his haze of semi-consciousness, Dalton found he rather liked lying on a woman's lap. It wasn't something he'd often had opportunity to do. Fuzzily, he decided to seek out more opportunities to do so in the future.

He could hear Mrs. Simpson rummaging through her reticule directly over him. Something plopped from her bag to nestle softly in his eye socket.

He reached up to fumble at the item on his face. A small cloth bag of some sort. The word *sachet* wandered through his cloudy mind, but that didn't seem quite right. Sachets were smelly in a good way. This was smelly in a sharp herbal way that wasn't pleasant at all.

"What's in here?" he mumbled. "Is it tea?"

"Oh, good, you're awake again! No, that isn't tea, it's catnip."

He pondered that for a moment. "Why do you carry catnip?"

She was still rummaging. "For the cats, of course."

That made sense. Rose liked cats, too. "Do you have many cats?"

"Oh, no, none at all," she said absently. "Beatrice won't allow them in the house."

Dalton tried to figure that one out, truly he did, but it was simply too difficult. He fumbled for his jacket pocket and dropped the small gathered pouch inside. Wouldn't want to lose the catnip.

"Aha! I found it!"

The reticule came to rest on his brow. If it hadn't been for the beads dangling into his eyes, the cool weight of it would have felt soothing on his throbbing head. Then someone drove a spike through his nose into his brain and he forgot all about the bag.

"Bloody hell!" He sat up abruptly, knocking away the reticule and the offending hand that hovered before his nose. "What'd you do that for?"

"I had to wake you up."

"I was awake. At least, I think I was awake. Now I wish I wasn't!" His nose burned and the pounding in his head had increased until he worried that his eyeballs were being knocked from his skull with every beat of his heart.

How he hated this woman. He could quite confidently vow that he had never hated anyone more in his life, with the possible exception of that pimple-faced boy from school. The one who had nicknamed him Dolly Dalton and had pushed him down at every opportunity.

That is, until Dalton had grown two inches taller and had sat on the boy once for an entire afternoon while he studied his lesson book. When the boy had finally agreed to choose a more pleasant nickname, "Monty" had been born. Thus had begun a brief period of acceptance from the other boys at school.

Of course, he'd left Monty behind many years ago. There was no room in his life for boyish distraction and amusement. Life was far too serious a matter to waste on such unimportant things. Liverpool's voice echoed in his head, from the occasion of his being called to discipline a young Dalton for the single boyish prank of his life.

"There's too much to be done to spend time on frivolities. When you are ready to take your seat in the House of Lords, you must remember this. A man is only as good as his mind. School the mind and you school the man!"

So Dalton had put away his heart and his soul the way that he had put away his cricket bat and his skates. Monty had gone into a storage trunk as well, never to be heard from again.

Until two nights past.

"Sir? Sir, are you still with me? Shall I apply the smelling salts again?"

Dear God, no. With difficulty, Dalton pulled his wan-

dering mind from the past to find that he was once again
comfortably ensconced on a nicely padded lap. She was
the perfect level of softness, he decided dreamily. Too
thin and he'd feel her bones. Too plump and he'd not
have room to roll his head so luxuriously into her mid-
riff, where he could press his aching forehead into her
pliant belly.

"Ah, Sir Thorogood?"

"Mm-hmm?"

"Are you—are you *nuzzling* me?"

Nuzzling. What a perfectly charming word. "Yes, I
believe I am."

"I see. Are you sure that's quite proper?"

Proper. Proper was not a charming word. *Proper* was
a stifling, cold word. In fact, *proper* was very likely his
least favorite word of the King's English.

"Sir? Don't go back to sleep, sir."

"Then talk to me. Tell me . . . about your husband."

Cool fingers on his throbbing head. "Very well, if it
will help you stay awake."

"How did you meet him?"

"I'd known his sister for some time, for I'd been volunteering at the hospital. She invited me to dinner on
several occasions where I met her younger brother Bentley."

"And you took a fancy to him?"

He felt her shrug. It did delightful things to her mid-
riff.

"Not at first, though most considered him handsome
enough. I'd had so little attention from men that I certainly didn't expect any from him. He seemed friendly,
that was all."

"How did you come to marry him, then?"

"Just before my father . . . died, Bentley's outfit was

called up. He was off to war and full of fire and romance at the thought. At the funeral, Bentley asked me to marry him before he left for the Peninsula. I think I accepted out of sheer surprise. And relief."

"Relief?"

Her fingers continued to trace through his hair. He wondered if she even knew she was doing it. She seemed very different in the fog, more . . . agreeable. Kind, just as Agatha had described her.

"Relief that I would have a home of my own, I suppose, some chance at a future. A family."

"And then he was killed?"

"Yes. And I was left dependent upon Beatrice's kindness." She remained silent then. Dalton missed her soft voice, for listening to her made the pounding in his head ease and his mind sharpen.

"Tell me about your drawing."

She seemed to stiffen briefly. "There's little to tell."

"But you are so interested in drawing, and your niece told me that you are quite good. How did you learn to draw?"

He felt her body relax beneath his head and shoulders and her fingers took up that lovely motion once more.

"My mother loved to draw and paint. My earliest memory is of her holding my hand while I held a pencil, helping me draw a flower. When she died, I drew because it helped me remember her. Eventually, I drew because I had no choice in the matter. Drawing was a way to leave my life for a while. A way to dream."

"And what did you dream of?" he whispered.

She didn't answer. "I believe the fog will lift soon. I think it is growing brighter already."

Dalton opened one eye, then promptly shut it once more. The light was indeed brighter, and therefore even more painful to his damaged brain. He began to lose his train of thought. The fog had left the landscape and clouded his mind instead.

He felt a cool hand cup his cheek. Cool hands and a warm lap. How he loved this woman. What was her name again? Rose?

"Sir, do you think that the footpads are still out there?"

Footpads. No, he must tell her—

He stirred, reaching his hand to hers once more. "When the fog lifts . . . call for John . . . get out of the park and send someone back for me . . ."

"Shh. I'll do no such thing."

"You don't . . . understand. I think someone is trying to . . . you're not . . . safe with me."

"Those men were after you specifically? I thought they were simple thieves."

"Even . . . footpads stay home . . . in these conditions." He gripped her hand earnestly. "I think . . . it's the cartoons. Someone wants them stopped. I can't . . . my head . . . if they're waiting, I can't . . . fend them off."

Guilt rushed through Clara. This was her fault. Then the real truth struck her. Oh, dear God. They weren't after *him*. They were after *her*!

Someone wanted her dead.

Chapter Twelve

Mrs. Simpson took her footman's hand and alighted from the carriage before the Trapps' house. With a worried expression, she turned to regard Dalton still seated inside.

"Are you sure you will not come in and allow me to call for someone? What if you lose consciousness again?"

She and John had managed to get him on his feet and back to the carriage when the fog had lifted. He'd remained conscious the entire way while John drove her home, but he remembered the alarming way he'd faded in and out on the footbridge.

He looked at her, for a moment having trouble placing her name. "Why would I do that?"

She stepped forward and removed the reins from his unresisting hands. "I insist that you stay. John can fetch one of your people back here in no time."

He nodded. "My people." Then his gaze sharpened on her suspiciously. "My . . . people?"

Dalton pulled himself back from the brink of revealing the truth about himself. He must concentrate! What should he do? How could he reach James?

"My . . . friend Mr. Cunnington." Focus, damn it! "He can be reached at the gentlemen's club that I . . . frequent." Had he given too much away? No, no, there was nothing unusual about having a friend at a club.

Mrs. Simpson nodded briskly. "Excellent! John, help me bring Sir Thorogood into the house." She turned back to Dalton. "Will you let me bring in a physician, as well?"

Dalton shook his head vigorously. It made his head throb worse. Damn, he did need a doctor, but not one of Mrs. Simpson's choosing. She'd likely bring in some quack who'd bleed him dry and ask too many questions, questions that he couldn't afford in his suggestible state.

"My friend . . . please, just fetch my friend." John was practically lifting him from the carriage. Dalton shook him off and descended on his own. The dizziness was easing, but he knew he should not be driving.

Inside the house, he was forced to endure the fluttering of Mrs. Trapp and her daughters until Mrs. Simpson shooed them from the drawing room. Dalton closed his eyes, grateful for the silence.

A cool hand settled on his temple, then laced gently through his hair to check his lump. He flinched, but not much, for the soft touch felt wonderful.

"Does it hurt you very much?"

The soft question was uttered from quite close by, and warm breath feathered across his ear. Suddenly Dalton was overcome with longing for more soft voices and gentle touches in his life.

All of its own, his hand crept up to capture the smaller one in his hair. He brought it to his lips briefly. The fingers in his fluttered slightly like a captured moth, then slowly pulled away.

Dalton sighed and let his head fall back to rest on the sofa's cushioned back. His head pounded still, but was settling into a bearable throb. "I think I should very much like a brandy."

A quiet laugh came from the booming silence. "And I should like a pair of wings, but I think neither of us will win our wish today. Spirits would be a very bad idea at this moment."

Dalton nodded carefully. She was quite right. "You are being very kind to me, Mrs. Simpson, especially after I was such horrid company on our drive."

"Were you? I'm sure I didn't notice."

That bothered him for some reason. He'd come to rather enjoy her flattering attentions, he mused, but now he seemed to have lost her interest.

What difference does it make? You have a mission!

Startled from his fog, Dalton opened his eyes at that thought to find Mrs. Simpson regarding him steadily. She tilted her head and gave him a tiny smile. "Your eyes are entirely too beautiful for a man. Why are all the gentlemen I meet prettier than I?"

He laughed out loud at that, then clutched his brain between both hands to keep it in his skull. "Ouch."

Clara shook her head, smiling. She wasn't sure at what point she had decided to forgive the man his posturing. Perhaps it had been when he'd told her that he'd been attacked because of her cartoons. Perhaps it had been when he'd thrust her behind him at the first sign of danger.

Or perhaps it had been the way he'd lain trustingly in her lap, defenseless but for her protection.

Whatever the reason, she found herself entirely able to smile naturally at Sir Thorogood without experiencing the desire to slap the curl from his powdered hair. So he'd assumed the credit for her cartoons—well, what of it? She had no intention of ever coming forward to claim her work. In fact, his charade only made her work easier, for now she would never be suspected.

She doubted she would ever understand what could make someone do such a thing, but her anger over the matter was gone. Let him bask in the glow for a while. If nothing else, she could be gratified by Society's wholehearted approval of her drawings.

Or disapproval—

If someone were after her . . . er, him . . . if someone were after Sir Thorogood, then this man was in danger because of her—despite the fact that he had willingly assumed the role.

She leaned forward, trying to decide how to warn him. "Sir Thorogood, you said someone was trying to hurt you because of m—your cartoons."

He didn't look at her. "I did?"

"Yes, on the bridge. If that's true, don't you think it might be wise to . . . well, make yourself a little less public?"

"Oh, nothing of the sort, I'm sure. Footpads, that was all, taking advantage of the weather to hoist a few purses and pocket watches." His tone was airy, if rather muffled.

"But you said—"

"Oh, a wandering mind might say many a silly thing, dear lady." He chuckled and waved a hand. "Silly things, indeed."

Oh, dear. The pompous poseur was back, and in good form. How tiresome. Just when she'd actually begun to like the man a little. "Your friend should be here soon. I told John to bring him straightaway. It is an interesting name, the Liar's Club."

Sir Thorogood mumbled something from under the hands rubbing his temples. Not so long ago she would have thought the name of the club suited him perfectly. Now she simply sighed, thinking that she would be off to the attic in a few hours to change into Rose.

She wondered how long it would be before Sir Thorogood's friend arrived. Edgy with anticipation, she considered her plans for the evening. Today was the first Sunday of the month. If Monty remembered what she had told him about Wadsworth's habits, he might decide to appear again tonight to learn what new documents had made their way into the safe box after Mr. Wadsworth's monthly accounting.

All she needed to do now was send Sir Thorogood on his way as soon as possible.

James knocked on the door of the Smythe Square house until the door was opened by a kind-faced butler. After introducing himself, he was led to a very comfortable parlor where he found Dalton enthroned on a sofa, attended by an attractive girl in a green dress.

She stood and moved toward him as he was announced, her hand extended. On second inspection, James decided that she was a woman, not a girl, though she had a youthful manner that had piqued his interest.

He sighed, thinking that, as usual, someone else had gotten to her first. All the quality females got snatched up by blokes like Simon and Dalton, leaving only the false-hearted ones for him.

"Thank you for coming so quickly, Mr. Cunnington. Sir Thorogood has had a blow to the head, but he won't allow me to call for a physician. Please appeal on my behalf, won't you?"

"Certainly, Miss . . ."

She blinked at him in surprise, then laughed at herself in a most charming way. "I beg your pardon, Mr. Cunnington." James found himself captivated by her intelligent hazel eyes and almost missed her introduction.

"—Mrs. Simpson."

James almost gawked. *This* was the "Widow Simpleton" that Dalton had described with such annoyance?

Mrs. Simpson took his silence for worry. "I'm sure he'll recover, but he's been fading in and out for over an hour. Perhaps you can reassure me as to his condition, you know him so much better than I."

She led him to Dalton's side. James spared him a glance, but aside from a certain pallor he looked all right, the hard-headed sod. James was far more interested in the pretty widow.

His curiosity was not to be assuaged, for Mrs. Simpson was already passing through the drawing room door. "I'll leave you to take him home, if I may? My footman suffered a mishap in the fog as well, and I'd like to reassure myself."

She looked to James as though she absolutely couldn't wait to leave. He could only nod, mystified by the conflicting impressions of Mrs. Simpson.

"Is she gone?"

The long-suffering growl came from the sofa, and James turned back to Dalton. "Yes, she's gone. I like her." He settled in a nearby chair. "Got conked, did you?"

Dalton raised a hand to his head. "Oh, I did my share of conking as well, thank you for your concern." With an expression of distaste, he flicked away the lap blanket that had been maternally tucked about him. "Get me out of this pink hell, will you? I've never seen so many women in one house before. Four of them! How does Trapp stand it, do you think?"

James looked about him at the comfortable drawing room. There was a certain amount of rose-colored decor, but it certainly wasn't the worst he'd seen. His own mother had been prone to pink, and he'd never much minded it.

Shrugging, he helped Dalton to his feet. "Perhaps Trapp thinks himself a lucky man, to have four women to fuss over him after a long day."

Dalton only looked mulish, so James dropped the subject. If Dalton was determined to dislike Mrs. Simpson, then more the fool he. James thought he himself might like to know her better. She was pretty, intelligent, and apparently *not* already under Dalton's spell.

James shook his head in wonder. "Your standards must be inhuman, old fellow."

Dalton brushed himself off and tugged his waistcoat straight. "I have no idea what you are talking about."

James pursed his lips, looking toward the door that the decidedly *not* simple Mrs. Simpson had disappeared through. "No, I don't suppose you do."

He turned back to Dalton. "Well, do you want to take your headache home, or do you want to double it by going to the club?"

Dalton closed his eyes. "Tell me."

"Oh, it's not so bad. Stubbs heard Fisher telling Kurt that Button . . ." Talking as they left the house, James kept one eye peeled for another glimpse of the Widow Simpson.

An hour later, Dalton sat at the manager's desk at the club and let the arguments swirl over his head. The factions of the club were becoming more deeply divided. The morale that had dropped after the losses suffered in the past months had struck a new low. Now the Liars were not only mistrustful of Dalton, they were beginning to be mistrustful of each other.

Fisher, the last living code breaker, had obviously spent far too much time alone in the coderoom. Dalton hadn't realized how haunted the poor fellow was by the ghosts of his predecessors. How must it feel to know that your department had been targeted more severely than any other, including the assassins?

Never a brave soul originally, Fisher had likely felt the seclusion of the coderoom had been a safe place from which to fight the war. In addition, he had only been an apprentice when his superiors had been killed off one by one. His sudden promotion to final authority must have been quite traumatic.

Kurt the Cook, the Liars' chef and premier knife man for many years, had taken exception to the quick rise of Fisher, and of Button, whose frankly effeminate ways did nothing to endear him to the gruff giant.

Dalton understood the man's desire for the proper order of advancement, and it was true that Button could be very wearing, especially since he had begun his involvement with the Liars through the acquaintance of Lady Raines. Agatha was a great favorite among the men, and Button tended to wax on about his close relationship with her.

These men needed someone to fight for, Dalton understood that. He simply wished they would all choose their own someone.

The volume of the argument rose around him. Button had resorted to standing on a chair in order to emphasize his point by poking his finger into Kurt's chest. Perhaps

Dalton ought to remind Button that a valet without fingers might find himself short of work.

Perhaps it truly was time to get women into the club. Preferably by the boatload.

Kurt had Button dangling by the scruff of his neck. Fisher looked tense enough to string on a bow. James sat in one corner with his head in his hands.

Where was the close-knit group that had worked like a fine watch to save Agatha a few weeks past? Dalton cleared his throat. Abrupt silence fell. "Dear Lord, I do hope we won't be needing to run a rescue mission anytime soon," he said with quiet disdain. "You lot couldn't band together to save a chunk of coal from the fire."

Fisher reddened but retained his rebellious scowl, Kurt growled incomprehensibly, and Button straightened his waistcoat with a twitch and a defiant sniff. Dalton looked at James, but found no support in those neutral brown eyes. So . . . not even James.

To hell with the lot then. Dalton rose. "I have a mission to run. I expect you all to work this out on your own. If anyone spills blood on the carpet, he'll be scrubbing it out with his own hands."

He stalked from the room and from the club without another word, but he wasn't fast enough to miss the sound of the voices rising behind him once again.

Clara was in her room when Bea's voice rose up the stairs.

"Claaa—raa!"

Refusing to answer in kind, Clara sighed and left her room to descend the stairs. Beatrice stood on the first step, inhaling once more.

"I'm coming, Bea," Clara said hurriedly. There was

no convincing Bea that actually climbing the stairs, or even troubling a servant, might be a more appropriate way to fetch someone. You could take a girl from the country . . .

"Clara, darling, you have a caller! A *real* caller!"

This was most embarrassing, as Clara had now descended far enough down the stairs to see a grinning Nathaniel—rather, Lord Reardon—standing directly behind Bea. It was fortunate that his lordship was not a "real" caller at all, or Clara might have been tempted to draw another Society Mama cartoon.

No, Lord Reardon was merely a friend, thankfully. He seemed amused by Beatrice but not unkindly so. Clara smiled at him gratefully.

"What fortunate timing. Have you had your tea, my lord? Would you like to join me?" Clara stepped down to his level and extended her hand.

Lord Reardon bowed over it and sent her a flattering look. "How charming to find you at home, Mrs. Simpson. I should be delighted to impose upon you for tea."

Observing all the forms, they retired to the parlor and Clara rang for tea. Bea couldn't quite come up with a good enough reason to include herself, and Clara didn't invite her. One mustn't encourage yodeling, after all. Nasty habit, unless of course one were Swiss.

Once they were alone, Lord Reardon leaned forward in his chair. "I came to return something to you and to beg a favor." He pulled a small wrapped parcel from his breast pocket and placed it in her hand. The flat soft item was no larger than a card.

Ah, her handkerchief. Clara smiled. "Aren't you the prompt one." She set the package to one side. "Now, tell me how I can be of service to you, my lord."

"This Tuesday I am committed to dine with my

cousin Cora. I should like to bring you along, if you don't object."

Puzzled, Clara blinked at him. "I certainly don't object to Mrs. Teagarden. Why would I?"

He laughed. "No, not object to my aunt—object to my blatantly using you for some intelligent conversation at the table. You have a very entertaining mind."

Clara sighed. "And here I thought you loved me for my exceptional beauty."

Startled, he blinked, then grinned. "Why aren't you afraid to tease me? Most girls do nothing but sigh and flutter at me."

"Well, I am hardly a girl, my lord." She shook her head at him. "Besides, you couldn't possibly be serious about courting me. Therefore, we may be friends and I may gladly provide distraction during your aunt's dinner."

"No," he said slowly. "I couldn't possibly be serious about courting you. Yet—"

She tilted her head and waited, but he didn't finish. He merely smiled and set down his teacup.

"I shouldn't keep you any longer. You've had quite a day already."

Clara nodded in agreement, then looked at him sharply. "How did you know that?"

His smile deepened. "I'm afraid your sister-in-law told me the entire tale about your ill-fated drive this morning. You were very brave."

"Well, I don't know how you came to that conclusion. Just a bit of fog that caused my companion to stumble and hit his head, after all." That was the version she'd told Beatrice, at any rate.

He gazed at her for a moment. "Indeed." Then he smiled once more. His eyes went rather dreamy when he smiled, giving him the aspect of a knightly angel.

Clara fought back a sigh of artistic longing. How she would love to pin him down for hours to model for her. Of course, she'd need a real studio. She could hardly ask him to sit in her bedchamber . . .

"I shall call for you at seven, if I may?"

"Hmm?"

"This Tuesday evening? Seven o'clock?"

Clara blinked. "Oh, yes, of course." She laughed at herself. "I'm sorry. Thinking about drawing you again, I'm afraid. I can be quite the goose when I do that."

His smile faded and his gaze sharpened. "Oh, no, Mrs. Simpson. Never a goose, not you."

After Lord Reardon had taken his leave, Clara remembered the little package. She opened it, expecting her own simple handkerchief. Instead, within the wrapping lay an exquisite bit of lawn edged in Brussels lace . . . it was the handkerchief of a duchess.

Clara held it gingerly in her hand and wondered precisely what Lord Reardon meant by the gift. He couldn't actually have formed an attachment for her, could he? A man like that? No, surely he'd only meant to show his appreciation for the drawing she'd given him.

The clock in the hall chimed and Clara smiled. Only six short hours to go until she could go back to being Clara Rose.

Tick-tock, she urged silently. Tick-tock in earnest.

Chapter Thirteen

Dalton went straight to his study when he arrived home, positively aching for some peace. As he relaxed into the dark green room that was filled with the smells of fine leather and good cigars, he felt his shoulders start to come down from around his ears.

The dispute at the club had left him exhausted and somewhat depressed. As usual, the men had spoken to him with scarcely concealed disrespect, calling him "the gentleman," an irritating reference that called to mind the class differences that stood in the way of his ever truly belonging.

In a few hours, he'd don his Monty costume for another midnight excursion. According to what he'd read in the files, Wadsworth was in the process of blackmailing someone powerful, although it was not clear who. Dalton was very interested in the progression of certain of his lordship's plans.

And Rose has nothing to do with that interest?

Dalton rubbed the back of his neck, being careful of his head although the throbbing had quieted somewhat. He wasn't quite ready to examine his attraction to Rose.

There was every reason to believe that he was only feeling a bit deprived. He wasn't a monk, after all.

Even Mrs. Simpson had an effect on him, which only went to show how far gone he was. Furthermore, by the time he'd been rescued by James this afternoon, he'd almost begun to like the woman.

Still, all the while in her company, thoughts of Rose had kept crossing his mind. He'd been itching to leave Mrs. Simpson in order to go to his saucy flower. To hear her soft laugh, see her outlaw smile . . . smell the scent of roses.

Funny valiant Rose, leading him by the hand through the darkness . . .

Lead me on, my flower. I'll follow you anywhere.

Which was precisely what he couldn't do. She was not for him. She was for a man like Monty, a free soul who could give her what she wanted, who could live happily in her world and never force her to live unhappily in his.

He rested his head back on the chair. Perhaps he was getting ahead of himself. She was only a useful informant, after all, a girl he liked and respected who'd helped him gain entry to Wadsworth's secrets.

If he could scarcely stand the wait before he saw her again, perhaps it was only his eagerness to get this case solved and prove himself ready to rule the Liars.

The fire in his study was warm and inviting. A few hours' rest . . .

He leaned back into the chair and closed his eyes, only to open them again immediately as the study door exploded inward and banged into the wall.

Dalton jumped up to land crouched on his feet facing the door, instinctively ready to do battle. The Sergeant stood just inside the gaping doorway, dripping and bleeding, his dignity in shreds along with the skin of his forearms. Something wet and furred dangled from his careful grip. "My lord, if you order me to try to wash this monster again, I must respectfully request that I be court-martialed instead."

Dalton was fairly sure it wasn't an idle threat. By the lifeless exhausted tone in the Sergeant's voice, it was a simple statement of fact. "But it was barely conscious when I gave it to you."

"It woke up right quick when we put it in the bath."

"I see." Dalton looked down at the writhing matted creature dangling from his majordomo's outstretched hands. "Are you waiting for me to take it from you, Sergeant?"

"Or put me out of my misery with a bullet. Either one will do." The Sergeant didn't sound as if he cared one way or the other.

Dalton looked from the animal's unsheathed claws to the red marks on the Sergeant's hands and arms. He himself had unbuttoned his frock coat and removed it along with his waistcoat when he'd entered his study a few moments before. He looked down at his shirtfront, then took another look at the bloody rips in the front of the Sergeant's sopping shirt.

Dalton put his waistcoat back on. Then he added his frock coat as well, buttoning it tight. Clothing could be replaced, but the Sergeant didn't look as though he would heal for some time.

"Uri, fetch some toweling," Dalton ordered.

The young footman took a step back. "M-me, my lord?"

Unbelievable. Uri was a former soldier, a brave and lethal swordsman, and an utterly dependable servant. Dalton glowered at him. "Coward."

"Yes, my lord."

"The toweling is for the Sergeant, Uri. And for me."

Uri gulped in relief. "Yes, my lord. Thank you, my lord." He tore off down the hallway, shouting for linens from the chambermaid.

When the toweling came, Dalton wrapped a portion of it around both forearms and carefully approached the long-suffering Sergeant. A deadly growl emanated from the dangling beast, and a claw swiped lightning-fast in Dalton's direction.

"Are you hurting it, Sergeant?" Rose wouldn't like it if her pet was damaged.

"Not at all, my lord. The monster's quite comfortable, aside from bein' wet."

"Ah . . . good." Dalton moved another step closer. Another slash and a truly unholy howl. Dalton took a breath. "Sergeant, may I inquire as to your previous strategy? So I know what to avoid, you understand."

"No, my lord, you may not. You're stalling."

Dalton sighed. "Yes, I fear I am."

"On the count of three, my lord, I am dropping the animal and running for my life. You may keep my severance to hire yourself an army."

"Really, Sergeant. There's no need for such dramatics—"

"*One.*"

"After all, it is only a cat—"

"*Two.*"

"Oh, very well!" Dalton lunged forward, his towel-wrapped hands extended. He managed to get some of the cloth around the back legs, pinning the shredding claws neatly down. That inspired him to fling the rest of the toweling snugly around the creature's front legs and head, leaving only a pink nose and half a set of whiskers emerging from the bundle.

It now looked as though he held a baby in his arms. A demon baby whose banshee howls were not muffled in the slightest.

"I leave you to it then, my lord."

The bundle twisted and screeched in Dalton's hands. "No, Sergeant, *wait*—" The Sergeant, a man who would have stood at Dalton's back were they outnumbered by one hundred, was gone, escaping down the hall like a rat deserting a sinking ship.

He was on his own. Carefully Dalton shifted the bundle under one arm. The toweling was already very damp and the room was chill. Cats liked warmth, did they not? He carried it closer to the fireplace, using his free hand to tug his chair around to face the coals.

He sat, gingerly letting the swaddled animal rest on his lap. In afterthought, perhaps not the best idea. A vulnerable spot, that. He made a long arm and nicked a cushion from the sofa, placing it between the cat and his personal effects.

Only then did he allow himself to relax the smallest amount. He could sit here for a time and allow the warmth to dry the creature. Perhaps the mishandled bath had been enough to clean it.

Weren't cats supposed to keep themselves clean? Life must have been hard indeed for the creature if it had given up on such a basic function. A flash of sympathy caught him unaware.

He ought to feel sorry for the Sergeant, were he to feel sorry for anyone. Or even for himself, for being stuck with caring for the beast until he'd kept his promise to Rose.

Rose. Dalton realized that he was smiling. He found

himself doing that more often recently, usually when he was thinking about a certain housemaid.

The cat had stopped its yowling and lay unmoving in the bundle. Worriedly, Dalton leaned over to peer through the narrow tunnel of cloth to see a single malevolent green eye glowing within. "Kit-kit-kit," he called softly.

The responding growl was so deep that he felt it rather than heard it. The sound made the hair on the back of his neck rise and he sat back quickly. Fine. No peering. No *kit-kit*. Understood.

Dalton remained where he was, carefully holding the bundle and feeling the warmth of the coals on his face. The house was silent. The servants were all hiding belowstairs, no doubt. Bloody cowards.

He ought to be at the club, or at least be pondering the club, but frankly he was bone-weary of his battle for the Liars' respect.

Liverpool assumed that Dalton wanted power and influence, that leadership of the Liars would put him in a position for advancement to Prime Minister someday.

Liverpool had it completely wrong.

Dalton's lap was vibrating. In astonishment, he looked down to find that he was absently stroking the damp bundle he held. Leaning closer, careful not to stop his rhythmic caress, he cocked an ear toward the cat.

The sound emanating from the animal was none other than a rusty purr. It *liked* him?

Dalton dropped his head onto the chair back and laughed out loud. Someone finally liked him, someone no one else could stand.

Except for Rose. "She likes us both, doesn't she?" The cat continued its deranged sawing sound. "The monster and the thief."

But would she like him if she knew he wasn't a thief?

Clara finally made her escape into the attic, but only after she'd told the edited version of her adventures to the twins at least five times.

This time Clara awaited Monty with an open window and a lighted candle. She'd had a very long day, however, and fell asleep on the pallet of old draperies that she'd scavenged from a trunk.

She awoke to find him kneeling over her, her cheek still tingling from the touch of his warm fingers. Lulled by her weariness, she only smiled up at him sleepily.

"Are you all right, rosebud? Did the master work you too hard this day?"

Clara nodded and opened her mouth to answer, only to be surprised by a sudden yawn. She clapped one hand over her mouth, embarrassed, but Monty only chuckled.

"You should be yawning. You're up very late."

"No later than you," she retorted with a smile. Oh, she was happy to see him. His gray eyes twinkled behind his mask and his teeth shone white in the candlelight. The light from the candle flame was small and dim, yet it was the brightest in which she'd ever seen him.

"You are handsome," she breathed, then caught herself. She blushed. "At least, I think you are. I wouldn't really know, now would I?"

Monty leaned close to whisper in her ear, his breath warm and caressing. "I'll let you take me mask off," he teased, ". . . last."

The very thought of undressing his hard body sent hot fire through her belly. Suddenly—*desperately*—she wanted him. He must have seen it in her face as he drew back, for his teasing smile died and his eyes grew dark. "I'm sorry, Rose. I shouldn't play—"

"Nay, you shouldn't!" She sat up quickly, giving his shoulder a shove when he remained in her way. Once she was on her feet she found it a bit easier to breathe.

Dalton cursed himself as he stood to face her. He had no intention of taking advantage of Rose, yet whenever he was near her he couldn't seem to help but speak with Monty's flirtatious manner. It was as if Monty were a real man, perhaps even the real man inside of him. After all, who knew what was left after the years of polish?

Sometimes he couldn't even recognize himself in the mirror, only a younger reflection of Liverpool.

Now his fearless Rose was looking at him with doubt and longing in her eyes. He was a bounder to string her along this way. What if she fell in love with him? What would it do to her to learn that he was a gentleman and a peer, miles above her reach, and had only been using her to gain entry to Wadsworth's house?

She could be sacked for what she was doing for him. *Or hanged!*

His breath left him in a hurry. Dear God, he'd never thought of that. He would get her out of this house directly, he decided. Not to hire her himself, of course. That wouldn't be right, feeling about her as he did— rather, with her feeling about *him* as she did.

He'd talk to Agatha and Simon tomorrow and ask them to take her into their household. She'd be well treated among that bunch of odd ducks, and he'd be able to see her on occasion—

No. It would be best not to see her at all. It would only confuse her further. She mustn't acquire any hopes in his direction at all. After tonight, he would secure her a comfortable position far away, never to see her again.

Then perhaps someday his chest would no longer ache at the thought of her.

Clara busied herself adjusting her cap while she recovered from her moment of yearning, then picked up the candle. When she turned back to Monty, she was quite sure not a bit of her feelings remained visible on her face.

"Do you wish to go to the study? His lordship was supposed to have had another meeting tonight." There, her voice sounded quite normal.

Monty looked at her oddly. "Don't you know if he did or not?"

Drat, she'd slipped. "I—I pled illness to come upstairs and wait for you." Indeed, the real Rose was ill with a terrible cold. Even now she was sleeping in Clara's attic with a warming pan at her feet and a poultice on her chest. "I'm sure the meeting occurred, for the cook has been workin' all day for it." The proof of that was in the smell of baking that had reached clear up to the attic this evening.

"Does he dine with them in his study?"

She laughed. "Of course not. They eat a late supper in the dining room, then retire t' the study with port and cigars."

He seemed intrigued. "Where's the dining room?"

"Come, I'll show you."

They traveled down the servants' stair to the ground floor, this time with the candlelight to guide them. Clara was quite sure that being in the dark with Monty was dangerous for both of them.

Thoughts of her handsome thief occupied her mind as she led him out of the hidden stair into the hall outside the dining room. The sconces were still lighted, so she doused her own light and left it on the stair.

When she opened the dining room doors she was stunned to see a fire blazing and the table all laid out for dinner in the bright light of the chandelier. Suddenly she realized why she could still smell a strong smell of cooking, even at this late hour.

"Oh, no!" She turned and pushed him back into the hall. "The meeting must've been delayed. Quickly, back to the stairs!"

He moved, but not swiftly enough. At the far end of the hall, the front door opened to admit a number of gentlemen who stood talking while Soames took their coats.

Clara yanked Monty back into the dining room by one arm and shut the door. He turned to run for the door in the far wall, but she held on and pulled him to a stop. "No, that's down to the kitchen! It'll be full of staff right now."

There was no help for it. Clara towed him toward her favorite hiding place in the sideboard. She'd emptied it of its dusty tureens and tablecloths months ago and none of the servants had so much as noticed. It was roomy for one. She only hoped it would hold two.

She opened the large cupboard doors on the bottom and made to shove Monty inside. He climbed in readily, but then he pulled her in after him and shut the door, trapping them together in the darkness.

Wadsworth's guests began their supper with a lively discussion of Sir Thorogood's drawings, which made Clara feel a tiny spurt of pride. Voices were rising outside the cupboard. She'd certainly managed to inspire some rigorous debate on hired love. Or were they talking about the war?

"I rather like the notion," one voice said. "A mistress is precisely what she is to me."

"Rather too poetic for my tastes, sir," another voice added, one that Clara recognized as Mr. Wadsworth. "I prefer to keep things businesslike. Payment for services rendered and so forth."

A third voice entered the discussion, a low cultured tone that made Clara think of fine drawing rooms and genteel strolls in the park. "Wadsworth, your plebeian roots are showing. I cannot participate in business at my status level. The very idea. No, I prefer to think of a good wine, beginning as mere fruit, then aging to something altogether more . . . rewarding."

This brought laughter and murmurs of agreement, although Clara was at a loss to understand why. She was finding it difficult to concentrate on anything but Monty. She was tucked deeply into the curl of his body, so deeply it was as if she'd climbed inside of him. His scent surrounded her and became her scent. His heat seeped through the layers of cloth separating them and became her heat.

"You're trembling," he breathed into her ear. "Only keep quiet and they'll not find us here."

He didn't understand. The last thing on her mind was fear. Perhaps there was a bit of it, but it only added an edge to the other tension thrumming through her nerves.

His hand shifted a tiny amount on her hip, and she jumped. He pressed her hip down firmly. "Shh."

His breath in her ear sent her thighs to trembling. She wanted him to move his hand. The only problem was, she wanted him to move it to a much more scandalous spot of her body. Several of them to be precise.

Chapter Fourteen

Dalton had a problem. And it was growing larger by the moment. Rose's warm firm body was driving him mad. He'd bent his head slightly to whisper to her, and he hadn't been able to make himself move away afterward. She smelled like warm heaven, like woman and rose petals and, rather suddenly, like passion.

The skin of her neck was so close that he could feel the heat on his lips. A fraction of an inch more and he would be able to taste her. And dear God, how he wanted to taste her.

The dining room beyond their hiding place changed tone with the clink of silver against china turning to the setting back of chairs. The dinner was over and the party would soon be moving to the study. They would be able to leave safely after the staff cleared the room.

He didn't want to leave. He wanted to stay curled with Rose in this tiny space with their mingled breath warming their faces and their every movement a fragment of a much older dance. And he wanted more. He wanted so much more. . . .

He succumbed. Just a brief stolen taste. Just a whisper of his tongue on her fragrant skin.

She jerked slightly and he pressed her still with his palm on her firm rounded hip. Held her still with strength and the fear of discovery for this tiny ravagement. God help him, if she had objected further, he was not sure he would have listened.

Instead, she let her head fall back on his shoulder, exposing more soft neck to his exploring mouth.

A near silent sigh escaped her, a sigh of submission and longing, or so he chose to hear it.

Clara had no senses available to her but touch and scent. The darkness was comforting in its anonymity. If even they couldn't see what they were doing, then perhaps on some level, it wasn't truly done.

Yet the heat of his mouth on her flesh was very real, as was the tantalizing pressure of his hand on her hip. Especially now that his fingers were tracing a matching spiral to the pattern of his tongue.

Every tiny stroke left a trail of flame on her. She imagined that if she were to look down at his hand, she would see ghost fire trailing from his touch.

She pressed her thighs together involuntarily and her hips rotated without command of her mind. He was hard behind her, as if she lay against a rod of iron.

If she were not mistaken, it was a rather large rod. She swiveled against it experimentally and felt an answering press of his loins against her bottom. Her own sex was hot wax between her thighs, swollen with unanswered need.

Her body was a stranger to her. Where had this need come from? Who was this woman pressed scandalously against a near stranger in the dark?

It was Rose. Rose who slid her hand up to cover the wide warm one on her hip. Rose who tilted her head to urge his hot mouth to her earlobe.

It was Rose who let the heat of him sink deeply into her and melt the frozen desires of years.

And it was Rose who slowly urged his hand to stroke up her waist, over her panting ribs to cover her breast.

She made a soft sound when he cupped her and rubbed his thumb across her nipple where it stood high against her bodice.

It was too loud, and they both froze, their passion ignited into heart-pounding fear for a long moment of suspense. But the murmur of talk never abated, and at last they allowed themselves to breathe.

Yet the momentary jolt of fear had only heightened their ache, had only made the future a more dangerous place, therefore providing an inner excuse to explore this tight, hot moment of erotic confinement to the limit.

Not content with the cloth-covered breast that filled his palm, Dalton slid his hand to her shoulder and began to ease down the neckline of the drab maid's gown. Every slow fraction of inch of shoulder exposed was met with a kiss of greeting.

His Rose was shaking fully now, and for a moment Dalton hesitated, though it tore him a slash in his soul. Was this fear of him? Was he forcing something upon her that she did not want?

As he hesitated, she made a small growling sound and rotated her bottom against his erection, nearly making his eyes roll back with unspent lust. He was harder than he remembered ever being and growing harder still, his desire a literal ache deep in his scrotum.

His breath quickened, and his pulse raced, until he felt dangerous with desire. Yet breath for breath, heartbeat for heartbeat, her desire seemed to keep pace with his.

The long tight sleeve of the gown slid down only far enough to pin her arm to her side. Her breast was now even more tightly confined, the neckline making a deep dent in the softness of her flesh.

Fortunately for Dalton, he was experienced with unbuttoning gowns in the dark.

Clara felt each button slowly give way with a sense of inevitability. It was as if Monty was caught up in the same dreamlike lure that she was.

"Sweet," he breathed as he freed her bindings. "My Rose by any other name . . ."

Shakespeare? Dear Lord, was there anything more alluring than a dashing masked thief who studied poetry? Clara's final iota of will melted away at his gentle whisper.

He would still feel the same if he knew who she truly was—wasn't that what it meant?

As would she.

The last button gave way, and the bodice of her gown fell forward. For a moment, she was reminded of when she came back to consciousness that night in the garden. Then the thought was burned away as his touch brought her to flames.

Her breasts were bare in the darkness. She could feel the soft movement of warm breath brushing over them as Monty returned his lips to her neck.

She'd never been bared for anyone in her life. She felt so wicked, unprotected yet free. When his warm palm cupped her, she jumped from the suddenness of his heat on her. Then his caresses began and she forgot all about the strangeness.

First he took all of her into his hand that he could

and squeezed gently. Then he let his fingers trail in a decreasing spiral until the tips of his fingers plucked gently at her nipple.

She squirmed and he took a soft bite of her neck between his teeth to hold her still. He moved his hand to her other breast and repeated the teasing, plucking motion. The tingle at her neck combined with the ache in her middle, along with the shocking pleasure of his gentle twisting of her nipples.

She was going to die. Right there, right then.

Then his hand left her bosom, and he released the bite on her neck with a kiss. She was shivering with longing, on fire with need. "Don't stop," she breathed.

He did not reply, only slid his hand down her side to the bend in her knees. She felt her hem rising up her calf. Her head fell back upon his shoulder. "Oh, yes," she whispered. "Please."

He shushed her again and drew her skirt above her knees, then above the tops of her stockings. She felt the cooler air on her skin, then his warm fingers stroked her inner thigh.

"Open," he demanded in her ear, and she obeyed. Why deny him when she was nothing but one vast ache for his touch?

She felt the faint brush of his hand on her curls, then a gentle exploring touch. Unerringly, he found the center of her pleasure, the one Bentley had never truly located. Swiftly he dampened his fingertips in her wetness, then drew them up and over her button in a caressing circle that took her breath away.

She twisted helplessly against him as he drove her higher and higher with his dancing, circling touch. She was only dimly aware of his own labored breathing and of the rigid erection that he pressed firmly to her bottom.

His mouth returned to her ear. "Don't make a sound," he ordered. Then he entered her with his finger in one deep plunge. A cry of pleasure welled up in her throat until she was forced to bite her lip fiercely to quell it.

That was the last of her control. She jerked and quivered helplessly against him in her release, her body throbbing tightly around his finger still thrust deeply within her.

She came back to awareness in the darkness, the only sound their mingled rasping breaths. Suddenly she remembered where they were and why.

"Did they hear us?" she whispered in horror.

He kissed her ear. "My fine flower, they're long gone. The help was clearing up when you came apart for me."

She felt his hand retreat from under the folds of her skirts and felt mingled longing and panic. What had she done?

When could she do it again?

"I think we'd best make for the attic, my rosebud."

"Y-yes," she stuttered. She opened the cupboard door a tiny crack and peered out. Once she was certain that no one remained in the room, she quickly scrambled out. Blushing furiously and completely unable to look Monty in the face, she made for the hall and the safety of the servants' stairs beyond.

He caught up to her on the stair and closed them both in the darkness once more. "I suppose we cannot light the candle now." He took her hand. "Lead me, then, my flower."

Clara couldn't answer. She could only climb the stairs in a daze of mortification and lust.

Dalton was still aflame, his blood still pounding. He tried not to let her sense the ferocity of his need. If she had any clue how profoundly he ached to raise her skirts again and press her up against the wall . . .

She'd been so hot and ready for him.

And she was no virgin.

The fact of her experience didn't resolve the barriers between them, and he still vowed to send her safely away somewhere. But there was no denying that it inflamed him deeply that were he truly Monty the Thief he might have shared sweet Rose's attic pallet tonight.

When they reached the attic, moonlight was streaming in through the open window. Silver glow glamoured the battered leftovers of the household until the raftered chamber had the air of a fairy bower. It was damp and chill, yet somehow the more magical for it.

"Oh!" She moved forward to lean her hands on the sill and raised her face to the sky. "I love the moonlight."

"And it loves you," Dalton whispered from behind her. She was so sweet in the pure light, a fairy maid, born of a rose and given to him by the moon for this one last moment.

A dream, he knew. Yet he felt as though if he lost this fantasy then he would face nothing but the dry fact of duty for the rest of his life.

"I'll not be back," he said. "This is becoming too risky."

She turned to him, her sweet face a delicate harlequin mask in the half-shadow. Still he had yet to see her in true light. "It's gettin' too dangerous for you?"

With a smile, he shook his head. "No, dear rosebud. It's too dangerous for you."

She studied him for a long moment, then turned once more to the moon. "So I'll not see you again, then?"

"No." It was better this way. He'd see to her improved employment anonymously and his life would be a little brighter, knowing she had some happiness.

"Then for this one night, Monty . . ."

"Yes?"

She turned and gazed into his eyes. "For this one night, will you be my lover?"

If Monty didn't answer soon, Clara felt as though she would burn away like paper from the fire inside her.

Perhaps he merely needed a little reminder of the pleasure they could share. She stepped closer to him and ran her palm under his coat, slipping her fingers under his rough waistcoat to trace a small spiral on his soft shirt over his heart. She could feel the rhythm beneath her fingertips. "Let me give you what you gave me, Monty."

His breath was coming harshly now. "But—I'll not be back, Rose. You'll—I can't do that and then leave you."

Her honorable thief. She leaned close to touch her lips to his throat. "Don't leave me unloved, darling," she whispered just beneath his ear. "I have never met a man I wanted the way I want you. I'll never meet another. Would you have me live my days never knowin' how wonderful it can be—*should* be—between a man and a woman?"

He was trembling now. She could feel his heart pounding beneath her hand, his pulse straining beneath her caressing mouth. Still he didn't touch her, didn't make a move.

She waited, counting the beats of his heart while he held himself stiffly from her. Nothing.

It was over, then. Clara pulled herself away from him and tilted her head back in defeat, closing her eyes against his rejection. "I'm sorry. I thought—"

He pulled her hard to his chest and kissed her. It was

a rough hungry kiss and she answered it with her own flaring need.

This time, both of Dalton's hands were free to caress her. He tried to recall why he shouldn't be running his palms down her slender back to her round bottom, but the fullness of her flesh in his hands sent the last trace of reason from his mind.

There was no Lord Etheridge. There was no Liar's Club.

There was only the ancient frigid void of his loneliness and the warmth of his Rose in the moonlight.

Clara had never wanted to touch a man the way she wanted to touch Monty. Her hands were shaking with her need to feel his body. She laughed a little at her trembling attempts to undo his waistcoat, but he only covered her smile with his hot mouth and tore his vest off, sending buttons spinning into the shadows.

She wanted him, oh, how she wanted him. Yet the power of her want seemed as nothing compared to the torrent of his need. She was being devoured.

Never had anyone craved her so. His desire was harsh, naked, and overwhelming. He stole her breath with his kisses, sent her into flames with his hands, and still it seemed he could not get enough.

She needed only make a motion to tug the tail of his shirt from his trousers to have him tear it off and fling it aside. The merest motion of her fingers toward the buttons of his trousers incited him to a flurry of action that left his hard, rippling flesh completely bare in the silvery light.

His body was astonishing. She'd never seen a fully naked man, had never been pressed skin to skin in an intimacy that shadowed anything she'd had with Bentley.

Monty was as bare as a Greek statue, but this was no cold marble beneath her seeking hands. This was hot rigid male animal, whose hardness left her melting with answering longing. If she could have, she would have drawn every inch of her naked God in silver ink to show the moonlight glimmering on the planes and dips of his bare and rippling strength.

Bare but for the mask. The mask that shaded his eyes in the dimness, the mask that hid his identity from her. The mask that, heaven help her, she made no motion to remove. The mask was the mystery and the dream that was Monty in her mind.

As much as she longed to see him, a part of her knew that when the mask came off, the dream would end. Then she must wake up and go back to being precise and proper Clara.

Somehow in the fray, her own clothing had gone the way of his, tangling together in the shadows while she and he tangled together in the moonlight. She was trembling in the attic air, but her shivers had nothing to do with the chill.

He backed her toward the pallet of draperies, kissing her fiercely all the while. She let herself fall, knowing that he would ease her gently down.

Once he lay above her with one hard thigh parting hers, she pressed him back for a moment. She needed her breath and her wits for just a moment more.

"I'll not conceive," she told him breathlessly. " 'Tis not the time."

Apparently the thought had never crossed his mind, for he only stared down at her for a long moment, his gaze unreadable behind the mask. Was he not much used to women? She herself had learned the trick of planned conception from Bentley, who hadn't been interested in immediate fatherhood.

Then Monty slowly lowered his mouth to hers and kissed her softly, his hard demand still present beneath the tenderness. "Were things only different, my flower, there'd be no finer thing than to make a child with you."

Tears came from nowhere and she impatiently brushed them away. "If things were different, my darling, I'd never let you leave me through that window."

She placed both palms on his jaw and urged him close for another kiss. "But we are who we are, love. This attic, this night, is all we'll have. Don't let us waste another moment of it."

Dalton could feel the trace of tears that her hands left on his skin and it burned him. What he was doing was wrong. It was unfair and untrue—except that it was the most honest moment of his life. His throat ached from the bright lovely truth between them.

Slowly he lowered his hot hard body onto her chilled soft one. He levered his thighs between hers and she welcomed him with the embrace of her legs about his hips.

"Come into me," she whispered. "I shall keep you there always."

Dalton felt a burning behind his own eyes at her words. This was no fevered coupling such as he had imagined on the stairs. This was a sacred moment, a promise. If he took part in this woman, he would never be the same.

He kissed her long and slow, then submerged himself slowly in her. It was like coming home.

Clara ached at his thickness, her hips twisting as she slowly accepted him. This was not Bentley, this was not some anonymous lover—this moment was as beautiful and unique as Monty himself.

Her struggle to take him eased and in answer he increased the pace of his movement until she was unable to think beyond his thick presence within her and his hard male beauty above her. She lost her mind, lost her every thought.

Every thrust was a revelation, every breath they traded a promise. Dizzily she ran her hands over him, memorizing every inch of him she could reach. Above her he rocked and drove into her with slow implacable lunges. His jaw muscles flexed in time with his thrusts, mesmerizing her even as it timed with her pleasure.

His sharp cheekbones glistened damp in the ghostly moonlight, a sculpted contrast to the shadow of his mask above. His eyes were mere glints in the blackness, mysterious and tantalizingly dangerous.

She should be appalled at herself, but she couldn't bring herself to care. She would *not* go on without this moment with him.

Then the drawing spreading pleasure captured her and she thought no more. Only sensation and pulsating connection existed.

Him. Inside. Above. His touch. His heat.

His love.

The peak approached and she stepped willingly over the edge, her gaze held by the glinting eyes within the mask. When she fell, it was with the knowledge that she loved him and always would.

She wrapped her arms about him, held him close and took him with her.

Chapter Fifteen

The room no longer spun about her, yet Clara's mind still whirled. What she had done should have been unthinkable. To take a veritable stranger for a lover?

Why did she feel no shame at all?

In fact, she felt the opposite. Bliss, perhaps. Or possibly even . . . hope. As if her weary heart had finally bloomed in the warmth—the *heat*—of his desire for her.

Outlandish plans swam through her mind, the kind she'd not dared believe in since her girlhood. She could go, right now with Monty. Marry him and live in some tiny room and live on nothing but love.

That was being a bit dramatic, of course. She did have some funds tucked away, and she was sure that with a bit of encouragement Monty would see the sense in a more conventional career.

Of course, he hadn't asked her to run away with him. But he'd said that if things were different . . .

You've never even seen his face.

Clara sighed. The tiresome little voice was right. Perhaps she was being premature. She rolled over into the warmth of Monty's body and rose onto her elbows next to him.

He was dozing in the moonlight, mask and all. His beautiful body was covered only by the merest corner of the velvet draperies. She eyed that small modesty for a moment, then flicked it from him with a snap.

"Hey, there!" His eyes opened and he grinned at her. "And here I was worried you'd be all proper again." He gave her own velvet covering a tug. "Sauce for the goose, now."

Clara laughed and allowed him to slide the cover to her waist. Then she put one hand over his to stop him.

" 'Tisn't gentlemanly, me being all naked when you're not."

He looked down at himself in surprise. Clara tapped her own cheekbone meaningfully. "What kind of woman does that make me, when I've never even seen your face?"

He raised one hand to his mask. When he hesitated, Clara's heart began to twist. Then he gave her a sheepish grin.

"Forgot I had it on."

"Oh, so you weren't born with it, then?" She poked at him as she teased. He retorted by wrapping one big hand around the back of her neck and pulling her down for a kiss that made her knees go weak and her legs fall open involuntarily. When she opened her eyes, the mask was gone. There was only him in the moonlight, every plane of his face as familiar as her own.

The pain was fierce and immediate as her heart broke quite cleanly in two.

Dalton waited in silence for her reaction, but except for a widening of her eyes he could see no change in her expression. He shifted slightly. Finally he had to break the silence. "You don't like what you see?"

"You're perfect," she whispered. "Quite the most handsome man I've ever seen."

Dalton raised his head to kiss her again. Her lips were cool for a moment, then warmed fiercely under his. He rolled her over, his erection rising instantly in response to the feel of her beneath him.

What this woman did to him . . .

Her arms rose to cling tightly to his neck and hold the kiss until they were both breathless. He pulled away, covering his astonishment with a small chuckle.

"If I'd known I'd get a buss like that I would've taken me mask off the first night," he teased.

She didn't smile, but only cupped his face in her hands. There were tears in her eyes that did not fall. He saw the glint in the last bit of moonlight left to them. A glance at the window proved that the sky had clouded. The light would be gone entirely soon. Darkness again for them, as always. He realized that he still had not seen her full in the moonlight as she had seen him.

Yet it was time for him to go.

"I'll be back," he promised as he reached for his clothes.

"No," she said. She stood and turned to pull her plain gown over her head. "There was only ever to be this one moment of Rose and Monty in the moonlight." Her voice sounded muffled in the fabric, almost as if she were crying. However, when she turned back to him, she seemed composed.

He moved to stand before her, wrapping his hands gently over her shoulders. "I can't just walk away—"

She covered his lips with the tips of her fingers. "I can."

It hurt to hear her say it. "You can?"

"You mustn't mistake fantasy for reality, S—Monty." She stepped back once, then again, letting his hands fall from her shoulders. "This attic was a dreamland, and you and I only a mirage."

For a moment, Dalton wondered at the new formality in her tone. Then the ache overwhelmed every thought. "I won't let it be!"

The last faint glow of moonlight died behind the clouds and she was lost to sight in the blackness that filled the attic. He heard a tiny creak, like that of old dry wood. Then nothing.

"Rose! Rose, we aren't done here. We can't be!"

His hoarse whisper echoed around the attic, bouncing back to him from a room that was as empty as his heart.

Dalton was stewing in his secret office in the attic of the Liar's Club when Simon tapped on the hidden panel and entered without waiting for an invitation.

"Damn it, Simon! This isn't your club anymore, remember? How am I supposed to handle Jackham with you running about, popping in and out of walls?"

"Jackham's gone off to Scotland, remember? Choosing a new liquor supplier, since the last bloke got picked up for smuggling French brandy. He prefers to see to the whiskey personally."

Dalton huffed. "To taste the whisky, you mean."

Simon shrugged. "Jackham thinks only about profit for the club."

"If I were Jackham, I'd be more concerned about club morale."

"Ah, the bliss of ignorance," Simon misquoted. "You forget that Jackham knows nothing more of the Liar's

Club than that we cater to gentlemen on one side of the wall, and thieves on the other."

"Thieves on both sides, if you were to ask Sir Thorogood."

Simon took the only other chair and stretched his legs out before him. "How is the Sir Thorogood case going?"

"Nowhere, quickly."

"Really? I thought you put a lovely pincer trap about the man, what with taking two identities and keeping a close eye on Wadsworth."

"Oh, I've discovered a good many juicy things about Wadsworth and passed them on to Liverpool, but I've found nothing to connect him to our cartoonist. Thorogood is more of a professional than I had anticipated. There's been no reaction to the impostor lure ... well, that's not entirely true."

Simon sat up. "What do you mean?"

Dalton rubbed his neck. "I've been attacked by footpads twice, once in an alleyway and once in Hyde Park."

"You? Or Thorogood?"

"Thorogood."

"Hmm. That could be chance, or possibly simple revenge for one of his cartoons."

"Precisely. It seems the man may have good reason to keep his identity secret. I certainly wouldn't want half of Parliament to be slavering for my hide."

"Surely it isn't that bad."

"I don't know. Someone's been following me—er, Thorogood. A fair man, who tries to pretend he isn't a gentleman."

"Can you describe him?"

Dalton shrugged, frustrated. "Fair, tall, good-looking sort. Youngish, but not too young. Which fits threescore members of Society. A description is no good. I'd have to spot him myself to apprehend him."

"How often have you seen him?"

"Twice, on the occasion of the first attack and . . ."

"The other time?"

Dalton described the near miss with the coal wagon, and the fair rider whom he had barely seen.

Simon sat back. "That is a bit thin, as far as evidence goes. Still, if your instinct tells you that it was deliberate, it probably was. You've a fine understanding of human nature."

Dalton covered his eyes with one hand. "After last night, I don't know if I believe that. At least not of my own nature."

"Last night?"

Dalton sighed. He didn't want to reveal his unprofessional act to Simon, but he needed help to sort it out. "Remember the source inside Wadsworth's that I told you about?"

"Yes, the housemaid Rose."

Dalton shook his head. "I know I shouldn't have done it. Even as I did it, I knew it was wrong—"

Simon recoiled. "You *didn't*?"

Dalton rubbed the back of his neck. "I did. On the attic floor yet. I feel like such an ass."

"You are an ass! What were you thinking, getting involved with a case in that way?"

Dalton snorted. "As if you haven't done it yourself."

Simon glowered but returned to his chair. "That's different. I was in love with Agatha."

That statement resonated within Dalton, but he shook off the feeling. "At any rate, Rose isn't a suspect. She's not involved with Sir Thorogood in any way."

"True. What are you going to do about her now?"

"I need to get her out of there. I thought about setting her up—"

"I can't believe it! You'd dishonor her by making her your mistress? She may only be a housemaid, but—"

"Shut it, Simon," Dalton said wearily. "I was going to say 'set her up with a new position,' you dolt."

"Oh. Sorry. That's a bit of a fiery point for me."

"I know. I must admit I thought about it, for I hate to give her up. There's just something about her . . ."

Simon blinked. "Have you conceived a passion for a housemaid, Lord Etheridge?"

"I hardly think so." Dalton steepled his hands. Looking down at them, he realized how much the gesture was saturated in Liverpool. He slowly flattened his palms on the desk instead.

"Regardless, I need to get her out of that house. It isn't a good situation, and what's more, I've put her in danger with my activities. If it ever came out that she helped a thief—"

"She'd be in the stocks," Simon finished. "Or worse."

"Can Agatha take her on? Find her something better?"

"A new job? Is that all you can offer her, Dalton?"

Dalton raised a brow. "What else is there?"

Clara threw the last of her sober half-mourning wardrobe into the carpetbag and knelt to reach under her bed for her secret chest. With a grunt, she tugged it out and lifted it to set on the bed.

Idiot. What had she done? She shivered. More to the point, what hadn't she done?

She hadn't once pursued the topic of precisely who he was working for. She hadn't once stopped to wonder why he never removed the mask in her presence.

Her hands fell to her sides for a moment and she closed her eyes. *You hadn't wanted to know.*

She'd been more than an idiot. She'd been thoughtless, foolish, and by heavens, *gullible*. She'd played into his game, confiding in him, towing him around that house—good Lord, she'd even given him her *cat*!

Oh, the poor thing. No doubt left to die slowly and horribly in some rubbish bin within seconds of his leaving the attic.

And all the time, he'd been hunting her.

The strength left her knees at the thought. She'd felt so sheltered and secure in her invisibility. So *stupid*. And now she was bound to pay for her folly.

Desperately, Clara suppressed her fear. She needed to leave *now,* for she had not only endangered herself in her madness, but the family who had taken her in when she'd most needed them.

She'd only thought of scandal at first, which was why she had retained her anonymity. But looking back, she realized that she had grown foolish in her zeal to uncover corruption. She'd made enemies. Powerful enemies.

She would never forgive herself if something happened to her late husband's family. Shallow and silly though they might be, they'd been nothing but kind to her through the last two years.

Even Beatrice's urging to investigate the marriage mart once again had been grounded in concern for her. Of course, male attention was the last thing she'd wanted.

Until now. Until she'd met this man and fallen under his manipulative spell.

"Aunt Clara? What are you doing?"

Clara spun around, placing herself between the door and her bag. It was Kitty, come to return the tracing supplies. With wide eyes, Kitty stared at the obvious preparations for leaving.

Clara moved quickly to take the girl's arm and pull her into the room. She shut the door. "I must go away for a while, Kitty. I've been very foolish and put you all in danger. If I'm no longer here when they come for me, perhaps you and the family will not be held responsible for my actions."

"What do you mean? How have you been foolish?"

Clara shoved the small chest into her bag with some force.

"Auntie, take care! You'll wrinkle your gowns."

Clara almost giggled in her panic. "The gowns don't matter, Kitty—"

"Don't matter? But Mama says—"

"Kitty, do be quiet and listen. If anyone should ask, you don't know where I've gone. You don't know when I'll be back, if ever. I kept to myself all these years, and you never liked me much anyway. Can you remember that?"

"But we do like you, Aunt Clara, honest! I know Mama can be difficult at times, but—"

The feeling of hounds nipping at Clara's heels increased. She gave Kitty an impatient little shake. "Simply do as I told you, Kitty. You know nothing about me, and you never cared to, do you understand?"

Kitty was obviously close to tears, but she nodded. "If you truly feel that strongly about it, then very well."

Clara pulled her close for a quick hug. "Goodbye, sweet Kitty." Then she hefted her case and made for the back stairs. Without a word to the staff she ran through the kitchen and halfway up the steps to the street. She stayed below street level for a moment, eyeing the surroundings carefully.

Everything looked normal, but what did she know of such things? Someone could be following her right now.

He could be following her right now.

The spike of pain in her heart threatened to overpower her panic for a moment. Then she firmly plucked it out. Monty was, and had always been, a lie. One could not love a lie.

Nor could one love a liar.

With a last sweeping glance at the street, Clara jumped up to hail a passing hackney. It was time to leave London but she had one stop to make first.

Dalton, dressed as Monty with his cap pulled down low, waited in the alley behind Mr. Edward Wadsworths' garden wall.

Stubbs ambled through the back servants' gate of the house and approached "Monty."

"Did you give her the message?" Dalton managed to keep a cool tone. It wasn't as easy as it should have been.

"Yessir. She said she'd be out in a jiff." Stubbs made to lounge against the wall next to Dalton. "Did you know you've got cat hair on yer coat, sir?"

Dalton gave him a long look from beneath the brim of his cap. Stubbs pursed his lips.

"Right, then. I'll be off." The young doorman shoved his hands into his coat pockets and moved off, whistling softly and emanating a deceptive air of harmlessness.

Dalton settled back to wait. He tried to remain distant and cool but the need to see her, be with her, touch her face—

A soft crunch in the gravel beyond the gate snared his attention and he stepped back into the shadow of the wall. The gate squeaked open softly on its iron hinges and a small form covered with a large shawl hurried through. A whisper came from beneath the head covering. "Miss?"

Dalton stepped forward. "Rose!" Unable to fight the impulse, he swept her into his arms with a glad laugh.

She squeaked and jabbed at him sharply with one elbow, kicking him away furiously.

"Let me go!" She gave him a push and backed away, all the while eyeing him suspiciously from beneath the shawl that half-covered her face.

There was no hiding her voice, however. He'd never heard this girl before.

"Oh, hell. The idiot sent for the wrong maid!" Dalton turned away heatedly. "Damn you, Stubbs," he muttered. "I said *Rose*."

"I am Rose," came a small voice from behind him. "What d'you want with me? I ain't . . . I ain't done nothing."

As Dalton turned to stare at the girl in astonishment, he thought she didn't sound too sure of that.

"*You're* Rose?"

She nodded and sniffled, pushing her shawl back and wiping her nose with her wrist. A fresh mark on her cheek overlapped an older bruise. She bore a superficial resemblance to his Rose, what he had ever been able to see of her. The same height and figure, the same dark hair, but there was no sauce in this girl's gaze, only wariness.

"And there is no other Rose in this house?"

She stared at him like a rabbit in a snare. "N-no. Only me. No other Rose. How—how could there be?"

Dalton knew fear of discovery when he saw it. He moved in, locking his eyes on hers. Dark suspicion began to twine through him. "Indeed. How could there be? How could a woman—who looks very much like you— gain entrance here, use your name, move freely through this house . . . and never raise the slightest alarm?"

He leaned close, pinning her with his gaze. He knew the effect his silver eyes had on people. All his life, the ignorant had made the sign against the evil eye when they thought he wasn't looking. This girl was no different. He saw her hand twitch at her side.

"Tell me, Rose." He was almost whispering. "Tell me who she is. I must find her. Please?"

He hadn't meant to say that last. Hadn't meant to let that note of longing enter his voice.

Suddenly the fear left her eyes, and she gave him a measuring look. "You fancy her, don't you?"

Dalton straightened. "That's not your business."

Rose ducked her head to hide her smile, but he saw it anyway. Damn. He'd lost the advantage. This never would have happened before. What was the matter with him?

Rose hummed to herself for a moment, then looked up at him again. "You know her and you like her."

"What makes you think so?"

"How could you not? Why, I'd not be alive right now if it weren't for her bringing me food and takin' care of me when I was sick! She's pure good, she is. A real lady, through and through."

A *lady*? Surely not!

Yet even as his mind denied it, his heart gave a leap of hope. If she were a lady, then she would not be so completely out of his reach. A lady—

Thrusting his distraction aside, Dalton appealed to the girl's loyalty. "I need to find her. She's—she's in grave danger." At the shadow of concern in Rose's eyes, he elaborated, weaving the lie with truth. "There are people after her, very powerful people."

"But—she wouldn't hurt anyone! She's good, I tell you!"

"I know that," he said soothingly. "If only I can find her first, I can protect her."

Rose chewed her lip uncertainly. "I don't know. I promised."

"You're very loyal to be protecting her. I want to protect her, as well. But I only know her as Rose the maid. If I can't find her—" He halted, damning the betraying hint of longing that had invaded his voice once more.

Fortunately, it seemed to sway Rose to his side. She gave him a look of wary sympathy. "I know," she said. "The lady just gets right into your heart, don't she?"

Dalton looked away when he should have coldly denied any such thing. Apparently that settled it for Rose. She leaned close.

"She lives next door. She's a widow, livin' with her husband's family."

Next door?

Rose continued. "I think the family is named Trapp, but my lady's name is—"

Dalton didn't need to be told. *"Clara Simpson."*

Chapter Sixteen

Later, Dalton scarcely recalled leaving Wadsworth's mews for the house next door. He'd given Rose several pounds, along with Agatha's card, and recommended that she get herself out of her situation immediately.

The Trapps' butler had a kindly mien, but Dalton was brisk all the same. "I am—Mr. Montmorency. I need to see Mrs. Simpson immediately," he said, barely able to keep a smile from his face.

His outrageous Widow Simpleton. His intrepid Rose. All wrapped up in one very suitable lady, just waiting for him to untie the bow.

The butler flicked his eyes from Dalton's boots to his cap, obviously weighing Dalton's manner and confidence against the common clothing. Dalton cocked a brow and tilted his head arrogantly. The well-versed Society butler should have no difficulty with this one.

The butler didn't quite smirk. "Yes, indeed, *my lord*."

Ah. Perhaps he'd overdone the arrogance a bit. This man was very good.

The butler showed him into the familiar parlor and left at nearly a full run. He reappeared almost immediately to open the door for a breathless Beatrice and Oswald Trapp. Blinded by his hauteur, confused by his attire, they didn't seem to see any resemblance to Sir Thorogood.

"How may we help you, my lord?"

Damn. Not Clara. "Where is Mrs. Simpson?"

The Trapps looked at each other uneasily. "Clara? *Our* Clara?"

No, my Clara.

Mrs. Trapp blinked at him, obviously mystified. "Whatever would you want with Clara?"

Oswald merely blew through his mustache like a rather confused horse.

Dalton could barely stand it. Drawing on his last thread of patience, he tried to explain without explaining. "I have some business with Mrs. Simpson. It is most urgent that I see her." *Clara-my-Clara.* "Is she at home?"

Oswald made another equine noise. "Hmph. No, not at the moment." He looked down at where his thick fingers entwined across his stomach. "No longer her home, y'see."

The man wasn't the most intelligent example of the species, Dalton knew, but he hardly expected Oswald to forget a relative in his own home. There was something going on here.

Trapp rumbled on. "She's gone off. Left this morning at daybreak."

"Gone?"

"Packed it up and left without a by-your-leave."

"She said goodbye to me," came a high, nervous voice from behind them. All eyes turned to the door. One of the Trapp daughters stood there, pale but defiant.

"Kitty!" Mrs. Trapp blinked at her. "What do you know about all this?"

"I know that Aunt Clara would never do anything truly wrong. She said she'd been foolish, and put us all in danger. She said if they came for her, that we were to act as if we didn't know her well and didn't like her very much at all. She said it would help."

A very odd sensation began to occur in Dalton's chest, a chilling of his heart.

The girl's chin quivered. "But I did like her! I won't say nay to it, not even if you throw me in the Tower!"

Beatrice moved to stand beside her daughter. "Neither will I!"

It seemed that Clara Simpson inspired loyalty in the most unlikely defenders. Still, it was obvious that the Trapps knew nothing that would help Dalton.

"May I see her room? She might have left some clue to her destination."

Beatrice looked as though she would have liked to refuse, but Oswald gave her a nudge and a growl. "The man's a *peer,* you birdwit! Show him the room!"

Clara's room was rather plain. Almost Spartan, for a woman. There was no lace except at the windows, and she didn't seem to be fond of covering her dressing table with fragile little oddments.

All in all, he would have declared the room's resident a very sensible woman.

Not the Clara Simpson he knew at all. His Clara was a mad creature, trading identities the way some women changed their gloves. His Clara was a risk-taker, a creature of danger and mystery.

The desk held all the implements of drawing, overflowing with charcoal and inks, pen nibs and papers of various types. Not hoping for much, he fanned through the stack of drawing paper. She might have left some sort of note, some clue—

It was like catching a glimpse in a mirror, if mirrors came supplied with black silk masks. And if they also furnished wicked glints in the eye, and grins full of mischief and flirtation. And removed one's clothing.

Dalton had spent hours in the last week pondering Sir Thorogood's drawings. He knew every stroke, every clever form, every light and humorous line. . . .

It felt rather like being stabbed with one of Kurt's long knives, that feeling of recognition and betrayal that pierced him. A very curious sensation, indeed.

He thought he might well bleed himself dry from it, slowly and forever. Abruptly he straightened and drew himself in. What a ludicrous thought. He was disappointed, that was all.

It was obvious to him now, of course. Memories of Mrs. Simpson streamed across his mind—questioning, pressing for a drawing, pursuing him like a love-maddened mink. And Rose—his Rose—sneaking through Wadsworth's house in the dark, leading him along, learning how to open safe boxes, by God!

Dalton looked back down at the illustration in his hand. The drawing was nothing more than a sketch, hardly more than a handful of lines, yet she had captured so much. Was this how she had seen Monty, this erotic portrayal of a dashing rascal? He removed the drawing and rolled it carefully, then tucked it into his coat.

Evidence, of course. He was in the habit of collecting evidence, it was his job. Nothing more.

And now his job was to collect a certain lying artist with entirely too much to say about the state of the government.

He turned to the three people waiting breathlessly in the door of Clara's room.

"Trapp, I have reason to think you have been harboring someone in your house who is acting against the good of the Crown."

The man paled, but his surprise seemed unfeigned. Beatrice staggered to a chair and sat gaping like a fish. Dalton waved aside their protests.

"I'm satisfied that you had no knowledge of her actions. I have reason to know that she can be very clever."

"She?" Trapp was still blinking at him in disbelief. "She?"

Dalton firmly suppressed his impatience. "She. Mrs. Bentley Simpson, to be precise."

"Clara?" The shriek threatened to tear the paper from the walls. It seemed Beatrice had regained her faculties.

Trapp's expression hardened. "Why, that sponging little—"

Beatrice slapped her husband on the shoulder. "Oh, posh, Oswald! Clara isn't a revolutionary. She's like a mouse!"

That hadn't been Dalton's impression of the Widow Simpson at all. "A mouse?"

Beatrice shrugged. "She was always hiding in her room, always drawing—"

Ah. Yes. Precisely.

Drawing.

Clara pulled the hood of her cloak closer about her face. She knew she looked ridiculous wearing wool on a fine summer day, but better that than to be recognized. She gathered up the last of her drawings. This string-wrapped parcel signified the final performance of Sir Thorogood.

She wouldn't even have risked bringing them to the *Sun* if not for her dire need of funds. There was no way to know when she'd ever be able to make any more. What she carried in her small chest might very well need to last the rest of her life.

She could always do tepid portraits of country folk in exchange for a chicken or some game, she supposed. To be honest, she wasn't quite sure what country folk did or how they lived. She'd been a resident of London her entire life, with only a few childhood journeys to Brighton to her name.

As she entered Gerald Braithwaite's office, she brushed by a small ragged man passing just outside. She ducked a quick apology and moved on, aware that the fellow had turned to watch her curiously.

Gerald took the packet glumly, not snatching it with his usual glee. He gave her a woeful glance. "They're after him, you know."

She gave a brief nod, pulling the hood more tightly. Gerald sighed and pulled the usual thick envelope from his desk drawer. He handed it to her, but didn't release it immediately.

"Is he done, then? Will there be any more to come?"

Clara shook her head quickly and tugged at the envelope. He released it and dropped his chin onto his knuckles, disconsolate.

Clara hesitated. She was rather fond of Gerald, for he'd been the first to see the worth in her drawings. He was a crotchety, foul-mouthed, belligerent old fellow, but he liked her work and echoed her cause.

She pulled back her hood and bent to give him a quick peck on the cheek. "I'll tell you a secret, Mr. Braithwaite," she whispered. "Sir Thorogood isn't half the *man* you think he is!"

At Gerald's look of shock and dawning comprehension, she gave him a quick wink before shielding her face and ducking from the office.

As she hurried to the front door of the building and her waiting hack, she heard Gerald's laughter boom through the halls one final time.

The ride had been long clinging to the back of the hired carriage, but as the small ragged man watched from his perch as the lady descended from the hack, he grinned to himself.

"The gentleman said 'Follow the maid, Feebles,' but methinks the gentleman meant 'Follow the lady.' "

Still, the case itself was none of his concern. His job was information, and he was fairly sure this information would be useful to the gentleman in charge.

He watched the lady enter the coaching inn that lay on the outskirts of London. The cabby followed with her bag, leaving the inn's hostler to water the horses. Good, then. She was staying the night.

Taking advantage of a chance for a brief rest, Feebles carefully stretched one leg to the ground, then the other. Then he ambled around the hack to cadge a chew from the hostler. That sort never smoked because of the chance of fire in the barn. Without a word, the hostler tossed Feebles a plug. The two men settled down to wait together.

The cabby came back, stuffing a wad of notes into his pocket as he jogged to his hack. Feebles hailed him in a leisurely manner. "Goin' back to town, are you? Mind if I come along?"

The man stopped with one hand ready to pull himself to the seat above. "Got the bob?"

Feebles shrugged easily. "Nothing but the lint in me pocket. But I'll promise good conversation if you let me ride up front. I might just know a tale or two you never 'eard before."

The cabby eyed him suspiciously, but Feebles was used to that. In fact, he cultivated it. He also purposely encouraged the next stage, which was dismissal.

The driver shrugged, accepting the very harmlessness that was Feebles, and vaulted up to his seat at the reins.

"Well, come up then. If you bore me, you're walkin' at the next crossing."

Feebles grinned and shot a stream of spittle to one side. It worked every time. He hadn't paid for a hack in years.

He clambered up beside the cabby. "Did you hear the one about the teetotaler and the tavern maid?"

The secret office above the Liar's Club was dark, but the intruder knew it well. It only took a moment to find the file containing the latest information on the search for Sir Thorogood. A quick scratch and light burst from one of the special friction matches that only the Liar's Club was supposed to know about.

By the time the wooden matchstick had burned down, the intruder knew everything about Sir Thorogood that the spymaster knew. A deep chuckle made the tiny flame sputter, then go out.

"Took you long enough, Etheridge."

There was a scrape, then a click.

Then the office was as empty as it should have been when the spymaster was a fast horse out of town.

Clara stood at the window of her little room at the coaching inn with no idea where to go next. All she could think of was how quickly her life had fallen apart. It had only been four days since she'd first seen Sir Thorogood at the Rochesters' ball! How had she managed to ruin everything in so short a time?

Clara walked to the wall, then turned and walked to the window, then back again. She'd never tried pacing before, but at this point she was willing to do anything for some inspiration. She'd stopped at this coaching inn just outside of London because she simply didn't have anywhere to run.

She'd tried making a list, but there was nothing to put on it. She'd been in this room for hours. Night had fallen long ago, but she had no way to know the time. She'd never needed a watch in town, for the bells rang the hours during the day and the watchmen called them at night.

No one called the hours here. In fact, there seemed to be no one about at all. She'd opened her window when she'd entered the stuffy room this afternoon. At that time there had been the everyday noise of carriages, horses, and the staff working about the place.

Now it seemed as though everyone in the world was asleep but her. Unfortunately, she was far too restless to prepare for bed.

If she leaned through the deep-set window she could just see the road shining white in the moonlight, stretching both ways through the mysterious hillocks and shadows. In one direction lay London and everything that was familiar. In the other lay all that was unknown to a woman born in the city.

Each stretch of road beckoned. Should she press on, living on what she had saved, eventually taking her chances on finding employment somewhere despite having no references or experience?

Or should she go back to where she knew the ways of the streets and the stones and the very air? Where she would live in constant danger of discovery, and quite possibly, attack?

Leaving the window and its beckoning possibilities for a while, Clara went to her case and removed a portfolio of sketching paper and a small box of charcoal. The accumulated candles in the room gave enough light when set together on the small writing desk, and soon Clara had lost her worries in the pure joy she felt in her drawing.

She drew Kitty the way the girl looked with her head angled over the keys of the piano and her lip caught firmly in her teeth. She drew Beatrice with one brow raised in an expression of mixed disapproval and amusement.

And she drew *him*, whoever he was. She drew him as Monty and as the pompous Sir Thorogood. But mostly she drew him as the devastating man beneath the mask who had kissed her with such damning false craving.

If she was ashamed of anything she had done, it was that she hadn't seen through the lie.

She hadn't wanted to see.

The drawing blurred before her. She pressed both wrists to her eyes. She would *not* cry. Her grief put up quite a fight, but ultimately she felt able to face his image again.

When she opened her eyes, the paper before her was blank, the sketches gone as if by magic. Had the topmost sheet blown from the table in a breeze from the open window? She looked to each side of her, but there was nothing on the floor.

"Hmm. I cannot deny that I am flattered."

Clara froze at the sound of the rich cultured voice behind her. Fear leaped high in her chest, ridden by an unmistakable bit of excitement. She stood, shoving her chair back as she turned.

The man who was not Monty stood behind her. Gone were the rough clothes. There was no trace of the laughing thief, no hint of the pompous poseur. This man was someone altogether new.

Chapter Seventeen

He was magnificent. He was everything that he had never been for her. Polished but tastefully elegant. Handsome, but somber in his perusal of her.

Had he always been so tall? So wide and imposing? So beautiful?

A trace of anger began to stir within her fear. So much of what she had given her heart to had been a lie. Monty's gentle humor, his flirtatious approval of her boldness . . . his desire for her. All a lie.

Had this man ever been anything but deceptive toward her? Had he ever said one thing that was true?

She backed slowly away as though he were a snake, until the small desk stood between them. He remained where he was, unimpressed by her caution, as a cat is unimpressed by the maneuverings of a mouse.

He merely watched her, then went back to examining the sheet that he held carefully by the edges.

"You're very good." He tilted the page to the lamplight, leaning to peer more closely at a thumbnail sketch of himself reposing nude in the moonlight.

Heat crept over Clara's face, but she tossed her hair

back and held her chin high. "You're very easy to look at, as I'm sure you know," she said, attempting a careless tone. "An artist's dream, really."

He merely made that noise deep in his throat once more. Clara twitched. Unwise of him. It made her want to fling something at him.

Preferably something heavy.

With spikes.

"I should very much like to title that page," she said, her voice straining to cover her turmoil. "Perhaps if you condescend to tell me who you truly are."

He finally looked up from the drawing and eyed her coolly. She couldn't keep herself from fidgeting under that silver gaze, but hopefully he couldn't see her fingers twisting behind her back.

He contemplated her for a long moment, his hands idly rolling the drawing into a narrow tube as he did so. Then he approached her, tucking the scroll into his coat as he drew near. He stopped just inches from her, so close she could smell the sandalwood scent of him. She turned her head away, but that only allowed his breath to brush her cheek.

Warm fingers caught at her chin and raised her face to the light. His touch was not rough, but there was no caress within it. He examined her as he had the drawing, with narrowed eyes that missed nothing.

She had the absurd desire to cross her eyes at him but until she knew his intent, it would not be wise to antagonize him. She must remain cool and retain her dignity, if only to save her heart from further humiliation.

Still her foot twitched with a suppressed longing to stomp his instep and perhaps have a go at bruising his . . . dignity.

He tilted her head from one side to the other. "I have

never truly seen you in good light, not without the face paint." He gazed at her dispassionately, his eyes shaded to gray as he stood with his back to the light.

Monty's eyes.

Pain slashed within her. She jerked her chin from his grip and looked away. How could she still long for someone who was no more than a figment of her imagination?

"You still haven't answered my question," she said, her voice flat. "Who are you truly?"

He lowered his hand and stepped back, as if surprised that he had ever come so close. Then he bowed formally, so deeply that it had an air of mockery. She longed to break a vase over his shiny dark head.

"Dalton Montmorency, Lord Etheridge, at your service."

She couldn't help a disbelieving snort. "Oh, very good. And I'm the Princess of the Moon."

He rose, his gaze intense. "No, you are a fairy maid, wild and changeable, born to taunt poor mortals to their ruin."

Clara nearly looked behind her to see whom he addressed before she realized he was most assuredly speaking to her.

"Me? A fairy maid?" She stepped away, eyeing him with new suspicion. "You simply cannot stop, can you? Lies fall from your lips like leaves in autumn."

He stiffened. "I have not once lied to you since coming into this room."

"That reminds me . . . how did you get in?"

He cocked his head to one side. "How do I usually get in?"

The window. Heavens, how stupid could she be? For someone like him, an open window was a virtual invitation. Then his words sank in. He was truly a lord?

He truly thinks me a fairy maid?

Oh, shut it, she thought to herself furiously. You have more important things to think about now. "Well, what do you want with me? How did I offend the mighty Lord Etheridge? I never lampooned you."

"No, you wouldn't have. I live out of sight for the most part."

"Yet you played the part of Sir Thorogood so well," she said bitterly. "You became quite the favorite of Society."

The corner of his mouth twitched. "Jealous?"

"I did not enjoy seeing a liar such as you showered with my success, no. But I never wanted acclaim or I should have stepped forward long ago."

"Then I doubt you would still be breathing today. Since I assumed Sir Thorogood's identity, there have been no less than three attempts on my life."

Concern swept her before she could stop it. Drat it, would she never get it through her head? This was no lover. This was an enemy.

She turned away, moving toward the window. The moon had moved to shine into the room, brightening that portion nearly as well as the grouped candles lit the other side. Could that truly be the same moon that had shone down upon Rose and Monty? Had that truly been only last night?

"It seems as if a year has gone by since I last saw you." His voice came soft and deep from just behind her.

Ever the silent-footed thief. She closed her eyes on the silvery glow and leaned her head against the window frame.

"You have never seen *me*," she whispered. "And I have never seen you."

"Are you sure of that?"

"Rose was a lie. The merry Widow Simpson was a lie. I am simply Clara, neither maid nor merry. In fact, I've been told that I verge on decidedly dull."

That surprised a chuckle from him. "Oh, that I doubt."

"My point exactly. You have no idea who I am."

"You are Clara Tremont Simpson, the daughter of Albert Tremont. You were once married, quite briefly, to an undistinguished young soldier named Bentley Simpson. Your father lost the family's fortune in a fraudulent investment scheme gone sour, losing much of the savings of his friends and neighbors in the course. He died poor and despised, with only you to look after him."

To hear Papa so disparaged finally brought the nascent tears to her eyes. Angrily she wiped them away. "You didn't know him, or you would never disrespect him so. He was as much victim as anyone in that investment."

"He stole thousands of pounds from people who trusted him."

Clara turned on him. "Then where did the money go? Was I draped in jewels and silks? Were marital offers pouring into my lap? That one *undistinguished* young man, despite your disdain, was the only man to ever look at me twice, the only one to ever want me! I married him because I doubted I would ever get another offer, and because after years of selling off our every possession one by one, my father couldn't live with what he'd done to my future and took his own life."

She felt the tears coming and looked away. "Does that sound as though we lived on ill-gotten gains? No, and I'll tell you why not. My father had a silent partner, a man who said being associated with lowly commerce would stain his reputation. A man, *Lord* Etheridge, whom my father dared not expose when the money was lost, for fear that he would never be believed when his word was pitted against that of an earl!"

She spun away, too furious and heartsick to hold her tears back any longer. Swiftly, he moved before her, wrapping his large hands over her shoulders.

"Who was it? Tell me the earl's name and I'll see him brought to justice and your father's honor cleared."

For a moment all she could do was stare at him. Then she gave a bitter disbelieving laugh. "Why? What could it possibly matter now? Being known as the daughter of a thief is the least of my worries. Do not forget that I am also a nearly penniless widow of unremarkable aspect in danger of my life from a man *who has just broken into my room in the middle of the night*!"

She laughed again, the sound like the crack of glass. "Do you truly think that proving my long-dead father's integrity is a priority at this moment?"

He did not release her. "You are in no danger from me."

"Then why are you here in the night? Why did you not call upon me downstairs in the morning, the way anyone else would have done?"

"I—" His hands slid from her shoulders, leaving them cold. He turned away with head down and his hands on his hips, breathing deeply. "I should have. Or I should have arrested you the moment I saw you."

"Arrest me? I thought you were here to kill me."

He spun back to face her. "Of course I'm not here to kill you. What do you think I am?"

She shook her head slowly, her eyes never leaving his. "I have absolutely no idea."

"I am . . . well, I can't tell what I am. But I was told to uncover Thorogood, and bring him—I mean, bring *you* before Lord Liverpool."

"The Prime Minister?" Clara searched her memory furiously. "I never drew Lord Liverpool, I'm sure of it."

"No, but you must have upset someone powerful, or I would not have been sent to find you. I am *not* an errand boy."

He said that last as though it were a point of contention, but she had no interest in reassuring him. Her own concerns loomed somewhat larger.

She was wanted by Liverpool?

She knew a bit about the man, but only what everyone knew. He'd been appointed after the assassination of Spencer Perceval and was widely known to be conservative in his views, particularly on the subject of class distinction and protection of the divine right of aristocracy to squash anyone who stood in the way.

In short, he promoted everything that she was fighting against. And he ran the government of England.

"Oh, dear." Blindly she reached for the spindly chair and sat. She'd most assuredly done it this time.

Dalton Montmorency stood before her. "You needn't fear Liverpool. He is a very honorable man. Cold, but honorable."

She shook her head. "And you think he will—what? Take me out for an ice and send me on my way? You've obviously gone to a great deal of trouble to find me. With that sort of manhunt, I should be surprised at anything less than a stay in the Tower."

"It is not against the law to scorn the well-bred."

"Oh, just listen to yourself! Well-bred! Which makes everyone else ill-bred, no matter their means or manners?"

"I didn't mean—" His face was in the deep shadow now, but she could feel him glaring down at her. "I needn't explain myself to you. I am here to escort you back to the city, where you will be turned over to the Prime Minister. Your safety is assured, so you have no reason—"

The attack came in an instant. A dark figure vaulted through the open window and flung itself at her. She had no time for anything but an intake of breath. However, Dalton reacted. She saw him fling himself bodily at the stranger, thrusting the two of them into the small writing desk. The spindly piece crashed to the floor, candles and all.

The room went black, all but for the patch of moonlight in which she sat. The struggle was brief and violent, from the sound of fists striking flesh and the final crunch of what she envisioned as something hard striking someone's skull.

Oh-dear-lord-let-him-be-well. She could not be shocked at the strength of her prayer. For all the lies, it seemed there was something between them, something true. "D–Dalton?" Her whisper seemed a shout in the darkness. She heard a scrape and a weary sigh.

"I am truly tired of being jumped by shadows."

Clara closed her eyes and sent a heartfelt thanks to the heavens. She heard the sound of something being dragged across the floor.

"Let's see who this mystery man is, shall we?"

Dalton backed into the patch of moonlight, tugging at the arms of a limp figure. The man seemed very large to Clara, but perhaps it was merely the threatening state of his dark clothing and the rough hood with raggedly cut eyeholes.

"Is he dead?"

Dalton gave a last heave and dropped the fellow. He gazed down at the man. "I shouldn't think so. I didn't hit him nearly as hard as I wanted to." He knelt and tugged at the hood. It came off, exposing a face with heavy features and a vicious scar that ran from brow to chin, passing like a trail over one undamaged eye.

Clara leaned closer, but she could quite comfortably vow she had never seen such a frightening visage in her life. However, Dalton passed one hand over his face and swore with a word she had only ever heard from Wadsworth's cook.

"What's wrong? Do you know him?"

"Yes. He works for me."

"Oh! Then we were in no danger from him at all."

"We were very much in danger. Kurt has only one skill other than cooking, and that is assassination. What's more, I did not order him here. The assignment must have come from above me in the chain of command."

He turned to retrieve one of the doused candles and lighted it with a coal from the grate. Then he moved swiftly about the room, gathering the few items that she had unpacked and shoving them into her bag. He took the belt from her dressing gown and used it to tie the hands of the large stranger.

Clara was a bit breathless at his efficiency. "Exactly how familiar are you with this sort of thing?"

He shot her a glance that told her nothing. "Come. We must leave this place. They'll be after us within the hour when Kurt doesn't return."

"Us? I thought you said this man worked for you."

"He did." He turned to pin her with his silver gaze. "Tell me now that you are innocent of any plot against the Crown."

Her eyes widened. "Plot? I draw pictures, my lord. I'm no spy."

The corner of his mouth twitched. "I am."

He hefted her bag and held out one hand. "Or I was. It seems I have just placed myself on the opposite side."

Chapter Eighteen

During the long carriage ride back into the city, Dalton studied all the options open to them.

Someone had given Kurt the kill order. There were only six men who could give that command, and he himself was one of them. That left only the Royal Four and Liverpool.

He ruled out Liverpool purely on familiarity with the man's methods. The Prime Minister would be ruthless enough to command an assassination if he felt the situation called for it. Dalton simply couldn't conceive of what would motivate that command in this case.

Unfortunately, it was his duty to report the night's activities to Liverpool. If only he could be sure . . .

No, it must be one of the Four. Unfortunately, Dalton only knew three of the men. One, Lord Barrowby, could be discounted completely, for the man was on his deathbed at his home in Derbyshire.

The other two he had known briefly while he had been one of their number earlier this year. Unfortunately when he'd stepped down to take over the Liar's Club he'd been excluded from further confidences.

He imagined that the others had chosen someone to fill the seat of the Cobra that he had left behind, but he had no idea who it was. Liverpool had not yet seen fit to tell him, and he'd been too busy trying to bring the Liars to heel over the past few weeks to divine it on his own.

So, three possibilities. Three men with the knowledge and the power to order a Liar to kill.

He wished he could have been sure if Kurt had seen and identified him. If not, then he could still expect help from his men, such as they were. If only he'd had time to win them over completely before this came up . . .

"We are going back? Why?" Rose's—*Clara's* soft voice interrupted his thoughts. He turned his head to see her peering through the gap in the shades that covered the windows of the carriage. She released the shade and the interior of the vehicle returned to near darkness.

Only the occasional street lamp shone through the parchmentlike shades, along with the slight glow from the carriage's own side lantern.

"Have you ever noticed that we are always in the dark together?" He kept his tone uninvolved. "In the attic, in the 'London particular,' in the Rochesters' garden—"

"In the garden?"

He couldn't see her face well, but her tone conveyed a wealth of consternation. "Ah . . . I forgot that you weren't entirely yourself that night. My apologies. I was merely worried for your health, bound as you were in that corset."

Something hit him and he clutched it in reflex. A glove, still warm from her hand. It appeared at least Rose's fiery temperament was a fact.

"Do not try to charm me. Why would you want to? You've got everything you wanted."

"Oh, yes," he retorted dryly. "I've more than a dozen spies and assassins on my tail. I'm on the run with a woman who despises me and makes no show of hiding it. I've nowhere to turn but to Liverpool for help, and I'm not entirely sure that my godfather is not part of all this."

"Your godfather?"

"Lord Liverpool."

"The Prime Minister? You are that high in Society? And you toyed with a *housemaid*?" Her voice painted a picture in his mind of her face, dumbfounded and angry. Then he felt her boot connect firmly with his shin.

"No. Apparently I toyed with an underhanded widow." Another kick to his shin and he'd had enough. He reached for her, gaining a few handfuls of something pleasantly soft in the process, until finally he had her wrapped tightly in his arms, facing away from him and nearly draped across his lap.

She struggled vainly for a while, cursing him until she ran out of breath.

He snorted dismissively, knowing it would drive her mad. "Very impressive. May I commend your grasp of foul words? Wherever did you learn them all?"

She twisted in his grasp one last time, then lay still against him. "Some from Gerald Braithwaite," she admitted finally. "The rest from Wadsworth's cook."

"It's really too bad that Kurt had to be left behind. He would have enjoyed that."

She turned her face to the side, brushing his cheek with her silken hair. "Who are you, that an assassin works for you?" she asked softly. "That the Prime Minister is a relation? That you steal into people's safe boxes, and take on false identities? You said you are a spy. Whom do you spy for and why?"

"I spy for England, of course."

"Then why are you hunting *me*?" Real confusion filled her voice.

He shifted uncomfortably. She was warm and soft against him and he was having trouble concentrating with the scent of her coming warm from within his arms. The rose scent was gone, but the underlying note of woman remained. She smelled like home to him, like flowers and firelight and long lazy mornings in bed.

"*Clara,*" he whispered experimentally. It suited her.

"I didn't lie about my name, you know." Her voice shook just the tiniest bit and he knew that being in his arms was affecting her, as well. "My name is Rose. Clara Rose."

He closed his eyes and fought the desire to flip her onto the seat cushions opposite and go searching inside her for his Rose.

But Rose had never been his. None of it had been real except for the revelation of his own loneliness and need.

He returned her to her seat before she could break down any more of his defenses. He was far too deeply involved in this case. His first case with the Liars, and he was breaking every rule in the manual. Some spymaster he was.

Rubbing the back of his neck, he forced his mind to focus. "You must tell me everything from the beginning if we are to discover who it is that is after you. When did you begin drawing the cartoons?"

Clara hesitated. Dalton shook his head at her silence. "I already know about the other Rose. I have given her what help I could to remove her from Wadsworth's. I know also that the Trapps had nothing to do with Sir

Thorogood. I assure you that no reprisal shall fall upon them."

She shifted in her seat for a moment, then sighed. "Very well, then. You know most of it. After Bentley's death I went into the attic . . ."

Clara told him everything. When she was done, the relief she felt was immeasurable. She sat back into the deep cushions, spent and liberated. She had never before realized how heavy her secret life had become. "So what now?"

Dalton didn't answer for a moment. He was glad of the dark, for he knew the relief he felt must show on his face. Her story had been simple, consistent, and ringing with truth. She was a mad, crusading tempest of a woman on a sure path to self-destruction, but she was no spy. Unfortunately, the Liars would not be convinced as easily as he had been.

"We need someplace to stay the night, and we need cash. The Liars are the best in the business, but I may know a few tricks they haven't seen yet." He'd never thought that his distance from the men would come to his advantage. Then again, if he'd ever truly gained their loyalty, he might not be in this position in the first place.

"If Kurt recognized me, then the last place they'll expect me to go is to a certain house in London. If he didn't, then we may as well spend the night in comfort while I contact a few people that I know I can trust. We must find out who has ordered the kill and why. Someone wants Sir Thorogood dead. The latest attack was definitely aimed at you, so they know the real identity of Sir Thorogood now."

She moved restlessly in the darkness, her action a rustle of fabric and a wafting of sweetened air from her person. The atmosphere in the carriage was becoming close. *Or perhaps not close enough.*

"I'm not sure I understand. How did they find me? How did you find me?"

"We've had someone stationed at the *Sun* for more than a week, waiting for the servant girl to drop off the cartoons." He shook his head. "You were very clever. We followed you once, but in that plain garb we lost you in the city immediately." Then he scowled. "You should never have taken such a chance. Do you have any idea what could happen to an unescorted lady in the city?"

"Lord Etheridge, do you send your servants on errands?"

"Of course."

"Are they always escorted? Can you honestly say that you have never sent a young housemaid alone into the streets, even inadvertently?"

Dalton opened his mouth to protest but found he could not. Although he certainly would never knowingly do so, neither had he ever given direct orders that it not be done.

After waiting a moment for him to reply, she continued. "If a lady is not safe on the streets, then *no one* is, be she peddler or princess. How can you be so hypocritical?"

His grip on his temper faltered. "You are the most annoying woman I have ever met."

She remained quiet for a moment as if stung. Then she said quietly, "I don't know why I say such things to you. I never have before."

What was the matter with him? He felt on the edge of combustion. He fought down his emotions. "Well, to your credit, you don't appear to be spiteful. Simply impassioned for your cause."

"Me?" The wondering tone in her voice almost made him smile, despite their predicament. "Impassioned? I'm not at all. I'm simply invisible Clara Simpson."

That brought a bark of harsh laughter from Dalton. "Oh, my dear Mrs. Clara Rose Thorogood Simpson, you are anything but invisible. You are mad, reckless, and outrageous but never, never invisible."

"I am?" She sounded inordinately pleased. "Imagine— me, outrageous."

"Do not forget reckless. I shall have to keep a very careful eye on you until we sort this out. You're likely to do something dangerous."

"I won't! I'm very careful—" She stopped for a moment. "I wasn't careful at all, you know. It was as if I thought nothing could ever happen."

"It's the first thing we try to teach our young recruits. That feeling of immortality is the gravest danger an operative can face."

"Did you feel that way, when you began?"

"Of course not," he said stiffly. "I am a most cautious person."

"Hmm. Very amusing coming from a man who is madder than I."

"How so?"

"I have only one thing to say. *Ruby pantaloons*." She snickered. "With a mustard waistcoat and emerald t-tails—" She dissolved into laughter completely. Nothing came from the opposite seat but soundless wheezing and the occasional snort.

Dalton pursed his lips. When she finally subsided, he cleared his throat. "I am not accustomed to being the object of laughter."

She sighed with great satisfaction. "I know. That's what makes you so very amusing."

He was not going to pursue that line of questioning. "What have you drawn lately that might have set off someone powerful?"

She remained silent for a moment. He could almost hear the gears of her clever mind at work. "Nothing, really. Most of what I drew only caused a bit of gossip, unfortunately. Mistresses, graft, that sort of thing. Only occasionally was I able to catch someone in an illegal act."

"Such as Mosely."

"Yes. I'm very proud of what Sir Thorogood did for that orphanage. But that was months ago. If Mosely were after me, wouldn't he have attempted something sooner?"

"The directive to find you came ten days ago. It could have been any one of several cartoons. Did you have to be so prolific?"

"Of course. Sir Thorogood is the most published cartoonist in London," she said stoutly. "The drawings were printed every other day."

"I wonder if you know how odd it is for you to speak of 'him' like that?"

"No odder than a grown man playing dress-up with a tricornered hat and a monocle," she retorted.

"Would you leave off about my costume? I upset my valet, if you must know the truth. He's a genius, but very sensitive to insult."

She began to snicker once more.

He leaned forward and spoke in a menacing tone. "Don't even begin."

There was an audible gulp, then silence.

"Thank you." Feeling better, he straightened his

blessedly short and tidy cuffs. "Now, tell me precisely what inspired the drawings that were published in the last two weeks. . . ."

At length, the hack drove up to a house that was stately and in good repair, but the plantings were small in the front, as though newly grown. Still, the house sat snugly with the others in its row, its brown stone lending it a warmth and permanence that made Clara's rootless soul twinge with covetousness.

They were admitted by a very fine butler whose dignity was not one whit impaired by his purple dressing gown and matching slippers.

"Pearson, I must see Simon at once." Dalton's urgency did not seem to disturb the man at all. The butler only nodded serenely.

"Of course, my lord. May I offer you refreshment while you wait?"

He was directing them to the drawing room when another man appeared at the top of the stairs. "Etheridge? What's afoot?" Tying the knot of his dressing gown, he came quickly down the stairs. "Is it the club?"

The other man was attractive, although perhaps his features were not so severely chiseled as Dalton's. But his smile was easy and welcoming and his blue eyes were indeed striking. Clara found herself gazing into them with dreamy fascination. Or perhaps it was with supreme exhaustion.

Had she seen him somewhere before? Her mind refused to work well enough to remember him.

Dalton cleared his throat beside her. "Simon, this is Clara Simpson. She's had a rotten night and she needs rest. If I could trouble you—"

"Dalton, don't be silly." The crisp feminine voice came from the stairs.

Clara looked up to see a delightfully familiar face. "Agatha? Agatha Applequ—"

"Raines, dear Clara. Lady Raines, to be precise, but you must call me Aggie now."

The man Simon turned to gaze at his wife with concern. "Damsel, get back to bed. You'll catch your death."

"Oh, don't fuss, Simon. It doesn't suit you in the least."

As Agatha made her way down the stairs, past history filtered through Clara's weary brain. "Oh!" She turned to Simon. "You're the Chimneysweep Knight!" Then realizing how that must sound, she blinked. "Oh, dear. How rude you must think me."

A rather astonishing smile flashed across Sir Raines's face, and he bowed in acknowledgment. "Not at all. You are most welcome to our home, Mrs. Simpson."

Clara returned his bow with a weary curtsy, then turned to Dalton. "I fear I've no sense left at all."

Dalton shook his head. "You'll have to do without for the moment."

Agatha had reached her by now and taken her by the elbow. "You look simply exhausted, Clara. Let me have a bath drawn for you, and then we'll tuck you into bed and you can sleep until noon."

"Oh, that sounds lovely." Clara fought back a tremendous yawn. Sleepily she turned to Dalton. "Good night, Dalton. I shall see you in the morning." She stood on tiptoe and kissed his cheek, then turned back to follow Agatha.

The stairs were far too numerous for Clara's teetering legs to carry her and it took all of her concentration not to sit down for a nap on the way up. It wasn't until she reached the top that she became aware of Agatha's startled expression.

"Why are you—" *Oh, no.* She hadn't truly done *that,* had she? The urge to look back at Dalton swept her, but she didn't dare. She followed Agatha on down the hall, resolutely not looking. What if he was wiping his cheek with a handkerchief? Or worse, yet, what if he was looking up at her the way part of her wanted to look down at him?

Chapter Nineteen

Gazing up the stairs after the two women, Simon shook his head. "Was that a kiss? I thought you didn't like the Widow Simpson? What about Rose?"

Dalton rubbed the back of his neck. "The Widow Simpson *is* Rose."

"Truly?" Simon raised an eyebrow. "I think I'm going to need a brandy. You, too. You look like a man who's had a shock."

Yes, a shock was quite correct. The way she kissed him, softly, casually, the way a woman might kiss her husband good night. . . .

He'd liked it very much. So naturally he forced himself to ignore it.

He followed Simon into the study, which resembled his own in its array of manly comforts. Good leather, good liquor, good books. He was always able to relax with Simon, who was perhaps the one person in the world who had no expectation of him. When he was handed a brandy, he quaffed it in one swallow.

"Rough night?" Wary amusement dripped from Simon's voice.

"The roughest. It seems someone has set an assassin on my tail."

Simon cocked a brow and settled back into his chair with his brandy. "That's new? I thought you suspected that all along."

"Yes, I did. But I never suspected that the assassin was Kurt."

"Kurt?"

"Got you there, didn't I? Yes, the assailant was Kurt, at least this night. I find it hard to believe a man as skilled as Kurt would have missed thrice before."

"But Kurt would never work outside the club!"

Dalton poured himself another brandy and sat in the chair opposite Simon, leaning back and stretching his legs toward the fire. "Precisely."

Simon rubbed his chin. "What did you do to get on the Liars' list?"

"I? Not a thing, until I knocked Kurt out and trussed him like a turkey. I believe it is Rose they are after."

"Clara."

"What?"

"Her name is Clara. You called her Rose just now." Simon grinned. "How many women are there in that bed of yours?"

Dalton carefully set his brandy glass down before he shattered it in the fireplace. "There are three women, if not in my bed, then yet in my head." He ticked them off on his fingers. "The Widow Simpson, Rose, and Clara. None of whom know the meaning of prudence."

"Well, what do you intend to do with your triplets? If Kurt truly is after them—I mean, her?"

"I forgot someone on that list. Sir Thorogood."

That finally drew a sound of surprise from Simon. Unfortunately, he was in the midst of sipping his brandy.

Dalton leaned forward to give him a good pounding on the back until he could speak again.

Simon wheezed and shook his head in amazement. "Clara Simpson is Sir Thorogood." It was a statement, not a question, but Dalton nodded.

"That's quite a woman you have," Simon marveled. "Yet how can you be sure? Could she not be posing as such, as you did?"

Dalton blinked. "I hadn't thought of that." Then he shook his head. "No, she's the one. She had access to Wadsworth's and the drawing style definitely matches." He patted the jacket pocket where he'd stored his evidence.

Simon leaned forward. "Show me."

Dalton looked away. "I'd rather not."

However, Simon looked so affronted—as if believing that Dalton didn't trust him—that finally Dalton handed over the two drawings he'd rolled and tucked into his pocket. "If you laugh, you're a dead man."

To his credit, Simon didn't laugh, although perhaps the hand clapped firmly over his mouth should have taken the credit. Still, his eyebrows rose to new heights as he examined the two pages covered with various sketches. His shoulders shook just the tiniest bit, however.

Finally Dalton could stand no more. "Enough!" He snatched the drawings and returned them to his pocket.

Simon still didn't speak but sat back in his chair, an enormous grin spread across his face. He closed his eyes and clasped his hands across his stomach, giving a happy sigh.

"What are you going on about?"

Simon shook his head, his eyes still closed. "You said I couldn't laugh. You didn't say I couldn't picture the moment when you show those drawings to Liverpool."

"Oh, dear God." Dalton contemplated the drawings with horror. He ought to fling them in the fire this very moment! But he had never in his career tampered with evidence and he wasn't about to start.

"Maybe she'll draw some more for you, so you won't have to use those." Finally a snicker broke through Simon's control. "Some with drawers on."

Dalton studied the fire without expression.

Simon took another sip of brandy. "Seriously now, you can't think to turn her over to Liverpool? He may have ordered the kill himself, you know."

Despite his own reservations on the subject, Dalton felt obliged to defend Liverpool. "No. I cannot believe it. Clara may be many things, but she is not treasonous. I'd wager my life on it. Liverpool might dislike her politics, but he'd never order an innocent woman killed."

"Well, as long as you're sure." Simon didn't sound too sure at all. "In my opinion, Liverpool is obsessed. Obsessed men can do strange things, if it feeds their obsession."

Dalton stiffened. "If Liverpool has an obsession, it is the safety and security of England."

Simon shrugged. "I never said it wasn't an honorable obsession."

Gritting his teeth, Dalton forced himself to take another sip of brandy, as if he was not feeling a most uncivilized desire to rub Simon's nose in the carpet for a while. A good row would—

A *row*? What was happening to him? He was thinking like Monty again. He rubbed his forehead as if he could rub Monty from his mind. How could an alias become such an insidious part of his personality?

Agatha entered the study and settled on the arm of

Simon's chair. "Clara is having a bath and something to eat. I daresay she'll sleep for hours. She's completely exhausted, poor thing."

Dalton didn't want to feel sympathy for Clara. He didn't want to feel this need to protect her. Where was his icy logic, his cool judgment?

He forced himself to focus. "What I need right now is information. Who ordered the kill and why, for a beginning. There's something not right here, something more than simply offended aristocrats taking revenge on a cartoonist—"

Pearson appeared at the door of the room. "Sir Raines, Mr. Cunnington is here to see Lord Etheridge."

James? Dalton looked up in alarm. "No, Pearson, send him away—"

Agatha raised one hand. "Why would we send him away when we just sent for him? He's been trying to find you since this afternoon."

Dalton stood. "Damn it, I didn't want James involved in this!"

"Well, that hardly surprises me," James said dryly as he lounged in the doorway. "You never want me to have any fun."

"James, this doesn't concern you."

"I can hardly refute that, since I have no idea what you are talking about." He held up a leather-covered file. "I've come because I have a theory that you should hear."

Simon perked up. "What theory?"

"I have reason to believe . . ." James stretched the moment out dramatically. "Sir Thorogood is a woman!"

Dalton nodded. "Of course she is."

James dropped his hand, his expression stunned. "You knew? How did you figure it out?"

"He didn't." Simon smiled. "He fell into it, face first."

Agatha patted Dalton's arm. "Don't feel bad. All men are dense when it comes to women." She turned to James. "How did you figure it out, Jamie?"

"I've been staring at these drawings for days, trying to figure out why they are so unique. Everyone loves them, rich or poor, male or female." He handed the file to Agatha, who undid the string fixture and spread the cartoons over the table. "Then I saw something that struck me, something that Ackermann lacks, as do the other popular cartoonists."

Simon moved to examine the drawings as well. "What's that, James?"

"Detail. To be specific, fashion detail. Whoever drew these is up on the latest fashion in women's clothing, shoes, and hair."

Agatha picked up a drawing of four ladies picnicking on top of a mountain of piled rubbish, with the sewage-laden Thames running sluggishly behind them. "He's right! How clever of you, Jamie!"

Dalton hadn't moved from brooding into the fire. "Yes, very clever," he snapped. "Too bad you didn't think of it two days ago."

James looked at Agatha and Simon. "What's wrong with him?"

Simon cleared his throat. "Dalton, perhaps you should fill James in. If the Liars have targeted you, then he's in the line of fire already as your second."

James blinked. "Targeted?"

Dalton turned from the fire and forced his fists to unclench. "First of all, you're right about Thorogood. The mystery cartoonist is really Mrs. Clara Simpson."

"Do you mean that little widow who's been plaguing you?" James's mouth twitched. "Well, that explains the attraction, then. She's been working you, trying to figure out what you're up to, right?"

"Despite your confidence in my charms, James, it's a bit more complicated than that."

"Stop dancing about it, Dalton." Agatha turned to James. "She's been posing as a maid at Wadsworth's as well. Dalton didn't recognize her until it was too late."

James grimaced. "Too late? What do you—" Then his jaw dropped. *"Oh."*

Dalton sighed. "Thank you, Agatha. I believe I can take it from here." He rubbed the back of his neck. "She recognized me first and made a run for it. When I caught up with her, so did Kurt. He tried to take us both down."

"You killed Kurt?" James looked shocked and just a tiny bit impressed.

"No, simply left him unconscious and bound to buy us time. So you see, I've placed myself on the wrong side of the line now. You might want to reconsider being involved."

"What are we going to do?"

Dalton looked at his second in command for a long moment. Determination hardened James's jaw, and he looked ready to take on the Liars single-handed.

"Thank you, James," Dalton said quietly. Then he turned to the stack of drawings. "Somewhere in this mess is the answer. There must be a link between one of these cartoons and the Royal Four. Someone issued that kill order and I want to know who and why."

"So do I." The soft voice from the doorway drew everyone's gaze. Clara stood there, clad in a fresh nightdress and wrapper. Her hair streamed loose about her shoulders. Dalton's fingers itched to touch it.

He scowled. "Why aren't you resting?"

She shrugged. "Oh, you know how it is. Conspiracy,

murder attempts, running for one's life . . . it's the little things that keep one up at night." She had a smile for James, however. "Hello, Mr. Cunnington. It is good to see you again."

"Indeed, Mrs. Simpson." James stared appreciatively for a moment, then looked at Dalton. "I still like her."

Dalton's scowl deepened. He was very conscious of how alluring Clara looked in her nightclothes. The last thing he needed was for James to take a fancy to her. "Well, she doesn't like you." He gestured sharply to Clara. "Take a seat, please. You may as well hear this."

She raised a brow at his peremptory tone. "Always the gentleman." She sat next to Agatha. "So how are we to puzzle out this mess?"

Dalton decided that he liked the way the candlelight brought out the red tint in her hair. He'd never seen it down before. She looked softer, warmer . . . fresh out of bed.

"Dalton?" James waved one hand before Dalton's eyes. "The kill order?"

Damn. He was forgetting his purpose. She was making him forget. Dalton forced his eyes from Clara and focused on the glow of the fire. *Distance. Control.* "The kill order is merely the symptom of the disease. This goes deeper than the danger to one woman. If one of the Royal Four has gone rogue, then the entire structure of the government is in danger. The Crown itself, perhaps."

Clara frowned. "Is that supposed to comfort me?"

Dalton shook his head sharply. "Comforting you is not my priority at the moment," he said. "There is more than your life at stake here."

He didn't look at her, but out of the corner of his eye he saw her flinch.

"Ah," was all she said.

Simon came to stand next to Dalton by the fireplace.

"I thought perhaps you were in love," Simon said too quietly for the others to hear. "It seems you are not."

Dalton tested the temperature of his heart. Cold as ice. "I never said I was."

"No, you never did." Slowly, Simon walked back to Agatha, who nested her hand in his as if for reassurance.

But Liverpool would approve. Dalton could hear him now, declaring his loyalty as he had done so many times in Dalton's youth.

"I should be happy to die tomorrow, should my king and country require it of me!"

Dalton knew it was true. He understood the Prime Minister, as perhaps no other person living did. Liverpool's faith was patriotism, his vocation the defense of England. Until this last month, Dalton would have claimed it of himself as well.

His life honed for one task, his very existence aimed at one goal.

Protect England.

But then you let her in. His every masculine instinct begged him to keep her safe, to protect her always. It interfered with his judgment—confused him and dangerously distracted him.

What did mere feeling have to do with this? If he would sacrifice his life—and he would—should he not be willing to sacrifice his heart?

Protect Clara he must. But his heart was already taken.

Again came Liverpool's voice, full of satisfaction and cool approval. *"Good man."*

No. He was not a good man. He was merely a loyal one.

When he turned, Clara had moved to the window to

look out at the darkness. He turned to Simon. "There's only a few hours left until dawn—"

"Dalton!"

The fear in her voice brought him to her side in an instant. She never took her gaze from the street, but reached for him with one shaking hand. "There! That man by the lamppost. It's *him*! It's Kurt!"

It was indeed Kurt. He stood brazenly in the circle of light cast by the street lamp, his face turned toward the house. Dalton watched as another man joined the giant assassin to gaze at the house. Stubbs. Then another figure. Then another, until the street corner was full of the most dangerous men in all of England.

This was what he had come to. Run to ground by his own men.

Simon had joined them, giving a low whistle at the sight. "I suppose we'd better ask them in and find out what they want."

Dalton turned on him. "Are you mad? It's obvious what they want."

Simon's face went very bland, which Dalton knew was a danger signal. "Those men were my friends and comrades-in-arms for fifteen years. Are you saying they've *all* turned rogue?"

"Of course not! But can you deny that the Liars follow orders, kill or be killed?"

Simon had no answer for that.

Dalton turned away. "The day you're forced to fight Kurt off Agatha, I'll let you ask me that question! Right now, I will not turn Clara over to them, and I will not bow to intimidation." He turned, pulling Clara with him. "We need to get out of here, and not by any way they can follow."

But how? The house would be surrounded in an instant if they tried to leave through any of the doors.

Clara turned to Agatha. "Quickly, are any of the houses on your row empty right now?"

Agatha blinked. "The family four doors down is summering in Bath this year." She made a gesture with her hand to the east. "But the house is locked up tight."

Clara rolled her eyes. "Are you people spies or not? Show us to your attic. Now!"

After giving James a brief set of instructions, Dalton gripped Clara's hand tightly as they ran from the room. He wanted to praise her for her quick thinking, but she wouldn't look at him. It seemed as though he had finally pushed her faith beyond its limits.

That was too bad, for she had never been as beautiful to him as she was now.

Clara examined the east wall of the attic, but could see no way that would allow them easy entry to another house. Simon's square was obviously of better quality than Smythe Square. Dalton pulled her away from her position peering at the solid brick.

"The fire wall won't yield to us, Clara. We must go another way." He towed her to the window.

She opened it and peered out, but shut her eyes immediately. "No. Too high. I cannot climb down."

He took her place at the window. "Not down. Up." With that, he'd climbed onto the window ledge and disappeared above it. Then his hand appeared from above her. "The roof. Take my hand, I'll pull you up."

Clara wanted to say no. She wanted to turn and run down the stairs as quickly as possible.

She also wanted to live. "Get on with it, Clara Rose," she whispered to herself. Then she hiked her nightgown and clambered onto the ledge, keeping her gaze on Dalton's wide palm.

She teetered, then reached for him with both hands. In a blink, she was beside him on the slick roof tiles.

The weather had turned since the earlier clear moonlight. Now there was nothing but the reflection of the city's street lamps against the lowering clouds. The slates were damp, and Clara's borrowed slippers had little foothold. Luckily, they were a bit tight on her. At least they would stay on.

She could see little but shadows. Hopefully, that meant that their pursuers could not spy them at all. Dalton kept his grip on her hand as they slid and crawled to the ridge of the roof.

He pulled her close for a moment. "Feel the ridge? Keep it between your feet. If you slip, try to let your feet go down either side so you won't fall."

She soon had reason to try out this advice, for he kept a brutal pace over the rooftops. More than once, he nearly tugged her arm from the socket when she slithered on the slates. What would have taken minutes on the ground seemed to take hours on the rooftops.

Finally, the fourth chimney came into sight in the dimness. Dalton left her straddling the ridge as if it were a recalcitrant horse, both hands seeking a grip on the slates.

He went down the rear slant of the roof and over the eaves. As he went out of sight, she shut her eyes, willing him not to fall.

Then he was back, scrambling up the pitch using both feet and hands. "Take my hand."

"I don't want to do this," she said as she released her grip on the ridge. "I truly, truly don't want to do this."

"I know. But the window is open now. I can drop you right into the attic."

Her knees were weak with strain and fear, but Clara forced herself to pull her opposite leg over the ridge until her feet dangled down the slates together. With one hand in Dalton's she let go of the ridge tile finger by finger.

Her tentative balance went awry as her weight shifted and she slid on one hip down the slates, gaining speed as she shot toward the edge.

"Clara!" Dalton's hand tightened on hers and her slide ended in a yank that almost dislocated her shoulder. Her body flipped, slamming her face down onto the roof. She looked up to see Dalton spread-eagled on the slates, his arms extended to hers, and one foot cocked over the roof ridge.

Her feet dangled in midair and the roof edge cut into her thigh. So close . . .

With effort she reached up to grab Dalton's sleeve with her other hand. He took her wrist and pulled her up until she could brace her feet in the gutter. He wrapped her in his arms, his own foot still hooked over the apex of the roof, and tucked her face into his neck as she struggled to catch the breath that had fled her lungs when she'd thought herself dead.

"I have you," he murmured. "I have you safe."

Then he helped her take a grip on the nearby chimney and regained his own balance. He moved around her, as able as a cat on the pitched roof, until he was beside her.

"We're just above the window and to the left a bit," he told her. "I'm going to let you down by hand. I want you to feel for the window ledge with your feet."

She surrendered her trust totally to him, allowing him

to dangle her over the roof's edge until her toes made contact with the stone ledge.

"Now, I'm going to drop you in. I want you to throw your weight in through the window. Ready?"

She nodded quickly but couldn't speak. One misstep, one wrong move . . .

She'd never been more frightened in her life.

"Now!"

She swung forward and flung herself in through the dark portal, landing sprawling on the dusty wooden floor of the attic.

He was beside her in a moment, pulling her to her feet. She clung to him, her fingers tightening in his waistcoat until they ached.

At that moment, he could have been the devil himself and she would have sought shelter in his strength and solidity. The fact that he murmured softly into her ear and stroked her straggling hair away from her face with heart-melting tenderness had nothing to do with it.

When she could breathe once more, she stepped back and straightened her spine. "We should move on."

He shifted in the darkness as if he wanted to reach for her again, but surely that was her imagination. "Right. Take my hand."

She rested her hand in his yet again and they made their way blind through the unfamiliar attic, stumbling and knocking shins until they found the door and the stairs down.

Her nighttime spying experience certainly was coming in handy on this adventure. Too bad she would never be using these skills again, just when she was getting rather good at it all.

They reached the ground floor and Clara ran out of ideas. "Now what?"

"We raid the house for a cloak for you and we hail a hack."

"A hack? At this time of night?"

"There's always a hack available in the residential district this late. All those husbands sneaking home late from their clubs."

Just as he'd said, once they'd made it to the street and fled around the corner from their pursuers, a hack came trotting down the cobbles in a leisurely fashion. Dalton raised one hand and the driver obligingly stopped.

Too grateful to marvel at their luck, Clara climbed inside and sank wearily onto the seat. She'd been through so much tonight, and it still lacked a few hours until dawn.

Part of her wanted to stay awake and note where they were going and how, but the rest of her fell victim to exhaustion immediately. She never even remembered lying down, but suddenly found herself being briskly shaken awake from her nap half-sprawled on the seat.

"Clara, come along. We must hurry."

"All right. Fine. Yes," she murmured, trying desperately to force both eyes open at the same time. Dalton pulled her from the hack and steadied her on the sidewalk as he waved the driver on.

The weather had deteriorated further. It was raining now, the chill needles striking her face and fully waking her at last.

Dalton began walking the opposite way from the route the cab had taken. He towed her along behind as if she had wheels. He ducked into an alleyway that allowed not a ray of street-lamp light within and made his way through the blackness as if he could see in the dark.

He led her around another corner, behind the building

she guessed, then climbed a box and hefted her up beside him. He took her hand and moved it forward until her fingers touched glass. A window.

"Don't tell me—we're breaking in again."

She heard a dark chuckle.

"I'm allowed to break in here. Or at least, I used to be."

His voice sounded grim, and for the first time she wondered what this never-ending night meant to him. From what she gathered, he'd lost his position defending her earlier. Fleeing with her again had likely only compounded the problem.

She tried to convince herself that it wasn't so, as he opened the window in some way that she couldn't see, and helped her through it. She wanted to believe that he hadn't lost anything important tonight, for it would be very difficult to resist a man who had sacrificed so much on her behalf.

Very difficult, indeed.

Chapter Twenty

Dalton felt the familiar air of the Liar's Club fold around him and ached for it. He'd come so close.

Now he had no idea what lay in his future. Would he be tried for treason? If he could not prove the identity of the rogue member of the Royal Four, it was possible.

Clara. What was he going to do with this maddening magnificent woman? She'd been so quick, so brave on the rooftops, with never a tear, never a betraying shriek that would have alerted the Liars. He shook his head. She'd have gone over the edge of the roof silent until the end, so as not to call attention to his presence there.

He still could not allow himself to care for her, but by God, she'd won his respect in that moment in a way that he'd rarely before esteemed a woman.

Holding his hand over her eyes in a last, rather hopeless gesture of secrecy—perhaps he ought to simply open the secret office to public tours—he led her up the narrow stair to the attic chamber. There he seated her on the old sprung sofa that probably predated Simon by many years.

She curled up, tucking her slippered feet under her

and wrapping the stolen cloak around her until he could only see her pale face in the glow of the candle he'd lighted.

Dalton rubbed the back of his neck, then untied his cravat and tossed it over the back of his chair. He sat at the desk, trying to think. It wasn't easy with Clara in the room. The air seemed charged with her, as if lightning were about to strike him.

She made him too warm. He shrugged out of his damp coat and forced himself to consider his options. How long could he remain in the club unseen?

Simon had assured him that no one but James knew of the existence of the secret office, even though one of the entrances went directly through Jackham's office.

Luckily, Jackham wouldn't be in until three days hence, for he was still on his liquor-buying trip. He was likely tippling in Edinburgh even now, for he insisted on personally trying every liquid that made its way into the club. Dalton still wasn't sure if the man was connoisseur or cozener, but it was just as well.

Dalton didn't trust Jackham, despite Simon's assurances that the man had no clue to the real purpose of the club. How could anyone work on the premises for years and learn nothing? The man was a common thief who had once lived for taking what he hadn't earned. If there were ever a leak in the club's security, Jackham would be the first person Dalton would look to.

So the office was safe enough for now. Taking Clara home to the Trapps would only put her back in the reach of the Liars. Their own territory would be the last place they'd look.

He hoped.

He glanced over at Clara. She'd melted into the sunken cushions like warm tallow, only her dark eyes wide in her pallor to show that she was still awake. She must be exhausted.

"When did you sleep last?"

She blinked. "Other than in the carriage?" She thought about it for a moment. "I had a nap Tuesday evening."

It was Thursday morning. Two nights without sleep. One spent with him, one night on the run. "What's holding you up?"

"Fear," she said promptly. "And I'm hungry as well, but you needn't concern yourself about that."

His mouth twitched. Only a small dig at his lack of hospitality. "There is a kitchen here. I'll find you some bread and cheese, if you like."

"And tea, please. Rather a great deal of tea." She snuggled deeper into the couch. "I feel as though I shall never be warm again."

"Ah, then, tea and a fire. Your wish is my command."

He was rising to leave, so he couldn't quite hear her murmured comment, but it sounded something like "I entirely doubt that."

True, he thought as he took the candle and left the room. Unfortunate, but true.

The fire was warm and the small meal heartening, but still something deep inside Clara shivered. Having discarded the wet wrapper, she sat on the floor in front of the fire, shrouded in her overlong cloak. She had braided her hair but had nothing to tie it with. Dalton moved restlessly about the room looking rather like a pirate in his shirtsleeves and unbuttoned waistcoat. She could just see the curls on his chest in the open throat of his shirt. Were his shoulders getting broader by the moment?

He was truly beginning to get on her nerves.

"Don't you have something lordly to tend to?" she snapped finally. "You'll turn me mad if you pace round me once more."

"James is securing your protection." His voice held frustration and the edge of something else. "There's nothing at all for me to do but guard you."

"Guard me how? Safeguard me, or prison-guard me?" She stood to face him. "I'm not going anywhere."

He stopped abruptly in his pacing and pondered her in a manner that gave Clara pause. "What is it?" she asked.

"To be truthful, you are going somewhere. I've decided to send you away until I can find the source of this mess."

She rolled her eyes. "You might have thought of that before you dragged me back to London. I was already on my way to the country to hide."

"I had somewhere a bit farther in mind." He looked away. "Scotland will do for now."

"Scotland?"

"Unless I need more time. If necessary I shall put you on a ship for the West Indies."

She glared at him. "Do I not have a say in this?"

"No. I need you off where you won't distract—I mean, attract assassination."

"And this has nothing to do with the fact that we were lovers?"

He stiffened. "Of course not. There is no point in bringing that up. That is irrelevant."

Her chill was complete now, all through her. "Ah," she said faintly. "It felt rather . . . relevant to me."

"Completely without bearing on the future." Then Dalton relented, facing her with apology in his eyes.

He reached one hand to tug gently on her raveling braid, turning her to the light.

Her face in the candlelight was pale and drawn, a stranger's face, really. But the flashing hazel eyes were pure Rose. "I've asked myself a thousand times . . . why didn't I see it? Why didn't I see Rose in the Widow Simpson?"

"I took care you shouldn't." Her words were a mere breath. If he'd been standing three steps back, he wouldn't have heard them.

"Perhaps. Or perhaps I wanted my fairy maid so badly that I didn't *want* to see."

Slowly she reached up and drew his hand from her braid. Her trembling fingers told the story that her rigid stance would not. She was as troubled as he. As anguished. As alone.

He took her face between his palms. "Who are you really?" His voice was hoarse even to his own ears. With his fingers he stroked dangling strands of damp hair from her temples. "All those faces. Are *any* of them real?"

She gave her head a tiny shake. "None. Or perhaps . . . all. I cannot say for sure."

"So there is some hope?" His thumb stroked away a tear. He doubted she knew she was crying. "My Rose is in there somewhere?"

"I don't know. In the end, it seems I am only Clara after all."

"Clara," he said, testing the name. Would Clara touch his heart? Would she soothe that dark place inside him that he'd never known existed until Rose showed him the way?

Could he afford the price? His life was already complicated beyond the telling of it. Could he devote enough of himself to her to keep her by his side?

More to the point, did he dare divide himself at all? It seemed the choice lay between Clara or England. Never both.

"Please try to understand, Clara. I cannot truly give myself. I simply cannot afford the distraction." He stopped. Yet he had already begun an affair—with Rose. When he spoke again his voice was regretful. "I can see how you might misunderstand the situation, but you must admit the circumstances were partly the cause. We were in a forced intimacy in the cupboard that got the better of our reason. It was simply an aberration, a misdeed that—"

"A misdeed? An *aberration*?" She stood awkwardly as the cloak tangled in her feet. In a fit of impatience, she pulled it off, then threw it to the floor. "You take what happened and you shrink it down to nothing so you won't have to admit what you did to me."

His jaw dropped. "I? Did to you? I recall you *begging*—"

She held up her hand to stop his words. "You did something that no one else has ever truly managed," she hissed. "You with your silver eyes and your lying passion." She was shaking with emotion. "You—"

She stopped, panting, choking on tears that she refused to allow.

He stood and stepped closer, until all she could see were his fine eyes. "I what?" His voice was low. Intense.

She couldn't bear it. She hated him more than she'd ever hated anyone in her life. She needed him so much she couldn't breathe. She shoved at him violently, pushing him away. Her pain welled up in a vanquished cry.

"You broke my heart!"

She'd thrown the cloak down between them like a

challenge glove. It was a challenge Dalton couldn't resist.

Logic, cold reason—how could they withstand the influence of this changeable enchantress?

He swooped down on her like a raptor, enveloping her in his arms, pulling her close for his devouring. His lips came down hard on hers, his hand in her hair rough and unbelievably full of need. He'd thought to conquer her, but from somewhere within him welled a hunger so powerful that he would have crawled in order to have her.

Almost angrily he fought it back, even as her hands came up to pull him closer. She wrapped her arms around his waist and slathered her body on his, as hungry as he.

Then they were down on the cloak. She tugged at his shirt, slipping her hands beneath it to warm them on his hot skin. His belly was hard and rippled beneath her touch, so she touched it more.

His mouth was greedy on hers and she fed off him in her turn. He rolled her beneath him, pinning her gown to the floor as his thighs parted hers. Unable to stop long enough to pull up her nightdress, he satisfied himself with rubbing the length of his own fully clad erection into the cleft between her legs.

It was torturous pleasure and she tore her mouth from his to gasp aloud. Her fingers fumbled as she searched for the buttons of his trousers. Eagerness and heat drowned out the warning cries of her mind. Only her heart and body were allowed to speak in this moment.

She gave up on his trousers and shoved her fingers into his hair, holding him close so that she could do to his mouth what she wanted to do to the rest of him. He groaned her name, her *real* name, as his hands cupped and massaged her breasts. His fingertips found her nipples, tugging and teasing until her eyes closed and her head dropped back to the floor.

Dalton took his kisses to her breasts, sucking and nibbling on her through the fine batiste of her nightdress. She felt his fingers curl over the neck of her gown, she heard the fabric rip—and only arched her back to ease his access.

Shoving her fingers into his hair, she held his head as he lovingly savaged her breasts. His lips, his teeth, the sharp burn of his incipient beard all combined in a storm of sensation that made her dampen and throb for him.

"Oh, God, Clara . . ." The rumble of his voice between her breasts vibrated directly through her. "I meant none of it. Forgive me."

"Dalton . . ." Her whisper was lost in his groan as he released his erection from its buttoned prison. She reached for him, not satisfied this time with ladylike discretion. She wanted to touch him, to take him in her hands.

Thick, hot male filled her grasp. She spared the grateful thought that it was a good thing she already knew he'd fit, or she'd have worried.

Going quite still over her, he shuddered as she stroked his erection gently. "Clara, I can't . . . I need . . ." But he made no move to pull away. She reveled in his pleading tone, in the knowledge that he would give her this small control.

"I need," she whispered back to him. "I need to see you. All of you."

He opened his eyes to read her face. She didn't turn her determined gaze from his. Smiling slightly, almost shyly, he rolled from above her to lie upon the cloak at her side, closer to the fire.

Clara rose to one elbow next to him, one hand reaching to take possession of his thick member once more. "Will you do as I say?"

He chuckled, half in alarm. "Really, Clara, you are the most outrageous—"

She kissed his lips closed. He deepened the kiss hungrily and protested no more. She pulled back very slightly. "You have much to learn about me, Dalton Montmorency, Lord Etheridge," she murmured against his lips. "As I do about you." She kissed his rough jaw and bit him gently on the chin. "You first."

"God help me," he sighed, then sent her a hot look. "You next."

Swallowing, Clara almost backed away from what she might be unleashing from within them both. Then her imagination blessed her with some of the lovely wicked possibilities and the heat within her bloomed beyond recall.

Slowly, she reached for his hands and unwrapped them from her hair. "You may not touch me yet. I am going to learn you so well I could draw you in the dark." She pressed his hands to the carpet at his sides. He made as if to raise them. "No," she said firmly, "or I won't do this."

She bent to take his flat male nipple between her lips the way he had done to her. His breath left him in a whoosh and she saw his hands flatten themselves to the floor.

I am going to learn you. I will know you so well that I will never forget an inch of you.

This was a moment stolen out of time—an interlude

of forever in this high windowless chamber snug against the rain. *Why was it always attics?*

He tasted salty and male to her tongue. She lapped his other nipple. The same. Her position was awkward so she rucked up her gown and straddled his stomach. He groaned and flexed his body beneath her.

"No drawers," he gasped. She pressed him firmly back to the floor.

"Of course not. I never wear knickers to bed."

If she'd thought his gaze was heated before . . . she looked away, that she might not see the black hunger she had made. She was almost frightened, yet so very aroused. She ducked her head down to his chest to avoid his eyes.

She plowed her fingers through the dark mat on his chest and gently bit his collarbone. "No more mystery," she whispered. "No more lies."

"No," he growled in return. "No more lies."

"Tell me then, Dalton. The truth. Tell me what you want."

He looked away. She raised her hands to his jaw and turned his gaze back up to hers. "*Tell* me."

His breathing deepened and his chest rose and fell between her spread thighs. "I like—I want your mouth."

She kissed him. "You have it. But that's not what you mean, is it?" She kissed her way back down his neck and down the central valley of his hard chest. "Here?" she murmured into his skin.

"Yes—no—"

Clara bit him just above his navel as she ran her hands over the marvelous ridges of his stomach. "Here?" She kissed her way down the tantalizing dark trail below, neatly maneuvering the lower half of her own body past a certain very large obstacle. Dalton groaned and twisted as she floated over his erection with only the trailing hem of her nightgown touching him.

"Clara," he warned, his voice a black growl.

She was pressing his control, she knew. The exhilarating feeling of authority became tempered with the desire to truly make him lose control. Only once had she caught a glimpse of the unleashed male animal within him. When first he'd kissed her after she'd made her offer in the moonlit attic . . . then, for mere moments, the façade was gone.

If there was only this one night, then by heaven, she wanted the real Dalton for her own. Not Monty, not Lord Etheridge. Dalton—hot, harsh, run riot.

It would cost her. She'd never reach him unless she released herself. No Rose, no Widow Simpson. Could she do it?

His tension-dampened flesh rippled beneath her palms and he began to grind his teeth in resistance to her.

"No." She ran her fingers into the waist of his trousers and drawers and stripped them from him. He moved to help her with his boots but she shot him a warning glare that made him lie back, laughing breathlessly at her ferocity.

Then he lay naked before her, every grand male inch of him. Hers, if she dared.

"You said you wanted my mouth." She ran one hand up a thick-hewn thigh as she crawled back up him. "Now where might that mouth go?" she mused. She kissed one hipbone. "There?" She kissed the other and tasted his skin in a slow stroke of her tongue. "There?"

"You are an imp," Dalton groaned. "You are a fiend sent to devour me."

"I'm not an imp. But I am hungry." His stiff erection

twitched before her gaze. He would never say it but she knew. *I want to learn you.*

She lowered her mouth to the swollen head of his member. He gasped, digging clawed fingers into the carpet threads and flexing his body upward. She pressed both palms over his hipbones to steady him. Opening her lips, she tasted him.

Salt. Musk. Sharp, tangy male. He pulsed against her lips. Fascinated, she took the entire head into her mouth, running her tongue curiously around the swollen shape.

Experimentally, she created suction, the way he had with her nipples.

Dalton nearly came up off the floor in one full-body spasm. He felt his mind slipping sideways. "Oh, *God!*" Not a curse but a prayer.

Her mouth was hot and wet and apparently naturally talented. Dalton had never experienced this particular pleasure before. Always so circumspect, always aware of his place, his proper cog in the great machine . . . never *allowed* himself this shivering ecstasy.

She pinned him more fiercely, pressing him down with her small hands as if she could actually keep him from rising. Yet, he would not stop her slow exploration for the world. Intrepid, even in this.

What a woman.

Not his woman, not past this night.

Tomorrow he would send her safely away until he could ferret out the rogue member of the Royal Four. But for tonight . . .

His thoughts swam away in the riveting eroticism of her wet mouth on him.

Tonight . . .

His body tensed, his breath shortened. The pulling, stroking exquisite torture never let up, in fact it deepened. He couldn't hold out much longer—

She gently raked her teeth across his flesh, by design or accident. The crescendo of sensations tore him from the dangling threads of his control, sent him spinning into animal darkness . . .

With a growl he was up and she was down. He tore her gown up and off her in a savage swipe even as he pressed his knee between her thighs.

Wait. Slow down. The last small protest of his civilization died away when she answered his primitive tactics with the tightening of her sweet thighs around his waist and a hoarse *"Yes."*

He drove into her with all the power of his coiled body, until she threw her head back with a gasp full of torment and wonder.

The hot tight slide of her body around his wrapped his mind in darkness and driving hunger. Each thrust was deeper and harsher still. Each withdrawal was faster and more torturous. He wanted to drive himself into her until the friction set them both aflame and they burned to ash . . . together.

Clara was on fire. She *was* fire, surely Dalton could see her glow . . . the pleasure of his forceful invasion was dark and seething, part exquisite pain and part wicked appalling fulfillment. She wanted his mad heat, his dangerous power. This dark anguished core of him was *hers*. Hers alone of all the world. She *needed* him to explode for her like a volcano too long dormant.

Her own explosion was almost upon her. With his fists entwined in her hair and his arms wrapping her immobile for his raw possession, she could only grasp mindlessly at his wide rippling back as his fierce thrusts forced her higher.

Higher. *God, she'd never known she could go so high—*

He threw his head back, his face tight with ecstasy above her. The look of him, the wild sweltering power of him, took her breath away, firing her with new possessive lust. He was a beast. He was *her* beast.

A rumbling harsh call came from deep within his chest, resonating through her fading awareness. Dear God, so *high—*

He swelled within her with his final plowing thrust and she was gone—spiraling up and out of herself in a wash of light and trembling ecstasy. *Higher.* She couldn't breathe—she didn't care—dimly she heard her own cry resound in the small chamber in unearthly harmony with his.

Limp, perspiring and trembling, Clara's body slowly regained contact with her mind. Her heartbeat boomed in her ears—or was that his? She couldn't tell where he ended and where she began. They lay entwined before the fire—panting, spent and far too blissful to sully the moment with a single thought.

Their hearts slowed together and their breathing softened and they slept—not hunter and hunted, not named, not defined. Merely man and woman—together.

Chapter Twenty-one

Dalton rolled over onto something clammy and unpleasant. He fumbled for it, then pulled it from beneath himself with a grunt. Slitting his eyes, he peered at it.

A slipper. Clara's slipper, blackened and ruined from her run across the rooftops.

Clara.

He bolted upright to cast a searching gaze about the office, then saw her. She was sitting tailor-fashion not three feet away, watching him.

Her smile of greeting warmed him within, until he saw the shredded nightgown she wore. Then his gut went cold. "My God. Oh, no." He scrambled to her side. "I—Clara, what I did to you last night—oh dear God."

There were faint scratches on her shoulder and her neck was reddened by the burn of his beard. He swallowed as he saw the small marks on the top of her breast, one pink dot for each finger of his hand.

She followed his gaze downward. "Ah. I should tell you that I do mark easily."

He wanted to take her into his arms but he didn't deserve to touch her. "I can't believe . . . I wouldn't hurt you for the world—" Yet he had. He'd taken her roughly, on the floor like a rutting beast. He sat back on his heels, unmindful of his nudity, stricken to his core with guilt.

"Dalton, I already told you . . . you didn't hurt me."

He shook his head. "I did. I used you shamefully. I—"

Something struck him on the nose. He caught it automatically when it dropped. A strawberry? He looked up to see Clara poised to toss another fruit at him—an apple.

"Now this . . ." she mused. "This might hurt."

"Clara, I know you're angry. I'm sorry, oh God, I'm so sorry—"

The apple struck his shoulder with some power. "Ouch!" He rubbed the spot with his other hand. "Stop. Please talk to me, Clara."

"Oh, are you interested in my viewpoint? I thought you were too busy wallowing in misplaced guilt." She picked up a grape. "This is small, but I think with enough force I should be able to lodge it in your ear. Hold still."

"Misplaced? My guilt is well aimed. Just look at you!"

She considered him for a moment, then smiled and popped the grape into her mouth. "Look at yourself," she said around it.

Not understanding, Dalton looked down. His first realization was that he was entirely naked. His second thought was of the old saying, "You should have seen the other fellow."

He was a mess. Teeth marks and the round red suction marks of her mouth were all over him. He became aware of a stinging sensation on his back and rolled one shoulder forward to look.

Welts the size and position of fingernail scratches decorated his back. "Oh, bloody hell."

She peered around him for a look. "Ah, I remember that." She grinned. "Want to do it again?"

He shoved away from her hastily. "*No.* Clara, it's obvious to me that I am far too dangerous for you. I've never . . . lost control like that before."

She looked obscurely flattered. "Why, thank you, kind sir."

"Clara, you aren't paying attention. That was—so—"

She reached into the hamper beside her. "I believe the word you're looking for is *splendid.* But I'll settle for *awe-inspiring.* Cheese?"

He shook his head quickly. She'd lost him again. "You . . . liked it? No, what am I saying, it must have been terrifying for you—"

She snorted. "I'll admit you're an impressive fellow, Lord Etheridge, but let's not get too full of ourselves." She dropped the cheese back into the hamper and unwound her legs. Rising to her hands and knees, she crawled toward him with a very odd little smile on her face.

The perspective down the torn neckline of her gown was most charming. It held him immobile a moment too long, allowing her to climb up and straddle his thighs where he knelt on the carpet.

She coiled her arms about his neck and gazed into his eyes. He didn't embrace her . . . but he didn't push her away, either.

"Dalton Montmorency, I want you to listen to me very closely. I liked it. I loved it. Perhaps it was a bit too intense for a steady diet, but I wanted to find the man within and I did."

Relief wanted to spread through him, but he couldn't allow it. "The beast within, you mean," he said bitterly.

She shook her head at him. "Poor Dalton. So many walls. Heavens, it took a great deal of imagination on my part to break them down, don't you think?"

Remembering the exotic pleasure she'd given him, he flushed. His muscles began to unknot. "I've . . . always wondered what that was like."

Her brows rose. "Oh, you've heard of it before?" Consternation brought her brows down again. "I thought I invented it."

Finally relaxing, Dalton wrapped his arms about her and pulled her close. He chuckled softly into her hair. "I'll admit you're an impressive woman, Clara Simpson, but let's not get too full of ourselves."

She bit his earlobe. "No, I'd rather be full of you."

He pulled his head back. "Aren't you . . ." Damn, there was no other way to say it. "Sore?"

She tilted her head and considered. "Well, I am . . . a bit." Then she touched her fingertips to his lips. Her hazel eyes grew dark. "But you said yourself you aren't looking for forever. And if I'm going away . . . I rather thought this time was all we—"

He kissed her. Softly, each touch of his mouth a caress of her swollen lips. He didn't want to think of her gone. He didn't want to think at all. "We have until this evening, when James will come to take you away," he whispered.

Her mouth trembled against his and her arms clung more tightly for a moment. Then she pulled her head back to look at him, her smile mischievous despite the dampness in her eyes.

"That's good." She wriggled on his lap. "Because it's my turn."

Clara delighted in the gleam that appeared in his silvery eyes. When he laughed out loud, she treasured the deep sound. One short day might be all she would have. She would not spend it weeping.

There would be plenty of time for that later.

With a deft roll, he had her on her back on the floor. "You're not naked enough."

She aided him in pulling off the ruined nightgown. He posed her then, stretching her legs out straight and her arms above her head. She saw his gaze falter for a moment when he noticed the other marks he'd left upon her. She made a long arm to retrieve another grape, then threatened him with it until the darkness left his eyes.

He leaned forward to take the grape between his lips, then kissed her fingertips and put her hand back over her head. He shook one finger at her. "Don't move, remember?"

A shiver went through her. "I do believe I've created a monster," she said faintly.

He ran his palms slowly up the insides of her legs. His thumbs stopped tantalizingly short of her cleft. "Clara." He smiled down at her. "You're next."

She shivered again. Seeing it, he rose to pile more coals on the grate. Then he gathered cushions from the sofa and oddly, the picnic hamper. He returned to kneel beside her with his spoils.

"What is that for?" she asked, her voice breaking very slightly.

He put a cushion under her head and put another under her hips. She began to feel odd for the first time. He was being so methodical. . . .

"You didn't answer me." She gestured toward the basket.

He took her hand and placed it back above her head. Then he gazed down at her hungrily. "I'm going to play with my food."

That's just what he did. Strawberries became small cool tents over her nipples. Her navel held a grape. Apple slices framed her nest and he crumbled lump sugar to rain down over her entire torso.

Throughout, he would lean down to kiss her mouth, or flutter a touch over her cleft, or take a soft nibble from that sensitive place where her neck became shoulder.

By the time he finished his task, she was shivering from everything *but* the cold. She wanted to squirm, to press her thighs together, to pull him down to her—but he was implacable. He would not allow her to move.

Then he drew out the cream puffs.

"French pastry is Kurt's specialty," he said conversationally. "He comes back from every mission with another recipe or three." Then he tore the small round bun in half to squeeze out the center of sweet thickened cream.

"Oh . . . my." Clara swallowed. What was he going to do with *that*?

He licked a bit from his finger and leaned down to share a sweet taste with her. She lost herself in the kiss for a moment—until she felt his fingers, cool and slick with cream, slide deep within her. She started and gasped, her cry lost in his mouth.

After such a long period of tantalization, she was more than primed. It only required a few deep strokes of his fingers to make her shudder and writhe, her hands twining together over her head in a pantomime of binding.

His mouth never left hers as he took her orgasm in a kiss. She relaxed after a long quivering moment and opened her eyes to smile up at him. "That was lovely. I never thought—"

His fingers went deeply into her once more, stimulating her wildly from within. Caught by surprise, overwhelmed into reaction, she threw back her head and cried out as she peaked yet again.

He soothed her down once more—a kiss, a caress, a murmur of endearment. She finally lay quiescent, limp and exhausted from her twofold flight.

At that moment he began to feast on her. His mouth was everywhere, teasing, tasting, turning her skin into a sheath of pure sensation. Then he reached the apples.

Then he found the cream.

At one point he was forced to stop in order to take the pillow from under her head and place it over her face so her hoarse rising cries wouldn't reveal their hiding place.

Finally, he lay down at her side and wrapped himself around her quivering damp body while she recovered her breath for the last time. He lifted the pillow. "Are you going to be quiet now?"

She nodded weakly, so he tucked the pillow beneath both their heads and pulled her closer.

She protested. "I'm sticky . . . the sugar—"

He chuckled. "No, I think I got every bit of it. You do make a lovely breakfast."

"Hmm." She lazily reached for the basket at their feet. "Time for mine."

They lay entwined, feeding each other bits of food between kisses and confessions.

"So Monty was your name at school?" Clara could picture him, lanky and too tall for his age, distanced from the others by rank, wit, and some portion of shyness.

"I had a brief period of camaraderie with the other boys then. Liverpool scotched that when I was caught during my one and only misdeed."

"Which was?"

"Which was a most ungentlemanly visit to an upper room of a local tavern when I was fourteen. Or rather, to a handy spot in a tree just outside the window."

Her brows rose. "A spy even then, my lord?"

"It was an act with a long tradition, actually. Likely generations of schoolboys had sat outside that window, for the tree limb showed considerable wear. It is no longer there. Liverpool directed it cut off immediately and my status with the other lads dropped accordingly, I'm afraid."

"Why were you caught and not the others?"

He didn't answer for a moment. "I . . . climbed onto the window ledge and entered the room."

She laughed. "You bold fellow! Did you interrupt anything interesting?" He didn't answer, only lay silent next to her. Her smile faded as she sensed his stillness. "Dalton?"

"A rape," he said flatly. "I interrupted a rape."

He started to shift away from her. She reached to pull him back to her. "Will you tell me?"

"I'd rather not."

She touched his face, directing his gaze to meet hers. "I want to know. Please?"

He nodded. Carefully he tucked her head into the hollow of his chin. "I was so inexperienced that I didn't know what I was seeing at first. The girl was quite young. I should have known she wasn't a tavern wench. The brute pulled her into the room and threw her down . . . I couldn't see well then. So I climbed onto the ledge."

His voice faltered. "I was . . . excited. I thought I was going to see a willing couple. . . ."

Clara felt him swallow hard.

"He was pulling at her clothing. I was so diverted— I'd never seen so much as a woman's calf before, much less what he revealed of her."

Clara stroked his chest. "Young men can be distractible in that regard, I imagine."

"I was too stupid and too aroused to grasp it. And then it was almost too late. He was about to take her when she finally screamed. I was through the window in an instant . . . almost too late."

Clara said nothing. A young man's first encounter with carnality . . . and he'd witnessed a rape. Had even been stimulated by it at first, all unknowing. For a sensitive boy, the guilt must have been astounding. Hence his dread of his own darkness, his own animal drives. She was beginning to understand what she had done to him last night.

She rolled onto his chest and raised her head to meet his eyes. "Dalton, you did not rape me. Not last night, nor in the attic. You couldn't, not you. Don't you know that?"

He smiled and stroked a strand of her hair from before her eyes. "I know that now. In fact, I'm not at all sure it wasn't the other way about."

"Good." She laid her head down to listen to his heartbeat. "Why did saving that girl get you into trouble? I would have thought you'd be a hero."

"Ah. Well, it turned out that the fellow was a spoiled

young marquess—an upperclassman at school—and the heir of a duke with whom Lord Liverpool was negotiating support for some law in his favor."

"I don't think I want to hear this," Clara murmured.

"He'd stolen a young farm girl from a field and paid the innkeeper a hefty sum not to interfere. Unfortunately for him, I didn't care who his father was, or how wealthy. Blue bloods bleed just as red, after all."

She raised her head and narrowed her eyes at him. "He was older and larger, wasn't he?"

Dalton shrugged. It did lovely things to the hard muscles of his chest beneath her hands.

"He was a bully and a coward. Still, if I had not had righteous anger on my side, it might have come out differently."

"Did you make him bleed?"

"Rather."

"Good," she said fiercely. "But surely Lord Liverpool does not approve of rape?"

"No, not in theory. He simply didn't see the point of such a fuss over a common farm girl, not when so-called larger issues were at stake."

"What did he do about it?"

"He forced me to apologize to the marquess, of course."

"He *didn't*! What did you do?"

"I apologized." He chuckled darkly in memory. "Loudly and publicly. I told him that I was sorry he was so poorly endowed that no woman would have him unless forced to it."

She laughed and wrapped herself more tightly around him. He stroked her hair in silence for a moment.

"Your turn," he said. "What was the largest lie you told me?"

"Hmm. It isn't so much what I said as it was what I did. Your Widow Simpleton is not at all like me. I'm afraid I'm not fashionable at all. I never wear face paint. I rarely tighten my corset. Most of my clothing is demure and dull . . . excepting the green dress, of course."

"What green dress is this?"

"Oh, sorry. I wore that one for Nathaniel, not you."

"Who is Nathaniel?"

"Nathaniel," she said smugly, "is my beau."

"Is that so?" he growled. He rolled her over in a quick movement and covered her with his body. "Your beau?"

She grinned up at him, glad to lighten his mood with a bit of teasing. "You're jealous."

"No, only amused. Nathaniel is no threat whatsoever."

"Oh? How can you be so sure?"

"Because I made you squeak."

Her jaw dropped. "What?"

He nodded arrogantly. "Indeed. You squeaked several times. Quite loudly at that."

"I did not!"

He leaned to nuzzle her ear. "Eeeee . . . eeeeee," he teased softly.

She hit him on the shoulder. "Stop that."

He shifted himself to lie between her thighs. He was hard and swollen, pressing gently against her sensitized cleft. "Eeeeee . . ."

She hit him again, and this time when her body stirred with her blow, he slipped a fraction of himself within her. He was so thick that he parted her deeply even so. A jolt of pure sensation shot through her. She gasped and clutched at his shoulders. He raised his head to smile down at her. "Do you know who's next?"

"Who?" she asked faintly, stunned at the instant awakening of her desire.

"We are." He arched his body to kiss her as he began to press gently but inexorably into her body.

She squeaked.

Chapter Twenty-two

Pulling on his wrinkled clothing, Dalton tried not to listen to Clara bathing with the cold water in the basin. Her gasps of chilled surprise were very nearly erotic.

When she finally allowed him to turn around, he found her wrapped demurely in the stolen cloak.

"What are you wearing under that?" Her nightgown had been put to its final use as her washcloth.

"None of your business," she said primly.

"Well, don't catch a chill in that damp cloak. And don't let James get so much as a peek of you under that when he arrives. He should be here with your things soon."

"Dalton . . ."

Her tone was serious. He gave her his full attention. "Yes?"

Her chin went up. "I don't want to go."

Damn. He'd thought it had been too easy. "You must. Going into hiding until I uncover the culprit is the only way to keep you safe."

"I don't want to flee. It will only mean they win, don't you see? The men like your marquess and my father's earl—if the people who see them for what they are hide away, then who will speak out? Who will save the innocent and the gullible?"

She was so valiant and so naïve. "Who will save you when Kurt comes after you again? How can I both protect you and solve this?"

"I can help you. I'm very good at what I do, Dalton. In the months that I've been doing it, I've never once been caught."

"It only takes once," he said grimly. How was he to turn her from this? "Clara, you will leave with James this evening if I have to tie you in a sack and strap you on top of the carriage."

She gazed at him evenly. "You would force me?"

It was an unfair card for her to play and she knew it, for he could see the darkening of shame in her eyes. Damn, she was stubborn.

"If you won't flee to safety, then—" He couldn't bear it. He spoke before thinking. "I can think of another way for you to secure your future."

"What is that?"

"Wed me."

She could not help a disbelieving laugh. "I could not."

He was affronted. "Why not? As Lady Etheridge you would be nigh untouchable." He warmed to the idea even as he spoke. "It is the perfect solution. You could live far from town. I have several estates for you to choose from. That way you would pose no distraction to my work. I would care for you beautifully. You would have everything. You would have such wealth you would never need to draw again—"

She flinched. "No, not everything. I would not have you. Nor my self-respect."

"As my wife, you would have everyone's respect! I offer you my name and my fortune."

"How can you think I would accept? You offer me desert and sand, and call it paradise."

"You think my offer bears no worth?"

"Your offer is an affront. I don't want your pretty exile, Dalton." She sighed, obviously reaching for restraint. "Your sense of responsibility is commendable, but I will not sell my future for your peace of mind. I deserve more than that."

"You are impossible!"

Her gaze turned to stormy green sea. "You are entirely possible, and that is my misfortune."

He gritted his teeth. "You feel nothing for me?"

She only looked at him. "I feel a great deal for you."

He thought of this Nathaniel, for whom she had worn green. "Is there another you love better?" He clenched his fists, fighting for control over the wildness and desolation inside of him. "Tell me who! I must know who it is that I lose you to!"

She paused. "Myself."

He couldn't answer that, couldn't justify a single argument in his mind. They stood unmoving, facing each other, together yet very far apart.

A click resounded in the silent room and a panel in the wall opened. Clara blinked. For the first time she noticed that the room had no obvious door. She'd been imprisoned all night and never been aware.

James poked his head through the opening, eyes tightly shut. "Are we all quite decent?"

"We are," Dalton said tightly. "It remains to be seen about you."

"Ah." James swung Clara's case into the room, careful not to make a thump on the floor. He then passed through the opening carrying a thick folio and another hamper.

"Here are your things, Mrs. Simpson. Agatha told me to tell you that she sewed your notes into a false bottom. It wouldn't pass a real search, but it'll keep them from the light-fingered."

He handed her a stiff card, printed with two passages on a ship leaving that night for Scotland. "This is for us. I thought we'd travel as brother and sister."

She carefully put it down on the desk. "Thank you."

James dropped his heavy file next to the ticket and pulled out a sheet of paper. "Dalton, I think you'd better see this."

Dalton reached for it, but James shot Clara a glance. "Outside."

Clara waved them on. "Go. I need my privacy for dressing anyway."

Dalton gazed at her for a moment, then followed James through an entirely different panel in the wall. Clara blinked. What a maze of secrets this place was.

After she was sure they were gone, she shed her damp wool cloak and pulled clean clothing from her case. She was just tying the waistband on a fresh set of knickers when she accidentally knocked James's file to the floor.

Sir Thorogood's cartoons flew in a scattered swath onto the rug. Sighing, Clara knelt to pick them up. The last thing she wanted at this moment was to be reminded of what she'd already lost.

As she gathered them up, she absently named off the faces she'd drawn. Mosely . . . Wadsworth . . . Nathaniel . . .

She stopped. *Nathaniel?* She'd never lampooned Nathaniel. Flipping back through the stack in her hand, she pulled out the drawing. Then she laughed.

The sheet was upside down. At this angle it only *looked* like Nathaniel. Shaking her head, she turned the Fleur cartoon upright to sort it into a neat stack with the others.

The face did not change. She held it closer. The jaw . . . the brow . . .

Clara had only seen this mysterious character once, during one of Wadsworth's meetings. The three men had bored her silly by arguing over some woman. She'd avenged her boredom with a scathing drawing that had made quite a splash when published ten or twelve days ago—

The same time Dalton had been ordered to find her.

She sat back on her heels, thinking furiously. Someone wanted her found. Someone wanted her dead. Could it be Nathaniel?

In her mind she saw that brief flash of intensity in his eyes when he'd watched her draw.

He'd known. Right there in the park he'd known. Heavens, she'd even presented him with the evidence herself!

And then he'd pursued her. Calling on her, gifts, extending invitations . . . as if a man like that would be seriously interested in her.

Dalton is. The obnoxious little voice was back. *He wants to marry you.*

"No," Clara muttered. "He wants to bind me up in cotton wool and *preserve* me, like a boy collecting a butterfly."

But what could Nathaniel want, other than to lure her out where he could stop her pen forever?

She placed the drawing on top of the others and finished dressing quickly. As she dug through the case for a warm gown, she pulled out her servant's dress. She held the simple muslin in her hands for a long moment.

Nathaniel was dining with his cousin tonight. He'd be out for hours. She could investigate—find out for certain before accusing the man to this half-mad spy guild.

She impulsively pulled the garment over her head. She needed out and away from Dalton at the moment, and this would help him in his goal as well. Not to mention, it was certainly an improvement on being shipped off like an embarrassing relation.

Clothed and shod, she pulled on her own thankfully dry cloak and moved to the first panel in the wall, the one that James had come through. She pressed on a bit of carving the way she'd seen James do to the other on his way out and the narrow door popped open.

She'd made her way out of the attic study. Now how was she going to get out of the club?

Miss Kitty Trapp threw herself down belly first across her mattress and glared at her sister's tidy bed across the room. Bitty was already petitioning their parents to move into Aunt Clara's room—which was larger and had a lovely big window—even though poor Aunt Clara had only been gone for two days.

Her sister would likely get the room too, for Mama and Papa were still angry that she hadn't told them immediately when Aunt Clara left.

They'd let that tall man into the house and called him "my lord," but darling Lord Reardon hadn't been allowed to so much as put a toe over the threshold when he'd come calling yesterday afternoon. Kitty didn't think that Papa really believed all that talk about treason, but still he'd canceled all outings and callers until he could decide what to do about it.

So here she was, banished to her room when she could be sitting in the parlor with the handsomest man on the face of the earth.

Kitty sat up and moved to the dressing table she shared with Bitty. Turning her chin this way and that, she wondered if Lord Reardon liked blondes. She fancied her hair was ever so slightly shinier than Bitty's, for she brushed it one hundred times every night, while Bitty sometimes skimped.

Other than her hair, what had she to compete with Aunt Clara? Her aunt was very smart and talented, but her figure was only adequate, while Bitty's and Kitty's threatened to be nearly as rounded as Mama's . . .

Kitty sighed. There was no point in deluding herself. Lord Reardon had never so much as glanced her way when Aunt Clara was in the room.

Bored, she wandered to the little desk and sat down to finish tracing the cartoons that Bitty had claimed first. Bitty always claimed things first, just because she had been born a few short minutes earlier than Kitty . . .

As she began to trace a very scandalous drawing that she was sure Mama would confiscate if she ever saw, Kitty wished she had thought to ask Aunt Clara to draw Lord Reardon for her. He was so divine, with his noble brow and his perfect jaw and lips that quite frankly fascinated one—

Kitty frowned down at the paper before her. Her tracing of one of the faces in the cartoon looked very much like Lord Reardon. Hmm. If she filled in here and drew this line a bit longer—there! She had her own portrait of his lordship and she'd done it herself.

With the help of the cartoon, of course. Silly, though.

Lord Reardon couldn't possibly have anything to do with a cheap hussy like this Fleur person. Mistresses went for those rich men who didn't have wives and whose titles made them so important that they didn't care what anyone thought and . . .

Men exactly like his lordship. Kitty's lip trembled as she looked at the drawing of *her* Lord Reardon—a lewd, immoral, awful *womanizer*!

Tears welled up in her eyes as she contemplated her betrayed love. Deceived by a scoundrel, a blackguard! Well, he wouldn't get away with this! Hiding his face behind that fat hussy's rear wouldn't keep him safe when Beatrice Trapp got through with him. Mama knew everyone who was anyone. She'd fix that worthless rake!

"Maa-maa!"

Dalton stood very still in the secret office, hating himself. She was gone. Gone into the night and the rain without leaving a clue. He had lost his maddening, magnificent Clara. He should not have left her. He should have stayed by her side until he could see her to permanent safety.

Dalton stared down at his desk where lay the one sodden slipper he'd found on the floor this morning. He gently laid his hand over it. His palm and fingers outstretched the small silken object by a good inch.

He'd lost her. His fingers slowly curled into a fist, crumpling the soft slipper until a puddle formed on the desk beneath his fist.

James stood silently watching him. The stolen cloak lay over one arm of the chair, wrinkled from its stay on the floor of the office and its turn beneath their tangled bodies.

Clara. Dalton knew that he must stay in control, must quell the wildness in him that was part panic and part rage. His hands clenched more tightly, desperate to wrap themselves around the throat of whoever was threatening Clara.

James cleared his throat. "Just tell me where to start, Dalton. You know I'll help."

"If I knew where to start, I would be there now," Dalton whispered.

James laid his hand on Dalton's shoulder. "Then we must think. She must have left on her own. Who could have known she was in the club?"

"Agatha and Simon. You and I." He'd been so bloody careful. "And whoever has been reading my files." He'd been so bloody *stupid* not to see the hole in their plan. The rogue player knew too much, and knew it as soon as Dalton did. He'd thought Feebles the leak, or even Stubbs.

It hadn't once occurred to him that his secret office had been compromised. James had found the kill order right in the Liars' files downstairs, phrased in the usual euphemistic way. "Mrs. Clara Simpson is to be accorded the greatest of courtesies" meant the honor of meeting Kurt's knife in a dark room.

What's more, the order had finished with Dalton's name, signed in his own handwriting.

Someone knew everything about him, and the club, and very likely Clara. Now she was out there, foolishly running from the very people who could keep her safe.

He shouldn't have pushed about her leaving. He certainly shouldn't have proposed! God, what had he been thinking? She didn't need him, with all the complications in his life. Her own was entirely too problematical as it was.

He rubbed his face. "If only someone on the street had seen something. Then I would know if she'd been kidnapped, or fled, or . . ."

"Or disloyal?" James's tone was reproachful. "Dalton, you can't possibly still believe that."

Dalton did believe in Clara. How could he not, after the last tempestuous twenty-four hours? "The important thing is to recover her."

But recover her how? He still didn't know who had ordered him on the case, or who had ordered the kill. Damn, but he was sick of fighting blind! He felt like a puppet who couldn't see his own strings. Or the ground below his feet. Or the sky above.

Who was pulling those strings and why?

He unclenched his fists and rubbed the back of his neck. "Until we find who took Clara, we have nothing."

And there was nowhere to begin.

Things were going well until Clara tried to get into Lord Reardon's house.

She had managed to work her way quietly out of the club by peeking around corners and had finally followed a whistling young man who was obviously carrying out the rubbish. She'd ended up in the alley behind the building, probably the very one she'd walked through the night before.

Getting to Lord Reardon's exclusive square had required a good bit of walking, but it was still fairly early. She didn't think he'd be done with his visit to Cora Teagarden yet. A servant scurrying on his way had pointed out his lordship's house and Clara had entered the rear delivery gate without causing any suspicion.

The house was quiet, with only a few rooms lighted

that she could see. Of course, the house was very large and grand and extended all the way to the street. It was twice as wide as the Trapps' house and likely three times as deep. As she took stock of the situation from her hiding place behind a box hedge she was stumped.

She couldn't pose as one of Reardon's servants without considerable cooperation, which she didn't think forthcoming. She certainly couldn't climb the wall and enter through the attic the way Dalton had. The parlor-level windows to the garden stood rather high for her to climb into, but it seemed she had no choice. Eyeing them carefully in the dimness, she thought she saw a slightly wider dark line between the two swinging panes of one window. Well, it was as good a place to begin as any, she supposed.

She made her way to crouch at the foundation of the house but there she hesitated. Something was different and it was not simply the fact that she was quite literally breaking in. There was something different within her.

Although she was resolute, she was without her former assurance, that blithe confidence of one who has never been tried. "Well, Dalton," she whispered. "You'll be glad to know that I no longer believe in my own immortality."

Breathing deeply to steady her nerves, Clara began to climb the wall, pressing her fingertips and shod toes into the even breaks between the great rectangular stones. The window was just above her head, so she needn't climb too far—

With a very unladylike grunt, she managed to slap one palm onto the stone sill of the window, then the other. Using every muscle in her body, she pulled herself chest-high to the window and balanced herself on her elbows, toes precariously wedged between the stones.

She hadn't climbed anything since childhood, and even then only the rare conveniently branched tree. Clara took a moment to inhale a congratulatory breath and to inspect the unlatching possibilities of the window.

It was latched, but poorly. Clara leaned her torso on the biting stone edge of the sill and inserted her fingertips into the gap. She pulled steadily. The window remained latched. She pulled harder, almost groaning in frustration.

The window sprang open. Clara jerked her head back to avoid being struck in the face—and overbalanced. As she felt herself slip, her heart stopped and she went back to that dreadful moment on the roof, but there was no one to catch her now—

She landed hard on her rear on the soft lawn beneath the window. Stunned for a moment at the brevity of her fall, she sat unmoving. Then she chuckled at herself. No one to catch her? How overly dramatic. "Let's not be too hasty with the symbolism, shall we?" she muttered as she rose from the grass. Her rear throbbed and she'd bitten her tongue, but she looked up at the open window in triumph and began the slow climb upward again.

A few moments later she threw one leg over the sill, then the other, and then let herself slide to the delightfully firm floor. Dalton could keep the climbing, she decided. She was going to leave by the door if she could manage it.

She shut the window but left it unlatched, just in case. Then she turned, dusting her hands. There, safely in.

Abruptly Clara had never felt more unsafe in her life. She was in the grandest house she had ever seen. Even in the darkness she could see the gleam of real gold on the plaster walls and hear the chime of the chandelier crystals as they moved in the breeze she had allowed into the room. Nathaniel's place in Society was made clear by the very beauty and luxury of his home.

She did not belong here. Reprisal for being found in this place illegally would be swift and certain.

Then again, Mr. Wadsworth would have been rather unhappy with her as well. She shrugged away her intimidation and stepped quietly through what looked like a small music room.

There were several parlors in a row, each grander than the last. She smiled as she imagined the butler sorting guests by status into their respective rooms. She wondered into which one she would have been placed had she come calling?

The house was empty enough—it nearly echoed—so the servants were likely gathered in the kitchen enjoying an evening off from his lordship's demands.

The next room was the one she had been looking for. The study. And yes, there was the handy candle in its stick next to the door. She had to stir the coals vigorously to find a live one, but then she had her light.

Quietly she circled the room. There was little to see other than good paintings and lovely subtle wallpaper of a green-on-green pattern.

What was it about men that all studies looked the same? Same big desk—size dependent on the importance of the man, of course—same blotter, same oversize chair before the fire, same shelves of the same books, same paintings behind the desk covering the—

The safe. Oswald kept his safebox covered by a painting behind his desk, as did Wadsworth. Clara quickly stepped around the desk to haul the large painting to one side.

Behind it was the largest safe box she had ever seen. She dipped to reach beneath the hem of her skirts.

Tucked tightly in her garter were her own homemade picks. She hurried to the safe box, levering the heavy painting out of the way with one shoulder. The lock resisted her every effort, until she was cursing most obscenely under her breath. This might require more than a hatpin and a scissor blade.

Then she remembered the trick she'd discovered in Oswald's study. Perhaps if she thought of Dalton in some improper way, she'd be able to manage the lock.

"Lord Etheridge," she swore in a whisper. "I vow if my very life did not depend upon this, I would never think of you this way again as long as I live." She rubbed her forehead on her upraised wrist, as if to rub the thoughts from her mind.

Then she let herself dream. Nay, not dream . . . remember. She remembered his large hands on her skin, the way his heat had jumped to her as if by a live spark, to ignite her own increasing need.

She remembered the way her heart had opened for him, and the way her body had softened for him. She remembered the way she'd taken his breath into her own lungs as they'd mated like beasts on the floor. The way she'd clung onto his shoulders as he'd lunged within her and the way his muscles had rippled under her hands.

She remembered how deeply she had fallen for his dark and lonely soul. How she missed his rumbling voice, and the way he'd seemed to see right into her, the real woman, not the lady, not the maid, but her secret heart.

And she remembered how it would never be again. . . .

By the time the lock went *snick*, Clara's face was wet with tears.

She wiped them away, pulled a number of files from the safe and began to read, sitting in a small circle of light in the large darkened study.

Chapter Twenty-three

"I've got it!"

James's jubilant voice rang through Dalton's office, startling Dalton from his thoughts.

Dalton had been reading a message from Liverpool that James had brought with him. It had been very clear. He'd been ordered to drop the entire mission and any inquiry into Thorogood's location.

There was no turmoil, no conflict within him at the notice. He knew precisely where his duty lay.

With England, as always. The fact that serving Clara and England was one and the same at the moment didn't signify.

Still, the message made him question everything he'd ever understood about his mentor. Dalton looked down at his clenched hands. Gone were the days of the steepled fingers and cool consideration. All he seemed to have now was rage and fists.

James's shout interrupted his circling thoughts. He jumped to his feet to look down where James had spread out the collected drawings of Sir Thorogood on the floor.

James was waving a scrap of paper far too quickly

for Dalton to discern the drawing itself. He reached out and snaked one hand around James's wrist. Dalton brought the drawing, wrist and all, closer to the light.

The cartoon was one that Dalton recalled had caused quite a furor. It was more risqué than usual, with a half-dressed female figure dominating the scene in more ways than one.

" 'Fleur and Her Followers,' " read Dalton. He scanned the entire drawing, but could see nothing more than a few wealthy fellows who were likely to get in trouble with their wives. "Why this one?"

"I told you that I spent some time investigating everyone who appeared in the drawings, didn't I?" At Dalton's nod, James continued. "Well, this is the only drawing that contained any mystery at all. See this fellow right here?"

James pointed out the man behind Fleur. His face was partially hidden by the opera dancer's rounded buttock. Dalton turned James's wrist sideways to get a different angle on the fellow. "Who is he?"

James plucked the drawing from his captured hand with his other, then handed it to Dalton to hold himself. "I was never able to learn his identity. Likely Clara herself didn't know, or she would have drawn him in more detail."

Dalton frowned. "That's a bit thin, James. Why didn't you simply find this Fleur and ask her?"

James snapped his fingers. "Because *there* is the mystery! There is no Fleur."

"Could it be a stage name?"

James shook his head. "We couldn't find her. We even had Button ask around, and if Button doesn't know someone in Covent Garden or Drury Lane, they don't exist. No one has ever seen her or heard her name before this came out in the newspaper, although there are now a number of girls who call themselves Fleur after the popularity of the cartoon."

That was indeed mysterious. Dalton examined the drawing once more. "Well, we know who these two are."

"Yes. Sir Foster, a courtier and generally useless hanger-on, and Mr. Wadsworth, that manufacturer of muskets whom you've been investigating."

Dalton rubbed his chin. "I had thought I'd found indications of blackmail in his safe but discounted it. The man is richer than Midas. Wadsworth makes a large portion of the arms for the British troops."

"One would consider him a loyal citizen, then."

Dalton grunted. "And Foster is a friend of the Prince Regent, or at least he was in the past. I don't think he's been in favor for some time, come to think of it."

"I think we should call upon Sir Foster, Dalton. It would only be the sociable thing to do, since we've a friend in common. He has a house not far from the palace."

Dalton turned to gaze at James in surprise. James flushed. "I haven't had anything better to do during the past few weeks."

Dalton raised a brow. "Have you considered becoming an analyst, James? The Liars could use just that sort of information breakdown."

James looked horrified. "A *desk* job? God forbid!" He looked at Dalton pleadingly. "Sir, I'm a saboteur, not a numbers man!"

Dalton cut him off with a sharp gesture. "Later. We have two suspects to speak to."

Clara had sorted through the files that seemed to pertain to Nathaniel's holdings and set those aside. Some were obviously to do with laws and other items currently before the House of Lords. She was curious about what went on in that exclusively male chamber, but forced herself to set those aside as well. She could study politics in her own time.

That left her with a most remarkable stack of dossiers. She didn't know all of the names, but it didn't take her long to realize what she had in her hands.

James Cunnington, Simon Raines, Kurt (no surname), and most interesting to her, Dalton Montmorency, Lord Etheridge.

This was going to be fascinating. She set the candle closer and bent to read.

Nathaniel knew everything about Dalton's club. He knew of the entrance from the back alley, he knew of the secret office, he knew of the—what was that word? Cryptography room? Heavens, what went on in *there*? One hoped it had nothing to do with crypts.

Clara had suspected Nathaniel of some involvement, but this was nothing less than full-scale espionage! Dalton needed to know about this immediately.

She gathered the files and reordered them as best she could. Somehow she thought Nathaniel might keep track of that. Placing them back into the safe the way she had found them, she carefully shut it and inserted her picks to trip the lock once more.

She heard a sound behind her, a faint click. She stilled, listening. She'd just decided that it had been nothing but a structural creak when she heard the slow scrape of wood sliding on wood.

Whirling, she fisted her hands around her picks. "Who's there?"

A man stood in the shadows. Only the faintest glow

of the candle reached him, enough to show her that he was well dressed and quite tall.

Scream! But the long habit of silence supported her in this instance. She was not supposed to be here, after all.

The man pulled a pistol from his coat and aimed it at her heart. "I presume you have a likely explanation for your presence here?"

The breath left her in a nearly hysterical *whoosh*. "What a ridiculous question. It's night, I don't work here, and I'm standing in the study. I'm obviously trying to open the safe." She was surprised at herself. When had she attained such composure, staring down a gun and giving saucy replies?

Especially when this particular view of a pistol made her spine dissolve with fear. Odd how the black hole in the barrel seemed to take up the entire room. She could hardly breathe as she realized that one twitch of a finger and her life would end.

The man moved one step forward. "Perhaps."

The light fell somewhat brighter on his face, and Clara recognized that line of jaw, that cheekbone, that high brow.

"I know you," she breathed.

"Of course you do." He stepped fully into the light. Clara's heart nearly shuddered to a stop. Lord Reardon. *Nathaniel.*

"Well, this is a surprise. What can I do for you, my lord?"

"I'm sorry to inconvenience you, Mrs. Simpson—"

The formality struck her as still more ridiculous in her panic. "Oh, please call me Clara," she blurted, her hysteria rising.

That surprised a smile from him and her pulse skipped a beat. Even while standing behind a weapon, he was breathtaking. She shook her head. "A face like an angel. It's truly too bad that you intend to kill me, for I should very much like to draw you again."

He stepped closer and carefully returned the painting to the proper position. "I'm not going to kill you, Clara. But I have been wanting to speak to you privately. Won't you sit?" He indicated the small settee with a courteous wave of his hand.

Her knees were not cooperating. "I don't mean to be difficult, but I'm far too terrified to move a muscle."

Again that archangel smile. "You certainly don't look it. In fact, you look surpassingly angry but not frightened at all."

An interesting statement that she must consider more fully at another time. "Nonetheless, I shan't be walking anywhere while a gun is pointed at me. I simply cannot."

He looked from her to the pistol and sighed. "Clara, I don't want to hold this pistol on you. I simply need you to talk with me without raising a row. If I put this away, do you think you will be able to oblige?"

"You're asking a great deal of me, my lord."

"Oh, bloody hell." He shoved the pistol into his waist-coat and swept her into his arms, carried her to the settee and deposited her on it. "There. Dilemma resolved."

I've been captured. And she'd done it all herself. There was no possible way for Dalton to know where she'd gone.

Every time Clara's captor turned her way in his pacing, she sat very still, her eyes on the carpet at her feet. Every time he turned away, she cast her eyes desperately about the room looking for something, *anything,* to help her from this pickle.

It was a lovely study, a manly woodsy room, without a single dratted weapon in sight. Not a vase, not a figurine, not a single candlestick graced the mantel.

Nathaniel called for tea, but despite his claim that he wanted to speak to her, he didn't say a word for a very long time.

His butler hadn't turned a hair, but only brought tea and biscuits, then removed himself by backing through the double doors and closing them.

"I must say I feel quite the dunce for not dressing for the occasion. Tea with his lordship," she muttered, her anxiety forcing her to break the silence, although not enough to beg for her freedom.

Nathaniel turned and gazed at her for a moment, then shook his head. "You look angry again. From that, I gather that you are very frightened."

"Aren't you the clever one?"

He paced before her once more. "Your safety may depend upon your cooperation. Are you willing to talk to me?"

"I have no idea what to talk about."

He stopped and turned toward her. "How did you learn about Fleur?"

"Fleur?" Cold fear had her muscles tensing beyond tolerance, causing her to tremble. *Fleur.* For some reason, that one cartoon had begun this chain of events. She'd been hunted, attacked, and now captured.

Living until tomorrow did not seem terribly likely.

Lord Reardon knelt before her, staring into her face with green-eyed intensity. "Tell me. Who told you about Fleur? Was it your brother-in-law?"

Clara hesitated. He was obviously trying to follow the trail back to the person he thought had betrayed him.

She could not let Oswald take the blame for her own foolishness.

She shook her head. "No one. I was there with you, at Wadsworth's. Listening from a hiding place. I entered through the connecting attic from the house where I live."

He rubbed his face, then regarded her soberly. "You've been watching Wadsworth. So you know a great deal, I imagine. That is not good, Clara. Not good at all."

"Oh, I don't know so very much," she blurted. "Not much at all."

"You must tell me everything you know about Fleur." His voice was all the more terrifying for its calm, even tone. "Your life rides on your answer, Clara."

"I don't know Fleur, I never met Fleur, I wouldn't recognize Fleur if I saw her on the street!"

Nathaniel stared at her. "Her?"

"Isn't that who you are asking me about? Fleur, the opera dancer or mistress or whatever she is?"

His mouth dropped open. "She?" The smile returned, stretching across his face until he looked like a blissful Greek statue. "You believe Fleur is a woman?"

He rose, then took one step back to sit in the chair across from her. He laughed. It was a deep-chested guffaw of unadulterated relief.

Clara told herself that affronted pride was a low priority at this moment, when she might be dead before morning. Still, she squirmed as he laughed on.

And on.

And bloody on. "So happy to divert you, my lord," she snarled.

Nathaniel sighed gustily as he wiped his eyes. "Oh, Clara, you are a delight."

"Please don't stop on my account," she growled.

"My apologies. But you have no idea how you had us worried. How fortunate that you took us literally. We thought the cartoon was allegory."

"We?"

He fixed her with a fond gaze that was belied by the steel in his voice. "Do not inquire further, my dear. It truly would not be healthy."

Fear tingled through her and she realized that she had almost begun to believe his vow that he would not hurt her. "Is that why you've been trying to kill Dalton, and then me? Because you thought Sir Thorogood knew too much about Fleur?"

"Clara, you don't want to know any more." Shaking his head, Nathaniel leaned forward to take her hand. "My God, you're like ice! Here, move closer to the fire. I'll ring for some more tea."

He urged her to the best chair and arranged a soft rug over her lap. She watched him, confused. "Well, I suppose you wouldn't bother to coddle me if you still planned on killing me."

"I've told you. I have no intention of killing you."

"Well, someone sent Kurt after me," she grumbled as she reached her hands toward the coals.

The next moment, she was standing with Nathaniel's hands hard on her shoulders. *"Kurt?"* His face was granite, all angelic resemblance gone.

Clara felt her stomach lurch. "Y-yes, Kurt. That's what Dalton called him. He said there must be a k-kill order." She couldn't help it. A tear began to trace its way down her cheek. She'd had a very long night . . . or was it two? And for the first time, the words *kill order* seemed distressingly real.

Nathaniel's face softened at her fear. He pulled her

close, wrapping his arms tightly about her. "Shh. Don't cry now, Clara, not after all your bravery. I didn't mean to startle you."

Confusion writhed within her. He was embracing her? *Comforting her?* Was this some diabolical gesture to earn her trust? Because despite herself, she *was* comforted.

A bit.

"I cannot return you now and I cannot keep you here," he murmured in her ear. "I must send for someone who will know what to do." With that, he turned and left the study and shut the doors once more. This time she heard a distinct click as he locked her safely inside.

Clara looked down at the small scissor blade she still clasped tightly in her palm. He hadn't noticed it. She tucked it quickly into her waist as the door opened once more. She looked up at Nathaniel pensively.

"I simply cannot determine which side you are on," she told him. "You know so much about Wadsworth and the others. You know so much about Dalton Montmorency and the Liar's club. And you know more about me than I do."

She tucked back a strand of wayward hair and contemplated him. "Why do you need to know so much?"

Lord Reardon cast a glance at his now-covered safe box. "I was too late, I see. You should not have done that, Clara."

Clara folded her arms. "Do you know what, my lord? I am becoming rather weary of being told what not to do. And I am definitely becoming weary of all this secrecy. If you are on the side of good, then what have you to hide?"

He cocked one eyebrow at her. "Do you truly need to ask that, Sir Thorogood?"

Clara inhaled quickly. "Ah." He did have a point, drat him.

Lord Reardon stood. "I'd thought to take you to my superior, but now that Liverpool—"

His superior? Connections fell into place in Clara's mind, snapping together like links in a chain. She leaned her head back to stare into his face. "You work for Liverpool, too, just like the Liars! And Fleur—Fleur isn't a woman, it's a plot!" She stumbled to her feet and backed away from him.

"Clara, wait—" He stepped forward to catch at her hands.

She pushed at him, hard. "You *are* against me! Let me go!"

Surprised, he released her immediately. She scuttled backward, stumbling over the sodden trailing hem of her dress.

"You and Liverpool! And Wadsworth! There is a plot against the Crown, and Liverpool is behind it! I've heard he was ruthless and power-hungry . . . but to plot against the Prince and King!" She gathered up her skirts and made a break for the door. She was through it and down the hall before Nathaniel could grab her.

The front door was locked, but the key stood out from the hole. In her haste she turned it the wrong way at first, then reversed it. The lock clicked and she tugged at the handle, but the door did not move.

Looking up, she saw a wide palm pressed against it above her head. She whirled and flattened herself against the wood, staring at Nathaniel not ten inches from her.

He gazed down at her. "Clara, you must believe me. We take no part in a plot against the Crown. Liverpool is as loyal as they come, as am I."

"Loyal to whom? Napoleon?" She aimed a kick at his

shin, but only succeeded in bruising her toes. The pain made her all the angrier. "You're mad, that's what you are! I've gone from one madman to another for days and I've had enough. Enough, I tell you! Let me go this instant, or I'll—I'll eviscerate you in my cartoon!"

"Clara, you must listen to me. You're truly in danger. You have no idea how much. There is no authority that you can run to now to save you, not a soul in England who can defend you." He reached one hand to push back a lock of hair from her face. "No one but me."

Foster was not at home. Dalton and James couldn't so much as gain entry. His house stood empty in the midst of an ostentatiously fashionable neighborhood. There was no one at all in residence but a man raking up the debris from last night's storm.

"No, milord. Sir Foster done left days ago. Told 'is lady to pack for a long ocean voyage and warmer climes, 'e did. They put a man to sellin' what was left so I don't expect they'll be back."

The old groundskeeper nodded constantly as he spoke, rather in the manner of a bored horse. Dalton tossed the fellow a coin and left with James.

"He must have left soon after the drawing came out," James said.

"I agree. I think we've found Sir Thorogood's offense. However, Foster couldn't have had anything to do with the attempts on my life or Clara's disappearance."

"There are two other men in the picture."

Dalton nodded. "I wish she'd seen the third fellow better. Only a quarter of his face is showing, as if she only saw what might show under the hood of a cloak."

James pulled the rolled drawing from his breast

pocket and examined the third man. "I can't stop feeling as though I know this bloke. She didn't give much detail yet he still seems familiar somehow, even only with a few strokes."

"I know. She's really quite amazing, isn't she?"

James flicked him a look. "Pure genius, but is that really the point right now?"

"Wadsworth."

"Yes."

"We're on our way."

Chapter Twenty-four

They made good time through the city streets. The evening traffic was heavy as usual, but Dalton paid his driver well to see them at Wadsworth's door within the hour.

Before they knocked, Dalton put one hand on James's shoulder to halt him. "Tell me, James, if a man made his pounds from the sale of muskets, would he be in any hurry to end the war?"

James tipped a brow. "Would he be in any hurry to prolong it, do you think?"

"Depends on the man, doesn't it?" Dalton had a very bad feeling about this. "From what I know about Wadsworth, he's a hard man—all business. Keep your eyes open and your pockets buttoned."

"My thoughts precisely."

Clara had been gone for too long now. She could be out of the city—hell, she could be in some ship's slimy hold on her way to France!

Fear for her churned inside him like too many fish in a pail. Ruthlessly he tamped it down. Later. He would deal with that later.

Finally Wadsworth's butler answered the door. Dalton presented his card and he and James were shown to a richly appointed drawing room. By the time the polite amenities were observed and the butler withdrew, Dalton was fairly burning with the need to tear through the house calling Clara's name.

"Well, this would make a lovely prison," observed James idly, cocking his head and examining the richly painted ceiling. Then he looked at Dalton. "Oh—sorry."

The door opened and a stout gentleman in his fifties entered. He was tastefully dressed, if a bit formally for this time of day. Intelligent black eyes glittered from the round folds of his face as he steepled his hands before him and affected a bow to them both.

"It is my pleasure to have you in my home, Lord Etheridge, and . . ." He raised a brow at James, obviously expecting an introduction. Dalton didn't bother.

"Mr. Wadsworth, we are here to inquire into your involvement with Fleur."

If Dalton had been expecting surprise and consternation from Wadsworth, he was disappointed. The man only nodded serenely and gestured to the lush chairs pulled close to the fire. "Of course you are. I've been expecting you for over a week."

Dalton and James exchanged a glance but took the seats indicated. Wadsworth remained standing with one arm draped on the mantel and one hand tucked into his waistcoat pocket. Since Dalton had virtually invented the commanding fireplace pose, he was not impressed. James had seen it a few too many times as well, for he only leaned comfortably back in his chair and pondered the ceiling once more.

After a long moment of silence, Wadsworth gave up the ploy. "Ah, well. One never knows when that will work." He took the chair nearest the grate and gave Dalton an inquiring glance.

Dalton only returned the man's gaze. He was here under false pretenses, having absolutely nothing to go on but the clue in the cartoon. He didn't want Wadsworth to know that, however.

Wadsworth smiled. The man was as experienced a manipulator as Dalton himself. With a nod, he conceded the point. "I gather you've learned of my youthful association with the Knights of the Lily, then?"

Dalton nodded sagely but his mind was racing. Knights of the Lily? What the bloody hell was that? Some sort of gentleman's club? A religious sect?

When Dalton didn't respond further, Wadsworth blinked. "Well, you can imagine my surprise when Sir Thorogood associated me with Fleur after all these years. I haven't a clue where the fellow got that idea." He continued to gaze at them serenely. "It's been years since I've had anything to do with that lot. It was just boyish play, you understand. Nothing serious. When certain authorities became aware of our little game, we were encouraged to disband."

The first sign of disquiet crossed Wadsworth's face. "Some of us more rigorously than others." Then his untroubled mien returned. "That all happened long ago. I'd forgotten all about it until that silly cartoon brought it all back."

Dalton glanced at James. James, after reading the look he'd been given, took up the supportive role. "I suppose it was simply chance that you met some of them here at your house, then."

Wadsworth's eyes shifted but he remained perfectly relaxed. Amazing. This fellow was as cold as January in the Yorkshire Dales.

The arms merchant smiled. "You're fishing. You won't like what you'll find, you know. By whose authority are you here, by the way?"

"We are on a mission for the Prime Minister," offered Dalton. After all, his association with Liverpool was rather well known.

"Ah." Wadsworth smiled. "Lord Liverpool has no idea you are here, I imagine."

Since that was precisely the case, Dalton had to wonder at this. What was going on that he didn't know about? Why was he being kept in the dark?

Wadsworth stood and crossed to the bell pull. He rang for his butler and requested a carriage be brought round immediately. "Fetch my hat and stick." Then he turned to James and Dalton. "Let's go and see him, shall we?"

Dalton held up one hand. "I am happy to accompany you, sir, but perhaps you would be good enough to satisfy my curiosity on one point before we go."

Wadsworth nodded warily. "Of course, my lord."

"Why have you been trying to kill me?"

It was a shot in the dark, based on gut instinct and wishful thinking. It hit center target with a *twang*. Wadsworth stiffened, his face darkening.

Dalton continued, pushing the man. "You thought I truly was Sir Thorogood, didn't you? You sent the footpads after me twice, and I think you may have had something to do with a certain ale wagon as well."

Wadsworth was silent, but it was a sullen burning silence this time, all serenity gone. He made a sharp gesture with one hand. Suddenly Dalton felt the cold steel of a pistol barrel pressing to the back of his neck.

"James!" He was too late. James stood with his chin raised at an odd angle prompted by the glint of knife steel held at his throat by another flunky.

Wadsworth made an effort to return his expression to that of kindly uncle and stepped closer to Dalton. "I shouldn't recommend that you put up a struggle, my lord. Bligh has missed you thrice before. His reputation is now at stake, and he'd very much like to repair it." Wadsworth's tone turned richly smug. "Wouldn't you, Bligh?"

The man behind Dalton answered, "Indeed, sir." The chuckle was accompanied by a gale of the foulest exhalation Dalton had ever had the pleasure of holding his breath against.

The man deserved to die for that act of pollution alone. The pistol was jammed hard under Dalton's ear. "The master wants you in the carriage, Your 'Ighness. Get your rocks movin'."

James cast Dalton a questioning look from the corner of his eye, but Dalton shook his head slightly. Being taken at the point of a pistol wasn't his preferred method of gaining information, but it was an effective one. It was surprising what people would reveal when they thought their audience wouldn't see another sunrise.

He and James were being kidnapped, perhaps the same as Clara had been kidnapped. Dalton fought down the image of her probable terror that rose in his mind. He needed to keep his head clear. If he and James were fortunate, they would be taken to the same place that held Clara. Then they must all escape together.

From some unknown place, from unknown number of guards, with Clara in unknown condition.

Again, not his favorite method.

Wadsworth donned his hat and hefted his jaunty walking stick. Dalton and James were shoved into the carriage like a duo of recalcitrant pigs going to market. James looked distinctly concerned at their predicament, but all Dalton could think about was that he was finally on his way to Clara.

Nathaniel took Clara's hand and towed her unwillingly back to the parlor. She resisted. He looked back at her and laughed, shaking his head. "My dear, you look like a reluctant child."

"I hardly care—what you think," she puffed, pulling and twisting her hand within his. "Better to look foolish than to look dead."

He made an exasperated sound, then swept her into his arms again. She wriggled, but he calmly toted her down the hall. "I've decided that this is simply the best way to transport you. A dreadful liberty, I know. Still, I rather like it."

He stopped in front of the fire. "If I sit you down, will you stay?"

She only struggled harder. That turned out to be a mistake, for he only shrugged, lifting her as easily as he did his shoulders. "So be it."

He sat in the chair and plopped her across his lap, still holding her nearly immobile with easy implacability. "I want to try to make you understand, Clara. You may even find that you want to help me."

She tilted her head back to give him a disbelieving glare. "I will not! How can you possibly expect me to—"

He kissed her, a quick soft press of his lips on hers that left her startled to the bone.

"Clara, I am a gentleman, but even gentlemen have their limits. I am in a deserted house with a pretty woman on my lap and nothing better to do. If you don't want my mind to wander further in this improper direction, I suggest you stop wriggling your bottom against me."

She froze. "No wriggling. See? Not a bit."

He laughed. "How flattering. Do you have any idea how adorable you are?"

Clara looked away. Dalton didn't think she was adorable. He thought she was reckless and outrageous—even dangerous. Upon reflection, she decided she preferred dangerous.

Still holding herself immobile, she sat stiffly on Nathaniel's lap. "What did you want to tell me?"

Nathaniel watched her for a moment, only the clenching of his jaw revealing his uncertainty. "Tell me this now, Clara, and I shall never ask again. Have you any involvement with a plot against the Crown?"

Clara threw back her head with a noise of exasperation. "*Why* does everyone keep asking me that?" The ceiling held no answer so she looked back at Nathaniel. "No. I am not plotting against the Crown. I dislike it when the privileged abuse the underprivileged, that is all."

He blinked at her. "Doesn't everyone?" Then he smiled. "I'm going to do a very bad thing that will likely get us both into serious trouble."

"Oh, lovely," she muttered. "I cannot get enough of *that*."

"I am going to tell you about a group of young revolutionaries which was composed of Wadsworth and a number of other young miscreants with ties to France." Nathaniel shifted a bit beneath her and Clara realized that he'd not exaggerated the improper route his thoughts had been heading. She held herself like stone.

He gave her a bemused look and continued. "They

called themselves the Knights of the Lily. The *Fleur-de-lis*, to be precise."

At first Clara couldn't move, couldn't react.

Fleur.

What in God's name had she drawn herself into? "No!" she protested. "I expose pilferage and—and venality. I don't know anything about revolutionaries or—or—" Her hands flew to her mouth in horror. "Oh no! And it sold two thousand copies!"

"Nearly three thousand, from my calculations. Not to mention all the tracings that were passed around." He sighed. "Now, to complicate matters, I must add to this the story of a young man, not much more than a boy really, who in a moment of rebellion against his powerful father took up with the wrong sort of people. People who wanted his father—well, let's just say they wanted the power out of his father's hands.

"To the young man, this plan to foil his father was like a game. It was great fun, what with all the secret meetings and the messages that must be burned at once. It wasn't until he became bored and attempted to stop playing that he realized that his erstwhile comrades had not been playing at all.

"He didn't know what to do. If he turned to his father, his father might suspect the betrayal to be very real because of their past conflict. The punishment would be swift and permanent if that were so. His life as he knew it would be over. Yet if he did nothing, the group might very well succeed against his father and he would be guilty forever of betraying the man he loved most in the world."

"But didn't you say he disliked his father?" Despite her predicament, Clara found herself caught up in the story. What a terrible position to be in!

Nathaniel gave her a sad smile. "Things between fathers and sons can be very complicated. Admiration can turn to disillusionment in an instant, and usually does, for what mortal man could sustain the illusion of heroism every moment of his life? In their turn, fathers have such expectations of their sons, as if they believe that a young man is a mere extension of themselves, able to perform with all the wisdom and experience that they themselves possess."

His gaze was now fixed on the fire and Clara could see the grief and regret in his eyes. "So what choice did you make, Nathaniel? Did you choose your father or yourself?"

He opened his mouth to answer, just as a fracas erupted out in the hallway. The door burst open and two bound men were shoved into the room to stagger before Lord Reardon and Clara.

She gasped. "Dalton!"

Dalton straightened, his eyes traveling slowly over her as she sat on Nathaniel's lap in her maid costume. Cold ice went through Clara as she realized what he must think. "I don't—he isn't—"

Nathaniel chuckled deeply, his grip upon her tightening. "Oh, but I am," he said, his gaze upon Dalton. "Or at least I'd very much like to be."

Dalton was so glad to see her alive and well that he could have laughed out loud. She was pale with dark circles under her eyes, but she was composed. Most of all, she was blessedly, thankfully safe.

He wanted to run to her, to sweep her close and hold her close until every cell of his body believed she was well.

Instead, he could only stare as another man held her in his arms. She looked back at him so worriedly, thinking he would blame her for her predicament. Loyal Clara.

One corner of Dalton's mouth quirked. "Let me guess. You fell off the roof and landed there by accident."

"No." The fair-haired man, who held Clara still closer, leaned back in the chair to regard Dalton. "I put her here, and here she'll stay, for the moment."

Dalton eyed the man he recognized well from the attempts on his life. "And who the bloody hell are you?"

Clara gasped and looked back and forth between them. "Don't you know him?" The fair-haired man only tightened his embrace on her and continued to regard Dalton steadily.

Dalton shook his head, but James Cunnington nodded. "I do. Nate Stonewell. Haven't seen him for years."

Dalton jerked. *Nate Stonewell?* Ah. The pieces all began to fall into place. Randolph Stonewell had been known as the Old Man, the spymaster of the Liar's Club before Simon. Nate Stonewell would be the wayward son.

The man quirked a brow. "I go by Lord Reardon these days."

"You look so surprised, Lord Etheridge." The mild voice of Mr. Wadsworth came from where he lounged in the doorway. "I've known of Nathaniel's connection to those odious spies of yours for years. Why else do you think we recruited him for the Knights of the Lily?"

James turned to Wadsworth. "*You* recruited him?"

Wadsworth came off his shoulder to stroll into the room and stand just behind Nate Stonewell's chair. "Surely you must realize that he is far younger than the rest of us. Why, he would have been a mere child when we were originally disbanded."

Yes, Dalton remembered, Nate Stonewell had been a child. The child that Simon Raines had rescued from kidnapping so many years ago. The son who had rejected his father and everything the Old Man had stood for. Who had left home at a young age to undertake his education on the Continent. Who had inherited his title and wealth from an uncle and who'd determined to enjoy every useless privilege of such without taking any of the responsibility.

Lord Reardon was what Dalton himself might have become, had it not been for the strict guidance of Lord Liverpool—a careless, easily manipulated tool of traitors.

Reardon eyed Dalton with curiosity. "And you are Lord Etheridge, the new master of that band of misfits otherwise known as the Liar's Club."

James shook his head sorrowfully. "Oh, Nate. You never did get it, did you?"

"Get what? Get that my father preferred all of you to me, his own son?" Reardon stood, lifting Clara from his lap and setting her aside.

Dalton looked her over quickly. She was pale and obviously very confused, but seemed well enough. Her wide questioning gaze shifted to him, but he could only give her a tiny shake of his head. She slowly knelt and reached for the lap rug that had fallen to the floor. In the course of her action, she managed to move two steps closer to him.

Clever Clara.

Nathaniel strode angrily to stare into the coals, bracing one fist on the mantel. "And then to make matters worse, there was Simon Raines. A boy from the streets, a ragged little beggar. *Simon.* His project, my father called him. He cleaned him up, schooled him, involved him in his work nearly every day. I, on the other hand, was expected to keep up my studies on my own and be a good example of a young British gentleman, pursuing all the useless things that such louts do. I was in line for a title, you see. My mother's brother was a lord with no issue and no desire to have any. I was groomed from birth to take my uncle's place. I felt sometimes as if I'd been given away in exchange for a title in the family."

Clara took another small step closer to Dalton as she drew the wool over her shoulders. Dalton could barely see her now without turning his head, which he dared not do for fear of alerting someone to her actions.

Reardon turned from his tragic pose to see what Dalton imagined were four distinctly unsympathetic expressions.

He shrugged. "Ah, but I was excited by my possibilities, of course. I enjoyed them to their fullest. I was a right little snot, taking care to rub that street boy's nose in every privilege and advantage I possessed. It never truly helped, however. Simon was always the son my father wanted, and I was merely the pawn in the power match."

Dalton saw Clara nod slowly. "I know precisely the feeling," she said.

Reardon looked up then as if pulling himself from the past with an effort. "Yes, I imagine you do. I hadn't realized . . ."

"Enough whining, my lord." Wadsworth waved his pistol to capture Reardon's attention. "What do you propose we do with this lot? We could throw them in the Thames. Or we might be able to pass it off as a carriage accident."

Reardon considered the three of them. "Faking a carriage accident would be too tedious. I don't care if anyone knows they were murdered. The suspects in the murder of *Sir Thorogood* will be so numerous that no one will bother to dig very deeply."

James groaned. "You've been keeping up with us every step of the way, haven't you, Nate?"

Reardon turned. "Of course. I've known the secrets of that club since I was a child. My *father* didn't tell me, of course. I had to follow Simon to learn anything. It wasn't difficult at all. People never really see children, do they? Or if they do, they don't take their activities seriously." He shook his head. "If you were going to live past morning, you would do well to take note of that."

Dalton closed his eyes for a moment in regret. Reardon was entirely correct. His pose as Sir Thorogood would bite him back now, for Thorogood had more enemies than Napoleon.

Wadsworth smiled. "Very well, then. Would you like to do the honors?" Wadsworth gazed coolly at Nathaniel and held out his own pistol. "Perhaps it is time that you prove your loyalty to the Knights of the Lily."

There was a long pause. James and Dalton tensed, but bound and against so many, what could they do? Dalton heard Clara whimper and cower behind him.

Whimper? Surely not his Clara? Then he felt a rhythmic motion against his bonds and realized that she had found a blade somewhere. A flare of hope ignited within him.

Faster, Clara, he willed, as he kept his eyes on the tableau before him. Wadsworth was watching Reardon closely, and the two thugs were preparing to enforce their master's will.

Then Reardon made a tiny bow. "As you wish." He

took Wadsworth's pistol and stepped back, aiming directly at Dalton.

Clara gasped. "No!" Dalton turned to see her go pale with alarm. He stepped in front of her once more.

"You said you wouldn't harm anyone!" Behind Dalton, the cutting became ever more furious as she pleaded. "Nathaniel, you don't have to do this!"

Reardon shook his head, but Dalton didn't think he seemed all that regretful. Bloody *hell.* If he was shot, the chance of James's and Clara's escaping would decrease drastically, if it had ever existed at all.

"I'm sorry, pretty one." Reardon took a step farther back. "I thought I could keep you out of this, but . . . alas." With the heel of his left hand, he pulled back the hammer of the firearm.

Dalton watched Reardon's finger tighten on the trigger. He readied himself, although there was no way to avoid the bullet at this range.

"No!" Clara's cry was followed by the explosion of the shot, and Dalton felt a violent push from behind.

Clara. There was no time to stop her. All he could do was twist to break her fall as she lunged into him, taking them both to the floor, toppling a nearby table with a crash.

Dalton lurched to his knees, his arms still bound. "Clara!" She lay limply before him. Blood welled from her side. There was a glint of gold and he saw a small blade in her hand, no bigger than a leaf of grass.

No. She couldn't die. He couldn't breathe, not even draw a breath. A vast band of pain and regret wrapped around his heart. *He couldn't lose her.*

Chapter Twenty-five

"Clara!" Her name was torn from his tight and aching throat. Her eyes opened and she gasped.

"Good heavens, that hurts!" She pressed a hand to her waist. Red seeped through her fingers and dripped to the carpet.

"Oh, damn," Reardon said faintly.

Clara peeled her bloodied fingers from her waist. A bloody slash cut into her skin, but there was no bullet hole. A flesh wound. Nasty but not deadly, as long as she did not take infection. Dalton closed his eyes with relief, bending to touch his forehead to hers in a silent moment of thanks to the divine.

"Damnation! You mucked it, you idiot!" Wadsworth was livid. He strode forward to yank the pistol from Reardon's hand. "Bloody amateur!"

"Well, it wasn't my pistol! I can do better with my own weapon." Reardon reached into his vest to pull out a pistol. "I'm more accustomed to the sight on this one."

Then he calmly levered it and fired once more. Wadsworth's servant Bligh went down like a felled tree. Reardon blinked and turned to the sputtering Wadsworth. "Oops."

"Why in the bloody hell did you do that?" Wadsworth looked from Bligh to Reardon in astonishment.

Dalton took advantage of their distraction to pull violently at his half-cut bonds. He felt some skin go with the rope, but he finally broke free.

Then he lunged for Wadsworth.

The spent pistol spun off into the corner and Wadsworth went down hard. Dalton saw James fling himself bodily at the second flunky and go down in a pile of broken furniture. Dalton didn't worry. Even bound, James was dangerous.

Dalton had pulled back one fist, ready to see how many pieces a man's face could be broken into—when the double click of another pistol resounded through the taut silence. Still gripping Wadsworth by the throat, Dalton looked down into another steel barrel just like the first.

Wadsworth lay in his grasp, calmly aiming the matching pistol directly between Dalton's eyes. "This is one of my own designs. Nathaniel may have bungled his shots, but somehow I don't think I shall miss mine."

Smoothly, the trigger began to slide back before his eyes.

Dalton grinned. "That depends on whether or not your design accounted for this—" He gripped the pistol backward, shoving his thumb *under* the trigger. Glaring, Wadsworth struggled to pull the trigger all the way back, but the mechanism wouldn't fire without full release.

Dalton twisted the pistol from Wadsworth's hold and stood. "Have you any more of these about your person?"

Wadsworth only glared and reached for his fallen

walking stick to help himself stand. Dalton went to where James lay half-sprawled on the floor. The other lackey was out cold, his nose bloody and his temple swelling.

Dalton knelt to untie James. "Did he get you?"

James was pale and sweating. "No," he gasped. "I believe I got myself. Fighting with my arms tied behind my back played bloody hell with my shoulder." When he was untied, he hissed as he used his good hand to drag his injured arm forward. "Damn. Another three weeks in the sling, I'll wager." He looked up past Dalton. *"Look out!"*

Dalton rolled just as he heard the unmistakable *swish* of a sword through the air. On his back on the floor, he raised the pistol in his hand and fired almost before he registered his target.

The narrow blade fell to the carpet. Wadsworth followed it a moment later to land half on the rug and half on Dalton and James. Dalton struggled to free the two of them from Wadsworth and to stand once more.

Something moved in the corner of Dalton's vision. *Reardon.* With the speed of a whip, he was across the room and had the man by the throat.

"Too bad," came a cultured voice from the door. "It was a lovely carpet."

Dalton turned. Liverpool stood just beyond, holding the sword that had fallen and gazing down at the body on the floor. Blood seeped from a bullet wound in the man's chest. Behind Liverpool stood two Royal Guardsmen, who quickly helped James to his feet.

Liverpool approached Dalton calmly, taking a handkerchief from his pocket to polish the slender blade in his hand. "Your coat is ruined, as well."

Dalton rolled one shoulder forward to find that his

silk coat was slashed across the back of the collar. Apparently Wadsworth hadn't known how truly difficult it was to behead a man. Dalton was very glad he hadn't had to find out, either.

Liverpool glanced down at Clara and then over at James. "Obviously a trying day had by all." Under one arm he'd tucked the business end of Wadsworth's silver-handled walking stick, which Dalton realized had concealed the sword.

James pursed his lips in an awed whistle. "Where can I get one of those?"

Liverpool shot him a quelling look. "Etheridge, do let Reardon go. He's on our side."

Startled, Dalton turned to stare at the man he still held by the throat. Reardon, growing purple but manfully trying not to show it, gave a careless wave of his hand. Dalton looked back to Liverpool. "But he shot Clara!"

"I'll be all right, Dalton." Clara came toward them, a handkerchief now pressed to her side, the other side supported by James. She was pale and her eyes were wide, but she looked wonderful to him.

Reardon took advantage of this distraction to reach up to peel Dalton's fingers from his throat. Wheezing just a bit, he shook his head. "I didn't intend to shoot anyone. I was going to very carefully miss you. It was all I could do to pull the pistol aside as it was." He took a step toward Clara, but Dalton moved into his path.

Reardon shrugged. "I only want to apologize. Shouldn't we fetch a doctor for her?"

"It's nearly stopped bleeding already," Clara said. She looked down at her ragged, filthy, rain-soaked and wrinkle-dried, bloodstained self. Then she looked back up to Dalton. "However, I think I need another change of clothing already," she said faintly.

Dalton felt his throat tighten at her bravery. What heart his Clara had!

Clara watched the look in Dalton's eyes go from worried to proud. Warming inwardly at his approval, she forced herself to turn away from him when all she wanted was to run into his arms. She moved to stand before Lord Liverpool.

Her side burned badly, and she was beginning to feel a bit faint, but primarily she found that she was terrified of the man before her. She could scarcely draw breath her throat was so tight, and she was sure her hands were shaking.

She put them behind her back and raised her chin, making sure not to look away from Lord Liverpool. "There is something you must know, my lord."

Lord Liverpool turned to her. To her surprise, he was not much taller than herself, yet he emanated such a presence that she'd expected someone more on Dalton's scale.

He stood before her, looking her over with his flat gray gaze. "Sir Thorogood, I presume?"

Clara didn't answer, her throat too tight to speak.

He gazed at her for a long moment. "Humph."

Clara swallowed. "Lord Reardon is not on our side. I've learned that as a boy, he joined a revolutionary group that intended to kill his father, who is apparently someone high in the government. He claims it was only a boyhood prank, that he was never serious about it. Yet I saw him meeting secretly with Wadsworth not two weeks past."

Liverpool only gazed at her impassively. Clara swallowed the dryness in her throat and continued. "If you read certain documents in his safe, you will see that they most definitely confirm him as a traitor."

Reardon looked from one person to the next. "That story does not refer to me."

" 'A boyhood prank,' " quoted Dalton softly. Clara watched him turn to gaze at Liverpool. "No. It doesn't refer to Reardon. It refers to Prince George, doesn't it, my lord?"

Liverpool shot Dalton a look full of warning, but Dalton continued.

"That is what all this is about, isn't it? Hiding what George did at the age of sixteen. You set me up, hunted Clara, twisted my Liars into knots, all to conceal George's association with the Knights of the Lily." He shook his head. "Poor George. He never took anything seriously. What a moment that must have been, when he realized that he was about to murder his own father, his own king."

"That's when he came to my father," said Reardon, nodding. "Prince George confessed his foolishness to my father. Father sent for Liverpool immediately and chaos reigned for one entire day. My father and Lord Liverpool dispersed the group, sending some of the young men as far away as America, forcibly if necessary. George was upbraided for several hours straight and put in the keeping of a rather fierce and watchful tutor. The King never learned of any of it."

Clara looked from a silent Liverpool to Nathaniel. "And now?"

Nathaniel gestured for her to sit on the settee facing the fire. Gratefully, Clara sank onto the cushions.

Continuing, Nathaniel looked up to include Dalton and James. "I'd only recently returned from persuading the Austrian Emperor to declare war on France. A month ago I was approached by the few surviving members of Fleur about their plans to blackmail the Prince Regent.

They knew I'd severed my ties with my father and assumed I was of like mind. Of course, I remembered the entire fiasco from my childhood, although I was not supposed to know anything about it at the time."

He snorted. "As if I could avoid it. The door nearly fell in with the force of Liverpool's pounding. I've never seen him so livid, before or since. You could hear him bellowing at poor young George all through our house." His lips twisted as he regarded Lord Liverpool, who stood silently watching them all. "I'm sure it will be my turn now that I've told you all of this."

James looked at Nathaniel, curiosity etched in his face. "So you don't hate the Liars?"

Nathaniel grimaced. "They aren't my favorite branch of the government, but no, I don't *hate* them."

James didn't back down. "Or Simon? Because you were awfully convincing just now."

Nathaniel looked away, then back. "Simon Raines was just a boy who had finally found a home. I couldn't hate anyone for that."

Clara chewed her lip. "But I saw you there, talking to Wadsworth and his guests. You seemed one of them to me."

"I was posing as a sympathizer in order to learn more of their plans. They have the potential to do the Prince Regent a great deal of damage, should word of his participation get out."

"But he was only a boy! Surely no one will hold it against him!"

Dalton shook his head. "No, Clara. The public would not be nearly so forgiving. What if it caused his regency to be stripped from him? It could happen, if public opinion turned too far against him. As regent, he is the guardian of his very ill father, our king. What would people think if they learned that he had once actively plotted his own father's murder?"

"No wonder you were all in such a frenzy to find me!" Clara chewed her lip. "But who signed the kill order?"

Behind her, Dalton shifted. "I did."

Clara turned, lips parted in shock. Dalton didn't look at her. "Didn't I, my lord?" His tone was light, almost bored. Clara knew by this that he was utterly enraged.

Liverpool gazed back at him. "Did you?"

"It had to have been me, sir." Dalton's tone was most polite. "For the only other explanation is that it was you."

If possible, Liverpool's gaze was icier than ever. "I don't think you have sufficient evidence to make such a dangerous accusation, boy."

Clara looked back and forth between the two men. "Then there is no rogue member of the Royal Four?"

Nathaniel turned to shoot her a horrified look, then ran both hands over his face.

Now she had their attention. Liverpool stared at her, his jaw working in his otherwise expressionless face. He finally spoke. "You know who the Royal Four are, child?"

Clara went cold. There was something resigned and deadly in his voice, as if her knowledge had just passed the point of no return. "N-not *who* they are, no. I simply know of their existence." She was fairly sure of the identity of one of them now—although Nathaniel had been very convincing as a villain—but she thought that Lord Liverpool really didn't need to know that.

"Mrs. Simpson, you are a very dangerous woman."

Inside Clara's stomach, ice churned. This was not good, not good at all.

Then Liverpool turned to the others as if she'd ceased

to exist. "Well, now that you lot have disturbed a very old dog, we must see what can be done to send it back to sleep again."

Dalton worked his jaw, but nodded. "Certainly, my lord. As soon as I've escorted Mrs. Simpson ho—"

"Mrs. Simpson is no longer your concern. I will conduct her to Westminster Hall, where she will receive medical attention . . . and where she will remain as the guest of the government until further notice."

Clara turned to appeal to Dalton but halted at the remote expression on his face. He didn't so much as glance her way. "Very well, my lord."

The two guards stepped up to escort her from the room. Looking over her shoulder from the other side of the red-coated young giants, Clara felt a sharp cold pain, as if she were being cut from him by a surgeon. She hardly dared think past that at this moment, or she felt she might collapse in a quivering pile of abject fear.

Dalton remained impassive. Nathaniel stepped forward to take her arm. "Come along, Clara." His tone was regretful but his grip was firm.

As Nathaniel led her away, she closed her eyes against the cold still expression on Dalton's face as he let her go without another word.

Her last near-hysterical thought was that at least she was leaving by the door. . . .

Dalton strode from Reardon's house, his gaze unseeing, his face grim. James caught up with him on the walk outside. The new day threatened to dawn as gray as Dalton's face.

James eyed him warily. He had never seen Dalton

like this. "He can't keep her locked up, can he? She's not guilty of any crime, not really."

Dalton shook his head. "In Liverpool's eyes she is." The life was gone from his manner, his voice as colorless as his eyes. "First, she's an overt reformist. That's dangerous to an old conservative like our Prime Minister. Secondly, I've just sealed her fate by displaying my attachment."

"Dalton, I know Liverpool has been something of a mentor to you over the years, much as you are to me—"

"Nothing like. You are one of my men, James. A brother. Liverpool considers me a tool in his hand. Rather he did until all this. Now I imagine he considers me a powder keg. He'd like to keep me far from the fire."

"Far from Clara," James said.

"Precisely."

"So what will you do?"

"What can I do?" He turned on James and cocked a brow coolly. "I'm a peer and a gentleman. I have rank and responsibilities. Do you expect me to break her out of there in the dark of night?"

James stepped back. "No, no, of course not."

"Good."

James could have sworn those silver eyes began to glow.

"Then Liverpool won't expect it, either." Dalton gave James a fierce grin. "Suit up, Griffin. We've a wall to climb tonight."

Clara's room in the old palace was not much more than a comfortably furnished cell. She was up in the rooms reserved for visiting diplomats, far from the busy corridors and overcrowded meeting rooms of Parliament.

Her window held a soaring view of the Thames and the rooftops beyond. She was more than five dizzying stories high and she could barely stand to look through the glass, much less escape through it.

The single door was guarded by her own stoic pair of redcoats, who met any request from her with politely bland refusal. The physician had come and gone, leaving her with a bandage and the assurance that she would only carry a minor scar.

She tried to tell herself that she had nothing to worry about. Dalton was where they were likely discussing what to do with her, and he wouldn't let anything happen to her.

Would he? He was a man torn between heart and duty and she truly had no idea which way he would turn.

Her baggage had been delivered to the room along with herself. Apparently, these four papered walls were going to be her only home for a long while. Resentfully, she wondered what Liverpool would say if she drew all over them.

Thorogood's version of the Sistine Chapel. Which she would likely not live to see. Clara lay back on the silken coverlet and contemplated the gilded ceiling.

In that plain plastered portion over there, she would depict the young Prince, held mesmerized by a young Wadsworth, their revolutionary plans spread before them. Then another drawing, of a shame-faced George confessing his fears to Nathaniel's father, while a child with Nathaniel's green eyes peeked from behind a door to observe.

Perhaps a border around each vignette, filled with tiny figures portraying the Liar's Club and their activities. It would take a very long time, but she likely had it to spare.

In the far corner, she would draw Nathaniel infiltrating the Knights of Fleur while a craven figure crouched in the sideboard, furiously scribbling away.

And she would draw Dalton as a man of light and shadow, torn between loyalties, torn between love and honor, perhaps even with herself as wretched harpy, shredding his shadow half with teeth and claws.

She'd mucked it all up severely these past weeks, and good men were suffering because of her.

At this rate, she ought to be able to bring the entire country of England to its knees within the year. Napoleon really ought to thank her for doing his work for him.

She rolled over, unable to bear the reproach of her imaginary drawings above her. How had she come to this point?

Breaking into the vicious Wadsworth's in order to right a few wrongs, how could that be so bad? Helping Rose had been undeniably good. Sir Thorogood's cartoons had done good as well, even if only bringing the plight of the disadvantaged to light.

Yet there had been one night of intrigue, one misunderstood conversation, one drawing too many.

One drawing too many . . .

She sat up, lethargy gone. One drawing had begun the entire chain of events. One drawing could stop it.

There was no paper in the room. Liverpool had taken even the ink from her when he'd left. Ruthlessly, she peeled a section of patterned wallpaper from an inconspicuous spot behind the bed. The back was blank enough if she was willing to disregard the dried glue. Then she gathered scraped soot from the fireplace with the heel of her shoe, catching it in one of the tumblers that had accompanied her request for a pitcher of water.

She added water a drop at a time until she had a thick paste of decidedly unattractive ink. It didn't matter, for the engraver could correct vagaries of the lumpy lines. What mattered was getting Sir Thorogood's final drawing on paper as soon as possible.

She used a pin from her hair as a nib. Bending close over her paper in the small light from her one candle, she carefully delineated four figures on the paper, inch by scratching inch.

One on a center pedestal, one partially cloaked behind, and two crouching on either side, reaching desperately for the standing figure.

Everyone would remember "Fleur and Her Followers" at the sight of this drawing, but this gave an entirely new slant on the topic, one that just might undo all the trouble she had caused.

She worked late into the night, until her eyes ached and her candle was a mere lighted wick in a puddle of wax. Finally came the last stroke of her clotted "ink" on her stolen wallpaper, the last flicker of light from her dying candle, and she was done.

As the room flickered to darkness, she laid her aching head down on her arms, her heart peaceful at last.

It was a very good cartoon, if she did say so herself.

Chapter Twenty-six

Dalton strode into the Liar's Club with James fast behind him.

"Are you quite sure about this?" James tossed his coat over one of the chairs in the club room used by "customers" and loosened his cravat. "Last night you thought they were going to kill you, remember?"

"How can I expect them to trust me if I don't trust them?" Dalton smiled grimly. "It's good advice. You should keep it in mind when you're spymaster."

"Me?" James's jaw dropped. "I'm still under consideration?"

"We'll discuss that later." Dalton pushed open the door into the private segment of the club, the part that the louts and lordlings knew nothing about. The room was full of men, Liars all, obviously holding some sort of conference. They froze at Dalton's entrance.

He strode to the front of the room where Stubbs stood conducting the meeting. "Wondering what to do about me?"

Stubbs blinked, then conceded the invisible podium with a glance at Kurt and moved to sit at a nearby table.

James seated himself in another chair, idly rubbing his shoulder and pretending interest in some dark and uninspiring portraits lining the walls. Dalton knew that his calm pose hid a burning curiosity held barely in check.

Dalton turned to face the Liars. They gazed back at him, waiting as they had for the past several weeks.

Waiting for him to trust them.

"Gentlemen, I need your full attention, for we have an operation tonight."

They sat in silence, unresponsive. Dalton took some encouragement from the fact that they weren't trying to kill him.

Yet.

It was progress of a sort. Now to rally them to follow him. Dalton's mind swerved through argument and reason. What words could he use to inflame them? What rhetoric would dim the last mismanaged weeks of division?

Trust them.

His thoughts slowed. Calmed. There was only one way to gain their trust. He knew that now.

"Gentlemen, there are some things you ought to know."

He stood before them and told it all. From the moment he'd been asked to step into Liverpool's position in the Royal Four and his subsequent leadership of themselves to his true reasons for running the Thorogood mission himself to the moment when he'd been forced to watch Liverpool capturing Clara.

He spared himself nothing. Every error, every moment of mistrust, every self-serving impulse was laid before them in precise detail.

"You have me at a disadvantage now," he finished. "I need you, but I have nothing to bargain with. I don't even know that I will be your spymaster once Liverpool sees to my reprimand. If you follow me tonight, you may very well be setting yourselves up against the Crown itself, or at least Lord Liverpool."

He fell silent at last, feeling rather like a spent pistol. It was in their hands now, this motley group of loyal madmen. The only question was . . . loyal to whom?

Several men glanced at Kurt, waiting for his reaction. Dalton waited. The Cook had more years in the organization than any other. The survival rate was not high these days, but Kurt had always seemed untouchable, a rock in the changing tides around him. Who might influence Kurt?

Then Kurt looked to James. Surprised, James gazed back at the big man as if to say, "Who, me?"

Then James stood. Dalton waited. James had ever been a puzzle to him. He was supportive in private, yet never once had he aided Dalton's rise into leadership.

James cleared his throat. "I—I don't know why you care what I think, having cost you all that I have."

Kurt grunted. "Old news, boy."

James's gaze flickered over all those present. Dalton imagined that James could also see all those not present.

"I say he's in."

Kurt nodded once. All eyes turned back to Dalton. Stubbs leaned forward. "Well, what's it to be, guv'nor?"

Feebles tugged uncomfortably at his fine new waistcoat and fingered the cravat at his throat. He felt like a fox caught in the lamplight, despite Button's reassurance that he'd fit right in the halls of Parliament. He certainly didn't look like himself, with his hair neatly parted down the middle and slicked down with oil. The plain glass spectacles that perched on his nose further painted the picture of a lowly secretary.

Think bookish, he reminded himself. Think desk man, paper diddler, a pale and pottering sort who worked late into the night arranging another bloke's affairs.

Lord Liverpool appeared at the top of the grand entry stairs, finally leaving for the evening. Time for the show. Feebles clutched his stack of papers to his chest and began to scuttle up the steps, muttering to himself in his fussiest manner.

One . . . two . . . He reached the step below Liverpool. Three. He let one toe catch under the lower step and faked a perfect stumble directly into the man on Liverpool's left. The fellow jerked instinctively aside, allowing Feebles to shower his lordship with a flutter of paper.

Feebles had practiced only one phrase in correct "priss-bookish" with Button's help.

He began to industriously brush off his lordship as if the paper had been the contents of a dustbin. "Oh, dear, how clumsy of me. Oh dear, how clumsy of me. Oh, dear. Oh *dear*!"

Liverpool retreated a step with a pained expression. "I am quite well enough, my good man. Perhaps you should devote yourself to putting your papers in order?"

Feebles looked down at the mess and squealed in horror. "Oh, dear!"

Liverpool and his companion continued on their way without a single glance back, but Feebles continued his charade until his prop papers were all assembled and the numbered key that had once resided in Liverpool's waistcoat pocket had made its way into his own. Then he scuttled to the street exit where Stubbs awaited him with an unmarked carriage. Time to set the plan in motion.

Button fussed with the gold braid on the enormous red coat he was fitting on a fuming Kurt. Since soldiers were not encouraged to have long hair, Kurt had his tangled locks piled upon his head like a girl, ready to conceal under the tall helmet of a commander of the Royal Horse Guard.

The helmet was authentic, filched from the storeroom of the Guard itself. There had never been a uniform made, however, that could cover the gigantic frame of the club's premier assassin, so Button had fashioned one from red wool and gold braid, although he still worried loudly that the gold buttons were not a perfect match.

"Don't worry about it, Button. Do you think anyone staring into that face will be looking at the trim of his uniform?"

Kurt swung slowly to glare at James, bringing Button with him as the valet clung on during the slow turn. James only smiled at the big man. "Come on, Kurt. You know I love you like a brother, don't you?"

Kurt only grunted, then plucked Button from himself like a man forcefully removing a leech from his flesh. "It's good. Go away."

Button sniffed. "No one appreciates perfection. Why do I try, I ask you? Why do I even try?" He gathered his tailoring gear and left the room. They could hear his affronted muttering all the way down the hall. " 'It's good,' he says. It's genius, I tell you, but do I get a speck of credit? I don't think so. . . ."

James grinned at Kurt. "Best watch out. Remember how the genius valet dressed Dalton at the start of all this? How would you like flowing lace sleeves and high heels?"

Kurt grunted again, but said nothing. In truth, James doubted that he was in any danger from Button, since the valet had developed quite a passion for Kurt's famous *petits fours*.

Just thinking about Kurt's baking genius brought a growl to James's belly. Unfortunately, the assassin had been too busy preparing for tonight's venture to spare the time for any kitchen magic. Mournfully, James realized that he was going to have to wait until tomorrow for his favorite trifle with berries.

Kurt heard James's stomach growl and took it as due flattery, as it was. "Got gooseberries in," he growled, which was his normal mode of speech. "And fresh cream and butter."

James's knees went weak. "Maybe we'll finish early this evening?" There was always hope.

Kurt shrugged and pulled his tentlike cloak over his fabricated uniform. Tucking the hat under one arm, well hidden under the cloak, he turned without a word and left the room. James grabbed his own cloak and followed. "If you start the sponge cake tonight—"

Clara rolled her forehead on her folded arms. Something had roused her, but she couldn't seem to open her eyes. Perhaps there had been nothing at all—

The faint sound of a key in the lock of her door woke her like cold water down her back. She stumbled to her feet to face the door. Who could it be at this time of night?

The door swung open and she blinked against the glare from the lighted hallway. Then a giant stepped into the rectangle of light, a giant that she recognized with a stab of primal fear.

Kurt.

The breath left her lungs as her worst fears seemed about to realize themselves. Liverpool had made his decision. She was to be disposed of—

The big man stepped forward, looming so far above her that she was forced to tilt her head all the way back to see his frightening face. He looked down at her impassively.

Then his gaze flicked to the drawing on the table. Clara had left it out so that the rather terrible ink could safely dry. Oh, no. She ought to have hidden it somehow. If her one bargaining chip were taken from her she would disappear for certain.

Kurt's buttons seemed to shake before her eyes. Then she heard a sound emerge from deep inside his chest, rather like the crunching of gravel. He was . . . laughing?

Quickly she snatched the now dry drawing and rolled it in her hands, standing and backing away from him as she did so.

He watched her for a moment from beneath heavy lids, then turned to gather her case under one great arm as if it weighed nothing. "Time to go," he growled. Stepping forward with surprising swiftness, he wrapped one massive hand around her arm and took her with him.

He didn't hurt her, but neither did she have the means to struggle. Her toes were scarcely touching the ground as he walked her down the hall to another doorway. It was a plain narrow door, built to disappear into the paneling of the wall. A servant's passage?

Kurt tapped twice, then opened the panel. He thrust her inside, then shut her into the dark space.

A scraping sound met her ears and a small light flared. Before her stood a man holding a tiny slip of burning wood and a coil of rope, wearing a rakish grin on his face.

Her mind spun. "Monty?"

Dalton stilled and his grin wavered. "If you like."

She caught herself up. "It—I was only startled— I'm—" Why was she apologizing to a man who was kidnapping her? Again!

She shook off the last of her daze. "What is it you want, my lord?"

He narrowed his eyes at her. "I think I liked 'Monty' better." He touched the end of the match to a candle set on a crate. The closet looked like some sort of supply room for the palace staff. Dalton began running the rope through his hands, forming a sliding loop at one end.

Clara didn't know what to think. Kurt and Dalton, working together. Was that good news or bad? "What are you doing?"

He stopped and tilted his head as he considered her. He looked so dashing with his hard body outlined all in black that she lost a moment to useless fantasy. All they lacked were the silk mask and the privacy of their attic.

What about your sanity? For you are certainly lacking something! Clara put a rein on her wayward thoughts. As Dalton continued to toy with the rope, tying it into some sort of harness, she realized that once more he was stealing her away.

"I cannot leave! If I am in trouble with Lord Liverpool now, imagine if I attempt to escape!"

"Bloody hell." Dalton turned back to her with a grunt of exasperation. With one arm he swept her close and lowered his mouth to hers.

She could never truly remember the depth of her response to him until he touched her, and then it all came flooding back. Her knees faltered and her pulse climbed, and her arms rose all of their own to wrap themselves around his neck.

The taste of him filled her mouth, mingling with her own until she couldn't remember which was which. She felt weightless when he held her, insubstantial yet somehow connected to the earth in a whole new way. As if when he touched her, he created a current within her that—

He stepped back, pulling himself from her embrace. "Imagine if you don't," he said. It took her a moment to remember the thread of their conversation.

Imagine what would happen if she *didn't* attempt to escape Liverpool, he meant. Remembering her own sure knowledge of her doom only moments before, she nodded. "You may have a point."

She swiftly yanked up her skirt to tuck her rolled cartoon into her garter. When she looked up, she was gratified to see the same stunned-ox expression upon Dalton's face that had surely been on her own a moment ago.

She shook her skirts sedately down once more. "Shall we go?" She arched a brow at him, serenely holding out her hands to take the rope harness.

Wordlessly he helped her into it but she imagined that his breath was coming a bit faster than necessary and his hands lingered on her a bit too long.

Then he turned to wrestle with something behind him. Clara noticed an odd cupboard built into the wall for the first time. Then Dalton opened it to reveal a darkened shaft. Clara picked up the candle and edged forward to peer warily down . . . and down . . . until the shaft simply disappeared into blackness. A warm flow of rising air toyed with the messy strands of her hair. She smelled . . . lye?

She pulled her head back in and closed her eyes for a moment. "You're sending me down the linen chute?"

He nodded, obviously very pleased with himself. "We can get you all the way to the cellar unseen. No one will be working at this time of night, and we can take the tunnels to St. Stephen's chapel. Stubbs is waiting there with the carriage at this moment."

Clara sighed. "Someday, my love, we must discuss my feelings about using doors." But not now. Grasping the upper casement of the opening, she went in feet first with Dalton's help. Sitting on the edge of the hole with the wood biting into her thighs, she froze when he reached to touch her face.

"Be careful, my Clara."

Turning her eyes to his unearthly silver gaze, she blinked at the emotion she saw there. The mask, it seemed, was well and truly gone.

Clara looked about her at the most secret establishment in the history of England and marveled at her own presence here. She'd never thought to see the inside of a traditional gentlemen's club, much less be welcomed in a den of spies.

They were all rather darling in their way. The big frightening fellow, Kurt, had brought her a dish of cream puffs that she was certain constituted an apology for his attack. He only grunted when she praised them. She ate one to please him, trying desperately not to blush at the memories that filled her mind.

Button, a prim and elegant fellow, had entertained her with tales of his life in the theatre that he claimed would be perfect fodder for her drawings.

A scraggly little man who seemed vaguely familiar

shyly handed her a golden comb for her hair. She thanked him solemnly and forbore asking its origin.

"You done right, bringing the gentleman back to us," Stubbs said shyly. The young doorman seemed sincerely infatuated with her. Clara wagered with herself that he fell in love at least once an hour.

Dalton and James Cunnington remained in conference in one corner of the large room. Dalton kept an eye on her, she knew, for she would catch him at it every so often when she felt his gaze. Which was ridiculous, of course, especially since there could be nothing between them.

Except for his rather astonishing offer earlier . . .

She'd just arrived and had been introduced to the members when Dalton had pulled her aside.

"You should understand, this isn't over. I fully expect Liverpool to come after you." His beautiful eyes were worried.

Clara had nodded. "I know. We'll simply have to make him understand that he cannot rule our—my life."

"It isn't that simple, Clara. You're a complication. Liverpool dislikes complications."

"Oh, I think that there is one way to get Liverpool to listen."

She reached into her satchel where she had placed the piece of tattered wallpaper and handed it to Dalton. The bold ink lines made Dalton widen his eyes.

He shook his head. "This is dangerous! And some-how—I'm not sure how, precisely—it's treasonous. Have you any idea how dangerous Liverpool can be?"

"Seeing that I have been running for my life this past week, yes, I think I have an inkling," she retorted. "But how am I to go on to live a normal life when all this is done?"

"Not this way. I can't bear to think what will happen to you if you take this particular tiger by its tail. There must be another way."

"I suppose I could flee to the West Indies after all," she muttered.

"Come work for me." The words came out in a rush as if from somewhere secret inside Dalton that he hadn't been aware of.

She looked as surprised as he felt. Dalton continued. "The Liars have never had a good suspect identification system. I want to hire you to be the official Liar's Club artist and drawing teacher."

"Oh, posh, I cannot even teach art in a school, for I have no other real ability. My watercolors are tepid, and my oils execrable."

"Well, my mistress of the execrable oils, this is one place you could teach. It would serve our young Liars well to be able to sketch a suspect to share with the others. Had I that skill, James would have identified Nathaniel Reardon days ago, and saved us all much grief."

Clara had only gazed at him for a moment. "I don't think further association between us is a good thing. I would be miserable and so would you." Then she had turned and walked away, her heart weeping at every step.

Now, Clara could only play charming guest to the Liars, and try to ignore Dalton's burning gaze.

Chapter Twenty-seven

Dalton watched as Clara charmed his men with her pirate smile and her fey beauty. They were smitten to a man, particularly when she took a chunk of charcoal from the grate and began to sketch each Liar in all his glory.

They clamored for more, scuffling for place in line to be next to be captured by her swift strokes on paper. Maps and files were sacrificed to keep pace with her swift hand. Dalton found himself reaching into his own coat to touch the two rolls still hidden within.

He'd never taken his evidence to Liverpool after all. Inconsequential, for they all knew it was only a matter of time until Liverpool came to them. The guards would be well able to describe Kurt, for who else quite filled those massive boots?

Still, Dalton felt more comfortable facing down his former mentor on his own ground. He looked around him, at the smoky interior, at his men gathered around the woman whom he would have given it all up for, and still might have to.

His own ground.

His own heart and his own mind. He knew precisely what he wanted now, and what he was willing to pay for it.

Dalton looked back down at the two rolls of paper in his hand. *He'd never taken his evidence to Liverpool.*

Finally, the sound of marching feet drew near. Liverpool, with a silent Reardon at his side, had arrived with enough of the Guard to roust the entire Liar's Club.

Liverpool wasted no time on preliminaries. "I've come for the woman."

As one, the Liars stepped in front of Clara until her slender figure was out of sight. Dalton stepped to the fore and felt the warm strength of his men's support at his back.

"I'm afraid you cannot have her, my lord."

Liverpool gave a quick nod. As one, the Guard leveled their muskets at the wall of Liars.

"Must I repeat myself? Hand over the woman."

"Clara. Her name is Clara, my lord."

Liverpool gazed at him for a moment. "Do you realize precisely what you are doing?"

Dalton nodded. "Yes, I do."

Liverpool's calm broke first. His face colored and Dalton could see his hands twitching at his sides. "If you go through with this, it will be for your personal benefit. Not the Liars. Not the Crown. Not England."

Dalton shook his head regretfully. "Can't you see? She *is* England. The beauty, the fire, the *spirit* of England. When I defend her, I am defending my country. There must be more to us than simply hide-bound traditions and arbitrary borders. What are we fighting for if not the treasure of our finest women?"

"Your romantic ideas always did get you into trouble, Dalton." Liverpool's gaze had not softened, but Dalton started at the use of his first name, which Liverpool had not used since young Dalton Montmorency had first come into his title.

"If it is trouble that I am in, then trouble there may be, for I'll—" Dalton looked behind him and grinned. *"We'll* not give her up to you. Furthermore, should you try to take her again, remember that there is nowhere on earth you can hide her that we cannot find her."

A low murmur of agreement rose from behind Dalton. He stopped smiling to gaze at Liverpool with utmost gravity. "We like her and we mean to keep her."

Liverpool only scoffed. "As what? And why in the world would you trust her? I'll admit her covert skills are competent enough, but she will expect to continue as Sir Thorogood."

Dalton smiled. "Oh, she's not Sir Thorogood. And you cannot prove that she is."

Liverpool's eyes narrowed skeptically. "No? Then who is Thorogood?"

Dalton's grin widened. "I am."

James stepped forward. "No, I am."

Stubbs and Button moved next. "I am, guv'nor!" "No, sir, it is I!"

One by one, the Liars stepped forward, all claiming the same. Liverpool gave them all a disgusted glare. "This is not amusing. You do realize that I'll have no choice but to disband you for this mutiny?"

"No, you mustn't!"

Dalton turned to see Clara stepping out from behind her human shield, the rolled drawing in her hand. "Clara—"

She waved him to silence. Dalton subsided, but he did not have a good feeling about her plan.

Clara steeled herself for Liverpool's intimidating

presence and moved to stand before him, head high. "I want to bargain with you, my lord. My . . . cooperation for your lenience."

Liverpool nodded. "I'm interested. Go on."

"I want you to leave the Liars as they are. I want you to free Dalton from any consequence he may have earned in your eyes from his association with me. In return, I will give you this."

She handed Liverpool the drawing and held her breath. He took it carefully, ever suspicious, and turned away from his Guard to unroll it.

Clara wasn't sure, but she may have heard him curse. She could hardly blame him, for the drawing portrayed him very clearly, standing over four figures, one upon a pedestal, three surrounding it, all with their limbs tied with strings that led up to the giant Liverpool's mighty hand.

But Fleur was no longer an opera dancer, she was now a sad woman draped in the British flag. She was unmistakably England herself. And the three worshipping figures had weary, noble faces and were labeled "Right," "Truth," and "Justice."

In her lone deliberation of the ceiling earlier that evening, Clara had realized something about the rigidly principled Lord Liverpool. None of his pursuit of her was personally inspired.

From her own observation and from Dalton's stories she had suddenly understood that his lordship viewed people in only three ways. There were the harmless ones—who were to be ignored. There were the dangerous ones—who were to be eliminated.

Then there were the useful ones—who became his tools. She had wafted directly past harmless, and a kill order undoubtedly meant that she was dangerous in his mind. . . .

So she must find a way to become a tool.

Lord Liverpool swiftly rolled the drawing. "I shall keep this, I think."

"Please do." Clara nodded gravely. "I only meant it to demonstrate that if you chose, you could find me enormously useful."

Lord Liverpool gazed at her for a very long moment, until Clara felt herself want to fidget. She tightened her clasped hands and held very still.

"I agree to your terms on two conditions," Lord Liverpool said shortly. "One, after today Sir Thorogood will not draw so much as a bucket of water for the rest of your life."

Clara nodded. It hurt to lose that part of herself, but it was only what she had expected him to ask for.

"Two, you will draw one last cartoon, according to my direction. You have given me a way to dissolve every scrap of public curiosity that you stirred up about Fleur, and to finally bring the Knights of the Lily into the light of day, where they will disappear like the shadows they are."

"And you will not punish Dalton and the Liars?" Clara persisted.

Liverpool contemplated her for a moment. "Do you realize that you've asked nothing for yourself?"

Clara dismissed the comment with a shake of her head. "I only want to be left alone. Do you agree not to punish Dalton and the Liars?" She was prepared to stand there all day insisting on that, but Liverpool simply gave a sharp nod and gestured for the Royal Guard to leave the club.

Then he turned back to her, a chill light in his eye.

"Now you must draw for me." He turned to beckon to the silent man who had accompanied him. "Nathaniel, it is time."

"You want me to *what*?" Clara stared at Liverpool and Nathaniel in shock.

"Your final cartoon, Sir Thorogood," said Liverpool. "Consider it a last hurrah."

"But with Wadsworth as hero? What of Nathaniel?"

"Nathaniel you shall portray as the last conspirator."

The injustice left her breathless. She appealed to Nathaniel, but his set white face gave her no reassurance.

"It must be so, Clara. The Knights of the Lily must be exposed, or they will continue to work unseen. We cannot afford to lose one of the main suppliers of arms to the British troops. Young Wadsworth's support is contingent on the preservation of his family name."

"But Nathaniel's reputation will be ruined! He'll be destroyed!"

Liverpool nodded. "Reardon knows his duty."

Nathaniel shook his head. "The public curiosity about Fleur must be satisfied, according to *our* version of the facts. In addition, the Knights of the Lily must be disarmed. If the group is made a proper laughingstock, if anyone associated with it is run thoroughly through the gossip mill, the Knights of the Lily will die a public belated death. Unfortunately, it seems I have been recognized as the third man. Some gossip got hold of that fact and London has been abuzz ever since this morning."

Clara pressed one palm over her aching heart. "Oh, Nathaniel. I've ruined you."

Liverpool lifted a brow. "Quite. Perhaps that will

teach you to keep your nose where it belongs, young woman."

"My actions would have been entirely unnecessary were you doing your job!" Clara blurted.

"Clara!" Nathaniel took her arm and turned her away, putting himself between her and Liverpool. "Clara, this is not the time or the forum."

She looked away grudgingly. "He doesn't care about you, Nathaniel. He doesn't care about anything!"

"You're quite wrong, Mrs. Simpson." Liverpool's tone was chilly and expressionless. "I care about England."

Clara straightened her shoulders. "So do I, my lord." Stubbs entered warily, carrying paper and ink. Clara took her supplies to the large desk and sat behind it.

"If you don't mind, I'd like to begin." She looked up at both men. Her heart ached at Nathaniel's set face and raged at Liverpool's indifferent one. "It should not take more than an hour."

Merely an hour to destroy a man's life. How powerful she was. What an arbiter of change she had become.

When she was done she left the office to hand the last cartoon to Liverpool. She stared at him dry-eyed, her heartache too deep for release.

"Here you are, my lord. My betrayal of Lord Reardon is complete."

Liverpool's lips twisted. "Don't be so tragic, child. Reputations come and go. Reardon's will recover." He took the drawing and unrolled it, then nodded approvingly. Without a word, he dismissed her, turning to speak to Dalton.

Reluctantly, Clara turned to Nathaniel. "I have learned my lesson well. I shall never draw another political cartoon."

Nathaniel took her hand. He looked terrible, his own pain flashing quickly in his eyes.

"What will you do now?" she asked.

He shrugged. "I shall go on, I suppose. Liverpool actually thinks this is for the better, for who could suspect a traitor to be a member of the Royal Four?"

She gaped at him. "It *is* you? Does Dalton know?"

"He does, as he should. After all, I took over from him as the Cobra. Liverpool called me home to England as soon as Dalton stepped down."

Clara smiled. "Your father must be so proud."

Dark pain flashed across Nathaniel's face, just for an instant. "He doesn't know, and he cannot. His mind is not what it was and Liverpool fears that telling him will compromise me." Shrugging, Nathaniel gave her a forced grin. "It matters little, for my father never thought that highly of me in the first place."

"Oh, Nathaniel." Clara couldn't find the words. "I—"

He kissed her knuckles and released her hand. "Stop apologizing." With that, he was gone.

Liverpool was leaving as well. At the last moment, he turned to cast a disparaging glance over the massed Liars, then looked to Dalton. "Who would have thought that a boy I raised would ever lower himself to keeping such base company?"

Dalton eyed Liverpool solemnly. His godfather would never understand. "I am not you. I shall never be you. But I am of value to you all the same, as are they. I hope to further earn my place among them. They have yet to give me a Liar's name."

Liverpool sniffed. "Why you should want one, I'll never know. But carry on, amuse yourself with your disagreeable little club. Get to hell by your own road."

Dalton twitched one corner of his mouth. It wouldn't do to reveal his relief at this moment. "Thank you, my lord. I shall."

Liverpool turned his narrow gaze on Clara. "I suppose you'll be wanting some sort of reward for your assistance in the destruction of the Knights of the Lily."

Clara blinked. "I shouldn't think—"

The Prime Minister raised one hand to halt her. "I'll have you know that I don't hold with extortion. You'll get no more than any citizen would receive from the Crown coffers and like it."

"But—"

"Are you arguing with me, child?"

Clara subsided. "No, my lord."

"I'll be watching you, girl."

Clara raised a brow. "And I you, my lord."

Liverpool left, trailed by his Guard. Once they were all gone and he could breathe easily again, Dalton turned to see Stubbs, Button, and Kurt grinning at his back. At least, Stubbs and Button were grinning. Kurt had his single eyebrow drawn down in a frightening manner and some of his few unbroken teeth bared. Dalton decided to declare it a smile and grinned back. "What's with you lot?"

Stubbs shook his head. "You, tellin' his lordship you ain't got your Liar name."

Button laughed. "We thought you knew, you see."

Dalton's smile faded. The lack of a Liar name had bothered him more than he wanted to admit, even to himself. "Knew what?"

That sent Button and Stubbs into choking snorts of hysteria, with much don't-mind-us waving of hands and searching out of handkerchiefs.

"Shut it, you dolts." Kurt turned his lowering gaze on

Dalton. "You've 'ad your name, sir. We all been usin' it to your face for weeks."

Dalton blinked, still confused despite a glowing coal of hope in his gut. "You have? What is it?"

"We picked it on account of 'ow you can tear a strip from a bloke and never curse, not once. Never even raise your voice." Kurt waited expectantly, but Dalton still had no glimmer.

"I know." Clara stepped up, James close behind her. She folded her arms and gave Dalton the pirate smile of old. "You're the Gentleman."

The Gentleman. Dalton's heart slowed and a sense of peace descended on him. Of course. He had been accepted by the Liars all along. It had been he who had not accepted himself.

He turned to Clara and reached for her. Gently he let his fingers rest on her shoulder for a moment, then he ran his hand down her graceful arm and took her hand in his.

"This is all due to you," he said.

She shook her head. "This is your merry band, my lord."

He let his fingers twine with hers. Hers were shy, reluctant. "And will you join our merry band, my lady?"

She looked about her. Dalton could see many encouraging grins at the corners of his vision, but he did not take his eyes off her. He dared not, for oddly she seemed about to disappear.

"I don't know . . . I've never taught."

Dalton covered her hand with his two. "You have indeed taught, Mrs. Clara Rose Thorogood Simpson. You have taught me."

He knelt before her. She gazed down at him in bewilderment as the Liars burst out in broad cries of approval. "You are far more woman than I deserve, yet I must tell you." He brought her hand to his lips. "I love you, Clara. I love you and I want you and I need you quite without reservation."

He smiled up at her astonished expression. "Will you wed me? Will you join us as my Lady Etheridge?"

Clara could only stand and stare down at Dalton in shock. The cries of the Liars died away as her silence lengthened. They all stood around her and Dalton, watching and waiting. The pressure of their eyes added to the hideous strain of the past days made Clara shake inside from tormented exhaustion. She'd been hunted, hounded, held at the point of a pistol, shot, and dropped down a palace laundry shaft. Now she was being *proposed* to?

She parted her lips to reply but no sound emerged. She couldn't think. The only sound was Dalton's voice in her mind. *It is the perfect solution.*

"I am not a problem for you to solve," she whispered finally. Dalton's hopeful smile faltered and her resolve nearly did as well. "I need to leave." She eased her hand from his grasp.

"Leave?"

She couldn't look at him. "I cannot be here. I need . . ." Shaking her head, she turned away, almost staggering in her weariness. "I need to think . . ."

"Clara." Dalton was on his feet now, reaching for her worriedly. "I'm sorry. I didn't realize—Stubbs! Fetch milady a carriage!"

Clara flinched. "*Milady*," she breathed in alarm. "You presume, my lord."

"Clara? What is wrong? Tell me what I've done?"

She turned to him, gazing up into his silver eyes. She had seen those eyes seethe and she had seen them freeze.

She had seen so many faces of this man she could scarcely remember them all. "You? You've done nothing. I don't even *know* you."

He recoiled as if she had shot him with Wadsworth's pistol.

"I see." He stepped back from her. She saw his throat work as he swallowed hard. "Yes, you should go home. I shall call on you tomorrow—"

She flung up a hand. "*No.* I need time. Time to think."

Stubbs stepped up. "I've a hack outside for ye, milady."

Their sheer blind persistence made Clara's spine melt in weary frustration. She could only shake her head blindly and make for the door and her escape.

Chapter Twenty-eight

The reward she received was more than Clara had ever dreamed of earning on her own. Beatrice had urged her to take it.

"You should take the reward. Because of you, a threat to the Crown has been removed. And now you're famous as well."

She was now an independent woman.

She had returned to the Trapp house to take a whole new position within the family. She had pondered finding her own small house, but she couldn't bring herself to begin.

She had sought out Rose in order to invite her to come to live with her, but the little maid had turned spy trainee and was more than happy with her new situation.

"Milady thinks I have potential," Rose had enthused, her eyes shining behind her new spectacles. "I never drop anything now. And Milady thinks that my knowledge of belowstairs'll come in right—come in *very handily.*"

Rose had found her place in the world, and Clara could be nothing but happy for her. If only she could say the same. Independent life was full of freedom. The freedom to be desperately lonely in the midst of Beatrice's gossiping cronies. The freedom to spend her evenings trying her hand at true art, though most of it landed in the fire.

And the freedom to dream long lovely dreams in which she wasn't alone at all.

She was sitting in the front parlor one afternoon after a week of independence, pondering that she was determined never to be under anyone's thumb again, when it occurred to her that in all her life the only person who hadn't tried to control her was Dalton. He'd angered her, he'd driven her mad, he'd tried to protect her, yes—but never once had he tried to quash her.

Then again, he'd not contacted her either, not once. Which only gave credence to her suspicion that his offers of marriage had been merely dutiful impulse.

Her thoughts were interrupted by a knock at her door. Could it be . . . ? With a thrill, she ran lightly to the door.

It wasn't Dalton. Not even close.

Upon her step stood a bent old man with a delivery basket. "Be this the Trapp house?"

Clara nodded and accepted the basket. It was probably something else from Agatha, who seemed to delight in purchasing gifts for everyone of her aquaintance. Clara tipped the old fellow and turned to place the basket on the side table. She didn't much feel like opening—

The basket meowed.

Clara dropped to her knees there in the hallway to open the ties with trembling fingers. When she lifted the lid, the smooth beautiful face of a ginger cat looked up into hers.

Disappointed, Clara realized that it was not her dear rescued cat. For a moment, she'd hoped that Dalton had kept and cared for the poor slit-eared animal for her. Instead, he must have thought to carelessly replace her with this lovely creature.

The cat blinked at her with wide green eyes and Clara's heart softened. "I'm sorry. It isn't your fault that you're not my ragged little friend." She ran her fingers gently across the top of the cat's head, and scratched gently behind an ear. There was something wrong with the soft velvet flap. . . .

"What's this?" She reached into the basket to pick up the cat and carried her to the light of the window. In this glossy animal's ears there were unmistakable slits, the kind that never would heal completely whole.

Her eyes stung. Clara held her cat close, tucking the silky head beneath her chin. He had kept her trust. He had more than kept it, he had exceeded it. Only the finest of care could have resulted in such radiant health in her pretty marmalade darling.

Then her pretty marmalade darling dug claws into Clara's arm and sprang from her embrace. "Ouch!" Clara rubbed the scratch and watched the cat trot back to the basket and hop in.

And immediately hop out with a tiny mirror image in her careful jaws.

Clara ran to the basket to see one other perfect tiny creature, a tabby of a lovely dove-gray color. "Kittens? Oh, you clever, clever kitty!"

And beneath them, somewhat the worse for riding about with babies, was an envelope. Gingerly, she opened the outer envelope to find with relief that the inner letter was relatively undamaged.

In a large manly scrawl, she read, *"Never forget all of those whom you have redeemed. Your grateful liar."*

After watching the mother cat carry both kittens to a

new nest that she carefully made on Beatrice's best sofa, Clara turned from the basket and strode to the small study. She took a piece of stationery from her desk and with swift decisive strokes, she penned an acceptance of the one position that she had been offered since her world had been upturned.

"Dear Lord Etheridge..."

Clara alighted from the rented hack to find herself the recipient of a delighted grin. She smiled back. "Mr. Stubbs! How nice to see you again."

Stubbs blushed and stuttered, then held the door for her, despite the fact that the club had not yet opened. She supposed she didn't actually qualify as a member, nor precisely as a guest.

In his eagerness, Stubbs followed her inside and took her cloak. "The Gentleman's expectin' you upstairs."

The door to the kitchen opened slowly, for the width of mere inches, and she could see three heads backlit by the kitchen lanterns. She shook her head. Some spies they were!

"Good afternoon, Kurt. I trust you are well, Button? And James, it is always a pleasure."

She received two shame-faced greetings and one grunt in reply, which she accepted with regal serenity. It seemed that the Gentleman wasn't the only one expecting her.

She ought to have been nervous. Or excited at the very least. But frankly, all she felt was a tranquil certainty. She was precisely where she ought to be, doing precisely as she should. If Dalton Montmorency couldn't see that, then she was just going to have to convince him otherwise.

And wouldn't that be a lovely way to pass an afternoon?

She was here. Fisher, the code-breaker, had run upstairs to whisper it a moment ago, before casting him a thumbs-up and dashing away.

Dalton would have known anyway, for his senses hummed in that way they always did when she was near. He patted the pocket that held the ring. He checked the light, fiddling with the draperies yet again.

Dimness was more intimate, but he didn't want to seem to be setting some sort of sensual snare. Then again, the attic truly wasn't at its best in good light, despite the hours that the Liars had spent cleaning the place.

Apparently a dozen spies did not good housekeeping make. They'd finally brought in Agatha's new protégée, Rose, in an advisory capacity. She'd rolled her eyes and set the lot of them to sweeping and scrubbing all over again.

Agatha had then stepped in to choose a number of things to make the attic comfortable and useful. There was a fine easel and a variety of papers in a printer's stand. There were inks of every color and a lifetime supply of plumes and nibs for pen-making.

The rest of the attic's furnishings disturbed him a little. Apparently, Agatha had been inspired to create what Dalton thought of as Ali Baba's cave. In the far end of the attic there existed a fantasy of drapery and cushions that kept Dalton's mind turning back to the nest of old curtains where he had lost his heart to Rose the maid.

Rose the maid, and the merry Widow Simpson, and

the valiant Clara, and by God, even Sir Thorogood! All of them combined made for a fascinating woman, a goddess of justice and fey, sensual charm that he could not wrest from his heart, no matter that she loved him not.

Perhaps if he said he was not opposed to a long engagement, she might reconsider. He'd even accept a secret betrothal, if that was what she wished. If only she would give him another chance to make that divine request, the one he'd bungled so badly twice before.

Unfortunately, he hadn't a clue how to do it. So he'd decided to bribe her with this outrageous studio, and planned to promise to abide by her slightest wish, and . . .

There his inspiration stopped. He'd never been a glib man. People thought it was because he was too important to be bothered, but it was simply that he didn't know how. Oh, he could discuss the exports of China, debate the writing of a law, even argue down the Prince Regent himself if necessary, but on this . . . sensitive matter, he'd had no practice at all.

The door opened. He swung about with betraying eagerness, then cursed himself. He would not pressure her. He would not try to sway her with tales of his own loneliness and longing for her.

She entered from the dark narrow stair, blinking against the sudden glare of the sunlight shining through crystal-clean windows to bounce from whitewashed walls back into her eyes.

Damn, he should have drawn the draperies, he should have—

"Dalton, what is this?"

She was looking about her, her delicate brows drawn together.

He cleared his throat, which had closed at the sight

of her wide hazel eyes. "An artist needs a studio, does she not?"

She looked him in the eye and laughed, the sound bursting from obvious amazement. His heart fell with a sickening impact. "You don't like it."

Covering her giggles with her hand, she shook her head, looking around her at the mountain of supplies and the Bedouin nest. Then she must have seen his disappointment, for she composed herself quickly.

"It isn't that I don't like it. It's only that—" She looked around her in disbelief once more. "All I need is a desk and paper and ink. I could work in any corner, had I candles enough."

Ah, they had overdone it. He'd suspected as much himself. Cheering somewhat, he gestured to the printer's rack. "There. Paper." He patted the cabinet that held the array of pen-making supplies. "Ink! And should you need them on a cloudy day—" He threw open the cupboard door to show a solid two hundred fine wax tapers. "Candles!"

She gave up any semblance of control and threw back her head, laughing out loud. Dalton had to smile with her, for she was so obviously delighted with his excess.

Drawing one hand across her tearing eyes, she sputtered to a stop. "Dare I ask about the—?" She canted her head toward the shameless pile of luxury in the corner.

Dalton tugged at his cravat. "That was Agatha's doing, I fear. I swear I never told a soul about—"

"No, I'm sure you would never lack for subtlety, Dalton. Not like setting this stage in an *attic,* or some such."

Rubbing the back of his neck, he gave up and confessed. "Very well, then, I lack subtlety. But I also thought it had good light."

She gazed at him for a long moment. "Do you need a lesson in subtlety, my fine British spy?"

The sultry note in her voice made Dalton's trousers tighten. She smiled and came closer, removing her gloves one slow finger at a time. Had the removal of kidskin ever been so subtly erotic? Or was it simply that every move she made fascinated him?

She drew near and he caught a whiff of roses. The memories it evoked nearly knocked him to his knees. He closed his eyes briefly in an effort to control his thoughts and he felt her touch upon his hand.

When he opened his eyes, she'd already turned away to examine the easel, leaving him clutching the soft skin of her gloves like a man clinging to a lifeline.

The easel was crafted of fine ash wood, and she ran her bare fingers over it appreciatively.

God, he would kill to be that easel!

"So sturdy," she murmured. "Strong and tall and fine . . ."

His lips parted.

She laid her cheek against the smooth polished wood, closing her eyes with pleasure. "Do you not love to stroke a finely made piece?"

His hands started to shake. His neck was sweating and his chest felt tight. He was very careful not to look down at himself, for fear of what he'd see.

"I have a gift for you."

He opened his eyes to see that she held out a scrolled paper. A drawing?

Then his eyes widened. She had carried nothing when she entered the room. Where had she kept it? And how could he live with knowing he'd missed seeing her retrieve it? His mind occupied with visions of garters and fluttering petticoats, he absently reached for the drawing and unrolled it.

And nearly swallowed his tongue.

"This—this is pornographic!"

She gave him that wild-child grin and tilted her head at him. "Are you going to arrest me?"

He'd had enough. He reached for her. "No, I'm going to throw you down and turn this sketch into reality!"

She danced beyond his reach. "Not until you hear me out."

Anything, he'd promise anything, if only he could bury himself in her fire once more. He hadn't been warm in ages, perhaps forever.

His longing must have shown in his face, for she held up a hand to halt him. Then she faced him, her hands loosely clasped at her waist. She looked the picture of proper English womanhood in her lavender half-mourning and her prim stance.

Which made it all the more stunning when she said, "Will you take me to your bed until neither of us can speak a word of sense?"

He could only blink at her for a moment.

"For if you do not throw me down on that ridiculous pile of sensuality in the corner and make me beg for mercy, I think I shall die on the spot for wanting you so."

He needed no further prompting. Like a greedy man reaching for gold, he took her into his arms and drew her close. He kissed her, savoring the softness of her fine mouth and the feel of her eager body against his.

Kissing his way down her neck and up again, he nibbled gently on her earlobe. "Reach into my pocket, my fearless rose."

Surprised, she laughed. "Already?"

He took her soft skin between his teeth and bit down just enough to make her quiver. "My waistcoat pocket, rosebud," he murmured in Monty's jaunty tones. "And none o' your sass."

He felt her small hand twisting its way into his pocket.

"I feel something. What is this in your—" She halted with a gasp. Dalton smiled. Perhaps high-flown words were not needed between them.

The ring was a single brilliant emerald nested in carved gold. Clara felt her breath catch as she realized that the carving was a bounty of perfect roses, spilling from the gemstone down the arch of the ring.

"Once again, we have the same idea at the same moment." Dalton stepped back and took the ring from her. He raised her left hand to his lips. "I've not done well by you, my love. I want to start again. I want to court you properly."

Clara's hands began to shake as he slid the exquisite ring onto her finger. "I don't want to start again. I want to make love to you now."

He pulled her close, wrapping her tenderly in his strength. "Marry me?" His breath was warm in her ear and she felt her spine weaken.

"I love you, Dalton Montmorency, whether you be lord or thief. I will be your mistress. If you don't want a mistress, I will be your lover in whatever stolen time that I may have." *Please, no, for I would die by inches without you.*

Warm fingers caught at her chin and raised her gaze to his silver one. "You've never told me that you love me."

"Don't be silly. Of course I have."

He shook his head slowly. "No. This was the first

time. I daresay I would remember, since I suddenly feel thirteen feet tall and powerful enough to toss Kurt across the room." With a small smile, he stroked his thumb along her eyelash, taking up the single tear that had gathered.

She took a breath and twisted the ring on her finger. "Yes, I love you, but I fear I shall make a rather outrageous Lady Etheridge."

Dalton stilled, but did not release her from his embrace. "Look at me, Clara. Is that all you see? Lord Etheridge?"

She closed her eyes and shook her head. "That is who you are."

"Look beyond that, I beg of you." His voice caught, a tiny break of desperation.

It shot through her like an arrow. She was hurting him.

"Look beyond his lordship," he whispered. "For there I stand, without you."

He bent his head and brought his lips close to hers. "Marry me," he whispered. "For I love thee well, my flower, and cannot draw another breath without thee by my side."

His breath brushed her lips, causing them to tingle, and his words freed her heart and drowned her objection. She laughed shakily through her tears and reached for him.

"Very well, then, I'll marry you." She kissed him hard. Then she grinned dangerously. "How many cats will Etheridge House hold, anyway?"

Epilogue

Dalton stood in the doorway of the attic studio, watching his wife draw. She was doing very badly indeed. In fact, he'd never seen her do worse.

He'd come upstairs with a basket of Kurt's best and a bottle of wine, hoping to tempt Clara into a Bedouin picnic. And then some food.

Yet now he was too concerned to care about curling up with her for an afternoon of not napping. For Clara to be drawing so very badly, something must be wrong. Her talent had only grown in the month since their marriage, for she had all the time and resources in the world at her disposal in her position as identification artist for the Liar's Club.

It was working, too. Clara had begun teaching the trainees to draw, and was now herself able to draw a usable portrait from a mere verbal description. The Liars were all honing their observation skills in the process, as they vied to impress Clara with their prowess. Collis, who had recently entered training, was her best student.

But this . . .

"My flower, are you quite well?"

"Mm-hmm." The drawing continued, each line shakier and more incomprehensible than the last.

Dalton was becoming truly frightened now. He came quietly up behind her and took her drawing hand in his. Something was wrong, her fingers were not right somehow . . . he was holding the wrong hand!

"Why are you drawing with your left hand?"

Clara finally turned to him and smiled. "Oh, hello, darling. I didn't hear you come in."

"I know. You were concentrating too hard. Why are you drawing with your left hand?"

"For Lord Liverpool, of course."

"Liverpool? But why would he care—" *Oh, no.* "Clara, tell me that you aren't thinking what I think you're thinking."

"Well, truthfully, Dalton, he said that Sir Thorogood could never draw again. He said nothing about Mr. Underkind."

Dalton closed his eyes. "And who is Mr. Underkind?"

"You're holding him."

Dalton opened his eyes and looked down at the small smudged hand in his. Her left hand. Which would produce drawings nothing like her right hand, once she'd practiced enough.

Mr. Underkind meant trouble. Mr. Underkind would likely bring the wrath of Lord Liverpool down upon their heads just when things had finally quieted.

Mr. Underkind would drive Liverpool completely around the bend as he wondered who it was.

Dalton couldn't help it. He laughed.

"I think I'm going to like Mr. Underkind." He lifted her charcoal-smeared hand to his lips and kissed it. "How about giving Mr. Underkind a rest for a few minutes?"

Clara's brows went up. "But I only just taught him how to draw a good circle."

Dalton leaned close and whispered in her ear although there was no one else about. "I have cream puffs."

"Ooh."

He nibbled her earlobe. "And strawberries."

"That sounds lovely."

He worked his way down her throat and bit gently at that tender spot where neck became shoulder. "I'll let you be on top." He licked the spot where he'd just bitten. He could feel her breath quicken. "But there's only room for two in the tent. You'll have to leave Mr. Underkind outside."

"Mr. . . . who?"

READ ON FOR AN EXCERPT FROM
CELESTE BRADLEY'S NEXT BOOK

The Spy
(Book Three in the Liar's Club)

COMING SOON FROM ST. MARTIN'S PAPERBACKS

The evening after their adventure on the streets, Phillipa found herself putting Robbie to bed although she was fairly sure it wasn't a tutor's job to do so. Yet if not her, then who? Certainly not Mr. Cunnington.

"He's goin' out again." Robbie's face was entirely expressionless. The very portrait of accustomed loneliness. "He's always goin' out."

Phillipa didn't know how to comfort him. Robbie's guardian seemed fond enough of the boy, although she hadn't been about long enough to form an opinion on the matter.

Time for a change of subject. "You're not going out anytime soon either, Master Robert." She shook her finger in his face but not too close. He might yet prove to be a biter.

His little face paled. "You goin' to cane me, then?"

Cane him? For dropping in on Mr. Cunnington's club for his tea? Good Lord, where had this child been?

Still, she couldn't let him think he could pull that sort of stunt every day.

Propping both fists on her hips, Phillipa looked down

at her student disapprovingly. "You, me lad, are about to experience the patented Atwater tickle revenge."

Robbie jumped up to run, a giggle already bubbling through his mock fear. Phillipa snapped him up just before he made it to the door. He must not have been trying very hard, for he'd surely learned more speed than that in his nine years on the streets.

She swung him yelping into the air and brought him down onto the rug before the fire, her fingers raking his bony little sides.

Robbie screeched, his rusty laughter another reminder to Phillipa of his short hard life before she'd met him. Grinning, she almost let him catch a breath before she began anew.

"Robbie the Rebel, are you? Robbie the Great Know-it-all, are you? You look more like Robbie Twitter-on-the-rug, if you ask me!"

Time to go in for the kill. The volume of Robbie's screeches rose to full riot level. Phillipa heard another sound beyond it, but she didn't identify it as the thumping of running feet in the hall until the door of the schoolroom crashed open.

"What the bloody hell are you doing to him?"

Before Phillipa could turn around, she was lifted by the scruff of her neck and dragged from Robbie.

She found herself dangling from James Cunnington's grip, gagging on her cravat—which was apparently auditioning for the role as her brand-new Adam's apple.

Then her gaze sharpened on James and her eyes bulged further. It was probably a good thing she couldn't speak, for the man was more than a little naked. In fact, he was naked, but for a towel around his neck and a pair of drawers that clung to his bath-damp skin like paint.

He was revealed to her eyes in all his powerful

beauty. His wide brawny chest, his rippling belly, the dark trail of hair that led the eye below the sagging waist of his drawers which did nothing to hide the muscular thighs framing what could only be *It*.

Great Greek Gods.

She desired him. The realization sent fresh strength into her struggles.

She wanted him, when she couldn't bear to speak her own name in solitude for fear of discovery. When she couldn't allow her body so much as a moment of freedom from its bindings and trappings.

With more strength than she'd known she had, she pushed herself from his grip. James laughed, obviously realizing his mistake, and gave her an apologetic grin. Phillipa forced a sickly chuckle to hide her appalling new awareness.

She lusted for a man who thought she was a man.

What a fix.